JACKSON

ALSO BY MAX BYRD

Jefferson: A Novel

JACKSON

A
Novel

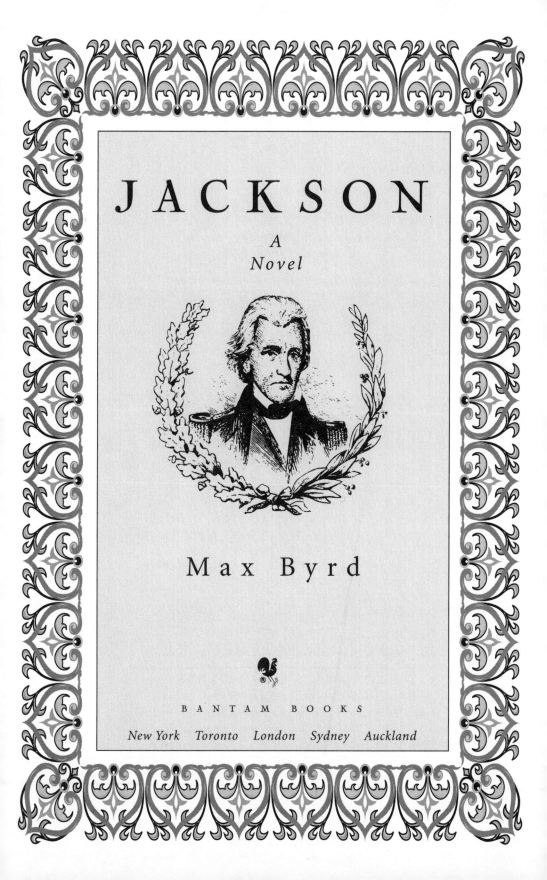

Max Byrd

BANTAM BOOKS

New York Toronto London Sydney Auckland

JACKSON

A Bantam Book/March 1997

BOOK DESIGN BY GLEN M. EDELSTEIN.

Library of Congress Cataloging-in-Publication Data
Byrd, Max.
Jackson : a novel / Max Byrd.
p.   cm.
ISBN 0-553-09632-X
1. Jackson, Andrew, 1767–1845—Fiction.   2. Presidents—
United States—Fiction.   I. Title.
PS3552.Y675J33   1997
813'.54—dc20   96-30534
                                                    CIP

Published simultaneously in the United States and Canada

Bantam Books are published by Bantam Books, a division of Bantam
Doubleday Dell Publishing Group, Inc. Its trademark, consisting of the
words "Bantam Books" and the portrayal of a rooster, is Registered in
U.S. Patent and Trademark Office and in other countries. Marca Regis-
trada. Bantam Books, 1540 Broadway, New York, New York 10036.

PRINTED IN THE UNITED STATES OF AMERICA

BVG   10 9 8 7 6 5 4 3 2 1

For My Wife Brookes

alors j'ai vu ma belle et la belle a souri

JACKSON

PROLOGUE

1854—Paris

If I were as clever (among other things) as Julius Caesar, I would be dictating these memoirs to two different secretaries at once.

To the first—let us say a slender, dark-haired young woman with a daughterly air of patience—I would recount the story of my thirty years' residence in Europe, my salad days, my fields of wild oats; and as I paced beside her table, hands clasped thoughtfully behind my back, eyes intent on my Turkish slippers, she would write it all down in ink the color of wine and in French, the language of farce.

To the second—let us say, with the precision of memory over imagination, a blond-haired woman of twenty-eight or twenty-nine, heavier of build, with the faintest voluptuary bulge of belly under her skirts (blue skirts, her favorite color) and a still fainter feather of feminine blond mustache across her upper lip, indescribably (to me) attractive. Let us seat *her* on the opposite side of the room, beside the window that looks out on the gray strip of mud and pleasure that is the Champs-Elysées in winter; and to *her*, passing and repassing in the little room, I would recount, in alternating sentences like Caesar, the story of my far shorter sojourn in Washington City, once upon a time, and she would write it all down in English, the language of hope.

Or perhaps, since she knows it already, "by heart" as the expression is, she would write nothing at all. She would sit with her long bare hands on her lap and watch the little black French sparrows whirling and spinning together in the sky, like thousands of musical notes slipped free from their perch.

Or perhaps again, better still, though she has heard it a dozen times before, she is kind, forbearing; she asks me to repeat a certain story that she knows I like. "Tell me again how the three Harvard friends, Ticknor the pedant, and Gray who became so rich, and you, yearning at twenty-two to be a great poet—how the three of you rode up the hill to Monticello in the War of 1812."

"It was *not* the War of 1812 exactly" (I would reply gratefully, taking a seat beside her). "It was early February 1815; and although not one soul in America knew it, the war was already over. A treaty had just been signed in Brussels, negotiated by John Quincy Adams and Henry Clay, but thanks to the slow speed of an Atlantic crossing in winter in those days, the news would not reach home for another month."

"If it *had* reached home in time?" she might interrupt.

"There would have been no Battle of New Orleans, no Old Hickory for President; no story. In fact, Ticknor, Gray, and I were on a journey south from Boston, and we had just made a detour from Washington City—a burned-out shell, still smoldering from the British invasion—a detour down to Richmond and then up the Rivanna Valley to Monticello. In the stagecoach we read a new poem, published that day in the Richmond paper, called 'The Star-Spangled Banner,' and we fretted aloud about the fate of New Orleans, where the British army was known to be massed—not much else was known—poised and ready to seize the Mississippi River, and with it the future, the western half of the continent, the whole untouched, virginal nineteenth century. No star-spangled banner if New Orleans fell."

"You were going to see Thomas Jefferson."

"We had letters; a letter of introduction from John Adams."

"And the trip was your idea?"

"Mine alone."

"Because then and now, forty years later, you, David Chase, felt that Jefferson was the greatest American who ever lived."

I will sigh loudly then, long-suffering, and begin to spread out my memories, like so many faded jewels on a carpet. Jefferson's glorious prose, his intellect, his house—more museum than house—which looked to the three of us young men as if he had assembled half the art treasures of Europe onto his walls; his vision of a democratic union, an American nation stretching from Atlantic to Pacific, the greatest field for freedom's experiment in all of history—

At which point Emma (let us give her a name) might press one soft finger to my mouth (the other secretary looking on, indignant) and cut me short.

"What did he—Jefferson—say to you, that you never forgot, about Andrew Jackson?"

I can be arch and cynical now, friends tell me—this comes of living in France, to a ripe old age. But in my youth I was earnestness itself; life had not yet carved its mask on my face.

On the evening before we left Monticello, not long after Jefferson, who was seventy-two that year, had retired to his bedroom, his grandson Thomas Jefferson Randolph rushed into the house with an earthshaking whoop. From under his armpit he thrust newspapers wildly in every direction, at every waving, scrabbling hand, then held one up for all of us to see: "ALMOST INCREDIBLE VICTORY! GLORIOUS UNPARAL-LELED NEWS!" In forty-point type we read it—everyone shouting at once—Andrew Jackson had just destroyed the British army at New Orleans; the British general was dead, their troops were retreating into the sea. "THE RISING GLORY OF AMERICA!"

But when we knocked at Jefferson's door and offered to read him the story, the old man called back that he could wait until morning.

And in the morning he ate his whole breakfast and took his usual ride before asking at last for the paper.

At noon, as we waited for the servants to bring our horses around to the west porch, Ticknor, who was our boldest member, cleared his throat and asked about Andrew Jackson—had not Jefferson known Old Hickory in Philadelphia, when Jackson was a senator and Jefferson was vice president? Were they not old friends?

To see us off, Jefferson was dressed in old-fashioned smallclothes, an ancient red waistcoat, and high sharp-toed boots called (from the days of his presidency) Jefferson shoes. To my eye, he looked for all the world like an elderly farmer about to visit his fields, not like an ex-President of the United States, whose words and name had circled the globe.

"Oh, I knew him well. I saw him often." The mild Jeffersonian smile, to which we had grown accustomed; but a curiously terse and un-Jeffersonian answer.

"They will talk of him for senator again, sir, will they not?" Ticknor persisted. "His political fortunes will climb."

"I would feel much alarm," Jefferson said with a sudden angry, stiff formality of language so unlike himself that the three of us started, "much alarm at the prospect of seeing General Jackson in high political office again." The horses arrived at the edge of the porch, but no one moved a step toward them. Jefferson looked at us in turn, one after the other, then settled an icy gaze on me alone. "Jackson's passions are terrible," he said. "Terrible. He cannot control himself. When he was a senator he could never finish a speech because of the rashness of his feelings. I have seen him attempt it repeatedly, and choke every time with rage. He is coarse and illiterate. He has murdered men in duels. He has very little respect for laws or constitutions. He is," Jefferson said, in a fierce whisper, as if addressing me alone, "the most dangerous man in America."

PART

1

December 1827–March 1828

CHAPTER

1

Andrew Jackson awoke leaning with his back against the barn door. His arms were flung forward across the side bar of a wagon. Sweat poured down his scalp and his neck and his chest in an amazing profusion for someone so skinny, so gaunt.

"You havin' the dreams again, Gen'l?"

The black slave squatting on his heels beside Jackson now rose and wiped his face with an old towel that seemed to glow pale white in the dark. Both men ignored the sickly sweet smell of Jackson's diarrhea, which ran down both pants legs, mingling with the sweat, and into his boots.

"Get me some gin."

"Yes, sir." The slave didn't move.

"Put some water in it. And go wake up John Coffee."

"Yes, sir." Still there.

"But don't wake *her* up." Jackson closed his eyes again as if to sleep. "Or I'll have your skin," he added automatically.

"Yes, sir." This time the slave, whose name was Alfred and who slept every night on the floor outside Jackson's bedroom, padded away on bare feet, toward the dark house.

Jackson shifted his arms so that he bent forward even more, at an angle of almost thirty degrees. He was sixty years old, and sometimes the pain was so bad it was still the only posture he could bear to take; back flat, knees flexed, arms flung forward over something. When he had fought the Creek Indians in 1814, he had often propped himself the same way exactly on a bent sapling while his officers stood in a half circle around him and wrote down his orders.

Those that could write.

Those that hadn't lied about that too.

Jackson blinked and stared up at the bleak, unfriendly stars, whose insides, somebody had told him, were actually made up of nothing but furious burning gases. Just like himself.

Crippled stars. Furious stars. Beads of burning sweat on the divine celestial face.

All his life, Jackson thought, slowly closing his red eyes again, he had been angrier and hotter than a star.

The Dreams of Andrew Jackson

Late September 1780, Waxhaw, North Carolina

WHEN COLONEL BANASTRE TARLETON—THE SAME REDHEADED, SIDEBURNED Tarleton who later chased Governor Thomas Jefferson out of his house and into disgrace—when that same Colonel Tarleton and his green-jacketed dragoons rode into Waxhaw one bright morning, every man and boy in the county took to his horse and his musket.

I was fourteen years old and too young to fight (they said), so my assignment was to ride hell-for-leather south to warn the next settlement. Halfway up Catawba Mountain I met a saucy blond-haired girl standing by the road, Susan Smart was her name, about my own age, her hands on her cocked hips, pert little backside round as an apple. I reined up, dirty, tired-looking, covered with grime, and wearing a yellow broad-brimmed hat that flopped over my face; no cavalier.

"Where are you from?" asks Susan Smart.

"From below." My heels almost met under my pony's belly, and I saw her peeking at them and laughing.

"Where are you going?" she asks.

"Above."

"Who are you for?"

"The Congress."

"Well, what are your people doing below?"

"Oh, we're popping them good," I say, pushing up the hat.

"*We,*" she snorts, wagging the hips. Over her shoulder, flouncing away, "Some poppin' *you'll* do, you skinny boy."

Six months later, when the British officer herded three of us into his tent and told me to clean the mud from his boots, I said I was a prisoner of war despite my age and ought to be treated with respect, like a man. I never saw a quicker explosion. The officer's cheeks went red, his teeth bared like a wolf's. He took one step back and without a word swung his sword—my left hand flew up, just the way it does in the engraving my people commissioned in 1824, *The Brave Boy of the Waxhaws.* His back-swing sliced open my scalp and gashed my hand to the bone. When I ride I finger the scars like beads.

Before that, at the Waxhaw Massacre, while I was on Catawba Mountain, Tarleton's cavalry had charged full speed into the poor old county militia, who had already put down their empty muskets and sat on the ground to surrender. One hundred and thirteen Americans killed outright, nobody could ever count how many wounded. They had to rip out the pews to turn the old log church into a hospital, and I remember that the floor was thick with straw and blood. To carry water I crawled on all fours through pools of blood and corpses; my mother floated beside me, nursing the dead.

CHAPTER

2

I'm afraid, Mr. Chase, that I don't speak a word of French."

Mrs. Sarah Josepha Hale put down her steel-nib pen, rose to her feet behind the desk, and bowed six inches forward, hands clenched in front of her waist, like a Chinaman.

David Chase, who was still brushing snow from his shoulders, tried to imitate her bow and succeeded only in stumbling on the carpet. He was cold, he was sleepy, and if the truth were told, he had no idea in the wheeled universe why Boston women bowed instead of shaking hands or nodding, as European women did.

Mrs. Hale was now moving around her formidable desk and motioning him to a chair. "But I do know a good deal of Latin," she said. She took his hat and sat down beside him. "My brother taught me secretly when he was at Dartmouth."

"I have forgotten every word of Latin that I ever learned."

Mrs. Hale had a quick, unexpected smile that flashed and vanished in an instant. "So have I," she whispered. She snapped away snow from the top of his hat with one efficient finger. "We shall have to do our business in English, Mr. Chase."

"*Englisch* it is," Chase said, and was rewarded with the smile a second time.

"You are much younger than I imagined, Mr. Chase, to be such a celebrated writer and cosmopolitan."

"As are you, Mrs. Hale," said Chase gallantly, though in fact it was true. "To have accomplished so much." Sarah Hale, he thought, was forty at least, but hardly looked it. She had brown hair worn in side-curls (an old-fashioned fashion that Chase hadn't seen in a decade); hazel eyes of great depth; and a delicate pink-white complexion that a girl of sixteen would have envied. Yet he knew for a fact that she had published one novel, *Northwood,* because he had bought and read it the day before, and had already worked a year and a half as founding editor of the *Ladies Magazine.* She was also the author of a nauseous little poem that had taken both English and American children by storm, "Mary Had a Little Lamb." Surreptitiously he glanced around the office for signs of lambhood.

"Well," she said, rising from the chair with the hat between her hands like a pie. "Well, then, that's settled. We are both paragons, are we not?"

Chase grinned and watched her deposit the hat on top of a bookcase and cross back to her desk. He had forgotten how much, despite their eccentricities, he liked the tart, dry voice of a native New Englander.

"My one concern," she said as she sat down again, "has been that you are too much of a *European* paragon—you have lived in France for these last nine years, yes?—and not enough of an *American* one. But you are a *very good* writer, I can see that, and your friend Professor Ticknor thinks the world of you. I don't like your poetry very much," she added rather brusquely, "to tell the truth. I don't understand what 'symbols' are. But then we are not asking you to write poetry, are we?"

Chase nodded slowly. In fact, he hadn't the least notion *what* they were asking him to write. But his bank account had now sunk so close to zero that anything short of a sequel to the mutton-headed Lamb he would undertake in a minute.

Mrs. Hale held up a cloth-bound book. "This is very good," she said, then used a word he had never heard before, "very readable." When she turned the volume sideways Chase recognized his little biography of the eighteenth-century statesman the Elder Pitt, published in London a year ago and disastrously stupid in its political judgments and facts. To his (and his publisher's) astonishment, it had sold more than eight thousand copies.

"You write *clearly*," Mrs. Hale told him, "and with a sure sense of moral value. And moral value is what we cannot, *in this country*, ever forget."

"No," Chase murmured. Ticknor had cautioned him that Sarah Hale was a patriot of the purest American kind. Almost single-handedly she had led a fund-raising venture among the ladies of Boston to complete the stalled monument on Bunker Hill, she was now busily campaigning to establish Mount Vernon as a government shrine, and she had just proposed in an editorial that Massachusetts's Thanksgiving Day become a national holiday. When she had gone to consult Ticknor about an anthology of the "world's greatest poetry," she had pointedly excluded all poets except Americans.

"In that unfortunate France where you have lived," Mrs. Hale began solemnly, and Chase hunched his shoulders (mentally) in preparation for yet another sermon on French immorality, a subject that appeared to fascinate and uplift Boston society. But before she could go on, the large brass bell behind her desk began to chime, and almost simultaneously someone knocked at her door and a rabbity young woman stuck in her head, glanced at Chase, then whispered very loudly, "He's *here*, Mrs. Hale—downstairs!"

Mrs. Hale quickly replaced the Elder Pitt among ordinary books and smoothed the skirts of her handsome silk gown. She would return in a moment, she said, if Chase would excuse her. Chase, on his feet as well, offered to hold the door, to wait outside, to vanish politely into thin air, whatever was required. Mrs. Hale only swept her hand in the direction of the window or his chair or both (the first vague gesture Chase had seen her make) and closed the door.

The window gave out onto Boylston Street. Boylston Street in turn gave onto the Boston Common, invisible from here; then Beacon Hill (a few slate and chimney rooftops in the distance), then the river, then Cambridge, and then at last the long, whiskery gray winter forests that ran up the rocky north shore toward Ipswich, where he had been born.

Looking straight down, he could see a triangular patch of colonial graveyard and an alley of trampled snow. Symbols, undoubtedly. An overloaded wagon of lumber rushed by, rattling the glass. Chase shivered and crossed the room to the bookcase beside Mrs. Hale's fireplace, and began to examine her books.

A true "cosmopolitan," he thought as he pulled out a volume at random, would have begun, of course, by examining her private mail on her desk, but he was clearly reverting already to ancestral Puritan ways. He held the book unopened for a moment. The bookcase was old and scarred and built of solid mahogany in a straightforward American pattern, for a lawyer or a serious bookman. Yet something in its design of carved columns and closed shelves struck him curiously. On top of it his hat still dripped snow. He rubbed the dark wood with one hand and felt the edges of his memory flicker and curl. He had seen such a bookcase somewhere before.

The book he had pulled out was *The Art of Writing* by John Jenkins, not a repository of professional secrets as it turned out, but a practical treatise on how to write a "fully rounded hand" using the new steel-nib pens such as Mrs. Hale had on her desk. Next to John Jenkins was a pamphlet by the president of Amherst College, *A Parallel Between Intemperance and the Slave Trade*. Then a *History of the American Revolution* by Mrs. Mercy Warren, in six buckram volumes, stiff as tombstones. The journalist in him couldn't resist trying to make an instant pattern: Boston in microcosm—practical, pious, obsessed with the bones of its past.

Pretty bad, Chase thought, bending his knees and grunting; though probably not quite bad enough to be published. The lowest shelf was stocked with what a ribald duchess he had known in England called handkerchief novels. He pulled out *The Power of Sympathy* by Anonymous, illustrated with an engraving of a young woman in a torn bodice and written, the title page explained, "to Expose the Fatal Consequences of Seduction." Chase tried to imagine the straight-backed, pink-complexioned, fully bodiced Sarah Hale yielding to the Power of Sympathy; failed completely. He had just pulled out a book of songs entitled *Home, Sweet Home* when voices sounded in the hallway and then, a moment later, the door swung open.

☆　　☆　　☆

"HERE is our writer," Sarah Hale said grandly, and it took Chase an instant to realize that she was referring to him and not to the tall but slightly stoop-shouldered and very white-haired old man beside her.

"And this is Mr. William Short," she said.

"Un grand plaisir de faire votre connaissance," said Short, extending his hand to Chase. *"J'ai lu avec admiration passionnée vos livres célèbres au sujet de la politique et de la biographie."*

Without any thought whatsoever Chase replied in French (home, sweet home). *"C'est bien aimable de votre part, monsieur, et également un plaisir."* He started to add a polite disclaimer—his books were far, far from *célèbres*—but stopped as Short turned to touch Sarah Hale lightly on the wrist.

"It was irresistible, but we must speak English, you know, Mr. Chase, though your French is exquisite to hear. It would be rude to exclude our charming friend." Short's French had been perfectly unaccented, bottled in Paris; his English had, unmistakably to a Bostonian ear, the lilting, sugary, and thoroughly implausible accent of the American South.

"Mr. Short," said Sarah Hale as she guided them both to chairs (the rabbit rushed in, poked the logs in the fireplace furiously, and glanced at Chase again before she rushed out), "will explain everything."

Short, however, settled himself deeper into his chair and, instead of explaining, rested both hands on the knob of an elegant black malacca cane and closed his eyes.

"David Chase," he drawled. He smiled without opening his eyes. "David is not really a common name in New England, is it? You like Josiah or Benjamin or Ephraim up here, don't you? Or that great dull Puritan monosyllable John. I've never known another David in Boston, I think."

"My late husband's name was David," Sarah Hale said from her desk.

"We want you to write a book, Mr. Chase." Short opened his eyes and put on a pair of extremely thick gold-rimmed glasses behind which his irises seemed to float like tiny drops of pale blue ink. "A book that Mrs. Hale will serialize in her magazine, beginning three months from now, and that I will then publish separately, through the offices of Mr. Osgood on Milk Street, and distribute all over the country."

"Ah." Chase cleared his throat and shifted his legs. If they had pulled out a press the next moment and started to set type, he would not have been surprised. The pace of journalism was obviously like the pace of everything else in America.

"It is a patriotic book," Sarah Hale assured him, taking his silence for resistance. "But you would have complete freedom."

For all his white hair and slender fragility, William Short possessed a physical force; he leaned forward and filled the room. "If there is one principle I have adhered to all my life," he said in the deliberately rising tone of someone accustomed to declaring his principles often, "it is Thomas Jefferson's principle of the sacred freedom of thought, the absence of censorship. 'Almighty God hath created the mind free,' Jefferson wrote. 'Truth is great and will prevail if left to herself.' "

A slant of ice-hard January light had found its way from the window and, in an eerie, spectral effect, now split William Short's face precisely in half; half shadow, half blazing white skin. "You will be the sole author of your book, Mr. Chase. I wish to finance it because I have confidence in your integrity"—Short raised one hand from the cane, either to forestall Chase's demurrer or else to block the January light—"and because I happen to think our country has reached a great point of crisis, a great crossroads. It is fifty-two years exactly since the Declaration of Independence was signed. We are entering into our second half-century. We have a momentous election before us. The question is whether we keep to our republican principles, as Jefferson established them, or whether we collapse into materialism and demagoguery."

"Mob rule," said Sarah Hale. "Posing as democracy." She was reaching across her desk for another book.

"I met Thomas Jefferson once," David Chase said. It was all he could think of to say. The truth was, he was not used to American ways anymore, he thought—female editors, political speeches, American bluntness. He wanted to go out the door and start over; wake up in Europe. In a little burst of recollection he turned in his chair and gestured toward the old-fashioned bookcase on his left, whose style and design he had suddenly remembered. "At his home in Virginia, many years ago."

"I know you did," Short said, nodding slowly.

"We want you to write a book about Andrew Jackson," said Sarah Hale.

Never, never, never!" George Ticknor said. "You must *never* do it."

Chase stepped over a pile of Ticknor's books on the floor and cocked his head (he trusted) noncommittally.

On Ticknor's sofa Francis Calley Gray stretched his long legs and propped his shoes against the fireplace fender like two upright brown squirrels. "Don't be discouraged, my dear fellow," he drawled, "by Ticknor's enthusiasm. Or if you are, hand me what's left of that bottle first."

"Andrew Jackson is a monster," Ticknor said. He gave Chase a bottle of claret from the mantelpiece, and Chase in turn passed it to Gray. "A brute, a slave-trader, a rabble-rousing demagogue. Don't you remember what Jefferson said the day we left Monticello? There on his porch—'Andrew Jackson is the most dangerous man in America.' "

"I have sometimes wondered," Gray said, "if the great Jefferson's nose was not a bit out of joint that day. Jackson had just stolen his thunder, no? New Orleans made Jefferson's protégé Madison look very feeble." He held the bottle up to the firelight and frowned.

"In the South," Ticknor said in a tone of deep disgust, pacing, "there are Old Hickory parades and barbecues every week. He makes speeches in favor of universal suffrage—'the will of the people,' he says. 'Every man is entitled to his vote.' "

"If I wrote the book," Chase told him, "I would be expected to investigate certain rumors."

"Namely? For example?" Ticknor's pacing had carried him to the table where they had eaten their reunion dinner. He stopped and glared over his shoulder at Chase.

"For example, did Jackson steal another man's wife?"

"Grand theft in Boston, of course." Gray poured himself a fussy half glass of wine. "But petty larceny in Tennessee. The papers have been full of that for a year, David, except nobody has any documents or evidence. Very shrewd of Monsieur Short. If you *proved* it—with evidence—you would pretty well stop Jackson's election forever, wouldn't you? At least in the North, and he still needs some of the North to win. What are the other rumors?"

"When Jackson took his army into Florida in 1818 and drove out the Spanish—"

"A highly illegal, unconstitutional, and extremely popular little war," Gray said. "This is terrible wine."

"The second rumor is that he profited from secret land speculation. Short has heard stories that Jackson took contributions from Tennessee banks in exchange for Florida land."

"And if you prove *that*," Gray said, "you would pretty well stop Jackson's election the other way too. Westerners will forgive a great deal in the private line, but not secret traffic with banks. And Jackson is, naturally, the sworn enemy of all banks. I confess I admire Short's mind. Sex and money. The two great themes of any book." He poured himself a second glass. "He must certainly be a Presbyterian."

"He is a land speculator himself," Ticknor said, returning to the fireplace. He rubbed his hands together briskly, professorially. "And fabulously wealthy," he added with vague Bostonian disapproval. David Chase studied his boot-tops and concealed his smile. Between Ticknor and Gray, he thought wryly, there was probably a million dollars' worth of invested property and funds, though the only sign of it in Ticknor's case was the Alpine range of leather-bound books that covered three full walls of his Harvard suite and marched in soldierly ranks along the floorboards, out the door.

"And in form it would be a 'Life of Jackson'?" Gray, who moved little but saw much, smiled at Chase's smile.

"An 'independent, objective, neutral biography.' I quote. William Short's patriotic contribution to the presidential election. He would pay my expenses to Washington City, and then to Tennessee, where I can stay with Andrew Jackson himself. Short would supply a letter of introduction from his own personal friend the great Lafayette, which will open every door."

"Ah, but who would read it to Jackson?" Ticknor asked sardonically. "The Great Illiterate. I don't like your project, David. Don't do it. Patriotism is the last refuge of a scoundrel."

"Ticknor," Gray told Chase, "if you haven't guessed, is an Adams man; though he never votes, of course. I think Jackson is a wonderful subject. My Tory cousin Daniel Parker met him once. It was love at first sight, such is the Hero's charisma, even for Tories." He lifted his glass in a mock toast. "*Charisma*. A word you must use on every page of your book. Ticknor is a professor. He lives in the past. He dreams of Washington and Jefferson and all the giants before the Flood. He doesn't accept that the Age of Reason is over. But the barbarians of personality are at the gates, the democratic *vulgus*, charismatic Jackson in their lead. How would poor old wooden-toothed Washington have fared in a true Jacksonian democracy? If you want to know the glorious—or appalling—future of your native land, write about Jackson; choose Jackson."

"On the whole, I think I would rather go back to France." Chase knelt by the fireplace and spread his fingers over the flames; his ears were cold, and despite the big coal fire his hands were growing icy. Unconsciously he imitated Ticknor's briskness. "I would *certainly* rather." Or would he? It was, in fact, a debate he had carried on with himself since the moment he was summoned to Boston—stay? Return? Home? Exile? His mind swung back and forth like a pendulum. Who had ever heard of a self-imposed exile from your own country? "I feel like a stranger here," he said, thinking of Paris, where the winters were warmer, the politics more intelligible. His gaze fell on Ticknor's Oriental carpet, Gray's supple, expensive shoes. "But I'm afraid I don't even have the price of my passage back."

"Your father left you nothing?" Ticknor was solicitous, but walked to the other side of the room. "Not even books? A library you could sell?" His hand caressed the haunches of the nearest bookshelf. "Books are valuable in Boston."

"My father was not much given to reading."

"The solitary vice," Gray murmured, finishing his wine.

"Well, if you do write it, you would bring a fresh eye to things," Ticknor said, giving way. "You've been abroad for so long, you would see everything fresh." A new thought gave sudden enthusiasm to his voice. "And Jackson really has committed the most terrible crimes—duels, murders, military executions—those are *not* rumors. But nobody seems to care. You could show people the *truth;* that's why Short wants you."

Gray put down his empty glass and stood, clasping his belly with both hands like a man with a ball. "You are to think over the offer and meet him at Fresh Pond tomorrow afternoon?" Chase nodded. "Very eccentric." Gray reached for his coat. "Very promising."

"Or you could write a chapter about Jackson and Aaron Burr," Ticknor said, now thoroughly caught up. "You know Jackson joined Burr's conspiracy in 1805 and just missed going to trial for treason himself—nobody remembers that now. The three of us were still in school. I change my vote. Write it, David. A truthful book might really stop his election—an *honest* book." He looked to Gray for confirmation. "David has always been the most honest one of us, yes?"

"He is certainly the poorest," said Gray, and shrugged on his coat.

Outside, Chase and Gray walked in companionable silence along one of the diagonal paths that crisscrossed Harvard Yard like a spider's web, under a matching web of glassy white stars.

At the corner of a brick dormitory Gray paused to shake something out of his shoe. "Theory and reality," he murmured. "The theory of the shoe, the reality of snow." He glanced at Chase, who was stamping his feet on the ground for warmth. "A Parisian war dance, no doubt."

Chase shook his head. He had almost forgotten how unstoppable Gray's irony was. "I'm still thinking of Jefferson," he said. "Jefferson and Jackson."

"Ah. The unholy duo. I always saw Jefferson as a democrat in theory, you know, but an aristocrat in temperament, a fine old slave-holding, book-collecting southern *seigneur*. The massa' of Monticello. Do you wonder, when he denounced the barbarous Jackson to us that morning, if he felt like Dr. Frankenstein in the novel—'Good God, what have I created?' You may use that in your book, David. 'Democracy is a coarse, misshapen, whiskered thing compared to one's ideals. Francis Calley

Gray.' Damn." He hopped a few steps and balanced against a lamppost while he pried at his heel.

Chase blew on his hands. Ten feet away the lamp's arc just reached the signboard on the side of the building. Stoughton Hall. Named, if he remembered correctly, for the judge who had presided at the Salem witch trials a century ago; *there* was a truly appalling piece of American history, to use Gray's word. How could Andrew Jackson top that?

"Double damn." Gray shifted his balance clumsily and held up his other heel. Past the brick archway that opened onto Harvard Square, a big twelve-passenger coach suddenly rumbled by at top speed, spraying snow in a white fan. Automatically Chase the journalist looked at his watch: 11:45, the New York express. When he had sailed for Europe nine years ago, the stage trip to New York had taken five days and departed just three days a week at noon. Now, he had learned from yesterday's Boston *Courier,* it took a day and a half and departed at all hours, thirty times a week. Or the steamboat would hurtle you straight down Long Island Sound in twenty-six breakneck hours. It was a whole new country, a whole new world, spinning like a demented top.

" 'Whom the gods would destroy,' " Gray said. He straightened up with a wheeze, adjusted his greatcoat over his belly, and started to limp forward. " 'They first make fat.' I would quote it in Latin for you, but I have forgotten; or better still, you would not understand. Ticknor and I are fat; you are lean as a post. Have you neglected the fleshpots of Europe? If so, a pity."

"I won't write the book," Chase said. "I've decided." He slowed his pace to match Gray's limp. Ticknor and Gray were aristocratic relics, preserved in amber. He didn't belong with them, he didn't belong with Short. "I don't seem at home here anymore. Everything's changed. I feel like Rip van Winkle."

"You are curious, however," Gray said. "Curious and loyal."

"No."

"I'll call your bluff. I'm rich. Come to my law office tomorrow and I'll give you the money for your passage."

Their steps crunched loudly on the snow. A barn owl clicked from the eaves of a building. Down Massachusetts Avenue, between hissing gas lamps, an omnibus loaded with passengers rattled around a corner and was gone. When he had been a student there were open fields from here to the Charles River, busy with nothing more than ducks and rabbits.

Now hasty, shabby clapboard and plaster storefronts covered every inch of Harvard Square; garish advertisements for patent medicines flapped on every wall; apparently the traffic never stopped, and all the new streets were duckless and raw.

"I would have to travel, interview, study American history." Chase thought of Mercy Warren's six enormous volumes. Had Jackson fought in the Revolution? "I'm too old."

"You are thirty-four."

The warmth of the wine had at last reached his brain. The appalling street bore down on him. He stopped in his tracks and gestured, waving it away. "The truth is," Chase said—it *was* a terrible, eye-popping, tongue-curling wine—"Jefferson, what used to be, democracy . . . I think I *hate* it here now."

"Of course you do, dear boy," said Gray, limping ahead. "That is precisely why Short chose you."

CHAPTER

4

In 1801, when Chase was eight years old, he had moved from Ipswich to the seaport town of Salem, where his father worked as a clerk in a shipyard owned by Gray's family.

What he remembered of his boyhood now was chiefly the landscape—the gray fists and knuckles of granite that broke through the thin Massachusetts soil west of Salem, the pale, underfed yellow pine forests that stretched westward and upward, over the coastal ridges and on and on (so he liked to imagine, as a boy), rising and falling, undulating like the ocean, over thousands of miles of American wilderness till they finally broke against the vast Rocky Mountains and dropped in a long green cascade toward the Pacific Ocean. He had been thirteen when Thomas Jefferson's agents Lewis and Clark had returned—Chase broke off his thought, bent forward, and blinked in the midday glare. Fresh Pond was a much bigger body of water than its modest name implied.

But this was Boston, he thought as his carriage left the Concord highway; the Valhalla of understatement. He shaded his eyes with one hand and estimated the length of the "pond," which he hadn't seen in years, as at least a mile and a half. Except that, of course, from December to March it was really a body of ice.

The carriage slid to a halt near a boathouse, and the black driver that William Short had sent for him jumped to the ground and flung open the door.

"He say meet him way over *there*"—a quick, cold-puckered grin, a white comma of breath—"jus' walk out on the *ice*, he say."

Chase followed the driver's pointing finger to a spot some two hundred yards out on the frozen pond. There a group of men and horses were gathered in a tight, busy knot, energetically doing something he couldn't make out through the glare.

"Growin' *ice*." The driver shook his head in tolerant amusement. "*Harvestin*' ice."

And in fact when Chase reached the group on the pond, those were the very words that William Short also used. "We are harvesting ice today, Mr. Chase. Welcome." Short stood at the center of a party of broad-shouldered young men, obviously Irish, all of them stripped down to shirtsleeves despite the cold, and most of them carrying long-handled wooden devices like brooms that Chase recognized as pushers for scraping snow. By contrast, Short wore a full-length black coat with a silver fur collar tipped up around his neck and a brushed beaver-skin hat that added almost a foot to his height. No one would have mistaken his malacca cane for a scraper.

"This is George Wyeth." Short introduced a boyish-looking man, Yankee, not Irish, who started to tip his cloth hat to Chase, then changed his mind. "George has invented a new way of cutting ice from the pond, and we're all here to see how it works."

"Waiting for Fred Tudor, actually," George Wyeth said, and one of the Irishmen spat on the snow.

"Waiting for Fred Tudor." Short pulled out a battered gold watch with a hunter's lid and a French design and cocked his head myopically as he studied the dial. "We can show you the plan at least, Mr. Chase, while we wait. You know in the past people have always taken ice from the pond with an axe or a saw, in whatever size or shape was convenient."

Behind Short, as if at an unseen signal, the workmen had spread out over the ice. Some were leading the horses into a line—there were three in all, each one trailing empty plow ropes—while others had started to scrape away snow from the ice, making a path in front of the horses.

"I didn't come to Fresh Pond often when I was a student," Chase said over the noise of the scrapers. "In Salem where I grew up, we never had much call for ice"—he smiled at Wyeth—"it's always cold enough in Salem."

"Plenty of call for it now," Short said. He took Chase's arm and guided him toward a stack of wooden box frames. "Or at least that's our bet, isn't it, George? The whole world is going to be calling for New England ice if we can just find a way to harvest it, ship it, and store it. And make a profit."

"Sell ice? At a profit?"

One of the horses stamped a single hoof, making a sound like a rifle shot.

"You've heard the saying, Mr. Chase, 'New England produces nothing but granite and ice'?"

Chase nodded and stamped his shoe on the ice like the horse; the scrapers were raising such a din now that he could hardly hear the older man's soft southern voice.

"A very unpromising landscape," Short said, looking out across the pond to its ring of sullen pines. "But the human thing—the American thing—is to turn even the limitations of nature to our advantage, yes? They are selling and shipping granite from Massachusetts all over the country now, everywhere. You will find Massachusetts granite in buildings from Philadelphia to New Orleans. George Wyeth and Fred Tudor intend to do the same with ice, only better." He gripped Chase's arm with surprisingly strong fingers. "They think you're a potential investor," he whispered. "But I asked you out here for a purpose."

By now Wyeth had lifted one of the wooden frames to the ice and knelt to attach it to a horse's plow ropes. He held it up for Chase to see: a plain rectangular frame mounted on top of two iron rods, twenty inches apart, like the runners on a sled. These runners, however, were sharply notched like saws, with bright, chisel-shaped teeth, and a little scooped mouth opened at the base of each tooth.

"You stand behind the runners," Wyeth said, clearing ice from the teeth with his fingers, "and plow just like in a field. We're going to put handles here." Under their feet the ice shook and groaned with the strokes of the scrapers.

"And the runners saw the ice into neat, uniform blocks," Short added, "which can be floated over to the dock and hauled and stored."

"And *then*," boomed a voice behind Chase's ear. He spun in surprise. "*Then* carried down to one of my goddamn ships, pardon my English, and loaded into the hull *systematically,* and shipped off to Cuba or Egypt or India just like a load of bricks. This your rich young man?"

"David Chase," murmured Short.

"Frederic Tudor," the newcomer growled. He swept past Chase and slapped a horse's rump, slapped George Wyeth's shoulder, stood on a runner, and spat, all in one agitated, fur-coated passage of energy.

"You're a world traveler, Chase," Tudor declared. "Ever drink iced tea in Cuba in the summer?" The Irish workers were moving purposefully behind him; even the horses were straightening their heads and looking alert.

"Never," Chase said, deciding to take the question as a joke. They were standing on a frozen pond on the twenty-third of January, under a pale white sun no bigger than a guinea, and the thought of iced tea and summer was as surprising and distant to him—he looked at the alien pines, the cold blue ceramic sky—as distant to him as Paris. *What* purpose? "Not once."

But Tudor wasn't joking. "You will. I want the whole goddamn world to drink iced tea whenever they want it. I want to change their tastes. *Create* a demand. Make 'em like *cold* drinks." He barked an unintelligible order over his shoulder and rocked up and down on the runner. "Know how all this started? Five years ago at Christmas my brother William looked out the window and said, wouldn't they like to have all that ice in the pond down in Cuba? Everybody laughed, but the next year I invested ten thousand dollars, every cent of my money, and shipped two boatloads of ice to Havana. Sold it for forty cents a pound. Showed them how to preserve meat, eggs, even fruit, and make ice cream. They loved it—the niggers down there went crazy, never even *seen ice before*—but where I lost my profit was in the transit. Not in my Cuban storehouse," he told Short, who was regarding not the horses and not the workmen, but Chase. "The storehouse was fine. I designed it myself, insulated everything with sawdust and straw and double roofs. But look here—" Tudor hopped from the frame and spread his arms over the ice. "This isn't wood. You chop at it with an axe, you get all shapes, all sizes of block, and then you load it in a ship's hold helter-skelter, you leave air spaces every-where, the cargo shifts, your money melts. George—"

On his knees Wyeth was hammering the last of two steering handles onto the frame, and his workmen were doing the same thing behind the other horses.

"Put on a show, George," Tudor ordered. He flapped his arms for warmth and stepped back while the teams moved into action. Wyeth gripped his handles, an Irishman seized the nearest horse's bit and tugged, and the runner blades started to saw the ice in long, deep parallel lines. From the other direction, at right angles to Wyeth's cut, a second team began to plow. And as its blades intersected the first set of lines, neat, square twenty-inch blocks of ice started to pop up and bob on the path of black water that had suddenly been created.

"Ten times the speed," Tudor shouted over the rip of the blades and the clop of hooves. "Perfect cubes, perfect size." He leaned toward Short. "Fellow opened a rival business in Martinique last year. I sold my ice for a penny a pound till I put him under. Same thing this year in New Orleans. I won't be beat. My seasonal loss from melting was less than *eight per-cent.*" He handed Chase a stiff white business card embossed with his name, *Frederic Tudor, The Ice King,* a Boston address, and an astonish-ingly long-winded motto: *He who gives back at the first repulse and with-out striking the second blow despairs of success, has never been, is not, and never will be a hero in war, love, or business.*

"All right, Mr. Short," Tudor said while the cutting teams crossed and countercrossed in front of them and the pond creaked and swayed under their feet. Instinctively Chase braced his legs for balance and hunched his shoulders, as if he were caught in a gale. "As far as investment goes, Mr. Short," Tudor shouted, "this is the time to fish or cut bait."

Short took the card from Chase and held it close to his glasses, then handed it back with a soft ironic smile. "Mr. Chase," he murmured, "welcome to the Age of Jackson."

✳   ✳   ✳

IN the private dining room of the Tremont House Hotel two hours later, Short ordered, from yet another black servant, a dinner of canvasback duck for both of them and a bottle of spectacularly expensive Chablis.

"You are not temperance, I hope?" Short poised the bottle over Chase's glass and leaned forward to peer at him. The Tremont House dining room was furnished with several dozen separate tables and two palely inefficient gas lamps on the walls; in their dim, flickering light Short floated like a white-haired fish. "You haven't taken the dreadful, unnatural oath?"

"I am a stranger in my own land," Chase told him sincerely. "I have no idea what the temperance oath is. I trust this wine has been chilled with Fresh Pond ice, of course."

Short smiled. "Temperance began in New York, but like all plagues it has spread quickly. I'm sure that Frederic Tudor has sold ice to the Tremont. To become temperance you forswear strong drink forever; you sign a pledge in front of twelve sober, unforgiving witnesses. There are in fact two different degrees of righteousness to it." He poured them each a very full glass. "You can swear mere temperance, which allows you to backslide and drink toasts at dinner if politeness requires it. Or you can sign the pledge with a capital *T* after your name, which means total abstinence. Then you are called a teetotaler and you go straight to the kingdom of heaven, where no grape grows." Short sipped his wine fastidiously. "Jefferson drank two glasses of red wine every day of his life."

"About my book," Chase began.

"About your book," Short agreed. "Have you looked at the book Mrs. Hale gave you yesterday?"

"Not yet."

"You should. It's called *Andrew Jackson: A Biography,* by John Reid and John Eaton. Reid died and Eaton finished it. It belongs to a new species of literature that you, in your blessed French exile, have been spared. The campaign biography—this one is extremely effective. It shows the reader that Andrew Jackson singlehandedly drove the British from North America in the War of 1812. That Andrew Jackson is a second Washington for greatness; more honest than Franklin, more intelligent than Jefferson, far, far more deserving of the President's mansion than the present incumbent, John Quincy Adams, he of the 'corrupt bargain' and the monarchist father. It says nothing at all about Jackson's duels, his illiteracy, his land speculations in Tennessee, his shameful treatment of the Creeks and Cherokees . . . about certain other things."

Chase put down his knife and fork. "I must tell you, sir, I know almost nothing about this, nothing—the names, the places, these are all abstractions to me. I want to be candid. I came home to be with my father while he died. I have no money whatsoever; I need your book. But I'm not the man to write it."

In the aqueous darkness of the gas lamps Short was cutting slices of duck and serenely eating them with his fork in his left hand, European fashion.

"I've no knowledge at all of the issues, let alone 'certain other things.' " Chase swallowed his wine in a gulp.

"You knew Thomas Jefferson." Short waved away the black waiter and refilled their glasses himself.

"I visited his home when I was young. *I don't know America, sir.*"

"As for that," Short murmured in the ironic voice Chase was by now used to, "who does?" He spooned a rivulet of gravy onto his duck. "You are perfect, perfect," he murmured.

Chase let his hands drop to his sides in frustration. Short looked up quizzically, then daubed at his mouth with a stiff white serviette, snowy as a beard. "Mr. Chase, I was Thomas Jefferson's personal secretary in Paris for five years, and afterward served in diplomatic posts abroad while he was secretary of state. When I returned home in 1801, he was President and we saw each other from time to time, then and later. I have in my home in Philadelphia a whole file of letters he wrote me; I sometimes make beginnings on a book of memoirs about him. Every feeling I have for this country is derived from Jefferson, from Jefferson's ideas. Left to myself—" In the poor light Short seemed to look away pensively, toward another table of diners, though Chase had begun to suspect Short couldn't see past the length of his nose. "I am not asking you to dig up dirt on Jackson," Short said. "That would be beneath you, that would be un-Jeffersonian. But we need an *honest* portrait, do we not, to counteract political fictions? Jackson as he *really* is—nobody seems to know him, you see. There are only legends, rumors, puffs. Jefferson trusted the people, on the condition the people would be rightly informed."

Short floated closer. "Your book, Mr. Chase, which I am too old and untalented to write myself, will be an act of repayment, say, on my part, to a country which Thomas Jefferson taught me to love."

"I am more European by now than American," Chase said, one last gesture of resistance.

"I think not, Mr. Chase. I've read your books. They're filled with a Jeffersonian love of country, though usually disguised as wit and irony, as love of anything ought to be." Short speared the last of his duck with the left-handed fork. "Beneath your skepticism there is also a streak of hero worship. You are far too democratic and kind to the Elder Pitt."

"I might be too kind to Jackson before I finish. I would insist on that right."

"The truth shall be our mutual guide," Short said so solemnly that Chase was sure he was quoting Jefferson. The older man pushed his plate aside and snapped two fingers to summon the waiter. "Actually," he said, "Jefferson quite liked Andrew Jackson. He told me so."

Chase stiffened in his chair as if it had turned to a block of ice. He started to speak; stopped.

"I have arranged for you to be in Washington City on January twenty-ninth," Short said. "Here are letters to the President, whom I knew quite well in Paris an eon ago. Here is a draft of credit on my bank. Your tickets."

The waiter materialized out of the opaque modern lights and Short pointed one long finger toward a cart of desserts on the opposite wall. "And the memorandum of agreement," Short said as the waiter turned toward the cart. "Your signature goes here."

Somehow there were also pen and inkwell on the table now. Chase took up the pen. The waiter wheeled over a little mountain of puddings, cakes, red-and-white confections of cream and sugar.

"Here," Short repeated ambiguously.

Chase read the very large sum Short had written on the top of the first page as his advance payment; mentally calculated how long it would last him in Paris, if he reclaimed his old flat on the rue de Seine and ate only one meal a day; inhaled softly; and signed.

"And port." Short bundled the papers back into his coat and nodded briskly to the waiter. "Leave the cart." He helped himself first to an immense slab of marbled rum cake, then apologetically handed the serving spoons to Chase. "Old men are always greedy for sweets," he said. "Forgive me. You understand, of course, that George Wyeth is the real inventor of the ice-cutting machine, but Frederic Tudor intends to beat him down and steal it away. He'll leave the boy a pauper in six months. I've seen the papers, all the contracts."

"And you haven't warned him?"

Short busied himself with pouring a slow, thick column of cream over his cake and said nothing.

"It is indelicate, perhaps," Chase said, wondering if his irony sounded sufficiently like Short's own, "to tell me of a crooked contract just after I have signed a document for you."

Short brought a spoonful of cream to his mouth and smiled. When he had swallowed, he daubed his lips again with his serviette and cocked his head at Chase, like a curious white-haired sparrow. "You are not married, are you, Mr. Chase?" he asked, as if in afterthought.

"No."

"Because," Short said, lifting another spoonful of cream, "there is a complication I forgot to mention."

CHAPTER
5

The sixth President of the United States, John Quincy Adams, looked longingly at the smooth-flowing brown stream of the Potomac River and wished that he could jump in.

Too cold, of course. Even in Washington, a so-called southern city, in February the river was too cold and the air was too cold and the hour, six-thirty in the morning, was too dark for swimming.

Satisfied with having made all possible logical objections and thereby deprived himself of a pleasure, Adams nonetheless stooped by the bank and paddled his right hand gently back and forth in the water. It was his custom when the weather was warmer to swim every morning in the Potomac for one full hour before returning to the President's mansion. He spilled water between his outspread fingers and contemplated the rock-hard orderliness of his schedule. Up at five; readings in the New Testament until five-thirty; meditations in his journal and prayer; then a solitary stroll along the bank of the river, four miles at least. Then breakfast. Then his desk. Then the unending (unswimmable) stream of soul-cracking visitors, whose names he recorded in the margin of his diary and whose business he knew, before they spoke, better than they did.

With a grunt, Adams forced himself to stand up. He clutched at a sycamore branch to steady himself until his usual spell of dizziness after bending had passed (a moral allegory? he wondered; upright he was never dizzy).

Over his shoulder the sunlight now threw itself in broken coins far out across the river, toward Virginia. Last year at this time, feeling braver, he had come down to swim but been prevented by a sweeping boat and a crew of sweepers, who were dragging their nets along the bottom in search of an old man reportedly drowned the night before. And while Adams had stood and watched curiously, the crew had actually come up with the body, about a hundred yards from shore, and after much fussing laid it on a blanket under the very tree he now clutched. The body of the man, a Mr. Shoemaker of Georgetown, was hardly marked, though there had been a dark flush of settled blood over his face, like a fever, and a few drops of blood issued from his mouth and one ear. There was nothing terrible or offensive in the sight, only in the information gathered next day from the press that "old" Shoemaker had been no more than sixty years old, one year older than Adams himself.

I should give up swimming altogether, Adams thought. I like it too much. It is too dangerous.

Dizziness had yielded, as always, to rectitude. He turned and began his solitary march back to the mansion, where breakfast awaited him; and also—he was systematic in his list—his worthy mad wife; his wasteful son John and his flirtatious, discourteous bride; and his son Charles, who might yet (if he did not spoil his chances) carry on the name.

He crossed a muddy field and wound around a trio of Guernsey cows grazing in an empty lot. In Paris, Adams remembered, his father had been fond of quoting a sarcastic French poem about the city's wretched climate—"wind and rain, rain and wind"—he had forgotten the rest. Anyone in his right mind, of course, would have exchanged Washington for Paris in an instant, rain or no rain.

The President paused at an unpaved road—there was in fact only half a mile of paved road in all of Washington City, and that was in front of Gadsby's Hotel—while a lumbering coach rolled by, full of sleeping, jouncing passengers. The arrangement—*deal* was not too strong a word—whereby the muddy and malarial District of Columbia had been made the nation's capital instead of Philadelphia or New York was one he had heard described many times. His father himself had told him the story. Jefferson and Alexander Hamilton had come out of George Washington's house in New York one fine spring afternoon in 1791 and commenced to stroll down Broadway, Jefferson tall and courtly and dressed to the nines in foppish French clothes, and Hamilton, no less foppish, but a good seven inches shorter, taking two steps for Jefferson's every one. If the secretary of state (Jefferson) would agree to the funding of Revolutionary War bonds at full cost (a measure designed to benefit Hamilton's friends, who had speculated in old bonds for years), then the secretary of the treasury (Hamilton) would agree to the removal of the capital to the very borders of the Holy Soil of Virginia, within sight of Washington's own house (a measure designed to satisfy the Virginians' feelings of dynastic destiny). The two of them had worked it out in less than five minutes and paused in the middle of the street to shake hands, an event noted by many observers, though none of them understood its significance.

Hamilton had been the ultimate loser, of course. His profits were soon gone—he himself was gone in a few years, shot dead—but the capital and its mud would be here forever. It had been Adams's experience that the shorter man, like himself, always lost out in the end to the taller.

As the President stepped through the mud and onto the sloping west lawn of his mansion, he also remembered Aaron Burr's first words upon seeing Washington City. *If this is not hell, it will do.*

⋆   ⋆   ⋆

IT will never do, Chase thought as he stepped out of the stagecoach two miles away.

"That one there is Gadsby's Hotel." The coach driver pointed his whip toward a ramshackle three-story building on the opposite side of the street. Then he looked down at Chase's battered portmanteau and spat. "But you ain't going to find a room in it."

Chase slapped at a mosquito on his cheek. Mosquitoes in February!

"Try the National Hotel down the block," the driver suggested, and spat again. "Or the Temperance Hotel, if you don't mind drinking water."

Chase gave him a coin and walked to the back of the stagecoach. In France he had read that Washington was on its way to becoming a great capital city; the plans of the French designer L'Enfant ensured wide avenues and inspiring vistas; the lofty domed Capitol and the President's mansion formed two splendid poles at the end of a spacious, carriage-filled boulevard. Crowds of senators and statesmen strolled in the open air, from embassy to embassy.

He shifted the portmanteau to his other hand. Spaciousness the city had. And possibly statesmen—the loungers on the wooden sidewalk in front of Gadsby's were dressed like farmers (and spat like stagecoach drivers), but in a frontier democracy who could be sure? On the other hand, the Capitol to his right rose on a bump of open grassland rather than a Roman hill; its dome, seen now through a fine mist of moisture and mosquitoes, was wide, flat, and black, like an inverted washbowl. The surrounding houses were few, and widely separated by open plots of grass. To his left, Pennsylvania Avenue (according to the sign) was wide enough to be splendid, but it was devoid of carriages, though not of pigs, and despite the clustered hotels and the stagecoach depot, most of its length was utterly bare and empty.

Most of *Washington* was empty, Chase thought, dodging pigs and gaining the sidewalk by Gadsby's. It had hardly changed since he had been here ten—thirteen—years ago, on his tour south with Ticknor and Gray. Then and now it looked as if the sky had rained a few dozen naked buildings on an open plain, then stopped.

But if Washington was empty, Gadsby's was full, as the driver had predicted. And so were the National and the Temperance (and a small annex next door designated "Native-Born Americans Only"). At last, opposite an open-air market where a crew of black slaves was busy unloading crates of chickens, he found Brown's Indian Queen Hotel, which announced itself with a luridly painted signboard of Pocahontas kneeling before her father. He signed the bar book, agreed to pay a dollar and a quarter a day, and received a pair of cloth slippers and a new candle to use in his room. And after depositing his grip and splashing his face with water, he returned to the street and oriented himself.

One *minor* complication, Short had said; but bring a bottle of something when you call.

The address Chase wanted lay fewer than six blocks away on his map; the walk itself took more than fifteen minutes, however, thanks to the condition of the sidewalks beyond Pennsylvania Avenue (mud interspersed with puddles) and a large open ditch across C Street, which was a construction project of indeterminate purpose, either recently begun or recently abandoned. Chase crossed a loose plank bridge over the ditch and passed, isolated from everything else, a druggist's shop whose window displayed a large poster advertising its own manufactured hair oil. In the same narrow building an optician's window had miniature busts of Franklin, Lafayette, and Washington, each adorned with a pair of tiny wire-rimmed spectacles. Washington's spectacles were colored white, Franklin's green; Lafayette's were clear.

Next to the optician's stretched a vacant lot big enough for two cows to stand in, grazing. Chase paused to ask himself if he had ever seen cows wandering free in Paris or London; if the next cows he saw would be wearing hair oil and colored spectacles. Then he reached the corner of New Jersey and F and entered a swaybacked clapboard building whose sign was hung from a single nail by the door: RECAMIER'S BOARDING HOUSE——ROOMS BY THE WEEK.

The clerk behind the desk answered his question by pointing wordlessly to key rack number fourteen.

Chase ascended two flights of stairs, groped his way down an uncarpeted hallway, and knocked twice at the door of number fourteen.

"Mr. Hogwood," he said brightly as the door swung open.

In front of him stood a woman about his own age dressed in a yellow gown of unmistakable French cut. Her blond hair was piled high in a chignon anchored with an ebony comb; her complexion was soft and clear, glowing in a ray of sunlight from a window to her right. Her eyes were flat and cold with dislike.

"Hogwood here!" boomed a man's voice behind her. "Come in! Come in!"

The woman stepped aside with a snap of her skirts, and Chase found himself staring at an enormously fat old man of sixty or more, stretched full-length on a divan and propped upright with half a dozen colored pillows.

"Like a Turk," the old man said to Chase, waving him in. Gravelly British accent; round pink face like a cooked moon. "You're thinking I look like a Turk snug in my coffeehouse, smoking my hookah." He smiled broadly, splitting the moon and showing yellow teeth and black gums. "Sorry, no hookah, no Turkee."

"I'm David Chase."

"Emma!" The old man's smile remained in place, but somehow grew harder and straighter. "Here's Mr. Chase come to put us in the poorhouse."

"I surmised," said Emma; she had disappeared behind a thin muslin curtain that divided the shabby room in half. Chase could see her figure move in silhouette.

"Come in, close the door, sit down," Hogwood said. "Do all the polite little things to make yourself at home. Emma will bring us tea."

Chase drew up a chair beside the divan. Hogwood's belly and legs were covered by a red-and-blue plaid blanket, not at all clean. He whipped up one corner to show Chase a swollen foot and ankle swaddled in white cloth. "Gout," the old man said calmly. "Gout or dropsy or cancer. Doctors can't say. Hardly matters, does it? Can't walk, can't travel. When it reaches as far as my heart, well, can't complain, eh?"

Chase murmured something and Hogwood dismissed it with a flip of his hand. "Sixty-three years old, abused my earthly vessel every single blessed day of them, *voilà*. You are carrying what exactly in that package, Mr. Chase?"

Chase looked down at his hands with surprise. "I thought—I passed a wine merchant's on my way here."

"Liar," Hogwood said happily. "Old Short—who is not short, by the way, did you notice? Nor is he fat—old Short—he *is* old—gave you precise instructions, I'm sure of it. 'Bring Hogwood intemperate beverages.' Must have written it on your contract." Hogwood unwrapped the bottle and held it up to the sunlight to read. "Burgundy," he said. "Very nice. From the Clos de Vougeot, which Napoleon is said to have made his troops salute as they marched past on their way to Russia. Lovely, Mr. Chase. I deeply regret that it is so early in the morning, not yet ten o'clock. Emma," he called. "Come place this exquisite bottle in our cellar so it can age." Hogwood winked at Chase. "I let most good wines age until noon, you know. Emma!"

"I don't really need tea, Mr. Hogwood."

"Of course, you don't. Terrible muck. But the *ritual*, my boy, a little ceremony of eating and drinking together instead of cutting each other's throats, as otherwise we might. And besides, there're not many pure ceremonies in America, are there? Dueling, of course, and tobacco spitting. But after that—Emma, put the tea here, the little cakes there."

Chase rose from his chair to assist her, but Emma was brisk, efficient, grimly tight-lipped. He watched a loose strand of blond hair curl on her throat. Her gown opened as she bent.

"This is plum cake," Hogwood said, heaping slices on his plate and gesturing for Chase to do the same. "That one is apple. Can't think how she finds the fruits this time of year, but she does."

"Mrs. Hogwood—" Chase began.

"Mrs. Hogwood's dead, my boy." The old man had shifted on his divan so that plates and cups rested on a wooden lap tray and his huge pink face could be turned directly toward Chase. "Emma is my daughter. Emma Colden. I made her take her mother's maiden name—you wouldn't burden a young girl with a name like Hogwood, would you? Her mother died in Paris twenty years ago. She was hit by a nobleman's carriage on the rue St. Honoré as she was crossing the street. Came out of nowhere, preceded by two barking dogs and racing footmen in uniform, supposed to clear the streets for him. A nice mixture of absurdity and tragedy."

"I'm sorry."

Hogwood balanced his teacup on his belly and grunted. "We are all flies in God's web. God the spider."

"I'll be at the market," Emma said from the door. She stood with one hand on the knob and looked at her father, not Chase. From this angle the sunlight coming through the window fell squarely across her arms and figure, but to Chase's eyes the yellow dress seemed almost dissolved by its intensity, and for a moment, from shoulder to waist, he had the illusion of gazing on naked skin. Then she moved entirely into shadow and vanished.

"She's angry with me."

Hogwood dipped cake in his tea. "You ought to see the central market yourself, my boy. Half the farms in Virginia sell vegetables there, flowers later on, mostly poultry now. Old Jefferson himself used to go from his mansion with a basket on his arm, they say."

"Mr. Hogwood—"

"My own practice, of course, when I could walk about, was in every new city I visited to go straight to the highest possible point and take a bird's-eye view of it. I went to the top of the State House in Boston, the roof of the Pennsylvania Hotel in Philadelphia, a church steeple in Charleston—what a dreary swamp that is. Notre Dame in Paris, of course. And the top of the Capitol here, if you don't mind high winds and the company of pigeons. Then, I like to go to the opposite tack for a low-life view. In New York I went to a slum at Five Points that equaled anything I ever saw in Europe. Found a beggar there with a reversible sign on his chest. One side read 'Paralyzed since the twentieth of March.' The other side said 'Blind since fifteen.' Very American, I thought."

"I believe we might still work together."

"No, we can't. Short is quite right. He hired me to write a book about Andrew Jackson and I haven't done it and I can't travel to Tennessee now, not in this condition. And time is running out."

"He said you had written something—possibly I could edit or build on it."

"I asked him to let Emma finish the book, that was my mistake."

"She is a writer?"

"She is a splendid writer. But she is a woman. And Short, although he lived in Paris and knew Madame de Staël and Adèle de Flahaut, all of the bluestockings—Short is very American now. 'Woman, climb up on this pedestal! Cover thine ankles! Flatten thy mammaries! Permit me to worship from afar thy Supremely Decorative Uselessness!' "

Chase grinned in spite of himself. "But he works with Sarah Hale."

"Oh yes. Short's a southerner and therefore completely inconsistent. That's one of the few things I like about Jackson. He makes no pretense of logic whatsoever. I was going to call my book, privately, *Old Hickory: Slash and Take.* But the divine Sarah Hale, you must understand, only employs women to write about *womanly* subjects. Politics are for men. I read your book on Talleyrand and Fouché, by the way, my boy. Thoroughly subtle. Rather passionate. I can see why Short would prefer you."

"I don't know your work. I'm sorry."

Hogwood looked suddenly tired. His moon face seemed to deflate like a ball. "I would open your wine, Mr. Chase, and ask you to stay. But the pain in my legs makes me a poor host sometimes."

Chase instantly rose from his chair.

"Before I came here," Hogwood said, "I wrote chiefly for magazines in Britain. *The Edinburgh Review. Blackwood's.* You are a Francophile, you wouldn't have seen my bits, though I've supported Emma and myself—until now—tolerably well. Now she supports me."

Chase looked about the little room, its muslin curtain, cheap furniture, boarding-house crockery. "What does she do?" he asked, aware that the question was presumptuous and rude.

Hogwood ignored it. From the plaid blanket he pulled a sheaf of oc-tavo-sized paper tied with a black ribbon. He handed it to Chase.

"This is part of what I wrote, Mr. Chase. Read it at your leisure. Treat it kindly." He wheezed dramatically and sank back in his pillows. "Think of my daughter."

CHAPTER

6

Half an hour later Chase sat down in his room at the Indian Queen and untied the ribbon around Hogwood's papers.

He held up the first page. The old man's handwriting was as tiny as he himself was fat. Chase let his gaze drift to the open window, where his vista comprised an unpainted shack, a shirtless slave leading a pig down an alley, a distant glimpse of the river curling in a great brown southern noose around the city. Paris on the Potomac. *Think of my daughter.* He slapped a mosquito, returned to Hogwood's first page, and in six lines saw why Short had dismissed him.

The Life of Andrew Jackson

Chapter One

ANDREW JACKSON WAS BORN IN 1767—NO ONE KNOWS EXACTLY WHERE, because the boundary line between North and South Carolina has been in dispute for decades. *He* says South Carolina, but he is a man notoriously lax with the truth.

In fact, I have heard people claim that because he speaks with a slight Irish brogue, he must have been born in Ireland (and so ineligible for the presidency) or on the high seas coming over, though the case is that the hills of North and South Carolina are swarming at this very moment with people who sound just like him. *Look* just like him, for that matter—tall and gaunt, with hard, angry, long-skulled, shovel-jawed features. Not an ounce of humor or art or generosity spoils the perfect *contentiousness* of their faces. I know the type well; in Britain we call them Scotch-Irish and stay clear, if we can help it, of their tough, vehement little world in the north of Ireland, where they migrated and settled from Scotland two hundred years ago, thanks to a decree of land to his Scotch soldiers by James I, of various memory.

Jackson comes of this belligerent stock. His grandfather Hugh Jackson fought the French in the great siege of Carrickfergus (in reality a trivial, farcical thing) and was later paid compensation for his "sufferings" by the British government.

His son, the father of our Andrew, finding no one to fight, joined the great wave of Scotch-Irish who descended on Pennsylvania sixty years ago, discovered it full, and wandered south to a backwoods region, either in North or South Carolina, called poetically, after a local Indian tribe, the Garden of the Waxhaws. (There is also a Waxhaw Creek, not much to look at; the whole area is generally styled "the Waxhaws.") True to their nature, the new settlers promptly started a local civil war between North people and South people and passed much of their free time raiding each other's towns and burning each other's crops (it took the British soldiers of '76, the great unifiers of this fractured country, to give them a common enemy).

An awful place to live, truthfully. I have often thought that the great curse of the South is not its climate, not its soil (like plowing red tar), not even its sad brown forests of scrub pine and oak—but its solitude. Six rude cabins make a town. Logs thrown "corduroy" crisscross in the mud make a road. No books, no theatres, no transportation. The little parties of settlers in the backwoods, like our Scotch-Irish pilgrims, simply sink into a perfect ferine isolation where all their appalling and violent Old World traits fester, fester. In the village where Andrew Jackson was reared, the local minister committed suicide by twisting a bridle ingeniously around his neck while he prayed. Six or seven months later the congregation decided it looked more like murder than ingenuity, and late one winter's night they dragged his young widow out to the gravesite and dug up the corpse.

In Ireland if she touched the skull and it bled, she was guilty.

The young widow got down on her hands and knees and extended one trembling finger to the forehead. No blood.

She started to rise and the nearest man seized her whole hand and *crushed* it into the skull. She wrenched away, sobbing, then waved her fingers under the torchlight—dry, innocent, matted with clumps of hair.

Jackson's father died two months before he was born. His corpse fell off the sled on the way to the funeral, but the pallbearers were so comically drunk, Irish-fashion, that they failed entirely to notice the body had disappeared. They found it hours later in the twilight, caught in the brush on the bank of a creek, covered with snow.

I count the boy's formative experiences—"the child is father of the man," the modern poet says—as three in number.

One. *Slobbering.* Hard to put it any other way. The boy Jackson was afflicted with several painful ailments—I have talked with the old slave granny who says she cured him of "the Big Itch" (all pause and shudder to imagine)—and he was from birth, evidently, not physically strong. Yet everyone agrees that his worst handicap was this: until he grew into adulthood, young Jackson spit and slobbered while he talked, literally *drooled;* and the harder he tried to control these sputterings, the more likely he was to explode in frustrated anger, forerunner no doubt of those terrifying fits of temper for which, then and now, the Hero is spectacularly famous.

I stop to muse. Of all this fragmented young nation's statesmen, Jackson is by miles and miles the least well-read. Let us not mince words: the closest to illiteracy. He attended a field school in the Waxhaw settlement for a few years only. There he picked up some fossilized phrases of Latin—I am told that the General often peppers his conversations today with *"ipso facto," "delenda est Carthago"*—and he learned to keep accounts. But as for real mastery of language—what other Hero has so mangled his native tongue? The General cannot spell an English word the same way twice. He wrenches grammar into agonizing contortions, leaves sentences incomplete, violates cruelly the tender domestic relationship of subject and verb. Compared to Madison or Adams or Jefferson—compared even to Washington, who spelled badly but quoted (bad) poetry from memory—compared to these paragons, Andrew Jackson, as far as language goes, is a coarse, unlettered ignoramus. In all the speeches and letters I have seen he has referred to exactly one book (Goldsmith's *Vicar of Wakefield;* dear God).

And yet, and yet: precociously he taught himself to read at five (this I have verified). In the years of agitation just before the Revolutionary War, the Philadelphia newspapers would find their way slowly into the Waxhaws backcountry, and then all the glowering Scotch-Irish farmers would put down their hoes for a time and gather in a house or church to hear the news read aloud, column by column. Every witness still living agrees: the person chosen most often to read aloud was skinny young Andy Jackson, whose voice was shrill, but who never faltered or grew hoarse; indeed, grew stronger as he recounted each new British outrage. In this dreadful year of democracy 1828, Jackson's "campaign managers" now write every letter and declaration that goes out over the Candidate's name (imagine someone revising Jefferson's prose), but Jackson's impromptu speeches in the field to his soldiers are legendary.

What to think? Inarticulation builds rage? Some men are born to books, others have books thrust upon them? Should we have a President who does not read and cannot write? But can *talk*? In mid-summer 1776 the nine-year-old Hero prepared especially hard for his reading one week, to an audience of forty or more gathered growling and muttering in his uncle Crawford's house, and thus began his long, ambiguous connection to the most literate and language-ridden President we shall ever see: "In Congress, July 4, 1776. The Unanimous Declaration of the Thirteen United States of America. When in the course of human events . . ."

Two. *The War.* I have an acquaintance who swears that for every story told about Jefferson there are always two contradictory versions: he fled like a coward from Banastre Tarleton's raiding troops; he stayed like a hero till the very last moment. He kept a slave mistress, he did not; he believed in God, he did not—endless tedious self-canceling scandals. For Jackson I hear much the same kind of paradox: he stole another man's wife, he was as innocent as Adam; he plotted treason, he breathes patriotism. But the one thing no one questions is the man's appetite for war.

The *boy*'s appetite, let us be accurate. Jackson's opponent in the coming election, His Rotundity John Quincy Adams, has vivid memories of being led through Boston by his kinsman Sam Adams and watching with wide round eyes the British redcoats parade on Boston Common. His mother took him by the hand to see (from a great distance) the Battle of

Bunker Hill, and he sometimes talks (with stilted, artificial memory, I fear) of remembering the cannon's flash and the black clouds of drifting smoke. But Andy Jackson was dragged by nobody to see a battle. Jackson, age fourteen, mounted a little "grass pony" and charged right in.

The stories of the backcountry war are dramatic enough: farmers splitting their saws in half to make swords; forts made out of cotton bales; militia going into battle with more men than muskets, so the unarmed ones watched by the sides until somebody fell, then raced in and snatched his weapon. Andy Jackson moved back and forth across the Carolina hills, as a spy, as a guide, in a high pitch of excitement. When Tarleton's dragoons massacred a troop of Carolina militia, Jackson and his mother nursed the wounded (and the dying) in a little church turned hospital and morgue. His oldest brother Hugh (Jackson witnessed it) died of heat and exhaustion after a skirmish beside a creek. While John Quincy Adams was being tugged by his mother back to his schoolbooks, Jackson and his other brother Robert were skulking along the backtrails of the hill country, trailing the enemy. He personally saw loyalist vigilantes hang a dozen suspected Tories from an oak tree, three at a time. Guarding a sleeping captain's house, he personally fired his musket into the ranks of a British patrol and felt the return bullets whizzing by his face ("the charming sound of bullets," Washington used to say). In the spring of 1781 he and Robert were trapped in a swamp by a British officer, who lost his grip on Robert's collar only at the last moment and fell from his horse, wounded by somebody's shot as the boys vanished into the mire.

Most dramatic of all: next day Andrew and Robert took refuge in a neighbor's house—only the wife and baby present—and a party of Lord Rawdon's dragoons tracked them down. I hold no brief for British conduct in these backwoods wars (my people, alas). They behaved with pure, unadulterated Saxon savagery. Stories are still told—a pregnant woman stripped of her clothes and the name "George III" carved with a knife on her belly; houses, churches torched; "rebel" infants skewered on a sword. Rawdon's men tore down the walls of Jackson's cabin and burned all the clothes and bedding. Famously, the officer in charge thrust a mud-coated jackboot in Jackson's face and ordered him to clean it, and the boy stood up straight and defied him. At which the enraged officer sprang back and swung his sword down like a club.

Jefferson and Washington and Adams never "ran" for President. They sat in their homes (reading) and waited for the citizens to vote. But those days are gone forever, transformed by Jackson chiefly, Jackson and his "campaign," his marching bands and rallies, his barbecues, his banners and posters and buttons and "Hickory" badges. You can buy, if you wish, a campaign engraving called *The Brave Boy of the Waxhaws*, which shows that British officer, sword swinging down, that brave boy Jackson, left hand going up to block the blade. Jackson still carries scars on his head and his hand. He would have remembered them at New Orleans.

The rest is quickly told. Marched as prisoners forty miles to the town of Camden, and incarcerated there with two hundred other rebels in the local jail, an unusually miserable affair without beds, fires, or any kind of food except stale bread, Jackson was robbed of his shoes and jacket. Evidently shaking with suppressed fury at his treatment, he nonetheless used his remarkable power of speaking (not slobbering) to persuade the British officer in charge to provide food and medicine at least.

In late April, through a hole in the wooden fence that he had cut himself with a razor (too young to shave), fourteen-year-old Jackson watched the American troops of General Nathaniel Greene pitch camp on the hill overlooking Camden. Greene commanded an enormous army, much bigger than the British garrison, and the prisoners were full of hope. Lesson of War Number One: while Greene camped and meditated on his superior position, Lord Rawdon's troops mounted a bold, supremely dangerous charge—and destroyed the American army. There was no substitute in war—in anything—for the direct, unforgiving attack.

Three days later, Jackson's mother arrived to take her sons home in an exchange of prisoners. By that time both boys were burning up, from the inside out, with smallpox. They journeyed back in a rainstorm, Robert lashed to the single horse she had brought, Andy and mother walking beside. In another two days Robert was dead.

And the Third Formative Experience. Brief, unendurable; everlasting. Jackson had never known his father. His mother (in the reading-aloud days) had imagined her youngest son would be a minister, and confided her dream to her neighbors, who laughed at the thought: Andy Jackson was the wildest boy in the Waxhaws, he cursed like a sailor of forty, raced horses and gambled; at age twelve he ran the largest cockfight in the county.

He had her red hair. He had the submerged part of her character that female decorum, even in the backcountry, so thoroughly obscured: fierce temper, fierce Irish courage; implacable determination to *grind down* any obstacle in her path. These, however, she kept covered for propriety's sake, much as she kept her Bible out of sight, Irish-fashion, covered on her lap with a piece of blue-and-white checked cloth.

As soon as Robert was buried and Andy was out of danger from the smallpox, Elizabeth Jackson set out on foot for Charleston to nurse captured Americans, two cousins among them, in a British prison ship.

Now, why do it? Why desert your only son and help comparative strangers a hundred and sixty miles distant? I am fat where the General is lean, I earn my living by words; I shall never in this lifetime travel in that bloody and pious Scotch-Irish mind. But it takes very little power of sympathy to ask these questions in the boy's place. Or to add: would it not leave you furious and helpless, torn apart with guilt and (because you could never, never name its true object) unquenchable anger?

In one of his numerous "official" biographies the General paints an affecting scene. "Kissing at meetings and partings," he says, "was not so common then as now." As if both were aware of what was coming, his mother wiped her eyes with her apron and stammered a few words of absolutely barbaric, un-Biblical advice: "Andy, never tell a lie, nor take what is not your own, nor sue for slander—*settle them cases yourself.*"

She died a few weeks later of "ship fever" and was buried in an unmarked grave in Charleston. In his prosperous middle age the General has looked for it twice without success.

CHAPTER
7

John Coffee turned his face a lazy six inches to the left and spat a brown bullet of tobacco over the side of the boat. Then he stretched one size-twelve booted foot along the damp cotton bale he was using as a bench and softly cursed all boats, all rivers, all political celebrations; his eye fell on James A. Hamilton, Esquire, of New York City, standing next to General Andrew Jackson at the boat rail: all Yankees.

As if he could read Coffee's mind, Hamilton turned and smiled at him. Smiled sickly, it appeared, except who could be sure? James A. Hamilton was wearing a beige-colored swallowtail coat with a matching velvet collar, an orange cravat, a pearl gray silk waistcoat, white duck trousers, and to top it all off a broad-brimmed beaver hat ten inches high and still covered with fur. He nodded and tipped his hat, and out from under its shadow his face now did look distinctly qualmish, which Coffee could well understand. The *Pocahontas* had been under steam for nearly two hours, rocking and slapping on the hard brown Mississippi waves, and if Coffee was any judge, Hamilton's elegant little pot-shaped New York stomach was beginning to shake like a churn on a mule.

On the port side a trim white steamer half their size was just now passing the *Pocahontas* for what must have been the fifth or sixth time since they had left Natchez. Fifty yards ahead, playing his game, the pilot cut straight in front of them, left to right, so that the *Pocahontas* suddenly bucked and seesawed in his wake and a great muddy spray of Mississippi water flew over the rails. Obviously ignorant of who was on board, the steamer's crew laughed and shouted something drunken and probably unprintable.

What would happen, Coffee thought, would be either that the little steamer's boiler would overheat in a while and simply explode—he had seen steamboats explode on the Cumberland River, and it was an awesome, satisfying sight—or else General Jackson would overheat and explode, and that would be a more awesome sight by far.

And in fact the General was now calling over one of the *Pocahontas*'s sailors, and Hamilton was raising his hands in alarm. Coffee lowered his boots to the deck and sat up straight. Hamilton was the son of Alexander Hamilton and reputed to look exactly like his martyred father—dark-skinned, neat, short, quick and fussy in his movements, the very opposite of Coffee himself, who was six feet three inches tall and carried his two hundred pounds with the shaggy deliberation (somebody had once told him) of a big bear in a small creek. But big or small, James Hamilton had known the General for exactly two days, and John Coffee had known him since 1790, the year they bunked together as bachelors in old lady Donelson's blockhouse, and nobody, certainly not a New York City Yankee, would get used to the General in two short days.

The sailor had reappeared by now, carrying Jackson's rifle. Coffee stood up, spat once more, though he disliked the taste and the habit and was trying to quit, then timed his walk so that he and Hamilton would meet just in front of the rail.

But timed it too late, he saw, because Hamilton was already on top of him, stumbling excitedly down the deck, clapping the beaver hat down with one hand against the wind. "He says he's going to shoot that pilot if he cuts in front of us again!"

"Well, he might."

Hamilton gripped the rail and swayed with the boat. "We don't need that," he said. He looked green in the face and prissy in the lips, but he held on fast to the rail, and for a moment Coffee indulged himself with the thought that he was truly looking into the great Alexander Hamilton's face, who had fought Aaron Burr in a duel and outsmarted Thomas

Jefferson. Hamilton squinted over his shoulder toward Jackson, now brandishing the rifle and shouting back at the little steamer's pilot. "We don't need to have the next President of this country shoot a man in the back on the Mississippi."

Coffee spat and bent down. "Tell him Aunt Rachel says she wants to see him."

Without warning the boat rolled and Hamilton pitched two slippery steps to the right like a man on ice and smacked straight into the rail waist-high. His head snapped forward and his legs went backward and the tall black hat took off like a flying duck.

"Shit! *Merde!*"

To Coffee's genuine admiration Hamilton glanced exactly once over the side, where the hat was now bobbing twenty feet away on a wave, then turned without another word and hurried forward again. In another minute General Jackson, followed at a distance by Hamilton, came striding toward the ladder, nodded at Coffee as he passed, and went below.

Hamilton stopped and this time allowed himself to stare ruefully out at his hat, and Coffee, rubbing his own bare head in sympathy, decided it was about time to act on the more or less clear orders he had more or less received in Nashville. "I imagine some good-lookin' ol' catfish will wear that fine hat by and by," he said, drawing it out and thickening his accent, because it had been his experience that the thicker you drawled, the quicker you disarmed a Yankee.

"That fine hat cost eighteen dollars and a half," Hamilton said, "at Stetson's store on Broadway."

"Well, you can buy a new one in New Orleans, French *à la mode,* and just charge the General for it."

"He's with his wife now?"

Coffee nodded toward the hatchway. "And Sam Houston and Major Lewis."

"Does he get like that often?"

"I have never been sure, in thirty years, whether General Jackson's temper is an affliction or an instrument."

"You mean he puts it on when he wants to," Hamilton said bluntly. Hamilton was Martin Van Buren's personal emissary, as Coffee well understood, and he was undoubtedly expected to report back to New York on every scrap of Jackson's character, so that Van Buren and his Bucktails could decide once and for all whom they were backing. Inwardly, Coffee grinned at Jackson's little display of temper: In politics, the General liked to say, it was always best if the other person thought he knew exactly how to manage you.

Hamilton checked through an open window above the deck. In the ladies' forward parlor Jackson and the others had just taken up chairs in a circle around Rachel. "She's lighting up another cigar," Hamilton snorted. He tugged at the velvet collar with both hands. "I've never in my life seen a woman smoke a cigar before."

Coffee kept his expression bland and unruffled. In New York they would want to know all about Jackson's temper, of course, his bad health, his tractability; but especially they would want to know all about Rachel, whose past, depending on what the filthy newspapers dragged up between now and November, could make Andrew Jackson President or . . .

"I like Mrs. Jackson," Hamilton was saying confidentially. "But I'm obliged to tell you, she is an uncommonly ugly woman." He turned a smooth New York face up to Coffee, as if a thought had just occurred to him. "Now she must have looked something different when she was younger." Coffee grunted, spat, balanced his big body on the rolling boat, said nothing. "Back when she was the scandalous Mrs. Lewis Robards," Hamilton added with a smirk.

The Mississippi rippled and sighed and spread out on its wide brown back in the sun, Coffee's absolute favorite river in the world. "Land him your own goddamn way," the General had said. But Coffee knew that a good fisherman never jerks the hook. He hitched his trousers and paused for a count of three.

"Mr. Hamilton," he said, smiling, savoring the name. He wrapped a huge bearlike arm around the bony little New York shoulders and put on a drawl as thick as hominy gravy, as thick as a beaver hat. "I would very much like you to know the truth about Rachel Jackson."

CHAPTER

8

One thousand miles away, in Washington City, Hogwood sat up straight and snapped the front page of his newspaper with one fat finger. "He's going to New Orleans," he said. "On a steamboat from Natchez! An act of sublime political deceit—you write poems, Mr. Chase, top that for a Symbol!"

Chase looked (he knew) puzzled and blank.

"*Jackson* is going," Hogwood said impatiently. He rolled about on his couch like a pink whale under a blanket. "Jackson is making a trip down the Mississippi to New Orleans. To celebrate—a month or so late—the Great Battle that made his fortune. But since he isn't a presidential candidate—"

Chase looked blanker still.

"Not an *official* candidate," Hogwood continued, "Jackson chooses the Evasion Direct. He travels the high road and lets Clay and the others grub for votes. Last year while you lounged across Europe some obscure tavern owner in Pennsylvania wrote him a letter and asked if he were *running* for President, and Jackson dipped his pen in Jeffersonian treacle and wrote back, knowing it would be published, of course, that nobody should *run* for the people's favor. He would personally *seek* no office, he said, but if the people in their democratic wisdom *chose* him . . . well, then."

"And in New Orleans—?"

"He has the perfect excuse." The eyes stayed closed. "Four days of speeches and festivities, the name of Jackson on every tongue, songs of Jackson, banners of Jackson, Jackson of very Jackson. But who could accuse the General of crass electioneering? He's merely commemorating the glorious American past, which happens to coincide with his own. Wonderful!"

"Here are my father's other chapters." Emma Colden placed a bundle on the little table beside Chase's chair and then took a quick step backward, brushing an invisible strand of hair from her forehead and lifting her chin as if she expected opposition. Chase stood up to bow his thanks. She was wearing the same yellow dress as yesterday, but no jewelry, no brooch or pin, not even a ribbon. Her pose was resentment embodied. Aloof, pale, icy dislike. Except that a visible strand of blond hair spilled irresistibly from her chignon and curled in a fine, wanton tendril to the base of her throat. Chase blundered through a series of clichés: Fire and Ice; Venus and Diana; Diana disrobed. He cocked his head and stared (he knew) like a pup.

"Now I gather that you haven't read my Chapter One yet." Hogwood made little effort to keep the disappointment out of his voice. "And yet here you are back for more."

Chase picked up the bundle of papers and selected, in honor of Jackson, the Evasion Direct. "I still feel guilty about taking your job, you know—your daughter is angry, you're not well." And the Vault Illogical. "So I thought if I read the whole manuscript at once, instead of in pieces . . ."

Hogwood grunted. He threw off the dirty red-and-blue blanket, then lowered his bad foot gingerly to the floor. In a yellow crackle of disapproval Emma had already retreated behind the muslin curtain that divided the room. It was human nature, Chase thought, to desire what stands aloof. Jackson. The absolutely gorgeous Emma Colden.

"I enjoy life," Hogwood said, "but I have had enough of it." He tested his weight on the foot and staggered upright. "Tell a lie. I'm actually feeling better and better. I could jump over a house. A small house. A one-story house. Now, Mr. Chase, your plan of research—ha!—is to stay in Washington a few days and interview people who know the great Jackson, yes?"

"Short gave me a list."

"A short list." Hogwood showed his man-in-the-moon smile and held his arms straight out as if he were about to break into a pirouette. "I can recite it backward, with scintillating annotations. Henry Clay, yes?"

"Yes."

"Has a mouth like a carp, great charm for women. A born gamester. Emma, is it not true that all true womanhood loves Mr. Clay?"

"He is said to gamble at cards." Emma was Delphic behind the curtain.

"And known to despise King Andrew. A rich source of dirt." Not spinning but turning somehow—like Humpty-Dumpty fired from a cannon—Hogwood suddenly crossed the room and began to fumble at a closet formed by a bedsheet hanging from a stick. He looked back over his shoulder. "John C. Calhoun, of course?"

"Yes."

"You will like him. He was secretary of war when Jackson first took up exterminating Indians. Everyone in Washington is in awe of Calhoun's logic and integrity. Translation: He will never be President. He is supposed to have written a poem once. Got as far as the word 'Whereas' and stopped." Hogwood emerged from the closet wearing a heavy black coat made of a slick leathery material that Chase had never seen before. He peered closely. Skinlike; no. Shell-like; no. "It's called a Macintosh," Hogwood said proudly, and fanned out the heavy black skirts like a genial bat. "The very latest British invention. Entirely rainproof. A rubber coat."

In her turn Emma had likewise emerged from behind the muslin curtain, in her hand an ordinary cane with a clouded handle.

"And since," Hogwood said, bowing and taking the cane, "I have suffered a temporary relapse into good health, I thought I would surprise you with an addition to your list."

"You mean, now?"

"I mean at this very moment, after you have bought me a lunch at Kinchy's ice cream restaurant on Pennsylvania Avenue."

Chase made his voice casual as he reached for his own heavy topcoat. "The three of us, of course—I'd be delighted."

"The two of us," Hogwood said, opening the door and beginning to roll away like a giant black ball. "Emma must go to work. But I promise to eat enough for three."

"Work—where?" But Hogwood was gone, and when Chase turned to look back Emma had once again vanished.

✳   ✳   ✳

KINCHY turned out to be, ten minutes later, a gracious white-haired mulatto with a cast in one eye, who presided over a single noisy room jammed with eaters of flavored ice cream, the grand dessert first introduced to Washington, Hogwood declared, by Dolley Madison, though Thomas Jefferson got all the credit. Kinchy led them to a table by the window, where Hogwood ordered, as lunch, a platter of Virginia ham, a "dish" (a tureen, Chase thought when he saw it) of vanilla ice cream, fried oysters, bread, butter, and a bottle of red wine. Chase ordered ham and bread and felt obscurely inadequate.

"I am monumentally fat," Hogwood announced. He studied his reflection in the window and clasped his belly with both hands, Francis Gray's curiously maternal gesture. "I have grown as fat as George the Third's old queen," Hogwood told the window. "And she looked as if she were bearing all fifteen of her children at once." He sighed and speared an oyster. "This is a lean country, however, Mr. Chase—shall I call you David?—the United States of Leanness, no place for a fat man. Your countrymen wear themselves down to shadows. Do you think Short fired me because I'm fat?"

Chase squinted unhappily at the window. Down Pennsylvania Avenue the black-domed Capitol sat on its dish of mud. "Perhaps Short would reconsider," he said, shaking his head because he knew Short wouldn't. "I haven't even begun—"

"Jackson is lean," Hogwood interrupted. "The perfect American, he has a lean and hungry look, he has the *corpus democraticum.*" His fork hovered above the oysters like a hawk. "He is six feet one inch tall and weighs one hundred thirty pounds. Such men are dangerous. Short, though old, is lean. Sarah Hale is lean—did she offer you grapes?"

Chase shook his head again. A hatless man (lean) strolled by the window wearing three silk waistcoats at once, each one evidently ornamented with a black-and-white portrait of Andrew Jackson's face.

"The latest campaign fashion," Hogwood said dryly, following Chase's eyes. "There were no Jefferson or Washington waistcoats, I dare say. Mrs. Hale had plates of grapes on every table in her office when I visited. A passion of hers, evidently, grown in a hothouse. She disliked me on sight—an English accent does not recommend one to Mrs. Hale—and she put them away when I had eaten no more than a bunch. And then, of course, I used the word *female* in her presence."

Chase was beginning to catch the rhythm of Hogwood's conversational gavotte. "Mrs. Hale objects to *female?*"

"It degrades women, she says, to the level of animals. I didn't pursue her logic."

"And Emma—?" Chase ventured himself onto the territory of Christian names. In Europe he had grown accustomed to the regulated world of ranks and titles, *Sie* and *du, vous* and *tu,* a thousand little turnstiles of formality. He would be Monsieur Chase even to the hangman. In America he was no longer sure how to speak his own language. "Emma agreed?"

"Emma was with Miss Wright," Hogwood said complacently. "Now we must turn to business. There"—the fork angled toward the Capitol dome—"is where we are going. When you have paid the bill. Washington's only free and uncensored theater."

"To hear a congressional debate?"

"To visit a representative of the democratic people. You are much more amiable than I expected, David. I share with you my secret. Before Short dismissed me, I had cultivated a promising acquaintance. Pure accident, pure serendipity. We met in the aisles of the Congressional Library, which is in the basement of the Capitol. Or rather, we collided. I was too fat—I am still too fat—for him to go around me, so we struck up learned conversation like two prisoners in a cell. We are soul mates in malice. He's dying to tell me something dark—he won't say what, he *hints*—to Jackson's discredit."

"A political enemy?"

"Better. A gossip. My friend supports Jackson, nominally, because he hates Adams. But he has the three things a journalist dreams of. He has information, he has venom, he has"—Hogwood grinned and pushed the bill across the table—"*documents.*"

He stood to reach for his cane and his rubber coat; in the window the grin on his pink face changed to a grimace. "I assume that my leg doesn't rise up first to smite me," he said, "like Jehosephat's bone," and Chase wondered how much pain the old man was secretly enduring for the sake of his lordly pose of good humor.

Outside, despite Chase's offer of a hired carriage, Hogwood insisted on walking the three uphill blocks to the Capitol. As far as Chase could tell, the rest of Washington, the town center included, consisted of occasional rows of buildings, five or six at a time, then long open spaces like missing teeth, then a few more buildings; then bare fields; then forest. By contrast, Capitol Hill was as crowded as Boston, crisscrossed with brick or yellow wood-framed houses that clung to its slopes like stitches on a ball. Beneath the great black-domed Capitol, wagons were parked or climbing everywhere; black-shelled hackney carriages dashed up and down like bugs.

At each corner Hogwood paused for breath and offered another nugget of information. They were going to Dawson's Boarding House—because single houses were scarce and expensive, nearly every member of Congress lived in a boarding house "mess" with like-minded colleagues, Jacksonians in some, Adams or Clay or Webster men in others, subdivided further by regions (Dawson's was for southerners) and tastes (there was, Hogwood shuddered, a temperance mess). His "acquaintance" was John Randolph of Roanoke, a senator from Virginia notorious for his satiric wit, his interminable orations, and his habit of striding into the Senate wearing full hunting garb and brandishing a horsewhip, followed by his dogs and a little Negro boy who carried a jug of port, from which he poured whenever Randolph held out his glass. He had been in Congress since Jefferson's first administration, and he had fought a spectacularly stupid duel with Henry Clay, in which neither man was shot.

"If America did not exist," Hogwood puffed at the door to Dawson's, "a novelist would have to invent her. The most normal thing about the gentleman we are about to visit—I make none of this up, David—is that his plantation house in Virginia is named Bizarre."

A green-and-white liveried slave boy (portless and whipless) ushered them into a private parlor furnished with a fireplace, which was not in use, three stuffed chairs, a desk, and a table loaded with tea and English biscuits.

"He has been telling you," said John Randolph as he rose to greet them, "that I am eccentric."

"I have been telling him," Hogwood replied, wheezing, "that for purposes of political gossip, you are a fish who feeds on the bottom."

Randolph smiled: not a fish, not quite a jack-o'-lantern—amazed, repulsed, Chase groped for an image. Randolph was at least six feet tall, slender as a string, gangling, ill-proportioned, with a small round head and a wide yellow grin. His coarse black hair (genuine, not a wig) was parted in the center Indian-style and formed two dark wings around the whitest, palest face Chase had ever seen. No chin, no beard; skin like withered parchment; small black eyes that darted from side to side. He wore an old-fashioned suit of heavy blue broadcloth, and a stiff white collar that reached to his ears, and he looked—Chase could come up with nothing better—like a waxwork ghost. The magnified waxwork ghost of a flea.

"I have laid on biscuits and honey and a pot of good China tea," Randolph informed them. "Knowing that Hogwood dislikes it."

"But I am English," Hogwood growled.

"And must therefore atone. Actually," Randolph said, shaking Chase's hand and simultaneously guiding him to a chair, "I admire all things English. I buy my books and clothes from England, and my paper and my soap. I won't *own* an American book." He snapped two spectral fingers and the little slave boy reappeared at the laden table and began to mix and pour. "And I serve good scotch whiskey in Hogwood's tea."

"Mr. Chase has lived in Paris for many years."

Randolph bowed. Chase had an impression of ghostly heels clicking.

"And he's now writing the book I couldn't finish, about King Andrew."

"I have known Andrew Jackson for twenty years, since he first came to Washington as a senator. I support him entirely. I say nothing against him—"

"Ballocks," Hogwood said.

Deep inside his collar Randolph showed yellow teeth. "I won't discuss politics on an empty stomach," he said, "or sober. I have too much disrespect for the subject. In France, Mr. Chase, did you ever meet Monsieur Talleyrand?"

"He wrote a treatise on Talleyrand and Fouché," Hogwood said through a mouthful of biscuit. "You should read it."

"Last year in Paris," Randolph said, waving away the suggestion with one cadaverous hand, "Talleyrand gave me dinner. The other guest of honor was Napoleon's younger sister Pauline, who was very proud of her back. She had come to Paris to have a nude statue made of her back. She was also proud of her feet. The next night she invited Talleyrand and myself to come and see them—*la toilette des pieds*. She had printed invitations made up. We found her with her little exquisite white feet displayed on a velvet cushion. At her command, three maids entered and washed the feet with sponges and dusted them with powder. Talleyrand held one of her feet like a little bird in his waistcoat."

"This will lead to Jackson," Hogwood murmured, and then without warning suddenly staggered upright from his chair, clutching his chest. He stabbed one arm toward the table, blindly; cups and plates went scattering, crashing. In another moment Chase had grasped his shoulders and pulled him back. At Randolph's bark the little Negro boy flew from the room.

"We'll have a doctor in minutes." Chase helped the old man stretch out on the carpet, then knelt by his side and loosened the buttons on his shirt. Rough, mottled flesh, slippery with sweat. Chase tugged at the collar, Hogwood pushed his hand away.

"I've made myself ill." His chest heaved and sank and he gasped for breath. "*A cause de gluttony.* Is that good French?"

"No," said Randolph, kneeling on the other side.

Hogwood squeezed his eyes into knots and spoke in a slow, determined rasp. "David can . . . come back later, to hear about Jackson."

"Of course."

A door slammed somewhere. Black voices swept by the window, running. Hogwood kept his fists closed, his eyes closed. When Chase held up his head, he struggled to rise to a sitting position, half choking, half coughing on saliva. But under his ruddy film of sweat the old man almost managed to grin. He clutched Randolph's sleeve. "He can come back with *Emma*," he said.

C H A P T E R
9

The Life of Andrew Jackson

Chapter Two

I HAVE A WORD: "WRETCH." FROM THE OLD ANGLO-SAXON "WREKKA," which originally meant a "kinless person, a person without family."

And I have a quotation, from a young British writer named Thomas Carlyle: "Isolation is the sum-total of wretchedness to a man. To be cut off, to be left solitary: to have a world alien, not your world, all a hostile camp for you; not a home at all, of hearts and faces whose you are! . . . Without father, without a child, without brother. Man knows no sadder destiny."

Now Andrew Jackson at fifteen was a wretch.

After his brothers and his mother had died, a distant backwoods cousin of some sort took him in, out of pity—here was a boy orphaned by the Revolution, penniless, friendless—and for six months or so tried to teach him the humble trade of saddler, but young Jackson soon quarreled with him (I shall write that phrase often) and went off to a yet more distant cousin, and then to nobody at all.

Henry Clay has devised the smug expression "self-made man" to describe himself (and annoy the family-made John Quincy Adams), but the real self-made man of the day, of course, has to be Jackson, who now found himself, one or two quarrels later, in full Carlylean sadness.

Full *southern* sadness. Southerners have a great dread of being alone. I attribute their insane love of dueling and codes of "honor" to their Scotch-Irish truculence and above all their rural isolation, which raises family connection to the highest possible importance (their insane "hospitality" is the obverse of their quarrelsomeness, of course). The Southerner invents cousins and aunts and uncles (whose honor he defends to the death) the way other men shake hands and bow; without kith and kin he hardly feels he exists.

Too much philosophizing. Forward.

While Jackson, aged sixteen now, stood solitary and southern in the mudpits of South Carolina, waiting for fate's next blow, fate (with her charming perversity) presented him with a surprise: the mails brought from Ireland a legacy of four hundred British pounds, Jackson's share of his Irish grandfather's estate. This Jackson promptly took to Charleston and squandered. First purchase, characteristically, a brace of pistols. Then fine clothes, wine, women—I find it revealing that he chose Charleston for his scene of gentlemanly dissipation; Charleston where his mother was (somewhere) buried, where his debauchery would feel most precisely like rebellion against maternal preachments. Within a week he had lost it all gambling, except for his horse, which he won back again in a desperate game of dice called "rattle and snap."

He drifted back toward the Waxhaws, he apparently taught school for a few months, worked in a store, organized cockfights, a bleak and aimless existence.

The cash crop of the South is not cotton, but lawyers. They spring from the soil like dragon's teeth. In London two generations ago, young Samuel Johnson finding himself similarly homeless and friendless said with nice irony, "possessing no skills or education, I therefore naturally became a writer." But that was London, a city. In the vacant brown hills of South Carolina, with a whole country organizing itself fitfully into a government, Jackson naturally became, like everybody else, not a writer but a lawyer. Slowly the character slips into focus: ambitious, angry, self-regarding—he went to Morgantown, North Carolina, and demanded without any prologue that the best-known lawyer south of Richmond, one Waightstill Avery, take him on as a student.

Wary of Jackson's non-credentials, which were outstandingly bad even for a southern lawyer, Avery said no. But on the day after Christmas, 1784, Jackson rode over to Salisbury, North Carolina and persuaded another lawyer, one with the arboreal name of Spruce McCay, to sign him up.

Now Salisbury had and has its pretensions. I have visited it. An old settlement for America, dating from a century before the Revolution. Large for a southern town, with all of eight hundred souls, black and white. Two broad, straight, shady streets crossing each other at right angles; a town pump in the center of the crossing; two ancient taverns, a newspaper, an academy—in all ways a step up from the log cabins and stump fields of the Waxhaws. Spruce McCay had a fine two-story mansion on one of the main streets, and in front, on the lawn, a little brown shingled house too small for a corn crib or a pig sty, fifteen by sixteen feet, in which Jackson and two other young scholars were set to work reading textbooks and copying papers.

Ambitious, angry, *wild*. They will still tell you Jackson stories in Salisbury. The first old man I approached (lounging like a straw-hatted lizard on the porch of a tavern) chewed his tobacco, spat somewhere near the cuspidor, and rolled his eyes. "Andrew Jackson," he said with true Southern deliberation, "was the most roaring, rollicking, game-cocking, horse-racing, card-playing, mischievous fellow that ever lived in Salisbury." Chewed, spat. "He didn't trouble the law books much."

"If Andrew Jackson can be President," sniffed a most respectable lady, "I guess anybody can."

Offenses: horse racing, to the point of obsession. Gambling. Cock-fights. Purchases of whiskey by the pint, quart, and gallon. Reports of a mulatto mistress. Incident at the Rowan House where Jackson and two friends smashed their glasses into the hearth, broke the table to splinters, then the chairs, then the bed, and finally stuffed bed, curtain, and blanket into the fireplace to burn.

Compensations: Only one. The politician's indefinite, all-important gift of—what is the right English word?—*presence*.

The Salisbury girls all loved him; the mothers clucked and prayed for reformation. The men allowed that he sat on a horse like an angel and had the coldest blue eyes in the South.

At the end of two years his fellow students passed their examinations and joined the bar. Jackson, however, left town owing money (one patriotic tavern-keeper showed me his yellowing bill with the totals crossed out and his own note scrawled above: "Paid at the Battle of New Orleans"). He migrated into the next county and spent six more months studying law with an eccentric old veteran named John Stokes, who had been wounded at the Battle of Waxhaw Creek, nursed by Jackson's own mother, and who wore in place of a missing hand a big silver knob which he was accustomed to pound on his desk like a gavel.

Now why quit Salisbury, really? Rumors of a quarrel with McCay, of course; bad debts—but as I grow older, I come to admire fate's tasteless, ingenious sense of humor. Two months before Jackson skipped to John Stokes, the Salisbury dancing school (another of the town's pretensions) decided to hold a Christmas ball. Jackson, leader of all the gay blades, was put in charge. He rented the hall, hired the music, ordered the bunting and punch—and out of some unplumbed reserve of anger against women or out of simple, sheer deviltry, he also sent cards of invitation to Salisbury's only white prostitutes, a mother-and-daughter partnership notorious for three counties. On the evening of the ball—they came! Dressed in all the colors of the rainbow the two whores strolled into the middle of the room, whereupon the music stopped, the respectable ladies withdrew to a corner buzzing, and ultimately a sheepish Jackson was forced to step up and explain it was all a joke—a *joke*! He led them away. Then left for good a few days later.

But what I like best, given the political "issues" of this Year of Democracy 1828, is the impish detail only a malicious fate could dream up. The whore's name was Molly Wood. The daughter's name was Rachel.

C H A P T E R
10

Better.

Chase put down the chapter and stared at no particular point on the wall. Much better, except for the gratuitous insults to Southerners. Hogwood's irritable voice fairly growled off the page (how had he ever gotten work published in England?), but it was a distinctive voice; you could hear the grumpy, undisguised passion behind it. A man like Short, with his dapper, deadpan irony—an *elusive* man like Short would recoil in horror. Why had he ever commissioned Hogwood in the first place?

Chase slid the manuscript under the pile of papers on the table. Second mystery: The first chapter had been written out by hand, in spidery blue ink; all of the others were printed on the long, narrow proof sheets that newspapers used.

They had taken Hogwood straight back to his room. The carriage driver had helped navigate him up the stairs and onto his couch. A doctor, summoned by Chase, had arrived a few minutes later, Emma (summoned how?) on his heels. Then confusion, bustle, dismissal.

Chase studied his watch (he was turning into Short, he was turning

into an American all over again). Ten minutes to four. Time is money. He
had chosen to read the new chapter downstairs, in the smoky bar of the
Indian Queen, because he liked its masculine rumble and American busy-
ness. To his right, one whole wall was devoted to a row of numbered pull-
bells on springs, which rang loudly whenever a room wanted service, like
a demented carillon. In the center a bartender stood cracking ice with a
hammer. Along another wall ran a single forty-foot table—the dining
room, in effect—where black waiters were setting out the dinner that,
take it or not, every guest paid for "American Plan."

Bells rang, men spat. A boy strolled by selling newspapers—
Washington City was a village of fifteen thousand people and had *six*
newspapers, three of them dailies. Chase scribbled on a margin *hôtel*, the
French word for a grandiose private palace; *hotel*, the American word for
a grandiose people's palace. Blessed are the takers of notes. He signaled
for whiskey and moved his gaze from nowhere in particular to the window just behind a table of beaver-hatted men smoking six-inch "seegars."
In every American hotel he had seen so far, the window shades of the
public rooms were constructed of leftover sheets of colored wallpaper,
rolled in a tube and suspended from the sash. Blessed are the journalist's
details. He scribbled again, automatically. If he didn't actually write the
biography of Jackson, he could sell travel stories to the French and English magazines. Wallpaper shades. "American Manners, By One Who
Was There." "Lambs and Grapes: The Patriotic Editrix of Boston."

"Sir?"

Chase turned to see a small black boy at his side, wearing a white shirt
and (supreme detail) the feathered Indian headdress of the hotel.

"Lady said for you."

Chase took the envelope the boy held out and fumbled for a coin. "Did
she bring this herself?"

"Blond lady brang it, yes sir."

"Is she outside?" Chase was on his feet peering toward the lobby.
"Stand here, watch these papers."

On the wooden sidewalk in front of the hotel a jumble of new guests
were admiring the Indian Queen sign. Chase pushed through arms,
shoulders, stumbled over a cairn of plaid carpetbags, and stopped. It was
raining now, lightly. To his left, in the distance, in the soft gray lattice of
falling rain a woman in a dark coat was just turning a corner.

He had taken three steps when he heard his name called out peremptorily, and he wheeled around to see a pale but serious young face leaning out of a carriage. An indisputably Bostonian voice repeated his name.

"It *is* David Chase, is it not?"

Chase cursed to himself and looked irresolutely first to the empty corner, then to the envelope in his hand: Chase. Pursue. By now the pale face had attached itself to a body and climbed down out of the carriage. A journalist's memory released its string of bubbles: Boston; Harvard; a dull, dull party in Ticknor's rooms. "Charles Adams," Chase said, extending his hand, forcing his gaze away from the street. "Of course. The President's son."

Charles Francis Adams possessed the family talent for disappointment. He wrinkled his nose and frowned. "You weren't going to remember my name," he said tartly. "I could see it on your face." Then he brightened. "You're going to freeze to death, out here in your shirt."

Chase looked down in complete surprise at his shirtsleeves.

"You're staying here," Adams announced. "I had to track you down. Gadsby's is better, but I guess it costs an arm." He brightened still more. "Is there a bar?"

Inside, Chase led him to his table where the small black boy still faithfully guarded the stack of papers and a newly appeared glass of whiskey. When he had tipped the boy again and ordered a drink for Adams, he sat down and propped the envelope by his glass.

Adams made no effort to hide his curiosity. "Work?" He cocked his head on his shoulder and tried to read upside down.

"Well, papers, notes—this just came." To a sudden chorus of room-service bells he held up the envelope in a halfhearted gesture of apology, then tore it open.

Mr. David Chase,

My father is much better and resting comfortably. In accordance with his wishes, I will meet you the day after tomorrow at Dawson's Boarding House at three o'clock.

E.C.

"I brought you another one." Adams passed over a sealed envelope. "You're a journalist," he added in his declarative fashion. "My father's read two of your books."

Chase frowned at Emma's letter a second time before folding it into his pocket. Not even a signature. E.C.

"So I assume," Adams began. He interrupted himself, threw back his head and drained the whiskey glass with one practiced gulp; then wiped his lips with the back of his hand. When he saw Chase's stare, the pale cheeks burst into two pink blossoms. "I'm an Adams on my father's side," he murmured, "but my mother is southern. I can drink like a Southerner."

"Ah." Chase nodded as if this made perfect sense. Adams wore a black frock coat and a stiff white collar that reached to his ears; his silk cravat was held in place by a badly clasped stickpin of ebony and gold. To Chase's eye he looked like a little boy caught wearing his father's clothes.

"So I *assume,*" Adams repeated, "that a journalist is in Washington to write about either my father or Jackson. There's nobody else."

"Did your father like my books?"

"He bought them, anyway," Adams said in a voice that unmistakably came from his New England side. Over the chime of bells he motioned to the bartender. "You're avoiding my question."

Chase nodded. "I am. What is this letter you've brought me?"

Adams grinned his own evasion. "Jackson is a hard man, a hard person," he said. "If he's your subject you ought to read what his people say in the *Telegraph* about my father. On the other hand"—he tipped up the second glass of whiskey and blinked slowly, Chase thought, like a baby owl—"politics are like that here. Jackson's the new-style American, if you want to know what I think. My father's the candidate from the eighteenth century."

Since this was beginning to be Chase's own view, he looked up at the pale Bostonian face with new interest. "Are you staying in the mansion with your parents?"

"Have to. I'm supposed to be studying law in Boston, but my brother John married two weeks ago and my mother's collapsed in disgust, and my father—he was a teacher when you were at Harvard, yes?"

Chase nodded. "I was never in his class. He was professor of oratory for two years."

"That letter's from William Short." Adams reached over his empty glass and turned the letter around in Chase's hand. "In Boston he came over and asked me to see that you got it."

Chase pulled an embossed card from the envelope and held it to the dying light of the window—in Paris it would already have been dark for hours; he imagined (what could hardly be true) a lonely blue and green globe spinning in space from light to dark, from past to present; a world split in half. "This is an invitation to a *levée* at the White House?"

"Tomorrow night." Hawklike now, Adams rose and hovered. "If I can ask a favor, speak a little French to my mother—she grew up over there, she *hates* it here. Make her tell you about her daring ride from St. Petersburg to Paris in the winter of '05."

"But the President's House?" Chase was doubtful. In Europe a ruler lived behind walls and guards. How rich could Short be?

"Eight o'clock, sharp. Half of Washington will be there, too, for the free food. I rode with her, you know, but I was only a baby." He looked wistfully at the bar and its lamp-lit portrait of the Indian Queen, whose dress was buckskin and whose flesh was pink. "I'm twenty-two now."

"I will come as your guest."

Adams hitched his trousers and dismissed the idea with a chop of his hand. "Anybody can come," he said magnanimously while the bells mocked. "Bring a girl if you know one."

*   *   *

HE did not. He dreamed of Paris and slept badly. Then awoke in the dark to the sound of barking dogs just under his window, and a moment afterward a loud, resonating bell from somewhere beyond the alley (the signal gong for Gadsby's Hotel, he was to learn later, calling breakfast servants in from Gadsby's far-flung annexes).

Chase lit a candle and splashed cold water on his face from a tin basin. Bells. For two minutes he sat in his chair and held Hogwood's next chapter in his hand while he stared through the window at the chalk-streaked sky. Fresh light, fresh from Paris. Abruptly he shivered and stood and snuffed out the candle.

Downstairs a dozing clerk behind the lobby counter yawned and frowned at the clock, then directed him through the side doors to a second alley, a stable. Ten minutes later he was on a hired horse cantering down Pennsylvania Avenue, in the capital city of his native land, without another human being or horse in sight.

At the President's House he slowed and turned in his saddle and yawned belatedly himself. When he had come to Washington thirteen years ago, on his trip with Ticknor and Gray, the President's mansion had been a blackened, burned-out shell. It was guarded by a ragged detachment of militia who squatted on the ashes and peered disconsolately down the road, as if expecting the British and their torches to return at any minute. Now it was rebuilt and enlarged, a three-story Georgian palace, painted a gleaming, Anglo-defiant white and surrounded by a low brick wall and iron pickets. *Domus democratica,* Chase thought, stretching for a Hogwoodian phrase. Impressive enough for a king.

But on closer inspection there was a rustic, unfinished, *American* look to the grounds. At least a dozen sheds of unpainted wood leaned against the brick wall at various places; one wing of the aristocratic mansion obviously still needed a coat of hard stucco. Bare timbers instead of columns supported the north portico. From the President's orchard a cow greeted the day with a groan.

At a muddy junction called Rock Creek he passed a large brick house set in the middle of an empty field, deserted except for a Jackson poster and a signboard that announced, English-style, the house's name: Kalorama. Chase crossed the creek and rode through the fields until he came in sight of the Potomac. He would make a circuit of the whole city, he thought, spirits rising; he would imitate Hogwood and gain the highest point, a bird's-eye view, a heightened vantage from which he would understand . . . what?

Kalorama. His mind jumped back. A made-up word, ignorant and pretentious. It irritated him pointlessly. In France, in Europe—he buttoned his coat and watched the cold, pink fingers of the dawn brush the eastern sky.

Six miles past Georgetown he found a tavern just opening, and he sat down at a table for a breakfast of fried bread and sausage. (The Parisian in him shuddered; the American picked up his knife and fork.) Through a window as he ate came the sound of another bell, not a breakfast gong, but a church bell two or three miles away. He paused, coffee cup in hand. It was not a Sunday, so the bell was tolling out the news of someone's death, he assumed. A sound familiar to him since boyhood, when the First Congregational Church of Salem had stood two blocks from his father's cottage. The code came back to him as naturally as breath: nine strokes for a man, six for a woman, three for a child.

He walked to the door and listened, but he had lost count. In New England a household in mourning would cover up all images—all mirrors and paintings—with white cloth. When his mother died, his father had gone methodically through every room. Details, or history? The question, Chase thought, was whether he really belonged where he thought he did, far away from the *domus democratica,* in another country; or whether he was like one of those North Atlantic icebergs that travelers wrote about, nine tenths of his nature submerged and frozen in memory.

He shrugged and finished his coffee. Memory could melt.

By noon he had reached a spot on the Virginia side of the Potomac where he could in fact look down and see the whole city spread out for miles, a Jeffersonian vista in which the Capitol dome, the river, the red bricks of Georgetown, the enormous theoretical avenues of the enormous theoretical city all made a beautiful abstract pattern of line and shadow. In the exact center, the journalist allowed himself to think, a small square gleam of white represented the President's House; rolling in from the west, behind a long, dark horizon of smoke-black clouds, was the nineteenth century.

He unfolded a campaign poster he had found on the road: a row of six heavily inked coffins and a blazing headline: "THE BLOODY DEEDS OF GENERAL JACKSON!!!" Underneath, headstones with skulls and crossbones, the names of men Jackson had supposedly killed in duels, a cartoon of Jackson running his sword through the neck of an innocent man.

Chase looked from poster to vista, then back again. What in Kalorama was he doing here?

CHAPTER

11

Well, anybody can come," John Quincy Adams said, reading
the invitation and handing it back with a frown. "You
didn't need that."

Chase took the slip of paper and found he had no idea what to do with
it. The President of the United States waited, arms stiffly at his sides,
while a servant dressed in blue and gold livery squeezed by them; his tray
of pastry and nuts passed just above the President's bald head, briefly
crowning him with a snowy peak of meringue. "I used to know William
Short," Adams said grimly. His eyes followed the tray as it disappeared
into a crowd of gaily dressed men and women, all of whom had their
backs turned to the President. "In Paris, when I was a boy. He always
called me Johnny."

Chase bowed in agreement, commiseration—he wasn't sure which. He
tucked the invitation back into his sleeve. "Yes, sir. Mr. Short was a
protégé of Thomas Jefferson then, or so he told me." One part of Chase
was intent on hearing Adams's low, surprisingly soft voice above
the hubbub of his other guests. A second part was trying to understand
how the ruler of a whole country could have a weekly open house to

which anyone at all could come. In Europe—he was not in Europe anymore.

"He was Jefferson's private secretary," Adams said, still watching the tray. "He wanted to stay in France as minister, but Jefferson never helped him along. Something about a woman. This is my wife."

Expertly a small dark-haired woman wearing a regal tiara and a modish French evening gown—the President himself wore a severely plain black suit—took Chase's elbow and steered him to the right. "I am Mrs. Adams," she informed him briskly. "And these are my children. John, his wife, Mary Hellen Adams, George—"

Chase bobbed down the line like a cork. At the end of it he accepted a glass of cold punch from another liveried servant and turned to look back. No Charles Francis Adams. The room was fifty feet long perhaps, thirty feet wide, a graceful oval jammed with at least three dozen people, and more guests were arriving every moment, in groups of two or three, simply strolling unannounced through an open door that led to the unfinished portico. Half of them seemed to ignore the President (a short bald crow), others made a perfunctory bow or curtsy before diving toward the food.

"The only requirement," said Emma Colden's bright English voice behind him, "is that a gentleman has to wear shoes. A woman, of course, must be escorted."

Chase turned to face her, discovered instead that he was facing a tall, broad-shouldered man of fifty, who looked down at him with amusement over a silk cravat the color of a sunburn. Lightly, intimately, Emma placed her hand on the tall man's wrist. "We were watching you," she said over the noise of the room. "Nobody but a novice goes through the whole receiving line."

"In the old days," the tall man said, bending close to make himself heard, "Jefferson shook hands with every guest. Madison was too shy, but his wife made up for it. All of the others have just bowed, like John Cranky Adams there, though God knows he's the stiffest. Monroe used to dress up in knee breeches and a wig and pretend he was George Washington."

"My friend knew them all," said Emma, patting the wrist possessively. "He's a thousand years old."

"I'm David Chase." Chase tried to avoid staring at the cravat by looking instead at Emma, who gave him a smile of dazzling indifference.

"Eph Sellers."

"Senator Ephraim Sellers," Emma said. "From Ohio."

The crowd was gradually driving them toward a wall (French paper, peeling, a design of Normandy farms—Chase found himself backed up against a Minerva clock on a shelf). "I remember when Jackson came through the door in '24," Sellers said, bending closer still. The senator had shrewd black eyes and whiskey breath and the politician's gift for boxing in his audience. Chase took a step sideways. "That door over there. The very night of the very day he'd lost the election to Adams, and suddenly, right here in the Oval Room, the crowd parted and there was Adams standing at one end, in his black frock coat and trousers, like a gunfighter, and Jackson, who had a lady on his arm, just walked up the length of the room and reached out and said, 'How do you do, Mr. Adams? I give you my left hand, for my right as you see is devoted to the fair. I hope you are well, sir.' And Adams smiled like a dying duck and bowed a New England quarter-inch and said, 'Very well, sir. I hope General Jackson is well.' "

"Mr. Chase is writing a book about General Jackson," Emma said.

"Put that in it," Sellers said smoothly, though the shrewd black eyes went instantly blank. "I saw it myself. The old Tennessee savage was as suave as a Frenchman, the Harvard graduate couldn't even shake his hand."

"Mr. Chase is also a graduate of Harvard," Emma said. Sellers looked at her curiously.

"I received your note," Chase told her. Emma brushed back the invisible strand of hair and lifted her chin. He had known many women more beautiful than Emma, he thought. Liar, he thought. "I'm surprised you were able to leave your father so soon."

"You two," said Sellers, more curious still, "seem to know each other. But of course in Miss Colden's line of work—"

"We were thrown together by accident," Emma told Sellers almost brusquely. "Thanks to my father's illness." Tonight she wore a dark blue gown rather than the yellow, and the color suited her better; the dress was cut very low at the neck, and beneath it she obviously also wore the tight corset known in France as the "divorce" because it separated and pushed up—Chase reverted instinctively to the discretion of French—*la poitrine*. As she spoke she was already looking away from both men, scanning the long, busy room. John Quincy Adams was a bald skull under a gas lamp. "Mr. Chase and I go tomorrow to interview John Randolph."

"The great orator of Roanoke," Sellers said, but there were no more senatorial reminiscences forthcoming. In another instant he had nodded, bowed (more than a quarter-inch), and followed Emma into the crush.

Chase put down his punch untasted. He turned to face (this time) the melancholy visage of Charles Francis Adams, who was watching Emma's bare-shouldered departure.

"I'm in love," Adams said. "I don't know if Ticknor told you." He pulled open a narrow door to the left of the clock and motioned for Chase to enter. "Come upstairs," he said. "See the rest of the palace."

Under the gas lamp, which hissed steadily above his left ear, reminding him of the fundamental incompetence of James Monroe's wife, who had insisted on furnishing the public rooms of the President's House with dangerous "conveniences," John Quincy Adams watched his youngest son and another young man go through the doorway that led to the stairs and his private apartments. Adams blinked at a proffered hand, bowed (his own hands clasped firmly behind his back), wished that he, too, could steal away to a place where there were no people, books only, lamps and guests that did not hiss.

"I am delighted to see you," the President said to an utter stranger. "My wife."

"I called on you yesterday, sir, about a place as Indian agent in Alabama." The hand (now joined by a florid, swollen, ticklike body) still hovered in front of Adams. "Name of Wragg."

Adams had been attacked in the *United States Telegraph* three days running for his lack of the "common touch"—something possessed to perfection, the *Telegraph* said, by General Jackson. The President had refused to interrupt a journey to Philadelphia to speak to a workingmen's club; he had been bred in European courts to a courtier's manner, he had studied at Harvard. Jackson would have seized the leprous, pestiferous hand extended toward him and pumped it till the votes gushed. Adams permitted himself a thin smile that he knew to be chilling and turned away unmistakably toward the next person in line.

"Emma Colden," that person said, and made a flawless curtsy.

One floor above, standing precisely over his father's head, Charles Francis Adams leaned comically into an open door, as if being pulled by the neck. "This is Madame's room," he said. "So you see I'm caught between"—as he tried several times to pronounce "Scylla and Charybdis," Chase realized that the President's youngest son was sublimely drunk.

"Because *that*," Adams said with a mock bow, toward the other side of the hall, "is my father's room. Monsieur. They've had separate rooms for the last six months, did you know that? Bit of news for the papers. Not, I imagine, like General Jackson and his volup—" Adams paused, ran his tongue between his teeth, tried again. "Rachel."

Chase felt himself torn between manners and snooping, the journalist's own Scylla and Charybdis. Unsteadily, Adams had begun to lead him across the corridor, almost entirely bare of furniture or paintings, Chase noted automatically, illuminated badly by old-fashioned whale-oil lamps suspended from pivots. More Normandy wallpaper, a worn Brussels carpet, an appalling dinginess for a President's home. Blessed are the details. He would abandon Jackson, write his impressions. *Scribo, ergo sum.* In his mind's eye, Paris rose over the horizon like a ship. His fingers fumbled for his notebook.

"In here." Adams stood aside to let him view the President's bedroom, faintly lit by another whale-oil lamp on a desk. Bed, mirror, bookcase.

"I have a filthy interpretation," Adams said slowly, drunkenly, to the mirror, "of the nickname Old Hickory. From Rachel's point of view."

"I ought not to be here," Chase said, bending down to look at the President's books.

"I myself am not inexperienced in physical love," Adams informed the mirror. His pale reflection winked at him lewdly. "I am officially engaged to be married. What are you looking for?"

"*The Power of Sympathy,* by Anonymous." Although Chase in fact had yielded to the impulse—irresistible—to see if John Quincy Adams by some chance owned a copy of *The Life of the Elder Pitt.*

"Here's Cicero," Adams said, abandoning the mirror. "My father's hero." He dropped to one knee and breathed whiskey in Chase's face like a senator. "The bald Tusculan. We disagree about Cicero. We disagree about everything."

"You're father and son."

"Do you know his daily routine? Makes a Spartan look volup—he wakes up between four and five, he walks for an hour and measures exactly how far he goes."

"Like Thomas Jefferson."

"Exactly." Adams looked briefly puzzled. "Then he comes in here and makes his fire himself. It teaches him humility, he says. Proudly. Then he eats breakfast and writes for an hour and goes downstairs and works until midnight."

"We ought not to be here." Voices, murmurs, ghostly and urgent, seeped through the badly carpentered floorboards.

"I write his journal out for him, from shorthand. He writes sonnets. He wrote a sonnet about my grandfather's death." Adams had wandered over to the window and parted the curtains. Chase cleared his throat, wondering how he would explain his presence in the President's bedroom if the President suddenly materialized, bald and Ciceronian, at the door.

"Capital of America," Adams said, "not a single light to be seen, dark as the moon's ass."

"Show me another room." The President's desk had two quill pens, a gold filigreed inkwell, a stack of blank sheets, and a buckram folder stamped (Chase opened and closed it in a single motion) *Political Correspondence.*

"I'll show you the orgy room," Charles Adams said.

Which in reality turned out to be, at the far end of the hall, over one of the unfinished wings, an almost empty chamber of modest proportions, bounded by tall windows on three sides and containing in its center, under a hanging gas lamp, one slightly battered green felt-top billiards table.

"This is the scandalous instrument itself." Adams smacked its wooden flank as if it were a horse. "You must have read about it in the filthy press." He had produced from somewhere a decanter of brandy and a glass, and with genuine Adams perversity seemed to grow sober as he drank.

Chase shook his head, trying to remember, but between Jackson and Adams, America was the Fertile Crescent of scandal.

"My brother John—he of the doomed marriage—I saw you shaking his hand downstairs—two years ago he sent to Congress an itemized list of all my father's purchases for the mansion, and even though my father had bought this table secondhand, with his own private money, eighty-four dollars and fifty cents, John brilliantly included it on the appropriations list."

"A scandal?" Chase asked.

"A scandal. Riotous, corrupt, undemocratic living. The kiss of electoral death. A *gaming* table in the White House. I am cursed with an excellent memory, Mr. Chase, I sat in the gallery of the Senate and listened to the forensic bilge as it washed back and forth on the deck of the ship of state."

Adams paused, looked pleased with his metaphor, and drank straight from the bottle. "Edward Everett of Massachusetts tried to defend us." Adams's voice dropped a whiskeyish octave and his mobile face grew long, solemn, and—Chase thought there was no other word for it—senatorial. " 'Sir, Dr. Franklin, no corrupter of youth, sir, was a great admirer of the game of billiards. Mr. Jefferson, I have been told, proposed to introduce it among the gymnastic exercises of the University of Virginia; whether General Washington played billiards, I do not know, but it is recorded of him that he played cards, which from a moral point of view is perhaps no better.' From the floor John Randolph of Roanoke intoned like a mummy, 'General Washington played billiards'—stop laughing, Mr. Chase. From the floor someone else rose to dispute the earlier gentleman—'Mr. Jefferson, suh, nevah, nevah played games of chance.' Actually, he used to play chess with my father in Paris. *Buvez?*"

"*Avec plaisir.*" Chase leaned across the table to take the bottle.

"They went on, thanks to brother John's literary ambitions, to read his rather lurid descriptive list. The *Congressional Record* declares the mansion to be 'furnished with choicest European fabrics.' " Adams made a slow, dramatic circle. " 'One room dressed in scarlet,' " he quoted, pointing the cue stick at an entirely unpainted wall. " 'Another in blue' "—the cue stick jumped—" 'a third festooned in orange.' " He stopped and smiled quite charmingly across the flat green surface of the table, still a little boy in his father's clothes. "This is, of course, the room *festooned* in hogwash."

Chase clacked two balls together in applause. Adams saluted.

"Why 'of the doomed marriage'?" Chase asked.

As suddenly as it had left, Adams's drunkenness seemed to return. He lurched forward clumsily and knocked the top of the billiard stick against the overhead lamp, sending it ringing and swaying.

"Mr. Short," he said. He dodged the lamp, ducked his head, obscurely angry. "Mr. Short told me several things about *you,* Mr. Chase. Sir." Between them the lamp swung like a ball of burning gas, hissing. Adams's thin face appeared, then disappeared in rhythmic flashes, black, white.

"He said you were quiet and ironic, you never stopped observing, and you nevah, nevah forgot. So I am nice to you."

"Mr. Short said that?"

"Man of disguised passions," Adams said. "You, not him. His very words." He slumped on his elbows and eyed the lamp as it came to a wary, trembling halt just above his head. "Some disguise," Adams said, and laughed out loud. "The way you *stared* at that girl."

✸   ✸   ✸

DOWNSTAIRS, under the north portico's overhang, Emma Colden stepped into her hired carriage and turned to look out again at Sellers.

"It would only distress and disillusion you," she said, smiling, not sure he could see her smile in the bad light, "to discover where I live. I prefer to be like Cinderella and disappear mysteriously after the ball."

Sellers leaned against the open door. "You quite charmed the President tonight then, Cinderella. He positively beamed."

"He is a prince of a President for beaming."

"He is a one-term prince," Sellers said.

Emma smiled again and reached a hand down to touch his shoulder. Ephraim Sellers was a politician to his bones; his gallantry and small talk swung invariably back to politics like the needle of a compass. He was also a man of average appearance who thought of himself as actually homely, so that for reassurance he needed a great deal in the way of little touches, attentions. He did *not* need the scarlet cravat that David Chase had stared at.

"I don't know a *thing* about that," she said. Sellers grinned, as she knew he would. They had met, become friends—were becoming more?—because, in the gallery of the Capitol where she was working one day, she had overheard his conversation, broke in, and correctly named the states that had voted for Jackson (she cared nothing for Jackson) in the corrupt election of '24.

"Not a *thing*." She put on a southern drawl. "I talked to the President about phrenology, which he distrusts, and quoted Cicero—"

"Whom he admires," Sellers finished. Around them other carriages were now backing and starting, wheels and harnesses were scraping in the equine minuet of a Washington party. "No, you don't know a thing about politics."

"I disliked Mr. Chase," she said abruptly, to reassure him.

CHAPTER
12

The Life of Andrew Jackson

Chapter Three

OUR RACHEL—*HIS* RACHEL—ENTERS THE STORY IN THE WINTER OF 1779, A twelve-year-old girl standing barefoot at the stern of the flat-boat *Adventure* as it plunges down the wild Tennessee River. Her hands are clasped to a bucking tiller, the air around her is seared with bullets and humming with arrows fired from the shore.

On the deck her father, her brother, her formidable fat mother Rachel Stockley Donelson are all firing back through gun loops along the sides of the flat-boat, as are the ten black slaves, the dozen or so other passengers, the nine more boats following close in their wake on the blood-streaked Tennessee.

Dear God, how did they ever make it? I can forgive much in America (there is much to forgive) when I think of the ordeal that emigrants like the Donelson party underwent in order to settle, to "develop" (as the new self-serving term has it) the wilderness.

Numbers. Take ten boats, three hundred people, a four-month voyage down the Holston River to the Tennessee, down the Tennessee to the Ohio, *up* the Ohio to the Cumberland, *up* the Cumberland to a curve and a salt-lick bluff later called Nashville where they were to *rendez-vous* with another party—total distance nine hundred and eighty-five miles; total losses, half or more of their boats and people.

My informant, since I have never seen Nashville and its salt licks, was a pleasant old Maryland woman (my age) named Mary Purnell Donelson, sixteen years old at the time of the voyage and the bride of John Donelson III. Mary's job was tending the sick, burying the dead, and nursing the babies—childhood, farewell—and she recalls wrapping her first corpse, a Negro man dead by frostbite, in a winding-sheet torn from the flat-boat's little canvas sail because no one had thought to pack shrouds or coffins. Another boat, carrying twenty-eight people, came down with smallpox and was left behind. Their cries could be heard around the bend as the rest pulled away; then the screams of the Indians descending, gunshots, nothing.

On the seventh of March a Mrs. Lemuel Peyton gave birth to a baby girl. Two days later the boat ran aground on a rock and the Indians crouching along the shore began to fire on it. To lighten the load, the panicked travelers flung whatever was at hand over the sides—with the blankets and bedding, in the hurry and confusion, accidentally went the new-born child. No turning back. They restrained the mother, shoved at the rock. Young Nancy Gower, two years older than Rachel, took the helm and steered the boat while the men rowed and fired. She was wounded by a ball passing through her thigh, but never a sound she made till her own mother saw the blood soaking her clothes. (Ah, Frailty, thy name is woman.)

And what, meanwhile, of Andrew?

By 1788, her father dead, her widowed mother settled on a vast holding of land east of Nashville, our Rachel was a married woman, living in Kentucky with her husband Lewis Robards. In North Carolina, our Jackson had received at last his law license; had wasted a year tending store off and on and looking for better work. Destiny, chuckling at her own subtlety, now decided to launch him west as well, in a slow, straight, comic line toward Nashville.

Now, the whole state of Tennessee had only recently come into existence. For several years after the Revolution the fiercely uncivilized North

Carolina territories west of the Cumberland Gap had been organized into an independent renegade state named Franklin (after the great Ben), whose governor was an Indian fighter named Sevier and whose official legal tender was otter skins (leading to considerable counterfeit money: raccoon pelts with otter tails sewed on) and "good whiskey." When Franklin was tidied up, given a clean collar, and reconstituted as Tennessee, Andy Jackson seized an appointment as the state's first prosecuting attorney for Nashville, in the desolate western division three hundred miles away. He called his pack of dogs, slung two pistols from his saddle, a rifle from his back, and stuffed half a dozen books in his bags. One of these was the student's popular crib, *Abridgement of the Law*, by one Matthew Bacon.

In Jonesboro, at the eastern end of the new state, Jackson stopped for a time to fit himself out as a proper gentleman. This meant buying a slave—a mulatto woman of eighteen or twenty named Nancy (*honi soit qui mal y pense*)—and a racehorse; and taking on a case or two in the local court, to show himself master of the law.

As it happened, in his first case the opposing lawyer was Waightstill Avery, the same old fox of a scholar who had a few years earlier refused to take Jackson on as a student. Lawyer Avery was amused, then and now, by Jackson's pretensions. In the courtroom, as our hero fumbled about with forms and motions, he twitted him unmercifully for his reliance on Bacon. Finally, unable to control himself any longer (I shall write that often), Jackson burst from his chair and swore, Irish accent sputtering, "I may not know much more law than Bacon, sir, but I know enough not to take crooked fees!"

A pleasant, soft-exhaling, bloody-minded Southern silence settled on the room.

Avery rose and asked—ominously—if Mr. Jackson meant to imply that *he* had taken illegal fees?

"I do, sir."

"Then it's false as hell!" shouted Avery.

Jackson ripped out a page of his Bacon and then and there, on the spot, wrote a challenge (a gentleman has a slave, a horse, and a duel).

Avery, who had indeed from time to time taken questionable fees, ignored the challenge.

The next day in court he likewise ignored the smoldering Jackson, who ripped out *another* page, wrote *another* challenge; and at sunset both men and their seconds met on a hillside south of town where they turned their backs, paced their paces, and at the signal turned again and carefully fired into the air.

Honor satisfied, they shook hands. Avery presented Jackson with a package and said, "I feared that in the event of my wounding you fatally, sir, you would be inconsolable in your last moments without your beloved Bacon." And Jackson unwrapped it to find a pound of smoked pork. The others laughed. Jackson, not conspicuous for his sense of humor, glowered at Avery as if he might take his shot all over again.

Nashville was still two hundred miles to the west. In the autumn of 1788, Jackson abandoned Jonesboro and its pleasures and joined a party of sixty families setting out with a hired guide.

No wagons, of course; no roads. Everybody, men, women, and children, proceeded on foot or horse, along hunters' trails. They stopped at "safe" campsites, put up buffalo-skin tents, cooked what they shot. Halfway into the trip, after marching thirty-six hours straight, the party halted and made a circle of tents around a fire, then crawled into them, exhausted. All except Jackson, who sat with his back against a tree, smoking a pipe. I don't like him, but he was a capable soldier long before he was a lawyer. Tennessee (I am told) has owls. The forest around the campsite certainly had owls, dozens of them, hooting louder and closer as the night settled in. Jackson smoked and thought; smoked and thought; then he picked up his rifle and crept to the tent of John Searcy, a popeyed little fellow who was to be a clerk of the court when and if they reached the fabled Nashville.

"Searcy," said Jackson, "listen."

"What is it?"

"Owls."

"That's natural."

"That's too damn natural. That's Indians, waiting for daylight."

On his own, iron in his voice, Jackson roused the guide, stomped out the fire. In half an hour he had led them all stumbling back onto the trail again, making for clearer ground. Behind them, toward midnight, a small party of hunters found their old campsite and took it over, and before dawn the Indians had in fact swooped down like the Assyrian wolf (or owl) and slaughtered them while they slept.

Jackson's friends were impressed by his woodcraft. I am impressed by whatever he has—I fall back on the despised word *presence*—that would make a hundred exhausted people get up in the middle of the night, on his say-so alone, and follow him without hesitation through the forest primeval.

We are closing in on Rachel.

CHAPTER

13

Halfway up Capitol Hill, Chase paused to wipe the perpetual Washington drizzle from his eyes and, in honor of William Short, check his watch.

Two muddy blocks away, at the end of an unpaved but cowless avenue, nudged and poked by stiff rows of yellow brick houses with pitched roofs and wooden porches, the enormous Capitol yawned and lifted its shiny black dome.

It was unfinished, of course; like everything else in Washington City, the Capitol was a marble mirage. On one of his walks Chase had been astounded to see that fourteen years after the British had burned the central section of the building down to the ground, reconstruction was still under way. From Delaware Avenue, where he now stood, the entire eastern half of the dome was covered by a web of scaffolds, ladders, and painted awnings, under which, even in the slate gray rain, carpenters and sculptors were apparently working.

Inside, he had found, it was better. The black dome covered a busy, dignified lobby. There was a chamber for the Supreme Court in the basement, a library for Congress between the two wings (where Randolph and Hogwood had met—Chase looked at his watch again and picked up his pace), and at the back of the so-called Rotunda a yawning crypt that was one day supposed to receive the mortal remains of George Washington himself, if his nephew at Mount Vernon would ever permit it. (But you would have to be crazy, Chase thought, turning a corner, dodging a splashing carriage, to leave the peace and quiet of Mount Vernon for this.)

He lowered his chin and pulled up his collar against a wind that had whipped itself to icy life somewhere north of Boston. Thirty yards ahead, directly in front of the red-bricked Dawson's Boarding House, the carriage skidded to a halt in four great fans of spray, and a moment later Emma Colden stepped out. She frowned at the sky and lifted her skirt from the mud.

"In Paris," Chase said, crossing to her, "there used to be burly young Savoyards who would stand on the corners and carry fine ladies over the mud on their backs."

"Are you a Savoyard, Mr. Chase?"

"A Bostonian. But I can offer one arm to the fair, like Andrew Jackson."

She stood out of the way of the horses, looked past his arm, and then stepped over the mud with a little skip that made her hips swing like a bell in her skirt. When Chase had caught up to her on the porch, she was removing her bonnet and shaking her hair free.

"Is your father well, or better?" Her hair smelled like lemon, an American smell, and her eyes, he observed for the first time, were slanted slightly upward, with a sleepy, sensual fold of skin under the lids. "I sent a note again this morning."

"Did you?" Emma dried one edge of her bonnet against her sleeve. Cold, aloof; colder than the wind. Chase felt a little rush of temper, but heard himself saying with mutton-headed mildness, "Since we're going to be partners for the next half hour, we might as well try to get along, no? Treaty? Truce?"

Emma flushed. She lifted her chin quickly, as if on guard. In her perfect English complexion her cheeks were like delicate pale rosettes.

"My father is as well as can be expected." She spoke, a degree less coldly. "The doctors have told him his heart is dangerously weak. They prescribe a treatment of rest and laudanum."

"I see. I'm sorry."

"It's not your fault, actually, Mr. Chase." Over her shoulder a black face peeked through a curtain. The wind dove with a shriek. "Nor the book contract either, to be fair," Emma added, shivering, ducking her head. "You're poor. We're poor. Do you understand what my father wants us to do?"

Father, daughter—it took Chase a moment to adjust to the rapid Hogwoodian shifts of conversation. "You are to charm scandalous Jackson secrets from Randolph. I am to protect you," he told her. He rapped at the big double door.

For the first time in their partnership she genuinely smiled. "Are you quite sure you haven't got that reversed, Mr. Chase?"

His fist stopped in midair.

Randolph's liveried slave pulled open the door, blinking at the wind and grinning.

In the private parlor everything was exactly the same as before, except for a small coal fire that now burned in the grate and the even more ghostly white of John Randolph's complexion.

"You must always wear blue, my dear," the senator told Emma as the two of them entered the room. "The color of the sky, except in Washington, and therefore remote and unobtainable and lofty. It will keep young men like Mr. Chase at a distance."

"Mr. Chase offered to carry me here on his back," Emma said, extending her hand.

"Mr. Chase is from Paris. Those are French ways." Randolph clasped her one hand in his two and cocked his tiny head against his collar. "Do you know Mrs. Bayard Smith, my dear?" Emma shook her head. "She has hair almost the same tint as yours, you see. But she always wears turbans instead of bonnets—" To Chase: "An item of feminine dress in fashion here until last winter." To Emma: "And places a jewel in the center, so." Randolph released her hand and touched an imaginary spot in the air above his head, then showed his yellow teeth like a horse.

They sat down with much fluffing of cushions, directing of teacups; they bowed over plates heaped with biscuits and nuts. Two days ago, Chase thought, the tall, slender Randolph, with his beardless chin and his shrill voice, had seemed amazingly boyish for a man of fifty; today, by the firelight, his face was old, powdery white, lined with a thousand fine wrinkles. If he wore a turban he would look like a mummy galvanized to life.

Emma cleared her throat and glanced sidelong at Chase, then put down her cup of tea. "My father is much better," she said. "You were kind to send your letter." Randolph waved a white, dismissive hand. Chase looked for unwinding bandages. "Now he sends *me* as his deputy."

"And what precisely can I do for *you*, my dear?"

"For us, in fact," Chase said, and likewise put down his cup. "For our book on General Jackson . . . Mr. Hogwood has begun it and I'm to continue it."

"And Miss Colden is Muse?" Yellow teeth.

"While her father is ill." Chase took two small dog-eared books from his coat pocket. "I've read all the standard campaign biographies—Isaac Hill, John Eaton, four or five more. But we're looking for anecdotes and facts—" he paused with what he hoped was Hogwoodian significance "—*documents,* something that hasn't been used before, something new. Last time you had just started to talk about Jackson—"

Emma broke in smoothly. "You have known him longer than almost anyone else in Congress."

Even a mummy was not without vanity. "Your lovely collaborator reminds me of my advanced age," Randolph told Chase. He hitched his chair closer to the fire and smiled as he spoke, but the elaborate courtesy in his voice had an edge. Emma's face reddened.

Chase stepped in. Partners. "I once heard Thomas Jefferson himself—speaking of advanced age—quote you, Mr. Randolph."

"Ah. Did you know St. Thomas of Cantingbury then?"

"I visited him at Monticello in 1815."

"You were a boy."

"A baby. He repeated your joke about discovering a new species of bird in Washington—"

"The war hawk. Yes, and I said you could identify the war hawk by its one monotonous call—'Canada! Canada!' Even after the British burned Washington to a cinder, half the members of Congress—not one of them ever in the army—were still demanding that we invade Canada. St. Thomas was one of them. He lusted after annexing Canada. Cuba, too. A deeply greedy man."

"Is Jackson?" Emma had recovered.

"There is no actual discussion of issues in this election," Randolph said, as if that were an answer to her question. He settled back in his chair and his hands made a little steeple of white bones. "It's the character of Jackson *versus* the character of Adams. Jackson has a committee of hench-men in Nashville—I call it the Whitewash Committee—that directs his campaign and sends out news stories and rebuttals as fast as Adams's committee prints its charges. And vice—so depressing—versa. Candidates have 'managers' now. The only real, the only great issue is ignored. Ad-ams has proposed a program of 'internal improvements,' as he styles it—he wants the federal government to build roads and canals, and he wants to subsidize a railroad to be called the Baltimore and Ohio; he even wants a national university, and scientific laboratories; he wants national observatories, which he calls, with the desperate Adams attempt at po-etry, 'lighthouses of the skies.' "

In his heart of hearts Chase believed that he had no political instinct whatever; he had drifted into writing books and articles about politicians because he couldn't live by writing poetry. Emma was looking puzzled. But he had heard New England versions of Randolph's complaint half his life. *These* politics he understood to the quick. "Federal improvements," Chase said firmly, quoting his father, "will destroy states' rights."

Randolph's mummified face came briefly to life. A pink tongue hissed between yellow teeth. "Yesss! If a state gives up any right to the general government," he said, "it gives up every right. John Adams tried to take away the freedom of the press with his Alien and Sedition Acts. John Quincy, the son, is, I truly suspect, a secret abolitionist. All Northerners seem to be reformers of one kind or another. His 'internal improvements' would lead step by step, if he could make them, to the dismantling of the states and then to the abolition of slavery, and I would shed blood to prevent that. Virginia would shed blood to prevent that."

Emma raised a hand in apparent protest.

"No," Randolph said. "*No*, asking a state to give up part of its rights is like asking a woman—forgive me, my dear—to give up part of her chas-tity."

"I had thought"—Chase hurriedly risked the transition—"that Mrs. Jackson's first marriage was the character issue."

Randolph stretched one long and disembodied arm toward the tea table. The arm poured honey-colored whiskey into his teacup. In the corner by the fire the Negro boy squatted on his haunches with a plate of biscuits in each hand and watched his master with round, steady eyes. "I knew Rachel Jackson," Randolph told them, "when she married Lewis Robards in 1785. Kentucky was still a part of Virginia then. Robards was, till the day he died, a suspicious, ill-natured scoundrel."

"It is said," Emma ventured, smoothing her skirt with one hand, "that Jackson seduced her away from Robards and that they lived together in . . . unmarried."

"They tell these tales about every politician." Randolph closed his eyes and smiled as if at some pleasantly scandalous memory of his own. Chase tried not to guess. "I have a dim recollection of talk in 1824. This time around, when someone—in Ohio, I think—first raised the matter, Jackson's committee planted stories of its own—that John Quincy Adams had pimped for the czar when he was ambassador to Russia, for instance. I remember earlier—the hazards, as you may say, of advanced age—that his father, old John Adams, was accused of returning from Europe with *two* mistresses, a German girl and a French one, and he sent home the German. John Adams, of all people, the Puritan Priest." Randolph grinned directly at Chase. "He was deeply flattered, I believe. He once told me the rumor had cost him the votes of the Pennsylvania Germans in 1800. But really I know nothing of this anymore. Washington is supposed to have had his Sally Fairfax, Jefferson his other Sally. I understand journalism and writers, my dears, but I know Jackson only in a public way. I can't think of any details—" he matched Chase's pause "—or *documents* that would help your book." He drained the teacup and replaced it on the table. "And in any case," he said, rising from his chair, "as General Jackson is reported to have said, 'I choose not to wage war against women.' " A final, impenetrable grimace.

At the door Emma gamely offered a compliment. "I've never yet heard you speak in the Senate, Senator," she said. "But I mean to come, and soon. My father tells me you are the greatest orator since Patrick Henry."

"The greatest orator I ever heard," Randolph said, reminding Chase that he would never, in his life, understand human nature, "was a woman. She was a slave. She was a mother, and her rostrum was the auction block. And she pleaded for her children and denounced the bystanders with amazing eloquence. Had she been my slave, I would not have sold her."

Chase pinched the bridge of his nose with two fingers, looked down at his shoes, admired Emma's cool self-control. She had no visible reaction whatsoever. "If you think of any incident or anecdote . . ." she said, putting on her bonnet.

"Or scandal." An ambiguous wag of the ghoulish head. To Chase: "Where are you staying?"

"The Indian Queen."

"Ah. With its famous signboard. I am, in fact, descended from the princess Pocahontas," Randolph told him and stroked one wing of his coarse black hair as if to confirm it. "You will find a far better representation of her, fully clothed, in the Capitol, just above one of Mr. Trumbull's malicious historical paintings. All compliments to your father, my dear."

Outside the boarding house a black landau stood waiting in the unpaved street, beside a little cherry tree in improbable bloom.

"You were very good, Mr. Chase," Emma said as they stood on the porch and she buttoned her coat against the wind. On the street the carriage driver came down from his seat and opened the door.

"Call me David."

"You were tactful, you were persistent. You've obviously done your reading."

"You were fine, too," Chase said, "except for the occasional bursts of flame from your eyes. He doesn't like women."

"No. He likes men."

They had reached the carriage and Chase stopped and put his hand on a wheel. "This carriage is from Senator Sellers." A statement of fact, not a question. Emma stooped and climbed in quickly. As he held the door open their shoulders grazed, and even in the carriage's interior shadows he could see the white curve of her throat and imagine curves whiter, softer . . . Colden, colder, coldest. I'm falling in trouble, Chase thought, right here in the city of mud.

"It belongs to him, yes." Emma adjusted her blue skirt over her legs. "So I can't offer you a ride. I'm sorry." She moved her head to indicate the scaffolded Capitol looming out of the twilight, as odd and unnatural as the painted backdrop of a stage. There, presumably, Sellers waited.

"*La belle dame sans merci*," Chase said and noted with disgust that as usual he had taken refuge in a joke and in French. "I would like to see you again," he said in English, seriously.

"I shall wear a turban, with a great jewel in the center." She latched the carriage door shut. "We are both very poor," she told him. "*Ecrivez votre livre*. Write your book." Then the horses snorted and the wheels turned and she was gone.

✷ ✷ ✷

AT the parlor window John Randolph watched them part, Emma in her carriage, Chase on foot. On the empty street the wind suddenly swooped and gusted again and flung a great swirling handful of cherry blossoms into the air, like a pink and white geyser twisting out of the mud.

He walked back to the little writing desk by the window and selected a sheet of his personal watermarked notepaper. In a tiny but exquisitely legible hand he wrote: *Dawson's——March 28, 5 P.M. Perhaps, my dear David Chase, there is one thing I can add to your book. Come and see me tomorrow night, after nine.*

Then he sat and looked at the fire and listened to the clock on the mantel click its brass tongue. After a moment he stood up with the note in his hand and walked to the fireplace and tossed it in.

14

The Life of Andrew Jackson

Chapter Four

Hogwood's Rules of Life.

RULE NUMBER ONE. A MARRIAGE WILL INEVITABLY SPLIT ALONG ONE OF TWO great fault lines: Bed or Money.

Lewis Robards had plenty of money.

He had a large stone house in Harrodsburgh, Kentucky, which he shared with his widowed mother; he had thousands of acres of land (all Westerners have land in quantities that leave an Englishman gasping); he had family connections stretching all the way back to Virginia, "old money," as old Virginians, powdering their old wigs, like to say.

And, of course, he had Rachel Donelson, favorite daughter of Nashville's founding patriarch. They had married in 1785, on the eve of Rachel's eighteenth birthday, she the belle of western Tennessee; Robards, the shy, lucky suitor. The same old lady who had floated on the flat-boat

Adventure with the Donelson party has written me a terse, rather disapproving recollection of Rachel before the marriage: "Medium height. Beautiful figure. Full red lips. Oval face. *She was irresistible to men.*" She was also an excellent dancer, a good horsewoman, high-spirited, vivacious; and a stem-winding, twenty-four-carat flirt.

As it turned out, precisely the wrong kind of wife for Robards.

In those days everyone in the West seemed to keep boarders, chiefly because of the Indians. Around the settlement of Nashville nobody went out alone, not women, not children, not even a strong man with a gun just to inspect his crops. The year of Rachel's marriage, if I've counted correctly from the back pages of the Nashville *Union*, a white settler, male or female, was killed by Indians on the average of one a week. Rachel's own father John Donelson was found dead by a creek, shot in the back with an arrow. So despite their wealth, like everybody else on the frontier the new Mr. and Mrs. Robards of Harrodsburgh took in boarders, not for the money but for the protection.

And one of the boarders, a young lawyer, name now lost to memory, found landlady Rachel wonderfully charming, found Rachel in fact irresistible; or so at least thought Robards, who glowered darkly and began to play the backwoods Othello whenever his wife spoke to the poor man or passed him on the path with a smile or allowed him courteously to light her corncob pipe. Another boarder, likewise a lawyer, is now one of Jackson's election managers, John Overton. He has compiled and published a formidable set of testimonials to Rachel's virtue—she was "completely, truly innocent," says the chorus (on oath), even Robards's ancient, respectable mother—and an equally formidable set of attacks on Robards's character, which was (on oath and on balance) "jealous, cruel, unkind, and unmanly."

No matter. Lewis Robards surprised his wife and the boarder one time too often for his tastes, and in the hot-tempered frontier way flung open the door and ordered young Rachel out of his house forever. Mrs. Donelson sent one of her seven strapping sons to bring her back to Nashville.

And three weeks later Jackson arrived.

Now Jackson was the new prosecuting attorney in Nashville. His daily business was in the courthouse (eighteen feet by eighteen feet, made of logs; windowless) that sat on a bluff behind the stockades, overlooking the brown Cumberland River. The widow Donelson lived with her family in a blockhouse nearly ten miles away, on the north side of the river.

Granted that Jackson needed a place to sleep. Granted that the evil fame of the Red Heifer Tavern of Nashville, opposite the courthouse, has reached even to me, flat on my back in Washington City (though something of a connoisseur of evil places). Still, the village of Nashville offered its pleasures, its stockaded walls, its private rooms to let—why in the world would Andrew Jackson settle ten miles away, exposing himself to a daily ride through Indian-infested forests, over a dangerous river ferry?

Was it Bed or Money?

I note first of all that though old John Donelson had been a better pioneer than businessman, by 1789 his steadier, less-restless sons had become astonishingly prosperous. Thanks to their business talent, Rachel Donelson Robards belonged to the largest land-holding family in Tennessee, and everybody knew it, for the princely Donelsons towered far above the rest of the great Cumberland Valley for social rank. They sent to New Orleans for their furniture, did they not? They bought their Negroes in Virginia instead of Tennessee (Virginia is the frontier standard of prestige in slavery as in everything else). They had begun to send their children east to private schools, and there was talk of West Point for one of the boys. There was even talk—the last democratic taboo—of ordering a Donelson Family Coat of Arms.

And here comes Jackson.

Jackson the orphan. Jackson the "wretch," the young man with the red blazing temper, the fierce sense of having been wronged by life so far, cast out and abandoned by father, mother, brothers. You may agree with John Quincy Adams, who thinks Andrew Jackson a coarse, unlettered, un-Harvard man; but Jackson is no fool, Jackson could look about him and literally see the lay of the land.

Since the day Jackson stepped inside the Donelson stockade, he has never been poor; or without a family.

And enter John Overton right on his heels (like an overwrought Shakespearean play, this—*Much Ado About Nothing*, perhaps; *Richard III* for the plot).

For hardly had Jackson taken up residence as a boarder in one of the outlying cabins, but a repentant and lonely Robards sends Overton down to Nashville to ask if Rachel will have him again.

She will, of course. What choice does a young woman have, even a Donelson? Marry or burn. At the news Robards himself galloped down forthwith from Kentucky and settled in with the Donelsons, wife and mother, and Overton moved into the outlying cabin with Jackson and a third young boarder fresh from Virginia named Coffee. I am tempted to sermonize here on the coming independence of women, the stupidity of marriage—why should a woman be at the legal mercy of a man, any man? Why should love be a golden cage? My prophet is Frances Wright; my text is "The World Turned Upside Down." But I pass on.

At first Jackson was away from the Donelsons much of the time. He rode a horrendous and horrifying five-hundred-mile court circuit from Nashville to Knoxville to Jonesboro and back, camping alone in the forests if he couldn't find company, eating whatever creatures he could shoot or catch. When he prosecuted homesteaders for debt (his usual job), they often responded with threats and fists. In the Knoxville courthouse an unhappy defendant stepped on his toes with the heel of his boot, and Jackson picked up a loose plank and flattened him.

When he returned to Nashville, the threats grew worse, because Robards had quickly resumed his jealous ways, alas. Jackson, by all accounts a conspicuously courteous man in the old southern way (if he was not flattening you with a plank), had now attracted Robards's green-eyed notice. Jackson was *too* attentive to Rachel, Robards declared, *too* courteous; he found them laughing together, they groomed horses together, they sat on the porch and smoked together (Romeo and Juliet with corncob pipes). It was too damn natural. More scenes, tears. Robards resumed another bad habit, spending his nights in the Negro women's cabin.

The faithful Overton remonstrated, to no avail; Coffee watched and brooded. And eventually Robards, shaking with rage, screwed up his courage and confronted Jackson directly, who offered (courteously) to fight a duel on the very spot to avenge the lady's honor. Because, Jackson thundered, *he* was innocent and *Rachel* was spotless; and if Robards said different, he would cut off his ears! Robards had him arrested for breach of the peace.

Now a nice scene. Jackson is supposed to enjoy the theatre and the company of actors. Having arrested him, a party of guards marched out of the blockhouse to escort Jackson and Robards to the magistrate in Nashville. As they walked downhill past a blackberry patch, Jackson stopped and rather theatrically asked for a knife to cut a few berries. Warily, the guards handed him one. Jackson tested the point with his finger; looked at Robards. Ran his thumb along the blade edge; looked at Robards. Gripped the handle—

Robards vanished full-speed into a canebrake, Jackson at his heels.

When he reappeared, Robards-less, a few minutes later, the prosecuting attorney pointed out reasonably to his guards that without a complainant the criminal charge was null and void. They took back the knife and agreed.

John Quincy Adams will have it (his campaign people will have it) that Jackson courted another man's wife, broke up a marriage, and lived with her in adultery.

Jackson's people say no, no, no, the marriage was over, Rachel was chaste, Jackson a pure, rescuing knight. How can you slander a victimized woman and call her, as the Adams papers certainly do, a "whore"? These are the simple *mores* of the frontier.

The undeniable fact is that in 1790 Robards asked the Virginia Assembly (like everything else in the world, Kentucky was part of Virginia) for permission to sue for divorce, the usual procedure, on the grounds that Rachel had "deserted" him for another man; and hearing *that,* Jackson took Rachel to Natchez on the Mississippi and married her there, so he said. There were no witnesses. Two and a half years later, when the couple had long since returned to Nashville and set up house, they learned that up in Kentucky Robards had waited and waited and mulled about, and only just then had he actually got around to filing his suit for divorce. Legally speaking—to everybody's pious horror—Rachel and Andrew were living in sin.

With Rachel in tears and Jackson in furious Scotch-Irish flames, for appearances' sake the humiliated couple had themselves married a second time by a justice of the peace. Half a dozen embarrassed Nashville witnesses were present.

The virtuous American people will overlook much in a President—duels and ignorance, of course; the wholesale slaughter of Indians—but not home-wrecking. If John Quincy Adams could *prove* it, if he could produce a witness (Robards is dead), a document, a *letter*—he would walk away with the election.

And if Jackson could persuade the *corpus democraticum* that he acted in perfect innocence, that a practicing lawyer, even in Tennessee, wouldn't know the difference between permission to sue for divorce and actual divorce, wouldn't even bother to *ask,* then he could probably sell sand in the desert, or ice in Boston.

In the new world of American politics it comes down to that in the end: salesmanship. Hogwood's Rule of Life Number Two. We hold this truth to be self-evident: all men are created gullible.

And thus on the one hand you have John Quincy Adams, pinched of face, wrinkled of skin, a disagreeable old New England toad, but superbly qualified, the most intelligent statesman since Thomas Jefferson; no salesman. And on the other hand, General Jackson, covered with blood and mud, fierce as Banquo's ghost, the self-styled champion of the common man, the people's furious friend.

In the Congressional straw vote as I write these very lines (March, 1828), the two candidates are dead even, going into the stretch.

I am heartily sick of Rachel Jackson."

James Hamilton put an elegant hand to his mouth, belched, and sat down. Coffee rescued the toppling plate of sherbet dessert from Hamilton's other hand and laid it on the floor, and when he looked up, Hamilton had somehow contrived to fill the hand again, this time with a glass of deep red French Quarter wine.

"I have heard," Hamilton said, raising the glass chin-high, right up to his orange cravat, "about ten thousand toasts to Rachel Jackson so far, and she wasn't even here at the Battle of New Orleans and we still have three more days to go."

"Aunt Rachel," Coffee said neutrally.

"Look at her." Hamilton tilted the glass dangerously forward, as if to indicate through the slowly revolving wheel of brilliantly costumed dancers the exact point where Rachel and Andrew stood on an elevated platform above the dance floor. "Fat as butter," he said over the silver thump of the band. Jackson and Rachel began themselves slowly to revolve in a kind of parallel dance to the one below them. "You told me on the boat she was the belle of Tennessee."

"She was, for a fact."

"For a fact, she's two hundred pounds of pious old granny," Hamilton said. He tilted the glass the other way and drank half the wine in a single New York gulp. "Won't let a man drink," he said, wiping his mouth with the lace cuff on the back of his hand. "Won't let a man tell a risqué story—'We don't *lahk* that kind of talk, Mr. H.,' she says. Church twice a day. Some damn belle."

On the platform Jackson and Rachel raised their linked arms to the crowd, which burst into deafening whoops of applause. Coffee had chosen a retreat as near as possible to a window—and all the windows of the Davis Hotel were flung wide open to the New Orleans night—but the noise and the heat of five hundred dedicated Jackson admirers were still too much to take. If he leaned his chair back any farther, Coffee thought, he'd fall in the bayou.

" 'And round and round the ghosts of beauty glide,' " Hamilton said as the music resumed, " 'And haunt the places where their honor died.' Alexander Pope. 'To a Lady.' "

"Yes, indeed."

"I can believe *Jackson* was wild. You just look at those eyes. I heard a story, General Coffee, about Jackson's eyes." Hamilton stretched out his empty glass and as if on signal the blackest servant in the whitest coat Coffee had ever seen materialized out of the swirling dancers with a brand-new bottle. "You tell me if it's true." Hamilton filled his glass. "Jackson was a judge in Memphis and a man named Russell Bean was hauled into court for cutting off the ears of his baby when he was drunk."

"That's right," Coffee said, and held out his own glass for a refill because neither tobacco nor spitting was allowed in the ballroom and his throat felt like a column of sand.

"And Bean walked right into town and stood outside the courthouse and cursed the judge and the jury and the state of Tennessee and swore he'd never be taken."

"That's right."

"And Jackson said send a posse, and the posse got scared, so Jackson yanked off his judge's robes and stalked outside with a pistol in each hand and marched up to Bean and said, 'Surrender this very instant, you goddamned villain, or I'll blow you through.' "

Coffee chuckled and sat up on all four legs of his chair to finish the story. "And when they asked Russell Bean afterwards why he'd given up to Jackson after holding off a whole damn posse, 'Why,' said Bean, 'when he came up I looked him in the eye, and I saw Shoot. And there wasn't Shoot in nary other eye in the crowd. So I said to myself, it's time to sing small, and I did.' "

Hamilton burst out laughing, and Coffee grinned. In front of him, because he thought his eyesight was going bad, the colorful whirling ladies looked like pieces of Creole candy dropped out of a box. Hamilton wheezed and drained his glass and wheezed again. There was *another* wild Jackson story Coffee thought he would pass over, for diplomacy's sake, the time at the race meet picnic by Clover Bottom, when the local tavern built a two-hundred-foot table under a tent, so the gentry could eat their meal, and while Jackson presided at one end, a fight broke out at the other, and Jackson, seeing he didn't have time to force his way through the crowd at the sides of the table, simply *jumped on top* and marched straight down, *slaughter* in every lineament of his face. Coffee could still remember how people stood with their food suspended halfway to their mouths while Jackson waded by. And when he got in range of the brawlers, he reached one hand behind his coattails where his pistol would normally be, and clicked his tobacco box loudly like a gun, and the whole cowardly bunch of them screamed, *"Don't fire, General!"* and ran like turkeys.

"She must have changed *after* the marriage," Hamilton said, with such a melancholy note in his voice that Coffee turned to look at him. "If she really was such a slender young beauty before."

The music jumped to a halt. The room shook again with shouts and applause. Coffee could feel the floorboards vibrate under his shoes. The whole building (anchored in bog, like everything else in New Orleans) was vibrating: lights, banners, candles, flags seemed to sway in one direction and then roll back like a wave in the other. Rachel had disappeared into the hands of her female keepers, but Jackson's tall spike of gray hair could be seen working through the dancers, toward them.

"You know," said Coffee above the noise, wondering if Hamilton were drunk and liable to be indiscreet, then bending toward him and taking the chance, "you know, I think she changed just about *overnight*. When I first came to the Donelson blockhouse she was a little bit subdued, of course, feeling the humiliation of being sent away by her husband. But then she perked up. She started to dance and go around and enjoy herself."

"Robards," Hamilton said. "Robards made her feel guilty."

"That's right. The day she learned that Robards had never filed for divorce, just out of meanness, that was the day the fun went out of her. One minute she was the respectable wife of Andrew Jackson, the next minute she was a notorious sinner. I heard her wailing all afternoon—'I thought he would kill me once,' she said, 'but this is *worse.*' "

"Drove her to the church," Hamilton said, and looked at his empty glass. Jackson had stopped twenty feet away, by a potted tree, where an ancient couple in striped Creole costume had caught him by the arm. "Made her pious. To live it down."

Coffee nodded once more and stood up. Close enough. He would have to repeat it all over tomorrow, he guessed, but politics was nine tenths repetition.

"Gentlemen," said Andrew Jackson as he reached their corner. He fanned his chest with his hand. "Who wants to be *me* the next dance?"

Hamilton was also on his feet and laughing and shaking his head in mock protest. On the trip south, once they'd passed Natchez, so many people had lined the riverbanks to cheer Jackson that they had all started to take turns impersonating the General. Sam Houston was all right. Coffee was too big, but it was hard to tell that from shore. But Hamilton, who must have stood five-four in his boots, had had to be boosted above the rail by Coffee and given Jackson's big plumed hat to wave. And still the crowds cheered.

"Are you all right, John?" Despite the sultry New Orleans heat, Jackson wore his dark blue major general's uniform, with a bright red sash, a white waistcoat, and yellow epaulettes the size of brooms. Just to look at him made Coffee sweat.

"I'm hot, General Jackson, I'm hot and dead, but it's a great day."

"Tomorrow morning early," Jackson told Hamilton, "we're going to the battlefield for a speech, and then to the Catholic church for a sermon. And then there's another dinner."

"I've written Mr. Van Buren about your reception at Natchez," Hamilton said, moving closer as the horns in the band started to play again.

Jackson lowered his head to hear whatever it was Hamilton had written, and Coffee watched the dancers reassemble and listened to the band and wished it was his hearing going bad instead of his eyes, because he had heard enough Creole music, he thought, to last a lifetime, and he had never liked the first thing about New Orleans, not its sponge-bath climate or its beard-moss trees and swamps and cabbage palmettos that looked soft and rotten all the way through, not even its vaunted French Quarter, whose endless shutters and closed verandas struck him as built for secrecy and whispers, not at all like the real France, he imagined. Hamilton had lived in France. He would have to ask Hamilton about the resemblance.

But Hamilton, when Jackson rejoined the crowd, had his mind on other matters. He turned his back to the dancers. Out of an inner pocket, with a little confidential flourish, he produced an elaborately printed card.

Coffee held it up to the window. It was so dark in their corner that he had to move a step toward the faint glow of an outside streetlamp. He would give anything to spit. Full, flowery script. Engraving of a black domino mask. "Admit One," he read.

The New Yorker beamed. He took Coffee's arm, like a brisk little spaniel leading its master out for a walk. "To the Mulatto Ball," he said, while the horns blared in alarm. Stage whisper: "Don't tell Rachel!"

✴   ✴   ✴

AND don't tell Mary Coffee either, Coffee thought.

He remembered the building well enough from 1815—a long three-story brick house on Orleans Street, with the ballroom on the second floor and spectators' curtained galleries on the third. And he remembered even better the one clear January night he had come in from his campsite on the Bayou St. John and climbed the stairs—just as he was doing this very minute with Hamilton—and taken a shocked front seat in the gallery.

Without a word their black usher drew back a velvet curtain and bowed them through. In a flash Hamilton was at the edge of the loge, peering down. Coffee blinked to adjust to the light, or the dark. The regular Mulatto Balls were held on a Wednesday, and only quadroon women and white men were admitted. For the Jackson celebration, he thought, they had obviously changed their rules—no sentry line of stern black mothers, for one thing, ranged along the entrance wall to receive the gentlemen's offers (and the gentlemen's cash). No corps of professional "introducers," either, who would lead you onto the floor if you were shy. Coffee struggled to recall the few words of French he had imbibed (and that was the very word) during the two and a half months when they liberated Old Babylon, as Rachel Jackson kept calling it, then and now. *Placées*. The quadroon ladies were called *placées* because they would dance, and smile, and curl themselves like honey around a young man, and if the young man agreed to set them up in a "place" near Ramparts Street in the Old Quarter, why that was a quadroon marriage.

"These," Hamilton said, gripping his arm again and dragging him forward, "are the most beautiful, tawny, *wonderful* women," and leaning forward with him, Coffee had to admit that if your taste ran to Babylon, here it was. Dozens and dozens of dark-haired, fair-skinned *femmes de couleur,* as the New Orleans expression went, sensual as roses. They wove gliding back and forth over the polished floor, under three dim crystal chandeliers, dancing to a Creole band with young men in coats and masks, or dancing with each other, or some of them languorously dancing all by themselves, like soft-spinning blossoms; blossoms on fire. There was a champagne bar in the corner, a brandy and absinthe bar opposite; between them a curving staircase led to the gallery level and private chambers. Under the nearest chandelier a girl's dress slipped from white shoulders to whiter—

"Praise to corruptible flesh," Hamilton muttered. He said something in French, then he leaned far out over the dancers and made the sign of the cross, as if he were blessing a ship. "Praise to quadroons. What the hell *are* quadroons?"

Coffee tried to explain, over the noise of the band and the clink of bottles and glasses as their usher reappeared. A quadroon was the child of a white and a mulatto. An octoroon was the child of a white and a quadroon. A tierceron of a mulatto and a quadroon. A griffe of a Negro and a mulatto—he stopped; he lost count and track. New Orleans had an official city code of fifteen racial gradations, which he had read, in 1815, with disgusted amazement and till that very instant, was sure he had forgotten. Somebody had lowered the gas lamps to a crescent-moon glow, and Hamilton was watching openmouthed a beautiful quadroon dancing alone just below them. Quadroon mistresses couldn't mix with white ladies, or sit down in their presence, or ride through the streets in a carriage. A white woman could have a quadroon whipped like a slave. Directly beneath them the girl's gown had now slipped all the way down to her waist. A young man in a wolf-head mask was slowly raising her hands.

"Jackson wouldn't come?"

Coffee shook his head. Hamilton was breathing hard, and Coffee was making a strong effort to remind himself that he was an old married man; life itself was nine-tenths repetition.

"He wouldn't approve," Hamilton said. "Afraid of the scandal." Hamilton had given a note and a coin to their usher. "Van Buren's like that."

"The General," Coffee said, wondering not for the first time at the single-track minds of politicians. Thinking of Jackson and Van Buren when he was ordering a whore. "The General has Spartan self-control."

"Not when he met Aunt Rachel," Hamilton cackled.

In the flickering light of the chandeliers they could see their usher handing the note to a black-haired girl and then glancing upward in their direction. "God bless her biblical bottom," Hamilton added.

Coffee laughed out loud at his New York bluntness.

"Come on, General, I'll pay for you too."

"No, no." Coffee cleared his throat and shook his head. Three years in the army had cured him forever of judgmental thoughts about what men (and women) did with themselves to please that corruptible flesh that he, like Hamilton, was perfectly willing to praise. It would be wrong to say that he had Spartan self-control; but he did have middle-aged inertia, and common sense, and Mary sitting at home. Hamilton staggered out with their Pandarus of an usher, and Coffee followed his progress around the gallery until Hamilton reached the curtained foyer at the top of the stairs, and the girl, and disappeared.

The Creole band launched into musical spasms. Coffee rose and made his way to the street. The truth was, he thought, coming out onto Royal Street and stopping to smell the exotic air; the truth was, except for that one big, brief flare of passion, Andrew Jackson was an undersexed man. You could blame his poor health, which would have killed anybody else thirty years ago. You could blame his political ambition, which knew that *another* scandal would certainly ruin him. Or you could even blame that same guilt about the divorce that had transformed Rachel overnight from a lively girl (of most corruptible flesh)—from a *flirt*, to use the pure English word—into a tedious, fat old churchmouse.

If you were a deeper student of human nature than James Hamilton, Coffee imagined, listening to his boots click rhythmically on the wooden sidewalk, you might even make one other connection. And then to his own surprise he paused and spat at last, and for once in his life allowed himself a disloyal thought about Andrew Jackson. Undersexed, he thought. *Overangered.*

*   *   *

WHEN Coffee saw Hamilton again it was half an hour past dawn, and they were both sitting down by arrangement to a cup of chicory-flavored *café au lait* in Maspero's Exchange Coffee House, next to the fog-shrouded river.

"You didn't indulge?" Hamilton asked, managing to yawn and look rakish at the same time.

"No, sir." To Coffee, the little New Yorker appeared, depending on your point of view, either totally disheveled or totally rejuvenated. "I went back to the Davis Hotel," Coffee said, "to see that the General was set up all right."

Hamilton clicked his tongue and ran his fingers through his hair, which had the tangled aspect now of a bird's nest glued together with pomatum.

"Well, I liked that place," he said, "last night. I like this town."

Coffee broke a sugared cruller in half and put a piece on Hamilton's saucer. "This café was here in 1815. The General actually did some of his planning for the battle in this very room with Jean Lafitte, the pirate."

Hamilton dutifully regarded the sand-covered floor and the open kitchen behind them where cooks in white French hats were banging kettles and pans. But after the indulgences of the night his mind had clearly swung back, like the needle of a compass, to politics.

"He'll make a speech this morning," he said, "at the battlefield. Is that right?" Hamilton gestured at the foggy levee beyond the window, more blue than gray in the rising sun. Coffee chewed on his cruller and made his face as reassuring as possible. Hamilton and Major Lewis, calling themselves campaign managers now, had written all three of Jackson's New Orleans speeches, the *only* speeches he was supposed to give, and their constant worry was that he might improvise on his own or stray from their text and offend somebody.

"Oh, he knows what you want," Coffee said. Over the levee's dark hump the smokestack of a waiting steamboat looked like an upended cannon. "He knows he has to appear 'above the fray.' Your very words."

"Presidential," Hamilton said. "He has to be presidential. Talk about the will of the people. Leave the filth to Henry Clay and Binns and Hammond."

Coffee nodded as if he would do just that. John Binns was the Philadel-phia newspaperman who had printed the notorious "coffin handbill" showing how many innocent men Jackson had supposedly executed in the war. Last year Hammond in Cincinnati had published the original stories about Rachel and Robards and had been fed his material, everyone in Nashville believed, by Henry Clay. When the first article came out, an enraged Jackson had wanted to take a cowhide whip straight to his office, but Coffee and Sam Houston had finally talked him into writing a furious, a truly sulfurous letter instead, which Coffee saw to it never got sent.

"You've eased my mind about that Robards business," Hamilton said with a tap of his finger. The little man liked things symmetrical, Coffee had noticed; he had now lined up his cup and spoon and the sugar bowl in a straight row, and he broke his half cruller into two more identical pieces. "I've written Van Buren. We're all right there."

"It was mudslinging pure and simple," Coffee said for the hundredth time. "Nothing else. You never saw two more *married* people."

"I sent Van Buren a copy of that little memorandum you wrote me." Politics or coffee or both had made Hamilton brisker, fussier. "About Rachel's first marriage. Very helpful, very clear. Well written. Thank you."

"That's all right." In his youth Coffee had written a few newspaper articles in support of Jackson and still kept them in a scrapbook, but he had been nothing but an ignorant, gruff old soldier ever since, and he was absurdly pleased by the educated New York Hamilton's praise. By contrast, Jackson had scarcely glanced at the memorandum. "Give Hamilton whatever he wants," he had said, thrusting it back, "keep the goddamned little man happy."

On the levee, sailors were setting up a gangplank to the steamship. Hamilton finished his cup and stood and added, with symmetrical afterthought, "You could write me another."

"All right."

Coolly, and somewhat to Coffee's awe, he named the man who had killed his father. "You could write me about Aaron Burr. The rumors about Jackson and Burr in 1805."

"I'll start it tonight."

"I'm a lawyer, you know," Hamilton said as they walked over the sand-covered floor toward the door. "I like to tie up loose ends and keep things neat. It runs in my family. Do you remember the name of that young lawyer who boarded with Robards up in Kentucky? The one that Robards first got jealous about?"

Coffee pulled open the door and felt the wet breath of the fog on his cheek; smelled horses and river and coffee all floating in the soft, sweet New Orleans air; smelled no trap, no ulterior motive. There was no reason not to be helpful, with a whole presidential election at stake.

"I do indeed," Coffee said. "A Virginia man. Name of Peyton Short."

PART

2

April–August 1828

CHAPTER

1

A bluebottle fly whizzed by like a bullet.

Andrew Jackson stopped halfway across the carpet and slapped, not at the fly, but at his coat pockets in search of tobacco.

Felt; fumbled; slapped.

Behind the big walnut table the Nashville Inn had sent up specifically for their campaign office, John Eaton rose and went rapidly through the exact same sequence of motions, like a man in a pantomime, and then pulled out a pouch of his own to offer.

Jackson noticed the unconscious imitation and said nothing; he had known John Eaton twenty years and understood him down to the bottom. He did mind the tobacco, which was heavily spiced with chicory bits, a New Orleans innovation that Eaton had picked up last month and that Jackson disliked intensely, as he disliked almost every spicy taste; but politeness dictated that he accept the tobacco and use it with a smile. Politeness counted for a great deal at any time, particularly in a room where everybody was hot and tired. "No man is a hypocrite in his pleasures," he had heard it quoted; whoever said that was not a polite man.

"General, sit down and let me bring you a gin and water to go with that pipe." John Coffee was as independent and calm, Jackson thought, as Eaton was insecure and anxious. He had known big John Coffee for over thirty years.

"Give him a cocktail," Sam Houston said, using the new word for a mixed drink of spirits, sugar, bitters, and water. A "Kentucky breakfast" was three cocktails and a pouch of tobacco. Like everything else that Jackson encountered these days, of course, it had a political side—the cocktail was of great use to a Democrat candidate, Henry Clay had reportedly said in Washington, because a person who has swallowed a glass of it is ready to swallow anything else.

Jackson sank back in his chair and accepted the drink—or cocktail—he was far too tired to tell. Through the open window, street noises drifted up with a curious disembodied, ghostly effect. If he closed his eyes and listened, it was like being dead while the rest of the world went on. Horseshoes ringing on stone. The arthritic creak of a loaded wagon. Black voices, white voices, a bang like a pistol shot.

When Jackson opened his eyes the bang was only the sound of Sam Houston closing a drawer at the table. Unlike Eaton and Coffee, who were dressed for the heat in light frock coats and riding trousers, Houston was in a new costume phase—Jackson had never known another man with such a love of wearing costumes—this time a peppermint-striped Indian blanket draped over a thin, collarless brown shirt; buckskin pants and tall boots; three or four Chickasaw necklaces made of green and blue stones and silver; and a flat, wide-brimmed hat with a single black feather for his nickname, the Raven. In his belt, as usual, was the wooden butt of a Derringer pistol.

"General," Coffee said in his mild voice that still carried right where he wanted, "we've got a bunch of letters you need to sign."

Jackson nodded and held out his hand. They had ridden up from a trip to Memphis and stopped at the Nashville Inn to see the new headquarters where Eaton and Major Lewis spent hours every day writing letters, clipping newspaper articles, and talking politics. As long as it doesn't *look* like electioneering, he had told Eaton, but now he was perversely glad to see that the room was absolutely papered with posters and banners and handbills. In front of him, directly over a glassed-in bookcase stuffed with folders, a six-foot banner:

ANDREW JACKSON

HIS TITLES ARE HIS SERVICES
HIS PARTY THE AMERICAN PEOPLE.

Jackson put down his pipe and the letters and closed his eyes on the dusty office, the heat, the murmur of men's voices under his command. He heard Rachel's name whispered; Henry Clay; the word *duels*. They were talking about campaign strategy, how to answer old slanders. It was ironic and infuriating, Jackson thought with the controlled, red-lidded tension that for him was the beginning of rest: In order to capture the insubstantial future, he had spent nearly four precious goddamned years defending the past.

The Dreams of Andrew Jackson

MOTE OF DUST. BLACK FLY, DRIFTING. A BONE-WHITE, YELLOW-TOOTHED unlined face that nobody has seen alive for twenty-two years.

Charles Dickinson by name. A young man in 1806, twenty-seven or twenty-eight, young compared to me, who was thirty-nine that year and old enough to know better. So everybody said. Another man would have simply ignored him because of his youth, first at the racetrack, where words heated up, flew about. Then later at Winn's Tavern in Nashville when he was clearly drunk and took *her* sacred name in his polluted lips. I should have ignored him because it was the liquor talking, and he apologized next day for it, and I nodded acceptance (no more) and that was that.

Except that his idiot friend Swann kept it up and sent *me* a challenge for words I had used, and I walked back into Winn's one Saturday noon and pulled out a cane and whipped Swann till he crawled, and would have whipped him out the door and into the street if my spur hadn't caught in a chair, and *I* fell down and he got away.

Except that I *hated* Charles Dickinson as much as I have ever hated any man, young or old, and I can't say why.

He reminded people of me, John Coffee said. At that age. Impulsive, a kind of an upstart, hotheaded, never sat on a fence in his life, but always took one side or the other and stuck. "Like you, General," Coffee says frankly, floating in front of me now, his big, mild face next to Dickinson's worm-stripped skull.

But Coffee was wrong. Charles Dickinson came from tidewater Virginia, not South Carolina. He was a rich *grandee*, a graduate of William and Mary College (like his hero Thomas Jefferson), Latin and Greek were his daily salt and pepper. Not poor, not an orphan; not abandoned by the world to make his own way. He had a large family, all still alive, his mother and father both still alive. And when he sent his letter to the Nashville *Impartial Review* calling me a "coward and a scoundrel," his wife was pregnant with their first child. I have no children of my own and never will, as Coffee knows, which is either Providence or Judgment, who can say?

And not like me one other way. I have handled firearms in anger all my life, since the day the British devils rode across Waxhaw Creek. But I am an indifferent marksman, lacking in skill (not anger), while along with his Latin and Greek, Charles Dickinson was widely known as the single best pistol shot in Tennessee.

He tried to frighten me.

Typically, he made a trip to Natchez before he published his challenge, and every day he practiced with his pistol and made sure somebody saw him and sent word back to Nashville. Because at the word of command, and apparently without aiming, Dickinson could put four lead balls into a space the size of a silver dollar, twenty-four feet away, and when he came back to Nashville he offered to bet anybody five hundred dollars he would finish me off with one shot. He never found takers. There was no doubt then in my mind or ever since that Charles Dickinson meant to kill me. Kill or be killed. Shake thy gory locks.

Coffee's face vanishes, popped like a bubble. And here is Aaron Burr's.

All during the year 1806 Aaron Burr is coming and going through Nashville. He warns that the Spanish are planning to seize New Orleans. He hints that the President has authorized him to scout up an army, privately, to counter any invasion and in return to seize Texas. Great events are set in motion, great forces, Fate is sweeping her torch across Tennessee. A man's life sometimes takes fire, I think, and burns like a tree. "Did you mean to kill him?" I rashly asked Burr. (I had been drinking, John Coffee had tried that year to stop my drinking, bet me a suit of new clothes, but I will either drink as I like or not at all.) "*Did you mean to kill him?"* Meaning Alexander Hamilton, of course, but neither of us used his name. Burr sat at my table with his glass of wine in his hand and twisted the stem between two fingers, a mannerism he had, and he said they had stood exactly ten paces apart on the banks of the Weehawken River in New Jersey and when the word "fire" was spoken, he raised his pistol and put his bullet exactly where he intended.

I woke up at five o'clock in the morning, May 29, 1806, and told Rachel I would be gone to Kentucky for two days and might see some trouble there with Mr. Dickinson. She never asked why. In Nashville, on the Courthouse Square, I met old General Thomas Overton. He was to be my second since Coffee was hurt, and we joined two or three others and set out for the Kentucky state line.

Dickinson took *eight* of his friends for company. Along the road he stopped four times and practiced with his pistol and left the targets on the trees. The last target was a piece of string hanging from a poplar limb, which Dickinson severed with one shot; he paid an old darky fifty cents to sit there and wait and show me the string.

"A miracle shooter like Dickinson," Overton told me in his old-country brogue, "always shoots fast."

I knew that.

"So you don't stand a chance if you try to shoot first, Andy."

And I knew that too.

We stayed in a tavern kept by one David Miller, on the banks of the Red River, and I smoked my pipe by the fire that night and slept so soundly they had to wake me for breakfast.

By six in the morning we were all riding downriver, to a point where a ferryman was supposed to take us over. But when no ferryman appeared, I spurred my horse into the stream and dashed across, followed by the rest, and we all dismounted in the poplar forest two hundred yards from the water, in Kentucky where affairs of honor were legal.

"How do you feel about it now, General Jackson?" one of the witnesses wanted to know.

"Oh, all right," I said, thinking for some reason of the Waxhaw Creek that Banastre Tarleton had dyed with my brother's blood, the first Red River. "I shall wing him," I said, "never fear."

Dickinson's second won the choice of position and he paced off twenty-four feet on the soft ground, still covered there with yellow poplar leaves like a huge smear of butter. Overton therefore would give the word to fire, which was what we had wanted. Each man was entitled to one shot.

Dickinson took his place. He wore a short blue coat and gray trousers. He was young and handsome and he had soiled his lips with her name—and mixed Robards's foul name with hers, I suddenly thought, realizing that here we were in Kentucky again, where it all began. Life turns in circles, wheel after wheel. "As for slander, settle them cases yourself," my mother said, her dying words. The songbirds were up. Some Negroes from a nearby field had crept over to watch. Dickinson chose his pistol. He adjusted his sleeves.

I was wearing dark blue trousers and a dark blue coat, which I buttoned once at the chest.

Everything fell silent.

Twenty-four feet. Eight paces, marked at each end by a peg. Our pistols pointed perpendicularly down to the ground.

I thought of nothing.

I thought if it were the great I AM himself who stood twenty-four feet away, I would still raise my pistol and fire.

"Are you ready?" said Overton.

"I'm ready," said Dickinson.

"I'm ready."

Instantly Overton shrieked in his old-country brogue, "FERE!"

Dickinson raised his pistol in one smooth motion and fired.

Overton told me later that he saw a puff of dust fly off the breast of my coat and my left arm came up with a snap and gripped my chest. But I otherwise never moved.

"Great God!" said Dickinson, stepping off the peg. "Have I missed him?"

"Back to the *mark*, sir!" screamed Overton, hand on pistol.

Dickinson stared at him; stared at me.

He stepped back to the peg, trembling, holding his pistol down, and averted his eyes.

I raised my pistol and aimed along the barrel till he sat on the silver bead. I pulled the trigger and the hammer snapped halfway with a loud "click" and stopped. Under the rules, a half-cocked shot didn't count. Dickinson stood with his pale young face to the woods. Coffee was right. He looked exactly like me. I sighted again and fired and he went down in a shower of smoke and blood.

I walked toward my horse, and two minutes later Overton caught up, puffing, saying, "He won't need anything more of you, General," and the surgeon who was walking on my other side said, "Look at your shoe, General!" Which I did, and it was filled with blood.

"Are you hit?"

"Oh," I said, "I believe he's pinked me a little." But the truth was, when they got me back to Miller's, Charles Dickinson hadn't missed; he had shattered two ribs and put his ball just one inch under my heart, where it sits this very minute, and I was bleeding like the Red River till they cut their bandages. "How could you stand there and aim and shoot when you had *that* in you?" Overton wanted to know, over and over. But I would have killed Dickinson if he had put a bullet through my brain. Such is anger. Such is will.

When I came home and walked through the door, Rachel fell to her knees sobbing and praying, "Oh, God, have pity on his poor wife, pity on the babe in her womb!"

And I knelt down beside her but wouldn't pray, such is love.

CHAPTER
2

John Quincy Adams was seated at his desk in the President's House, writing in his Diary, when he felt the floor, the chair, the desk itself begin to shake. The oil lamp beside him rocked. The window shutters rattled as if seized by the wind in both hands; the entire house heaved like a ship on the crest of a wave and lurched.

He recognized it at once as an earthquake, the first he had ever experienced. It lasted about two minutes by his watch, and then the house returned to its accustomed midnight calm.

Adams put away his watch and tried to recall a line of poetry that might deal with earthquakes. *If storms and earthquakes mar not Heaven's design,* he scratched in the margin of his page, *why then a Borgia or a Cataline?* John Dryden, he thought, but could not remember the actual poem. He lifted his head and gazed at the shadowy rows of books beyond the desk. An application? A moral? There were Borgias and Catalines conspiring all across the country, creating earthquakes. The earth shook with conspiracy against him.

Adams laid down his pen and crossed the hall to his wife's bedroom. To his surprise, although she was the most nervous and high-strung of women, she had slept straight through the earthquake, and was still sleeping now, before him.

In an uncharacteristically tender gesture, Adams put down his lamp on a table and sat beside her bed, to watch her sleep.

She lay on her back, arms outside the blankets. The pull of gravity had smoothed her cheeks and unfurrowed her brow, so that in the soft, forgiving glow of the little lamp she looked almost—not like a girl; Adams was too rigidly honest to think that—but like a young woman at least, like a bride, for example, of twenty-three or -four.

Adams sat carefully back, making not a sound. His wife was unaware that in the course of his rummaging a few weeks ago he had come across a manuscript in her hand, bound neatly between two hard white vellum covers: "Louisa Catherine Adams: The Biography of a Nobody."

He did not think it a violation of trust to read it. Louisa was his wife. She was deeply unhappy. Since the day they had moved into the President's House she had been melancholy and unwell; she refused to go with him on his annual summer trips to Quincy; from time to time she retreated to her room like an invalid and refused to see people, even to appear at their weekly receptions.

To his own mind Adams had been quite reasonably patient and understanding; he had, at some financial sacrifice, paid for her secret trip to Philadelphia and her consultation there with the spectacularly ill-named quack doctor Philip Physick. He had allowed her to go on a separate vacation to the New York lakes. But he recognized, with pursed lips, that Louisa thought this hardly sufficient. When their son Charles had become engaged last summer, she had written him a letter, and Charles, in one of his periodic fits of rage against his father, had shown it to him. Adams, who remembered everything he read, recited the words silently in his mind: *It is a painful thing to state, but it is nevertheless a fact that as it regards women the Adams family men are one and all peculiarly harsh and severe in their characters.*

Louisa sighed and stirred in her sleep. Somewhere far off a bell rang twice and then stopped. Washington was a city of bells; alarms. They were not a *romantic* couple; Adams would admit that. They were not Rachel and Andrew Jackson.

Out of old, unconscious habit he slowly moved the first two fingers of his hand from front to back, tracing the outline of his skull. When he had courted his wife in London, her whole family had assumed he was interested in the oldest girl, Nancy, until in his typical abrupt and "harsh" manner, in the middle of a family dinner, he had suddenly handed Louisa a poem he had written for her. Pandemonium ensued—the governess snatched the paper from Louisa's hand, the children were rushed from the table, Nancy dissolved in tears. In the first years of their marriage they had often left poems for each other on their tables, in their books. Louisa thought she had married a poet.

An earthquake, he had read, is followed by a series of diminishing shocks.

Adams took one last look at his sleeping wife's face and went out into the hall. The President's House creaked and muttered, from floorboards to ceiling. At the window he glanced out at the awful city. A few streetlamps winked near Gadsby's Hotel, a few more near Capitol Hill. Otherwise, as black and empty as the sea. If Americans thought the federal government was significant or powerful, they would have long ago flocked to be near it. If Americans thought the federal government was to be *permanent,* they would have built a real city around it.

He coughed and felt the painful rawness in the back of his throat that usually presaged a cold. Every member of his cabinet was complaining of illness. Henry Clay dragged himself by once a day to moan about his state of health, his general nervous paralysis; he, too, intended to visit the great Dr. Physick. Barbour was in perfect health, but had asked if he might resign the War Department for the post of ambassador to Great Britain. Rats abandoning a sinking ship, all of them.

Adams swallowed and made a face against the pain. No one was wearier than he. Morning would bring a renewal of visitors, problems, outrages, slings, arrows; his oldest son, George, in Boston, suffered dreadfully from depression of spirits. Adams wrote the boy weekly letters of counsel and advice, stressing the benefits of hard work, early rising, the ultimate goodness of Providence; these did no good, they were undoubtedly too harsh. And now, in his fifty-ninth year, the President recognized the same symptoms of despair and depression in himself.

He made out the pattern of a constellation above the Capitol dome— Orion the Hunter—and reminded himself of the blessings of his life and the example of his parents. Jackson would win. He, Adams, would be turned out of office, a failure. His sons would prove failures after him, and their sons afterward. Despite everything, as he stood with his lamp in the President's House, cares crawled over his soul like a nest of spiders.

CHAPTER
3

Two years earlier, pinched for money as always, David Chase had scribbled a hasty little article for the *London Tradesman*. He had also submitted a modest little title with it—"New Trends in Iron-work"—which, in the nature of the profession, his editor had slightly revised: "The American Revolution in Music!"

The article's subject had been, of all things, proposed to him by his father, the remarkable new technique for manufacturing pianos just invented by a fellow New Englander named (improbably enough) Alphaeus Babcock. The older way, of course, was to make them of wood and wire. The Babcock way was to string the wire to a one-piece iron frame, which a smith could mold in a forge for about ten dollars. Almost at once, Chase had seen, there were two revolutionary consequences. First, the new piano could stand up to a harder pounding than wooden ones (in Vienna the composer Beethoven was said to *wreck* a piano a month). And second, the new pianos were so cheap and easy to put together that almost every home could afford one. Chase had gone to a piano factory in Soho Square and watched them being mass-produced, a dozen a day.

He gave his hat to the black servant who opened the door, and when he glanced into the adjoining room he recognized at once the matronly profile of a Babcock Grand.

"Music starts in five minutes, sir. I'm putting your fine hat right over here."

Chase accepted his numbered brass tag, reminded himself that his behavior was utterly buffoonish, and entered the drawing room secretly blushing.

It was an ordinary bare-walled apartment, split in the middle by folding doors. At one end the pianist was showing her sheet music to the tenor, who held a foulard with both hands to his throat. In the middle, more black servants were placing little straight-backed chairs in double rows. At the far end, like a swarm of clean-shaven bees in frock coats and collars, twenty or thirty politicians and their guests had gathered around the inevitable bowl of punch, on a table.

This was Washington's "cultural" boarding mess, the journalist in him had discovered, and it boasted a small library, which he had already passed, and an authentic Rembrandt etching (hung permanently behind a velvet curtain) as well as the Babcock Grand. It was situated at the very top of Capitol Hill, in sight of the scaffolded dome, and presided over by four patrician senators, all from New England, three from Harvard. The journalist had hinted and flattered and dropped Short's name very hard indeed to come up with a ticket for their annual spring musicale. The journalist had no interest whatsoever in music.

"David."

"Nicho."

Chase accepted with a little bow the glass of punch that Nicholas Trist (with an identical bow) presented him. Trist was a man his own age who frequented the bar of the Indian Queen and worked in some not-yet-clear capacity for the secretary of state, Henry Clay. He had gap teeth and a mane of frizzy red hair, which Chase suspected him of curling, and an awesomely cynical turn of mind.

"I have something to insert in your book," Trist said, looking over his shoulder like a spy. "Irresistible." He ducked his chin and fumbled in his coat, then produced a slick brown envelope sealed with wax. "Coals to Newcastle," he said. "Sweets to the sweet."

"From a reliable source, I presume?" To the far left of the punch bowl, unmistakable in his red cravat and looking as black-eyed and shrewd as ever, Ephraim Sellers of Ohio was standing too close to three men and gesturing with senatorial vastness. Down the middle of the aisle, between the rows of chairs, walked Emma Colden.

Trist followed Chase's eyes and shook his hair, horselike, once. He flicked the envelope with his thumb. "The exclusive story of how Andrew Jackson skins, boils, and eats his young, with a postscript on the secret rites of the Nashville Committee of Abominations. We offer it purely in the public interest and expect no thanks. I know that girl."

Chase slid the envelope into his pocket without a glance.

"In actual fact," Trist said, "it's a set of verified and veracious anecdotes about Jackson's homicidal temper tantrums in the army. Mr. Clay thought the record should be complete. Print and be well, Mr. Chase. I see that girl with Eph Sellers all the time, our well-known widower and senatorial cipher—*he* has an independent fortune, elastic politics, and bad breath. Probably a Jackson man. *She* has a drunkard father and no money at all. Cool as a block of ice." Trist looked at Emma, then at Chase; then shook his head again. "I don't think so, my friend."

Chase handed him back the untasted punch and made his way down the aisle. People had begun to take their places—at the piano the tenor was making rapid little pipping noises to loosen his vocal cords—but there was still a chair free beside her. Be a buffoon and be well.

"The singer is undoubtedly French," Chase said. He assumed that the chair belonged to Sellers and sat down in it anyway. "Because I've never yet seen a Frenchman who hadn't got something wrapped around his throat."

Emma turned and looked at him without surprise. "Between eating and talking," she said, "it's the source, as my father says, of most of their pleasures. I haven't seen you in days, Mr. Chase."

"Nor I you. And it's David." Fatuous, untrue. Since he had gone with her to John Randolph's rooms that day, when he should have been writing his book, Chase had in fact been hovering like a moonstruck schoolboy outside her boarding house. He had watched her ride away twice in Senator Sellers's elegant carriage. Once he had even sunk so far as to follow her at a distance down Pennsylvania Avenue, on her mysterious way to her mysterious job, only to lose her in the market crowds at Ninth Street.

"I didn't know you were musical, Mr. Chase. David." In front of them the tenor progressed from pips to Babcockian scales.

"I've heard it has charms to soothe the savage breast."

"Ah. How *is* your research on Jackson? Shouldn't you be in Nashville by now, in search of scandal?"

"My cup of scandal runneth dry. I write ten artistic words every day, which I tear up every night. Mr. Short is impatient. If I'm lucky he's going to fire me. He's summoned me to New York anyway, for a conference, so I leave Washington tomorrow."

She pushed her skirt to one side to give him more room, a simple blue cotton hoop bound with an indigo sash that matched her eyes and set off her hair. She wore a single black ribbon around her throat, and compared to her the other women in the room were as alike as cabbages.

"No more interviews with John Randolph?" she asked.

"Not a word."

"When I was a girl," Emma said, "the London *Times* always printed its articles about sexual misbehavior in Latin, you know. My father would read them aloud to my mother." The pianist played a warning chord, and while Chase struggled to picture this scene from Hogwood's domestic life, the man in front looked quickly around and made a fierce shushing sound like a schoolmaster, one admonitory finger to his lips. Emma ignored him. "I wonder how you would say Andrew Jackson in Latin?" she said.

"Andy Jacksonus?" Chase leaned closer, tried to keep his voice low, and succeeded only in turning heads all around him. Flirt, flirtation. There was no other English word for what they were doing.

"You might try writing your 'Andrew Meets Rachel' chapter in Latin," she said. "*Veni, vidi, vici.*"

In the pure infinitude of silence between the tenor's clearing of his throat and the pianist's first note, Chase laughed out loud.

The schoolmaster whirled and hissed like a goose.

Emma broke into the widest grin in the world—"Shhh!"—and pressed her own cool finger against Chase's mouth.

"I believe you've taken my place, Mr. Chase," said Ephraim Sellers, tapping David's shoulder.

CHAPTER
4

C hase returned to Washington City three weeks later, on June 15, just in time to attend the grandest party of the season. He sped from his hotel to a carriage to a doorman to a hallway, deposited his hat, smoothed his hair, and walked into a book-lined room so elegantly furnished that it might have dropped out of the sky from Paris or London. Except that it contained, next to another Babcock Grand piano, thirty or forty Washingtonians, some in buckskin suits and Stetson hats and some in silk gowns, and all of them, every one, gathered in a circle around the high, stiff collar and pale, mummified figure of John Randolph of Bizarre.

Chase came to a halt on the threshold.

"In regard to the cub," Randolph shrilled, evidently in the midst of oration. He paused to spread his long, thin legs even wider apart on the carpet. "The *cub*," he declared, "is a *far* greater bear than the old one."

"Do you refer to John Quincy Adams?" asked Emma Colden from the edge of the circle. "The President?"

Randolph turned his small, unearthly white face slowly in her direction, a white bat finding its range. He studied her for a few seconds, then bowed deeply. "Indeed, I do, Miss Colden. This is the last year of the administration of the father renewed in the person of the son. I bore some humble part in putting down the dynasty of John the First, and by the grace of God I hope to aid in putting down the dynasty of John the Second. I mean to blow his administration sky high. Yes, sir"—he straightened and revolved his head in his collar like a turtle—"*sky high!*" And his voice rose to a falsetto pitch as if to follow John Quincy Adams off into the clouds.

Chase stepped around the buzzing circle of Randolph's admirers and made his way to Emma.

"You've returned," she said, smiling. "In time for the circus."

Chase took her arm, reflected for a split second on his boldness, and glanced about the crowded room for Senator Sellers. Randolph was laughing; a man in a coonskin cap was clapping. Chase led her toward French doors that appeared to open out onto an enormous manicured lawn. "I've survived New York the Damned," he said, "as my father invariably called it."

"Yes. And you've published six long articles in the *New York Sun*. You are the 'Spy in Washington,' are you not? And are you rescuing me from the party or only John Randolph?"

On the other side of the French doors there suddenly appeared a tiny white-haired man, dressed not in buckskin but old-fashioned colonial smallclothes, white silk leggings, and a black three-cornered hat, which he removed and stuck firmly under his left arm the moment he saw them. Chase guessed at once that this was their host, Major Peter Van Ness, the wealthiest man in Washington City.

"When I was in Congress," Van Ness said, looking at each of them in turn and blinking, "I always liked to go to President Madison's weekly *levées*." He had a face like a shriveled apple. He smiled at Emma and revealed a row of small, perfect white teeth, made out of painted wood. "You remind me of Dolley Madison, my dear."

"Emma Colden," she murmured.

"Lovely," Van Ness said, and took her hand to kiss in the Continental fashion; in the Continental fashion, Chase noticed, Van Ness in fact kissed not her hand but the back of his own thumb. "Your wife is lovely, Mr. Colden. Such beautiful hair."

Before either could speak he had beckoned a passing waiter to their side and, despite the hat under his arm, swept two glasses of punch from the waiter's tray. He handed one to each of them. "Years ago," he said, "at one of those *levées,* I saw Dolley Madison pause to say a friendly word to a shy young man from Kentucky, I think. He was trying to balance a cup of coffee on a saucer—the first china cup he had ever seen in his life—and he became so confused that he dropped the saucer on the floor and put the cup of coffee in his pocket!"

Emma leaned forward and touched the old man's hand with her own. "What happened then?"

"Dolley was the soul of tact. She looked up at the ceiling and pretended not to notice. Later she sent a servant around with a fresh cup." Van Ness beamed little white tombstones at Emma. "Now you young people stroll down to the river—just follow this path—and enjoy the day." And he clapped his three-cornered hat back on his head and disappeared inside the house.

"I was born in the wrong century," Chase said wryly, watching him go. "They were giants before the Flood."

Emma had already started down the path. "Giant or not," she said over her shoulder, "you mustn't let appearances deceive you. He was once the mayor of Washington as well as a congressman and a major in George Washington's army."

"A major mayor."

"He has untold millions, from his marriage."

Chase cocked his head curiously at something in her voice, but she was walking briskly ahead, blue skirt swinging over the graveled path that led down, through the center of the manicured lawn, straight to the banks of the Potomac. Major Van Ness had built his mansion at the bottom of an empty mud grade (Seventeenth Street, to the optimistic), and he had clearly used some of his untold millions to level most of the native trees and undergrowth and create an extraordinary panoramic view of the dark green hills of Virginia, on the other side of the river.

"That's the Lee family mansion," Emma said as he caught up again. She brushed a strand of blond hair from her neck and indicated a glimmer of white columns on a far green hill. "There are as many Lees as Adamses in American history, I think. They call the house Arlington, after Horace Walpole's outrageous house in England."

"The middle son Henry has joined Jackson's campaign staff," Chase told her. "He's *also* writing a biography."

"There have been five published so far. Yours will be sixth, his will be seventh. There will be Jackson biography factories on every block." They stepped around a whitewashed tree stump that reminded Chase of a Van Ness tooth. "Or have you abandoned Jackson?" Emma asked. "For your articles?"

"No more articles." Chase shook his head and winced. In New York he had promised an impatient Short to work on nothing but his book. "I don't see Senator Sellers today," he said, and cleared his throat.

"He's gone back to Ohio, for business."

"Ah." Chase walked three paces, decided against clearing his throat for a second time.

"He'll be gone for a month," Emma said, and then abruptly turned to face him. "Your book will be good." Her face was flushed, her hair transformed by the sunlight to fire. "We admired your articles, both of us. My father says you pick up things with amazing speed."

They had somehow reached the edge of the river, where Van Ness's gardeners had constructed a wooden viewing platform and a rail above the water. Without another word she swung her skirt over the walk-plank and gained the platform. Chase stood stock-still for a moment, did clear his throat, then stepped up after her. She put down her glass and walked to the far end; he was clearly not to reply or comment, so he craned his neck one way—behind them strolling guests now dotted the vast lawn like drops of paint—and inclined his head to listen to the rush of water. Since he had last seen her, he thought, he had in fact done everything with amazing speed, everything except write his book. He had read—twice over—every biography, article, and clipping about Jackson that Short could send him—and in New York Short had supplied a whole new stack, a stack as high as his waist; he had interviewed a score of Jacksonians in Washington; traveled by stage to New York the Damned; scribbled newspaper articles, notes, outlines, letters, titles. But not one word of the book, one syllable. New York the Damned, America the Rushed, Jackson the Unwritable. "I do indeed wonder," William Short had murmured, consulting his gold watch as usual when he intended to be ironic: "has the English girl proved to be a *distraction*?"

At that very moment the English girl surprised Chase utterly by leaning forward and gripping the rail with both hands. He thought of a preacher about to vault the pulpit. "In the royal county of Kent where I was born, Mr. Chase"—she moved two steps along the rail toward him, hands wide, but eyes intent on the river—"*every* square foot has been farmed for seven centuries. There's not an inch that doesn't belong to somebody, or somebody's ghost or somebody's plow."

Chase followed her gaze. He saw only a brown river, a few shabby boats, dark hills, a regiment of green pines marching over a ridge and south.

"But *here*—" Emma spread her hands as if to indicate space, awe; sublimity.

" 'Roll on, thou deep and dark Potomac,' " Chase said, trying for a joke, trying to recapture their flirtatious note. Stupid.

"This country is like a Time Machine, my father says. Here we are, not one mile from the President's House and the whole scene might have been discovered yesterday, absolutely free of the past. No lords, ladies, dukes, ghosts—"

"You're a radical," Chase said, at once amused and baffled; standing closer.

"Ah, no. Pardon me. An American." Emma smiled, not at him. "My father would go home if he could. He's seen all he wants to see. But I mean *never* to go back. My greatest regret about his book, Mr. Chase—your book—is that I can't go west to Nashville now and see the future."

Chase raised his eyes and looked again at the river, the hills. Felt . . . nothing.

When he looked back, Emma was studying him closely. "It doesn't move you," she said flatly, a declaration. With a snap of her skirt she had scooped up her punch glass and turned her back.

Twenty yards farther along the bank they stopped as if at a signal. From the house now came the strains of music, and around a curve, bouncing down the muddy grade from Georgetown, was a gilt carriage whose horses wore plumes and driver a set of crimson livery.

All over the lawn other guests had paused to watch. "Frances Wright," said Emma quickly, shading her eyes. The carriage reached flat land, tilted dangerously, then sped out of sight behind the house. Emma's voice rose with unmistakable pleasure—"Fanny Wright!"

In the drawing room a small orchestra had set up beside the French doors. Emma steered Chase to one side beneath a trio of very bad paintings (Van Ness ancestors, a Van Ness daughter in pink and white, holding a cat). "There should be a reception party outside first," she said over the music. "Fanny always makes the grandest possible entrance."

Chase glanced at the packed drawing room. More and more people had arrived, seeming to materialize out of nowhere. The black servants themselves had lowered their trays and taken up posts near the hallway entrance, from which voices and applause could now be heard. He wiped sweat from his eyes and squinted. The most interesting party, the party of the season—in his soft Virginia drawl, pulling out the invitation like a conjuror, Short had more or less ordered him to attend, notebook in hand.

"Do you actually know who Fanny Wright is?" Emma stood on her toes and peered down the hall through a canyon of heads and shoulders.

"In France"—Chase squeezed beside her and chose the most neutral of possible adjectives—"she is *bien connue.*" But in France, Fanny Wright was not well-known, she was notorious. She was the young, very young British companion of the old, very old Marquis de Lafayette, and five years ago she had published a book of wildly progressive views, in praise of Lafayette's beloved America, then sought him out in person, moved into his château, and finally declared herself in all the newspapers and journals, to the disgust of Lafayette's family, his "adopted daughter." Even in Paris tongues had clicked.

"I met her once," Emma said as the violins shuddered, then whinnied abruptly to a halt. "She spoke in Cincinnati when my father and I were there."

Chase nodded. The crowd by the hallway rocked forward, back; began to part. He looked past Emma for the angular black figure of John Randolph, but he had evidently vanished, or retreated to the lawn at Fanny Wright's arrival. Of all forms of modern life, Chase thought, Randolph would like least a female of wildly progressive views. The crowd sighed, the violins sprang into the "Marseillaise," and Fanny Wright appeared.

"Her hair!" Emma's hand flew instinctively to her own head.

Chase blinked. Fanny Wright was just under six feet tall (dwarfing the poor Major Mayor and his wife). She was dressed in a kind of Quaker uniform—a black coat reaching to the knees over a plain gray dress—and in contrast to every other woman in America her fierce red hair was cut very short, much shorter than a man's, and curled tight like a helmet just to her ears. She wore a soft black beret, which she removed with one hand as she reached the doorway; a theatrical gesture, Chase thought, beautifully timed.

The guests surged gently forward. Fanny Wright began a slow progress among them, shaking hands, nodding. Even over the orchestra's excited brays and the hubbub of other voices, her voice carried to every corner, rich, strong, an orator's voice.

"Miss Colden! *Quel plaisir de vous voir! Quelle surprise!*"

Emma shook hands, smiled; lingered an instant too long on Fanny Wright's short hair. "You remember me! I had hoped you would. We met in Cincinnati."

"And your father, your kind father?" Fanny Wright lifted her enormous gray eyes as if in search of him, but encountered instead, at her own height—

"David Chase." He shook her hand once, firmly, in the European manner. Fanny Wright inclined her handsome head in acknowledgment.

"My father is fine; he's very well." Emma started to say more, but the crowd surged again and Fanny Wright was forced to move—move splendidly, Chase admitted, move like a royal personage—forward.

In her wake Emma was lifting one hand to her own fashionably long blond hair. "You don't approve of her," she said. Another flat declaration.

"*I* don't approve," said John Randolph of Roanoke, appearing like a bad genie beside them. "I am just going to station myself by the door, in case the guest of honor is moved to speak *ex tempore.*"

A rolling food table pressed the three of them sideways, toward an alcove. "I didn't know, Mr. Randolph," said Emma, "that you were acquainted with lady radicals."

Randolph's grotesque white face had never looked more unhealthy, less human. He planted himself with his back to the room, blocking their view. "I had the honor of meeting the young lady four years ago, my dear," he said, "in 1824, when she escorted—shall I use the word *escort*?—that grand old soldier Lafayette on his triumphal tour as Guest of the Nation. I saw her right here in Washington, where she and her sister sat in the Senate gallery and had the good taste to applaud my remarks. I saw her at Monticello, when Lafayette called on St. Thomas and the two old hypocrites fell into each other's arms to the tears of hundreds. And I had the great good fortune to be present in Nashville one year later, when our friend—now traveling alone—called one fine afternoon on General Jackson."

Chase, maneuvering to keep Fanny Wright in sight, stopped in midstep.

"Ah, he smells scandal." Randolph stroked his own black wing of hair and leered.

"Jackson knows Fanny Wright?" Chase stole a quick glance. At the far end of the Van Ness drawing room, surrounded by a tide of admirers, Fanny Wright had now reached the French doors. She was just bowing to someone beyond them.

"Oh, yes. General Jackson himself received Frances Wright on the front porch of the Hermitage. I was there, I was"—he smiled at Emma—"a fly on the wall. Old Hickory meets the Priestess of Beelzebub. You know of her utopian community Nashoba?"

Emma was wary. She looked at Chase, at Fanny Wright, exiting through the doors. "I do."

"It was at Monticello," Randolph told Chase, "that I first heard Frances Wright's ideas—scarcely, in fact, had she looked about her before she plunged into a debate with St. Thomas himself *contra* slavery."

"She is an abolitionist, yes."

Randolph suddenly thrust his white worm's face out of his huge collar. "No, sir, she is worse than an abolitionist. She wishes to *mix* the races; she wishes to see an *amalgamation* of the races." In the alcove, turned away as they were from the room, the orchestra, the retreating party, his voice hissed with inexpressible contempt. "She chastised Jefferson for *keeping slaves,* she denounced *him, me,* all of us—Lafayette was mute as a stone. She recited her *dream of the future*—I have a cruelly accurate memory, I remember each infernal syllable: 'Let the olive branch of brotherhood be embraced by the white man and the black, and their children *gradually blend into one blood and hue.'* Nashoba was the name of the community she purchased with her fortune, for that nightmare of amalgamation."

"And Jackson?" Chase had found his notebook and pulled it out of his pocket.

Randolph's head swiveled in his collar and he smiled at the sight of the notebook. "Lafayette had written Jackson a letter asking him to help Frances Wright buy land in Tennessee. What the well-disposed biographer wants to know, I suppose, is whether General Jackson was aware of her vile plans beforehand."

"Was he?" But Chase had already guessed from Randolph's teasing grin. He closed the notebook with a snap. Ten feet away the late-arriving John C. Calhoun hurried past, in pursuit of Fanny Wright.

"He was not. *Quel dommage* for you. Jackson merely steered her to a land agent. She bought six hundred acres of forest near Memphis, far from Nashville. She bought twenty slaves in New Orleans. She imported a dozen white miscreants for that part of the brotherhood, and she promptly set up a commune, so-called, based on racial equality and"—Randolph's grimace was horrible to see—"free love."

Arms folded across her breast, Emma was literally backed into a corner shelf of Van Ness knickknacks and books, her way out barred by the two men. "I think you exaggerate," she said. "If I may say so, you exaggerate."

Randolph shrugged. "I have heard her speak, out of professional curiosity. She began by attacking marriage as an institution of oppression by the male over the female. I confess I left the lecture hall before she reached the interesting subject of miscegenation." He did not repress a shudder.

"She is a wonderful speaker," Emma said.

"She reminded me," Randolph told Chase, "of Dr. Johnson's remark about a woman preaching—'It was like seeing a dog walk on its hind legs. It was not well done, but you were surprised to see it done at all.' "

In spite of himself Chase laughed.

"You are both," Emma said, pushing furiously between them, turning toward the open room, "all of you men, trapped in the past."

Randolph's hand gripped Chase by the shoulder. Emma vanished. "Have I blown your romance, dear boy," he said, "sky high?"

CHAPTER
5

Technology," said Hogwood and looked about the room with great satisfaction. "The practical application of science. That's what we're here to see. A very old word, you know, forgotten for a hundred years. Brought up-to-date by you Americans."

"Technology," Chase repeated.

"Popularized in Boston, I'm told. By some Harvard man, no doubt, like yourself, Greek and Latin coming out his whiskers."

Chase mopped his brow and loosened his collar and likewise looked about the room. Although it took up the whole second floor of the building, Maelzel's Automaton Theater consisted of exactly ten rows of eight identical cane-backed chairs and a raised platform that would evidently serve as a stage. Over the platform hung a heavy purple curtain spangled with crescent moons and silver stars. The only light came from tall, narrow windows along the sides, through the nearest of which (as usual, he thought, in Washington City) Chase could see a grazing cow.

"Your friend Andrew Jackson, however, has coined an entirely new word," Hogwood informed him. In the blistering heat of the room, the fat old man paused to puff like a diving whale. Two men in shirtsleeves and straw hats squeezed in front of them. *"O.K."*

"O.K.?" Chase said, wondering if everybody who talked with Hogwood was eventually reduced to an echo.

"Standing for 'oll keerect,' according to his enemies." Hogwood wheezed and laughed at the same time. "Such is Jackson's luck—even his illiteracy pays a political bonus. I heard three innocent people use it yesterday."

"I saw John Randolph yesterday."

"Ah. Speaking of Jackson's enemies."

Chase twisted in his chair. The theater was almost completely filled now with men in shirtsleeves and a scattering of ladies, almost every one of them carrying fans or silk parasols that were no protection at all against Washington's brutal, impartial afternoon sun. "No, he's still a Jackson supporter," Chase said. "Or an Adams hater, at least."

"He's told you nothing? Not even a *soupçon* of scandal?"

"The day Emma and I went to his boarding house"—behind the curtain loud thumps and a metallic ratcheting sound were clearly audible—"I had the impression he might have said something . . . if I had come alone."

"Alone. Yes. Perhaps. Poor Emma. Randolph is one of nature's own bodyguard of bachelors, I fear, the great contrary of Fanny Wright." The thumps stopped, but Hogwood's voice continued at full volume. "He's supposed to have no testicles, you know."

On stage the curtains suddenly rose with a flourish and revealed what could only be Monsieur Antoine Maelzel, dressed despite the heat in a full-length claret-colored swallowtail coat and a voluminous cravat of white cambric that burst from his chest like an ocean wave. He stamped his heels (Hessian top-boots, gold tassels) for attention.

"Ladies and gentlemen," he announced in a high-pitched German accent, *"fellow Americans,* I introduce our Visitor!"

With another flourish he stepped aside. On the little stage, behind a seaman's chest, sat revealed the carved wooden figure, life-size, of a glowering Turk in flowing robes and a bright red turban. His left hand held a pipe close to his mouth; his right hand lay on the chest beside a chessboard, on whose ivory pieces his wooden eyes were grimly fixed.

"O.K.," Hogwood murmured.

On stage Monsieur Maelzel was busily opening three separate doors in

the Turk's chest and pointing out to the audience a clockwork arrangement of wheels, levers, and gears. From time to time he stooped to hold a
candle beside a door and thrust in his hand to show its depth. Then he
closed each door, placed a cushion under the Turk's right arm, and slowly
wound up the mechanism with a long brass key.

"Now, sirs, ladies, I challenge each of you, any of you to defeat the
Automaton!"

For the next full hour members of the audience filed onto the stage and
engaged in a collective game of chess. The Automaton took white and
made the first move, grasping the piece in its right hand and fingers
and placing it down with a click and a tap. After a move made by an
opponent the machine paused for a few moments, as if contemplating the
board. On giving check to the king, it raised its turbaned head in a signal.
A parasoled lady made an incorrect move, and the Automaton banged on
the chest impatiently and replaced the piece (a rook). At the close of the
game it reached for a knight and then, whirring and tapping, moved it
rapidly over each of the sixty-four squares of the board in turn, without
missing one or touching the same square twice.

Throughout the exhibition Hogwood, too fat and short of breath to
climb onto the stage, beamed and nodded from his chair. At the first
check he poked Chase with an elbow and winked, and when the Turk had
finished and raised its fierce head to the audience, Hogwood banged his
cane on the floor in applause.

Scarcely had the Automaton been wheeled offstage than Monsieur
Maelzel rolled out from the other side a new Automaton carved from oak
and dressed in the blue and gold uniform of the British Grenadiers. Once
again the brass key produced the familiar ratcheting and clicking, and
then a trumpet rendition of two marches and a popular song, "Home,
Sweet Home." ("His phrasing is good," Hogwood chuckled, "but
wooden," and applauded with his cane again.)

For his climax Maelzel at length brought out an enormous panoramic
box, tilted up at an angle for the audience to see, which he announced as
"The Burning of Moscow," and indeed the box contained a miniature
view of the Russian capital, complete with polished domes and minarets.
Then the bell on the model Kremlin began to toll and flames (shimmering pieces of colored paper) could be seen making their way from building to building. A bridge in the foreground was covered with tiny figures
clicking their way to safety. A regiment of French infantry whirred toward

the bridge from a burning barracks. Flames began to ascend the domes. Somewhere deep in the mechanism a music box played martial music, the bells tolled faster and faster, and as the last platoon of Frenchmen crossed the bridge the Kremlin itself blew up in a loud and smoky explosion, and at the same instant the curtains fell.

Outside in the bright summer air, Hogwood was still shaking his head in admiration.

"Technology," he said. "Not what Harvard had in mind, but wonderful, no?"

"Wonderful, yes." Chase steered him out of the sun and into the shade of a tree growing where the sidewalk would have been, he thought, in a real city.

Hogwood limped with his cane and wiped his cheeks with a handkerchief. "Washington heat," he said, wheezing. "Icehouses take fire and scream because they can't bear it. I like it. All Englishmen like it, we're all Druids at heart. The Automaton Turk, my dear David—?"

"Yes?"

"I've seen it three times now. Monsieur Maelzel always opens the cabinet doors in the same order, he always winds the key the same number of times no matter how long the game. I suspect, not technology, but trickery. A little person concealed in the chest, perhaps, and reading the board from underneath, then pulling the levers; but nobody else agrees. Will you sit on that bench for a moment?"

They had worked themselves from tree to tree as he talked, and the bench consisted only of a plank between two empty barrels in a vacant lot, but Hogwood sat down with a tiny smile of relief nonetheless.

"It's not Paris." He motioned for Chase to sit down beside him. "Or the Tuileries."

"Not even Boston," Chase replied. "Or the Boston Common." Yet in the distance the white haunches of the Capitol rose sphinxlike in something like real majesty, and the bottom of Capitol Hill leveled off into a long green prospect of meadow, road, and river that reminded him of Van Ness's mansion, or his ride to Kalorama. With a little imagination, faith, you could see it all in twenty years, fifty years, village to city, mud to marble. Emma could; probably Andrew Jackson could. But at the moment, such was the weakness of his own imagination, Chase thought, it was only a hazy, nondescript southern landscape shimmering in the June afternoon like Moscow burning.

"Tell me more about John Randolph," Hogwood said.

Chase closed his eyes. "I've run into him five or six times at the Capitol, elsewhere, yesterday . . . I heard him speak against the tariff—"

"Jackson is for a 'judicious tariff,' " Hogwood chuckled, "whatever that means."

"—against the Cumberland Road, the Baltimore and Ohio railroad. He quotes Voltaire and Gibbon, he defended Jackson's bad spelling, he said the proper role of the federal government was 'masterly inactivity.' "

"He knows something," Hogwood said.

Chase opened his eyes. "After one speech I saw him in the Strangers Gallery of the House. He told me Jackson is opposed by all of the banks, most of the newspapers, and four fifths of the churches, which is true. Then he patted my hand and said perhaps they were right, my dear. If there *were* a document or a fact, he said, it might be a duty to print it. He had a *dim* recollection of something happening in 1824."

"He's not *efféminée,* you know; he just teases, like a cat." Hogwood rubbed his face with his sopping wet handkerchief. "I believe I shall melt into wax. No, Randolph simply *dislikes* women—the natural consequence of looking, as he does, like Dr. Frankenstein's monster. He dislikes women, likes men; loves liberty, hates equality. He would turn on Jackson because he distrusts all Westerners and democrats. *My* theory is that he knows something disgraceful about Jackson's duels. I've made a study of duels—in England, when I was a wee publishing lad we had a rich assortment of duelists."

"You're too hot, even in this shade." Chase stood up decisively. The last thing he wanted was a second collapse of Emma's father.

"After Waterloo, for instance," Hogwood continued, remaining where he was, "there was a British colonel who killed three French officers one right after the other, in a simultaneous duel. He made his challenge by hitting them on the head with a baguette."

Chase laughed. "Not Jackson's style, I think. There's a saloon down this alley."

"An oasis," Hogwood said, finally struggling to his feet. "God the camel. There was a Scotswoman at the end of the last century who called herself James Miranda Stuart Barry and served, disguised as a man of course, in the army; fought dozens of duels over her squeaky voice. In Germany I witnessed an all-woman duel, swords, between the Princess Metternich and the Countess Kielmansegg."

"Down here." Chase led him between two empty wagons and into a courtyard where an unnamed tavern spilled out of a basement, Washington-style, and three or four plank-and-barrel benches made a beer garden. He signaled a waiter while Hogwood sat under a striped awning.

"In Ireland," Hogwood said, his face in the shade like a moon on fire, "Richard Martin of Connemara was known as Hairtrigger Rick because of his temper—I wrote an article about him once—fought forty-three duels in a year. Fought people, loved animals. Perfect idiot. He founded something called the Society for the Prevention of Cruelty to Animals, and when he died a few years ago he had a new nickname, much duller, Humanity Martin." Hogwood accepted a tankard of beer from a black waiter and lifted it in a toast. "To humanity and scandal."

"This miserable young book of mine. It's like blood from a stone. Writing it, or *not* writing it—" Chase broke off and stopped just short of full confession. Hogwood was not the man to moan to about your writing; Hogwood had never been at a loss for words in his life. Chase wiped his throat with the wet handkerchief. The Washington heat must burn up the words, he thought; the air was in flames from burning words.

Hogwood had meanwhile cocked his head and stuck out his lower lip like a pouting whale as he studied Chase over the rim of his tankard. "Now John Randolph is a man in conflict with himself," he said, as if Chase had asked a question. "Like all interesting persons. He's torn between being a Southerner and therefore in favor of Jackson, the Tennessee Attila, and being essentially an eighteenth-century Gibbon-and-Voltaire kind of creature of reason, and therefore appalled by Jackson's politics. This election should be labeled 'The End of the Eighteenth Century,' like one of Maelzel's exhibits. Sooner or later Randolph will stop hinting."

Chase wiped his mouth with the back of his hand. Found nothing to say.

Hogwood drained his tankard and raised one pudgy finger to the waiter. "You are likewise," he said, "my dear David, a person in conflict. Whether to keep at this tawdry book or abandon it. Whether to stay in your astoundingly vulgar native land or go back to Europe." The waiter was slow. Hogwood picked up Chase's tankard and poured half of its beer into his own. "If you go down this alley to Sixth Street," he said in a matter-of-fact voice, "and turn left, in the building across the way you will find Emma at work."

CHAPTER
6

Gales and Seaton, Printers.

Chase went up the steps two at a time and pushed open the door. From a corridor to the left came the rumble of machinery and the pungent black-gardenia scent of newspaper ink. He walked down the corridor, opened another, far heavier door, and entered a room like a furnace, shaking with noise.

For a moment he stood stock-still with the doorknob in his hand. Directly in front of him, snapping their jaws, spitting out paper, were two great black cast-iron printing presses. Each was manned—wrong verb—each one attended, watched, *womanned* by a team of young ladies dressed in light blue uniform dresses, printer's flat caps, and canvas aprons. Behind the presses, attached to them both apparently by short steel pipes, a furious red-hot Bolton-Watt steam engine, toad to their princesses, squatted between two massive bins of coal.

Chase approached the nearest clattering press.

"Emma Colden?" he shouted.

Without looking up the young lady pointed a finger. A neatly framed sign had been nailed to a pillar nearby, its message set in scornfully large type: GENTLEMEN ARE REQUESTED NOT TO STAND AND LOOK ABOUT,—BECAUSE THE YOUNG LADIES DON'T LIKE IT.

"I'm looking for Emma Colden!"

The young lady swung a lever. Despite the skylights over each press, the heat was stifling; their hair, dresses, arms were streaked with sweat. Where Chase stood they were feeding paper between the platens, while a few feet away two more workers rhythmically pulled and stacked the printed sheets as they came out. In the clamorous bang and blur of the action Chase could just read the title line as it slipped by: *The National Intelligencer.*

"I'm looking for Miss Emma Colden!" In Paris, when he first arrived penniless, sou-less, in 1819, he had supported himself by working in a printer's office on the Left Bank, a complex and labyrinthine affair of black rooms, tunnels, and furnaces that twisted in and out of a medieval basement like a burrowing dragon. The French were splendid printers; they loved all kinds of printing machines. A few years earlier Louis Herhan had invented a stereotype plate which he called the *cliché*, in effect a reusable wax mold for type, and with that and another device for making continuous rolls of paper a good French house could turn out two or three thousand impressions in less than a week.

But these presses—Chase could tell at a glance that they were faster, simpler: a crank acting on a toggle joint instead of the cylinder, an inking hose, a treadle to the steam pipes. Technology—the *speed* of everything in America now.

"She's in there!" The girl beside him wiped her brow with the back of her hand like a man and grinned. "Compositor's room! Are you Senator Sellers?"

"His saintly and devoted father."

The girl gave one short bark of a laugh and turned her back.

Another corridor, shorter, darker, and suffused with the unmistakable smell of urine, kept in buckets for cleaning the type. He held his nose and pushed through another door.

The compositor's room was no bigger than his room in the Indian Queen, but every wall was jammed floor to ceiling with equipment. To his left, cabinets of type, tools, a Dutch door. To his right, a little potbellied Franklin stove (in this heat a joke—but during winters in Paris you would hold your fingers against a hot metal bar until you could stand to pick up the freezing bits of type). And next to the stove, under an open window, two upward-slanting compositor's tables covered with type and paper. A miraculously tiny old lady wheeled around. She, too, wore a printer's cap, but also a faded scarlet dress from another century, ornamented across the sleeves and bosom with dozens of fluttering ribbons.

"You are much too young and handsome to be a senator," she said.

Emma Colden looked up.

"And much too intelligent-looking," the old woman added, coming toward Chase, removing her cap and squinting.

"This is Mr. Chase," Emma said from the far compositor's table. And *that,* Chase thought, is why her father's Jackson chapters are set in type. "He's a journalist, a writer."

"I am a writer," the old woman said. She shook Chase's hand once, hard. "Anne Royall. You've heard of me? I write books. I travel the country and write my impressions. Show him one, Emma." Without waiting for Emma to move, Anne Royall darted to the side of the compositor's table where she sat and came up with a thick octavo volume bound in cardboard. "This is the latest," she said. "It costs two dollars and contains my famous sketch of John Quincy Adams."

"I hadn't known," Chase murmured, looking at Emma but taking the book the old woman thrust at him.

"Two dollars," Anne Royall said. "I print them and sell them myself. He didn't want to talk to me, so I waited by the river early one morning till he went swimming—silly old man, swimming by himself—and I sat on his clothes. When he came back I said I wouldn't move till he gave me an interview."

"Mr. Chase is writing a book for Sarah Hale," Emma said.

"I've met her," Anne Royall said without much pleasure. "Do you know what she keeps in her desk drawer? Butcher's paper and a bottle of apple vinegar. Pats the vinegar on her temples with the paper, prevents—she *says,* I didn't notice—crow's feet."

As she talked Chase politely opened the book, turned pages. "John Coffee," he read. "Do you know him, Miss Royall?"

"One of America's gentlemen." Anne Royall pursed her lips and nodded. "I interviewed him in Alabama. An enormous tall man, but gentle as a nurse. In the army they used to call him Ajax. I tell the story of how he manages General Jackson—nobody else can, except *her.* Once at a racetrack Coffee decided Jackson was about to quarrel over a bet, but every time Coffee tried to stop him, Jackson just shook him off. So Coffee stepped up behind him and *lifted* Jackson up in a bear hug and carried him out, kicking like a baby."

Chase laughed and reached in his pocket for two dollars. At the compositor's table Emma had half turned away and her left hand was playing idly with a rack of type.

"A fine business for a President-to-be, of course," sniffed Anne Royall as she took the money. "Racetracks. On the other hand, once when I tried to see Adams he was being visited by a phrenologist."

"You mean he was getting his skull measured? The President?"

"He was," Anne Royall said with a brisk, emphatic nod. "Getting the curves charted to have his character read. I could see his bald pate through the window. It looked like a mule's egg."

To his horror Chase heard himself quoting a piece of comic verse:

Know well thy skull, and note its hilly lumps.
The proper study of mankind is bumps.

What was it, he wondered, flushing, that impelled him, as soon as he saw her, to act like a particularly brainless fourteen-year-old boy? But Emma, eyes fixed on her type, was smiling.

"*You,*" said Anne Royall, first looking at Emma, then at Chase, then cocking her head, "must be the one who's writing the book about Jackson."

"Well, yes. Slowly."

"His first installment will come out next month," Emma said, "in the July issue of Sarah Hale's magazine."

"Well, in fact . . ." Chase began.

"*I,*" announced Anne Royall, "am going to fetch Fanny Wright." And with another brisk nod and curious hop, she left the room.

"Fanny Wright is across the street in the main office," Emma said as she turned back to the compositor's table. "With Mr. Seaton. You've come in the rear entrance."

"And this is what you do, where you work? Your father and I finished at Maelzel's and he sent me here." Chase sat down on a stool beside her, fanning his face with his hand (Emma's profile was sharp and cool—she would stay cool on a tour of the Inferno) and asking himself why the

militant and impressive Fanny Wright would visit a printer's office, however advanced the technology.

"Mr. Seaton edits the *National Intelligencer* newspaper over there." She
indicated, through the open window next to her table, the street, a pig, a
two-story yellow frame building next to an alley. "He prints it here and
runs a commercial printing business 'on the side,' as you say. I learned to
set type when I was a girl, for my father."

"I imagine you in pigtails, tall for your age, with smudges of ink on
your cheeks."

"You are," Emma said placidly, beginning to set lines of type in a steel
tray, "impertinent."

"The *National Intelligencer* is an anti-Jackson paper."

"I have written for it." Her eyes moved steadily back and forth from
the type tray to her copy sheet while her fingers quickly picked and sorted
letters. "Short articles. Anonymously, of course. Virtually all of the printing in Washington is done by women, but Mr. Seaton is not sufficiently
advanced to allow a regular female journalist." She anticipated his question and looked up from the type for an instant. "Anne Royall he toler-
ates, as everybody does, and prints her books—she's the town's leading
eccentric, apart from the members of Congress, of course."

Chase handed her a one-inch slug of lead type. He cleared his throat.
"Yesterday, with John Randolph, I was obtuse. Insensitive." He cleared his
throat again and stopped.

An acute, sensitive silence. At the other end of the building the sullen
thump-thump of the steam presses came to a halt; on the street the pig
squealed once. Emma began to tap the slug of type into her tray with a
mallet. "You must understand, Mr. Chase," she said at length. "For myself I don't care whether Andrew Jackson or anyone else wins or loses an
election, so long as I can stay here, in this country." She lifted her face
directly toward him, blurred and lost in the strong sunlight from the
window, just as she had been the first time he saw her. "In England, in
Europe, I would be trapped, like any other woman. Here—"

"Here is Fanny Wright!" declared Anne Royall from the door.

Chase and Emma turned at the same moment, and Chase rose as both
Fanny Wright and a portly man in shirt and braces squeezed into the
room.

"This is Mr. Chase." Anne Royall pointed him out as a lively curiosity.

"But we've met, haven't we?" Seaton appeared less than delighted.

"Mr. Chase? At the President's mansion? Somebody's office?" He had round, mismatched eyes, one brown, one green, which he narrowed with the born distrust of a publisher. "You're the writer."

Then Fanny Wright, dressed in her same beret and black Quaker uniform, was pushing between them, nodding, shaking Chase's hand, and bending over Emma's type tray, all in one swift, energetic motion. "You're setting my pamphlet! This is the pamphlet I wrote on the ship—a defense of Nashoba, a declaration of *female* independence!"

"Miss Wright is giving the Fourth of July address next week in New Harmony, Indiana," Seaton told them and wiped his brow with a damp bandanna.

"The first woman to speak on the Fourth." Anne Royall raised one finger and abruptly sat down on a bench and spread her feet.

"You've lived in France for many years, Mr. Chase." Fanny Wright's rich voice made every statement an absolute. Chase nodded superfluous agreement. She held up a long sheet of proofs to Seaton, who blinked his brown eye shut, like an owl. "So you, like me, are a kind of foreign visitor. Let me ask you then: How do you find Americans, after your long absence? I myself observe three outstanding characteristics—Americans are deeply *insecure* as a people, they are *cruel,* they are *torn apart* by sectional rivalries."

"Insecure?" Chase looked up, puzzled by her statement; awed by her manner.

"I am constantly asked," Fanny Wright explained, "whether I find America *better* than Europe. Don't you find the same thing? A man in New York, during a rainstorm, asked me if we had better *thunder* than that in England. Yesterday Mr. Van Ness asked whether I thought the Potomac a greater river than the Thames, then he gave me his homemade cider and said it was better than any champagne in France. Americans are cruel because they tolerate slavery."

"Oh, I don't know," Seaton said unhappily. "People differ—"

"And duels," Anne Royall said.

"And duels." Fanny Wright was now reading her pamphlet and speaking at the same time. "A steamboat blew up in Long Island Sound two weeks ago and killed one hundred people, and when I told my companion he simply shrugged and said that was the price of progress."

"Will this be the message of your speech?" Beneath the rather shapeless and baggy Quaker dress, Fanny Wright clearly possessed a full, womanly figure. Chase studied her striking gray eyes, her great height—to hear her on the speaker's platform would be an impressive occasion, an event, John Randolph notwithstanding.

Fanny Wright smiled like the born politician she was, *ad seriatim;* at him, at Seaton and his bandanna, at Emma and Anne Royall. "In my speech on the Fourth of July, I intend to sketch, so to speak, the future history of this country. Because its faults, though serious, shrink to nothing compared to its possibilities. An awful responsibility has devolved on the American nation—the liberties of mankind are entrusted to it, the honor of freedom, self-government."

Chase let his right hand shuffle surreptitiously the bits of type at the bottom of Emma's tray. It was a skill like swimming, once learned, never forgotten. In mid-oration, Fanny Wright asked a rhetorical question; he nodded without hearing; his fingers spelled out—

Will you go with me to dinner tonight, 8 o'clock?

The heat of the room made his head ache. Fanny Wright turned from the American future to the oppression of women in the institution of marriage, and Seaton, who had listened intently till this point, now began to rub his neck with the flat of his hand. Anne Royall fanned her ribbons with a sheet of proof. Chase stole a sidelong glance. In the corner of his eye he could see a carriage bouncing past on the hot street. Two slaves, barefoot, in bell-shaped straw hats and dusty blue cotton shirts, lounged by the alley. Frances Wright's voice was musical, rhythmic. As so often happened, Chase felt his mind suspended, drifting, a mote of dust, unconnected to the scene around him. He had no business here, or anywhere. The history of the American future stretched out like the American continent, rolling inexorably westward, sun-baked under a hard-shelled and optimistic sky, while he himself retreated into a single dark point of consciousness, entirely alone and insecure. His eye fell to the type tray. Beneath his question Emma had spelled out—

Yes.

CHAPTER
7

The Life of Andrew Jackson

Chapter Five

AARON BURR POPPED UP IN TENNESSEE LIKE A GOPHER. Well, clearly the wrong simile for so malicious, witty, and well-dressed a madman as Burr, but let it stand. A dapper little gopher with a buff jacket, a scarlet cravat, very large, wet eyes, very sweet speech. Burr actually popped up in his unexpected way, not out of the red Tennessee soil, but at the window of his second-story room in the Nashville Inn, month of May 1805.

Down on the street, by the dawn's early light, Andrew Jackson and John Coffee sat on their horses calling Burr's name. Burr appeared, disappeared; reappeared on the street, strolling casually forward, hands as usual in his buff coat pockets, and Jackson whistled around another horse for him and led the way, laughing and hooting, back along the river to the Hermitage.

For Jackson had known Burr since the earliest days of his political career, when he served an unhappy half term as Tennessee's senator to the then-capital of Philadelphia, and Burr, also a senator, not yet a duelist or Vice President or Napoleonic conspirator either, most kindly took him in hand. I have met those who claim that Jackson's own very courtly and charming manners are modeled precisely on Burr's. If you saw them together, they say, you would recognize at once that the younger man apes the older (more peculiar; the taller man apes the shorter) like father, like son. In Nashville, where polite entertainment consists of a horse race or a duel, Jackson still talks about the brilliance of Burr's society dinners that grim Philadelphia winter, the glories of Burr's wines, sauces, epigrams.

What epigrams spilled from his lips as they rode back to the Hermitage that day in 1805 I cannot say. By then Burr was no longer senator, no longer Vice President; more like a fallen angel than anything else. In the amazing election of 1800, when the Senate went through thirty-six separate deadlocked ballots before choosing Jefferson over Burr, he had reached his political apex. (My favorite election, if I may digress: seven full days of voting, with Jefferson presiding serenely in the Vice President's chair over his own fate, a blizzard raging outside, thirty half-frozen senators sleeping on cots in the cloakroom between ballots; one poor senatorial soul, Raines of Maryland, dying of pneumonia, would rouse himself just long enough to scrawl "Jefferson" on a ticket, then fall back on his blankets, gasping. Democracy, to paraphrase Horace Walpole, is a tragedy to those who feel, a comedy to those who think.)

Burr. After his first term as Vice President—the reward for coming in second in the 1800 election—Jefferson sent him off into political limbo, i.e., the practice of law. Then came the failed run for the governorship of New York, the mad duel with Hamilton; disgrace. Except that to Jackson and the rest of Tennessee there was no obvious disgrace in a duel. And most certainly not one with that dark-skinned little Creole Alexander Hamilton, who had long turned up his aristocratic nose at the West and chosen to represent instead the eastern Banks and moneybags, while Burr, the Westerner's friend, had labored powerfully to see Tennessee and all her poor-but-honest neighbors admitted pell-mell into the Union; and Burr, moreover, was a decorated Hero of the Revolution, still an honored title in Tennessee, who had fought and slept in the field with his soldiers, far from the French luxuries, say, of a Monticello.

What was he doing in Nashville? This Jackson naturally asked over breakfast at the Hermitage, in those days a crude two-story blockhouse with one room on the ground floor and two rooms upstairs.

"Mexico," Burr whispered, looking carefully about. *"Texas."*

Jackson and Coffee leaned forward as one. Burr lit the first of the day's cigars and began to spin a tale as, evidently, only he can. I have always been fond of Talleyrand's remark that speech is the faculty by which men conceal their thoughts. No better speaker in that sense than Burr. He had come out, he whispered, on a secret mission—he flashed in the morning sunlight an impressive blank commission with the unmistakable signature of Thomas Jefferson. His assignment: to protect the city of New Orleans from ripening Spanish plans for *invasion,* and should the treacherous Spanish strike in the next few months, as Burr knew they would, strike before the Americans were ready, Jefferson had authorized him to lead a force of state militia against them, the vanguard of a federal army that would annex both Mexico and Texas in retaliation and *sweep* them into the Union.

Jackson sighed in wonder. Coffee scratched his head. Drive out the Spanish Dons—double the size of the country; these were a Westerner's themes. This, to a people who regarded the Spaniards as the only barrier between them and the Pacific, who looked over the wide brown border of the Mississippi with a land greed unparalleled in history . . .

I contemplate now, in the late spring of 1828, with genuine amazement the tiny size of the American colonies as they existed for two hundred years before the Revolution. Spread along the eastern seacoast, never more than a few hundred miles inland from the Atlantic—a remarkably small and narrow ribbon of civilization, not a great deal changed in its boundaries since the seventeenth century. But *after* the Revolution, *after* the new government had taken its chairs and cleared its throat, then the pioneers began to *swarm* over the mountains like lemmings. (Lemmings and gophers.) Land mania, land *fever* wracked the body politic. (Not for nothing was the first President a land surveyor by trade.) In 1789 you have thirteen states—just forty years later there are twenty-four, and no end in sight except the ocean. I myself arrived in America in 1825 and vividly remember the first public land office I ever saw. It was located next to my hotel on Broadway in New York. It was jammed from morning to night with shouting, scrambling men, and it flourished a huge canvas banner over the door with two simple words painted on it: "Go Ahead!"

I have seen it a thousand times since, and heard it *said* until my ears are withered. "Go Ahead—This is the Land of Go Ahead." By which is meant, Go Ahead and *Take* the land as fast as you can fling the Indians aside and grab it. In Cincinnati, as I walked down the street, a perfect stranger, shopkeepers would stick their heads out the doors and shout, "Hey! You want to buy a farm?" In Chicago—a lakeside village crawling with speculation—the times and places of land sales were announced by a black man dressed in scarlet coat and scarlet pants, carrying a long scarlet flag, sitting on a snow-white horse. He would stop at every corner and call out his announcements in a sing-song chant and people would flock around him to listen and then *rush* off to buy.

By 1805 the country had expanded so far that most people expected it would soon split into three or four independent republics. Madison thought so. Monroe thought so. Thomas Hart Benton said they should erect a statue of the great god "Terminus" on the Rocky Mountains and let somebody else start a new country west of it. Jefferson, always an imperial visionary, disagreed, of course; he wanted Jeffersonian democracy spread from coast to coast and pole to pole. And for once Jackson agreed with Jefferson, violently. (Jefferson's vision was founded on political theory; Jackson merely hates all foreigners, whether English or French or Spanish.)

"I have the authority," Burr said, that spring day in 1805, smirking unctuously and folding away his bit of parchment, "to call up a whole division of trustworthy soldiers."

"I can do that," said Jackson, who was a general in the Tennessee state militia, though not in the regular army.

"And to order five large flat-boats built here in Nashville, to float us down to New Orleans."

"We can do that," Jackson said, and promptly commissioned the general store of Jackson & Coffee, which operated out of a one-room shack in Clover Bottom, to build the flat-boats. Coffee rode off to round up workers; Jackson slid his arm cheerfully through Burr's and introduced him to Rachel ("She is short, plump, and smokes a corncob pipe," the amused Burr wrote his daughter Theodosia; "not quite the 'vamp' one had hoped for"). Later in the week Jackson threw an enormous dinner for Burr at the Nashville Inn, at which he introduced his friend to every political dignitary in the region and gave a memorable toast ("Millions for defense and not one cent for tribute") and thereby publicly, for all time hitched his wagon, so to speak, to Aaron Burr's dark star.

Off went Burr to round up other allies. Coffee promised the flat-boats in two months.

How to explain the subsequent turn of events?

The world is divided into two kinds of people. There are those optimistic souls who believe that the human personality is intelligible, readable like a watch, *explainable;* and there are those enlightened and skeptical souls like myself who believe that the human personality is by nature and definition elusive, irrational, essentially *unknowable.* It is the only sense in which man was made in the image of God.

Which Aaron Burr at once proceeded to demonstrate.

Because not a single word he had said in Nashville was *true.* Probably he intended to follow events in the land-hungry West and, if the opportunity really arose, seize Texas with the aid of his private army and declare himself king (or emperor or czar—Burr laughs a good deal at himself). Or perhaps he intended simply to embarrass or harass his enemy Thomas Jefferson, whose diplomatic caution with the Spanish had made him unpopular in the West. Or perhaps, like a small boy idly poking a big dog, Burr just wanted to see what would happen.

Alas for him, no one who underestimated Thomas Jefferson ever got away without feeling his elegant bite.

Poor Burr plotted too long, too scornfully. Jefferson sent out his own secret agents and pursued him from New Orleans (where that sensual and lymphatic city had never quite decided to believe Burr) all the way to the border of Spanish Florida. He was arrested one moonless night in 1807, accoutered un-Burr-like in an old blanket-coat and a floppy white hat, and charged with high treason.

A federal trial was ordered in Richmond. Chief Justice John Marshall, another of Jefferson's enemies, appointed himself head judge and set about calling witnesses. And prominent among them, of course, was Andrew Jackson.

Now, back in Tennessee Jackson had wavered briefly in his support of Burr, thanks to some damaging and truthful letters from the Secretary of War; but Burr had moistened his golden tongue and explained them away, and Jackson had joyously rejoined the fold. Burr was not guilty, that was all there was to it. When Jackson received his subpoena, he galloped to Richmond and strode into the courthouse demanding to be heard (you cannot help admiring Jackson as a natural force; he is as innocent of thought as a hurricane). When the judge told him to sit down and wait his turn, Jackson strode outside, fuming.

It was an American trial and therefore a species of circus. The splendid and eccentric John Randolph of Roanoke was chairman of the jury and sat with his riding crop across his knee and his jug of port at his side. Lawyers filed motion after motion for delay, all promptly granted. A cynical young journalist named Washington Irving wrote back to his New York paper that every five or six days the jurors were dismissed for a week "so that they might go home, see their wives, get their clothes washed, and flog their Negroes."

Meanwhile Jackson grew furiously impatient. He announced in the paper that he would address the people next day on the State House steps. The crowds gathered, drawn by curiosity and Jackson's reputation as a duelist, and promptly at noon he marched up the steps, turned, and launched into a brilliant and fiery speech. He denounced Jefferson, who was all old lady milk-and-water as far as American land rights were concerned. He praised Burr, who had never for a moment tried to divide the Union as charged (he *should* be hanged if he had, Jackson said).

Revelation, self-discovery—Jackson sawed his arms like a preacher, paced the steps, and whipped the crowd into a demagogic uproar. Not since those far-off days when he read aloud to the Revolutionary farmers had Jackson so felt the orator's unique power and thrill—for a full hour and a half he held Richmond completely under his spell. The prosecutors peered nervously through their windows and gauged correctly Jackson's threat to their case; next morning they informed him that, after all, his testimony wouldn't be needed.

"He can talk as well as shoot," marveled the Richmond papers, and one of them predicted that such a charismatic figure might one day be President.

That day approacheth.

Meanwhile Burr, acquitted but disgraced, as all the world knows, has popped up again in 1828 (like a gopher, after all), and it is widely rumored that he daily funnels secret advice and money into Jackson's presidential campaign. His principal agent, moreover, is thought to be a New York lawyer named James A. Hamilton Jr., son of that same Alexander Hamilton that Burr coolly murdered in a duel some twenty years ago.

History is a laughing god, is she not?

Fortune, turn thy wheel. Talk, shoot. *Go Ahead.*

Note to David Chase: This is the last chapter I have been able to write—use any part of it if you like. My invention flags; the days and nights go by me like waves past a Devon wreck. I tried to work in a line or two about Automaton Turks and games of chess, but A. Jackson resists all civilized comparisons, I find.

And yet the old scoundrel stirs me up and makes me reach anyway for my pen. There is still the question of Jackson's coffins, Jackson and New Orleans, Jackson's wife . . . What was it the Duke of Gloucester said when he received a gift of the Decline and Fall of the Roman Empire—*"Another damn thick, square book! Always scribble, scribble, eh, Mr. Gibbon?"*

CHAPTER
8

Andrew Jackson sat in his private room in the Nashville Inn and pried open his military watchcase with a thumbnail. Then he ignored the watch and studied instead the floating pink and gray color of the twilight, through the window on his left, and calculated that he had just about half an hour before the committee came to escort him down the street to the theater.

He snapped the watch shut and nodded once, vigorously, to confirm the calculation. It was quarter past seven. The play began at eight. He was not a man to arrive too early for anything, but he was also not a man to inconvenience the others in the playhouse by arriving late and causing a ruckus.

He dipped his pen in the inkwell and finished the last few words of a memorandum to John Eaton, which Eaton would in due course rewrite in better English: *It is very True that erly in life, even in the Days of Boyhood, I contributed my mite to shake off the yoak of Tyranny. . . .* He paused to wonder if that was what Eaton called a "mixed figure." *I support Our nations patriotic Eagles. I support Our nations army. If this gives me the characteor of a "Military Chieftain," as the National Intelligencer says, why I* am *one.* He pushed the paper to one side, scrawled *Coopy* across the bottom, and put it in his "Eaton" envelope.

John Quincy Adams, somebody had told him, liked to make fun of Jackson's bad grammar and spelling, and his bad habit of letting other people edit his letters. Jackson stabbed the pen into the inkwell and pulled out a fresh sheet of paper. John Quincy Adams was a base, slanderous skunk.

He wrote, *Memorandum to John Overton: The latest developement from Henry Clay will bring retributive Justice to vissit him and his pander heads,* and then he read the sentence aloud to the empty room. The word *developement* he pronounced "devil-*ope*-ment," which was the way he had learned to pronounce it fifty-one years ago at Dr. Waddell's country school in the Waxhaws. People occasionally tried to correct him, people who didn't know him well, but that only made him say it *louder.* Devil-*ope*-ment. Which by some trick of mind now made him think of the word *elopement.* Development. Elopement. Usually, if he considered the question at all, he imagined his mind as a tree that sent its roots down steady and slow, gripping into the rich soil of Experience, but once in a while it seemed more like some skitterish long-legged insect caught in a bowl and trying to make its way crawling and jumping up the side, but falling and slipping back. It was a skitterish trick of the mind that made him think of elopement.

No, it wasn't. Henry Clay's latest "developement" was to spread the rumor to newspapers that after she had left Robards, Rachel had actually lived in Jackson's Nashville house as Jackson's housekeeper for three full years, a kept woman, and that was so ludicrous and twisted, so easy to refute that he almost couldn't be angry about it. But the very absurdity of it made his mind jump in memory to the final court order granting Robards a divorce against his wife, and like everything else concerned with that event, Jackson remembered it nearly word for word: "Rachel Robards," said the Court of Quarter Sessions, Mercer County, Kentucky, "did on the sixth day of July, 1790 depart in elopement from her husband, the said Lewis Robards, with another man." And that man, of course, was Andrew Jackson.

Even people like John Coffee and Overton got the chronology wrong sometimes. They all thought "elopement" referred to the trip down the river to Natchez, on old Captain Stark's flatboat, after which the two of them were married. In fact, what Robards meant was something completely different. But Rachel and Robards had quarreled and got back together again so often in the summer of 1790, who could keep track?

Well, Jackson could. He scowled down at the envelopes and sheets of paper scattered over the writing table, then stood abruptly and walked in a tight, straight line to the end of the room, as if he were a sailor walking a rope. He scowled at the street too. It felt as though he had spent half his life in dreary, thin-walled hotel rooms looking down at streets full of other people, and probably he had. Wagons and carriages clattered along toward the playhouse. On the far sidewalk cotton-puff ladies swayed in white dresses that blossomed against the darkening buildings, men clustered like summer bees in front of a saloon door. The first time he had ever seen Rachel Robards she was coming down the well path at her mother's house wearing a white dress and a little lace collar and her face had a sunlit tilt to it, up and sideways, and her black hair was pulled straight back, Indian fashion, so that all you saw for a moment was her face and cheekbones and great brown eyes. And he must have stopped stock-still with the tin well-bucket in his hand and just stared, till old lady Donelson gave one of her barking laughs and said, some Indian lookout *he* made, and Overton, over by the fence with his gun, kind of frowned and snickered at the same time.

Jackson felt no hatred for Lewis Robards. And that was curious, because Robards had shared Rachel's bed for nearly three years before Jackson could come to her rescue.

Keep your anger for the living, his mother used to say.

He left the window and the stream of people heading to the theater and went to sit on the bed, where he took out the locket he wore around his neck and held it next to the bedside lamp. The old military watch was hard to open, but Jackson kept it for sentimental reasons. The locket, however, swung open at a touch. And there was Rachel, painted in Washington City in December 1815—that would be thirteen years ago, in a black dress with a white collar and a delicate white Spanish headdress, a mantilla, that tumbled down the sides of her kind face like a frothy waterfall of lace. He had bought the headdress for her in Pensacola, when he was the governor, and her soft eyes looked straight out of the little painting at him, loyal and sweet-tempered. The truth was, he had her with him always.

The real elopement had taken place *before* Natchez, when Rachel went briefly back to Kentucky for a reconciliation—he and Robards had been looking daggers at each other for a month, and Robards had even tried to have him arrested, no luck to him—and within a week of going back to her husband Rachel had written her mother that it was hopeless and come get her and take her to her sister Jane's on the Cumberland River.

Now, the obvious thing would have been to send one or two of her brothers, big, strapping lads who could protect any number of unhappy sisters. But old lady Donelson had her own ideas, and she actually drove over to see Jackson at the blockhouse by Mansker's Station where he was now living with Overton and Coffee. And she had called him out of the blockhouse, down to the road. He could see it this minute. His life with Rachel was like a play in his mind that he could start and stop whenever he wanted, a wide-awake dream. There sat Mother Donelson in her mule wagon, one dusty boot up on the brake board, reins in her hand, and in her blunt old frontier way she asked, without much ceremony, would he be willing to go up Kentucky way and bring Rachel down to her sister's?

That was all; there was no need to spell out the implications, what it meant for a single man, sent for or not, that had quarreled with a husband to come riding up to the house in search of the wife.

Jackson held the locket closer to the lamp and felt he could melt with tenderness. It had been the physical love, of course. Rachel was a beautiful creature; as a young woman she had a way of curving her head back that he would know from a mile away, and her hips had flared from her tiny waist like a bell. But physical love was only the beginning. Once he and John Coffee had taken an old slave with a gangrenous leg over to the doctor's in Nashville, and the doctor had amputated the leg just above the knee. When the poor old black man came out of his whiskey-pain shock, he turned his head and saw his leg lying on a table by the bed, and he blinked his eyes and said in total innocence, "Which one is me?" and that was exactly the way Jackson had felt when he first saw Rachel, so close they were.

"Rachel is a sweet thing," her mother had said, sitting on the buckboard with a letter for Rachel in her hand.

The sweetest thing in the world, twenty-two-year-old Jackson had thought (but not said). If he went to Kentucky, he would change his life forever; he would make the biggest decision a man ever makes.

"She stands in need of a protector," her mother had said.

Politics and ambition rapped at the hotel door.

I was born to be her protector, Jackson had either thought or said, and he stood up to open the door. But in his mind's eye, in his dream, he was swinging onto his horse and riding north to rejoin his love, and everything they had done or suffered since had only endeared her to him all the more.

CHAPTER
9

The universal human habit of stopping in the middle of a doorway—John Coffee broke off his thought and waited while James Hamilton, having come to a complete halt precisely between the doorjambs of the Nashville Thespian Theatre, now compounded the problem by standing where he was and slapping his coat pockets vigorously with both hands, evidently in search of his ticket.

"They won't ask for the stub this time," Coffee told his back. "Not for the afterpiece." Hamilton looked up over his shoulder, blinked, nodded once, and finally stepped through the door and into the lobby.

Murmuring reassurance, Coffee led the lawyer out of the crowd, now unblocked and streaming in by the dozens, and guided him past a wall of theatrical posters and placards (one long "Jackson and Reform" handbill had been nailed in the center, next to *King John*). They mounted a few makeshift steps and took their seats in the very last row of the orchestra.

It was a western custom—and Hamilton by this time had become an enthusiastic and thoroughgoing Westerner—to return to the theater after the main performance and watch a half hour or so of songs, patter dances, and sketches. They had seen a full-length performance of *She*

Stoops to Conquer, and now there was only this curlicue-tail of a musical afterpiece and they could all go home. Hamilton balanced his new cream-colored Stetson hat on his lap and consulted the program; Coffee glanced up at the boxes to check that General Jackson had taken his place safely (it was too much to expect that Rachel, who disapproved of the theater in principle, would ride all the way in from the Hermitage just to watch a godless abomination). Then Coffee pulled out his handkerchief, wiped his eyes, and tried to forget that this sweltering barn of a room had not that long ago been Smith's Nashville Salt-House and used exclusively for storing the salt excavated four miles away at Cumberland Lick. The stage and rows of seats looked professional enough, with their gilt wood and their green baize covering, and the boxes where Jackson sat were hung with banners and gay little pennant flags, but the floor was bare pine and still perfectly saturated with salt, which made it look wet under the gas-lights, wet and deceptively cool.

Coffee fanned himself with the handkerchief. The last time he had been here the play was an amateur production of Home's *Douglas,* and John Eaton and Sam Houston had both taken parts; no great surprise, he supposed, that professional politicians liked to playact, especially Sam Houston, who would go to remarkable lengths to wear any kind of cos-tume. But what was curious, Coffee thought, was the extent to which Andy Jackson, who would never have dreamed of being an actor himself, loved to watch actors perform, and liked to mingle with them afterward.

Jackson settled back in his box. The musicians filed into the pit. A flatboat man in linsey-woolsey clothing stood up and called something to the nearest fiddler, and that part of the audience burst into raucous laughter. Hamilton seemed not at all disturbed by the roughness and noisiness of the crowds—what were the real theaters like in New York, Coffee wondered, or France?—Hamilton was, in fact, leaning forward to exchange a few words with two old saddlebag trappers in the next row. Then suddenly the musicians started to play a march and the curtain rose.

Noah Ludlow, the singer who now strode onto the stage, was also the star of the play, but he had changed from his British vest and cravat into a buckskin hunting shirt and leggings, an old slouch hat on his head and a rifle on his shoulder. The audience saluted him with loud applause, both hands and feet, and long whoops and howls like Indian war cries. Ludlow stalked from one end of the stage to the other with his rifle while the orchestra played and the whoops, if anything, grew louder. He crossed back to the center and the music made an abrupt transition from march to a tune instantly recognized as "The Hunters of Kentucky."

The audience began to roar. Ludlow pranced left, then right, singing at the top of his lungs. "The Hunters of Kentucky" was by far the most popular of all the hundreds of ballads written about the Battle of New Orleans. Coffee had heard whole companies sing it, verse after verse, at Jackson dinners. Eaton had spent a ridiculous sum of money to reprint it and circulate it for free all over the West. A satiric Jacksonian had written another version called "The Voters of Kentucky," mocking Henry Clay, but nothing compared with the success of the original. Ludlow stamped his foot in time to his own singing—

You've heard, I s'pose, how New Orleans
   Is fam'd for wealth and beauty,
There's girls of every hue it seems,
   From snowy white to sooty.
So Packenham he made his brags,
   If he in fight was lucky
He'd have those girls and cotton bags
   In spite of old Kentucky.

The actor mugged and danced his way through three more verses, then came to the climactic lines.

But *Jackson* he was wide awake,
   And wasn't scared with trifles,
For well he knew what aim we take
   With our Kentucky rifles;
So he marched us down to Cyprus Swamp;
   The ground was low and mucky;
There stood John Bull in martial pomp,
   But here was old Kentucky!

As he delivered the last five words, Ludlow snatched his old slouch hat from his head, threw it to the stage, and swung his rifle up as if he were taking aim. At that, the audience came to its feet with a tremendous, deafening shout. Ludlow raised his left hand toward Jackson's box and the crowd turned, whooping and applauding. Amid an even more thunderous uproar Jackson slowly stood and extended his arms. By now even the orchestra was lost in the din, the building itself was shaking with blasts of sound. At the peak of the noise Hamilton grabbed Coffee's sleeve and pulled his head down close. So great was the clamor around them that Coffee could only make out a few words, mouthed, but unheard: "Quincy Adams . . . New Orleans . . . *could never top that!*"

*   *   *

IN the morning the two of them rode over from Coffee's house at Sugar Tree Hill to the Hermitage. Hamilton, quiet, a little under the weather, Coffee thought, from the exertions of last night, paid scant attention to the countryside as they rode; but Coffee, as always, studied the crops, greeted the slaves by name, reflected for the ten-thousandth time what a mistake the General had made to build the Hermitage at the *bottom* of a hill slope, where the rain could collect, instead of at the top of the hill like anybody else. But Rachel had wanted her home there, nearer a spring, she said, and the General had built his home for Rachel. Coffee spurred his horse through the narrow gate on the right, reserved for riders in single file.

Inside the house, which was unusually crowded with visitors even for Jackson, they found the General seated at his library table. On the couch in front of him John Eaton and John Overton were going over stacks of newspapers with two more men from the Nashville Committee. Richard Henry Lee, the newest biographer, sat to one side scribbling in his note-book, and Ralph Earl, easily the worst painter on the North American continent, was yawning and sketching from a corner as Jackson sorted his mail.

Hamilton took the leather-backed wooden chair by Jackson's bookcase. With scarcely a preamble, he launched into a detailed report on his most recent trip to the East. Meanwhile Coffee stood by the window and looked out at Rachel's garden. There two or three slaves had arrived at a state of pure physical motionlessness that he thought a Buddhist monk might admire, if a Buddhist monk ever somehow found himself in middle Tennessee on a slow, syrup-sweet June morning.

From time to time he listened to Hamilton's brisk New York voice; for the most part he imitated the Negroes. It was not so much, Coffee thought, that politics bored him as that in some primitive way they *dis-tressed* him; they brought up problems and ideas that were beyond his control and that opened up difficult vistas, so to speak, on human nature, on the American version of human nature. And unlike the General, he lacked the confidence—he lacked the *imagination,* he believed, though the word would flabbergast anti-Jacksonians—that allowed Jackson to deal so decisively with life.

"General, your principal liability in New York right now," Hamilton said, "is the rumor that Aaron Burr is backing your campaign."

"He *is* backing it," said old Judge John Overton, who was bald as an apple, and toothless, and who had come to dislike Hamilton in an obvious, fidgety way. But the New Yorker was too well connected to offend outright. Overton leaned forward and spat into the brass spittoon between his boots. "He sends us letters twice a week, he organized a committee of correspondence for Ohio, he puts his personal money into the election committee."

"Well, it hurts," Hamilton said. "People associate Burr—" he paused for a moment and Coffee watched every face in the room associate the seventy-two-year-old Burr with Hamilton's martyred father "—with threats to the Union. Plots to split the Union. The General's alleged part in the alleged conspiracy."

"And since the last tariff was passed," Eaton put in, "half the South is talking about breaking up the Union." He gestured at his stack of newspapers. "I've got clippings of anti-tariff meetings in South Carolina, outright calls for secession—Burr makes people nervous, rightly or wrongly."

Jackson picked up a small cardboard box wrapped in brown paper and twine. He inspected the address. "Aaron Burr stays in the background and gives excellent advice," he said, "as well as money." He looked over the top of his reading glasses at Eaton's plump, handsome face. "We don't have to win *all* the votes, you know, John."

Eaton nodded, Hamilton wrote something down. Coffee accepted a cup of hot tea from the tray being passed around by a servant. Jackson's voice, he thought, listening to Jackson, then to Hamilton again, was often described in the papers as "high-pitched," a thing that baffled him, since he had been hearing Jackson talk for thirty years and his voice was in fact quite low-pitched and deep. If you found a story about Jackson saying X, Coffee guessed, you could be fairly sure the truth was Y. He sipped his tea and pondered the ironic and unthinkable thought that when you came right down to it, the case was probably the same for John Quincy Adams or Henry Clay. It had certainly been true for Thomas Jefferson—amused, he watched his mind go from Burr to Hamilton to Jefferson—whom his mother had known back in Virginia; for every story good or bad about Mr. Jefferson, she used to say, she had heard the exact, absolute opposite from somebody else.

"Masons," Hamilton said significantly.

"That is still a problem." Jackson put down the package and ran a hand through his hair, which sprang back up like gray bristles on a brush. Two years ago a New York Mason named William Morgan had quarreled with his lodge and published its secret rituals in a pamphlet; a few months later Morgan had mysteriously disappeared, probably into Lake Erie, and half the country had broken into anti-Masonic clamor. "Now I haven't attended a chapter meeting of Freemasons in fifteen years," Jackson said with a definite edge to his definitely low-pitched voice. "Or a Grand Meeting in two or three. But I am on record as a member. I admit it."

"Adams has issued a statement denying he was ever a member, or ever will be," Hamilton told him.

"It's an irony," Jackson said to Coffee, and now his jaw had begun to go hard and his back military-stiff in his blue frock coat. He took off his glasses and jammed them into a coat pocket. "Adams claiming *I* belong to a corrupt conspiracy of the elite while *he* is the uncorrupted democrat."

"I was just thinking that the truth in politics is always the other way round," Coffee drawled, keeping his voice mild; there was nothing to be gained by encouraging Jackson's temper, not in front of the ever-officious Hamilton.

"Monroe," Hamilton said.

Jackson had gone back to the package and was now sawing the twine with a small ivory-handled knife. "You tell Van Buren *not* to say anything else about Masonry," he instructed Hamilton brusquely. "Masonry is going to fade as a campaign issue, the people are going to lose interest. As for Monroe—" Jackson cut the twine with a loud snap. "I've written Monroe. I've also written that two-faced lard-headed pink-eyed scoundrel that was his secretary of navy, S. L. Southard—" Eaton looked up in alarm "—I have great respect for James Monroe," Jackson said, "I would like to *keep* that respect. But if he's going to say in public, even at one of his little eastern *wine-drinking* parties, that I was no more than an agent of his orders at New Orleans, because I can *document,* by God, that which he never wrote me a word after November twelfth—"

As always, when Jackson's anger heated up, his syntax boiled, fell apart. Eaton, who was their man in Washington and who worried constantly that Jackson's intemperate letters might end up in the papers, was leaning forward, ready to interrupt. Coffee put his big hand on Eaton's shoulder. Hamilton checked off something on his list.

"Now look at this!" Jackson said, opening the package. He held up a ceramic whiskey flask, amber-colored, with white bas-relief profiles of Jackson and George Washington on opposite sides. "*This* is what you do about Monroe, Mr. Hamilton. Those people in the East are writing their editorials about the danger of electing a 'military chieftain,' isn't that right?" Hamilton took the flask, nodded. "You tell Duff Green to get out some editorials reminding the people of the *other* 'military chieftain' this country elected President. You find out who manufactured this flask, John Eaton, and see about distributing some on the Fourth of July." Jackson glowered at the bookcase and looked ten years younger. "You tell them to *get busy now,* goddamnit!"

☆　　☆　　☆

AFTER lunch Jackson organized a party for riding to Clover Bottom, where Noah Ludlow was giving an abbreviated matinee performance of some of his sketches.

At the Hermitage, Coffee stayed on to file a few letters for Jackson, then wandered down to the stables to inspect a mare he understood was almost ready to foal, but he had hardly climbed into the stall and started to look when Jackson's personal servant Alfred came in after him with a note.

"It's from her?" Coffee asked, just to be saying something, because Rachel's big looping scrawl, once seen, was unmistakable.

"That's about right," Alfred said, and sat down on a bale of hay.

"She's having one of the usual, I guess?" Coffee tore open the envelope and glanced at the single sheet of paper. He saw the name Jesus three times, printed and underlined, and the word *don't* underlined, and *precious precious Savior in the Blood.*

"Where is she?" Coffee asked.

She had been, according to Alfred, in Ralph Earl's room, in the back parlor, in the master bedroom, in the General's library, and when he had left the house in search of Coffee, she was going into the dining room. And in fact the dining room was where Coffee found Rachel five minutes later, sitting at one end of the long table with her Bible open in front of her and the pretty young niece Emily Donelson seated beside her, holding her hand.

He stopped for a moment at the door to look at her. Short, podgy, hopelessly fat. Dressed as usual in an old blue calico frock; gray hair piled in a haphazard bun on her head, no visible pin or comb, no jewelry or makeup or ribbon. The Siren of Nashville.

"Rachel, I got your note."

"I'm so fearful," Rachel said rapidly, breathing hard, not even looking up. Coffee motioned young Emily away and took her chair. "The enemies of the General have dipped their arrows in wormwood and gall and sped them at me, almighty God, was there ever anything to equal it, thirty years in happy social friendship with society, speaking or thinking ill to nobody."

"Now, Rachel." Coffee clasped one of her soft little hands in his own and she began to sob uncontrollably. He patted her hand gently. They were close to the same age exactly, he thought, he and Rachel; he had known her since he was eighteen years old. But do you ever really know somebody?

"I fear not them," Rachel said, trembling but breathing more slowly. Coffee could see the lines of dried and drying tears on her cheeks, under her eyes, like so many spidery lines in a pane of shattered glass. "I fear Him that can kill the body and cast the soul into Hell Fire. Oh, Eternity, awful is the name!"

"Has your aunt been like this all day?" Coffee asked Emily Donelson.

"She gets upset sometimes when the General has meetings," the girl replied. Long-necked, like all the Donelsons. Beautiful black hair. Coffee took up the corner of Rachel's Bible and pretended to read.

"They have offended God and man!" Rachel said, taking one deep breath and stopping.

"Amen to that," Coffee told her. "You don't want to be looking at those newspapers anymore, Rachel, you hear me? Or listening in on the General's meetings. You want to come on down to the stable with me and look at that mare that's about to foal. That's God's work, in the flesh."

"Making life," Rachel said, wiping her eyes.

Coffee nodded and closed her Bible for her. Making life. Making life was what frustrated and fascinated poor Rachel. If she and the General could ever have had children of their own, both of them would be different people now, Coffee thought, the General less angry, Rachel less fanatical, hysterical. He wiped her cheek with his handkerchief. Poor old thing, he thought, trapped in her piety like a rabbit in a cage.

"We'll get Lyncoya to come on with us," he said.

"Lyncoya's sick," Rachel said quickly, and for a moment Coffee was afraid she would start sobbing again. But the fit was easing. Sniffling, blinking, she smoothed her fat hands on the front of her dress—what Coffee's mother, he remembered, used to call the "stomacher"—and stood unsteadily up. Lyncoya was the Indian boy Jackson had brought home from the Creek Wars in 1814 and more or less adopted. But he was no son. Andrew Jackson Jr., an adopted white boy, was no son either, not really, not down on the level where Rachel suffered.

Coffee put his arm around Rachel's shoulders and Emily Donelson handed her an old, faded bonnet. She was crying softly to herself and murmuring, "Jesus, Lord Jesus" when Coffee glanced back, on impulse. There at the other end of the room, stopped once more in the middle of a doorway, stood James A. Hamilton Jr. Their eyes met. Hamilton's dark, fussy little face looked thoughtful.

"I came back early from the show," he said. He let his gaze drop to Rachel's trembling figure. He slowly took off his cream-colored Stetson. Then he raised his eyes back to Coffee. "I would admire a little conversation with you, General," he said, "later on."

CHAPTER
10

That night all the signs pointed toward a change of weather. The colony of summer crickets under Coffee's study window—crickets the size of bears, to judge by the noise they usually made—went abruptly silent. The sky grew overcast and bruised. Mountainous clouds, a dark, waxy purple in color, started to pile up across the western horizon, where the Cumberland Valley sloped downward to the prairie. Hot sweat. Still air.

Coffee poured a small measure of raw plum brandy into his black after-supper coffee and noticed that Hamilton, on the opposite chair, was making a face.

"Well, it looks pretty strange, I agree," Coffee told him cheerfully. "Plum brandy and coffee. But I like it." He sat back and wrapped his big hands around one of the delicate china cups his wife had brought out for company. "Who was it said, 'No man is a hypocrite in his pleasures'? One of Jackson's favorite sayings."

"Samuel Johnson," Hamilton said, and poured his own brandy into a conventional brandy snifter.

Coffee nodded and spat into his brass cuspidor. More pleasure. Samuel Johnson, the great dictionary maker.

"So," Hamilton said, and settled back into his chair. He had a big nose for a man his size, and against the glow of the oil lamp on the table his little profile was as sharp as a parrot's. "All the time I was telling Martin Van Buren that Aunt Rachel was the key to managing the General, all that time it seems *you're* the key to managing *her.*"

"She has these fits once in a while," Coffee admitted. A roll of thunder made him sit up straighter. He could hear a distant grumbling that finished in soft, hollow-sounding detonations. A windowpane vibrated in its frame.

"She reads things sometimes in the papers," he said, "about herself and Robards—we try to keep the papers away from her, but the General subscribes to over twenty, he has to have them—and she goes into a full prayer state, you might say. Most women reading in the public newspapers that they're a convicted adulteress, most women would get upset."

"Does Jackson know?"

Coffee nodded, although in the failing light he wasn't sure Hamilton could see him. Andrew Jackson had spent his share of time and more comforting his Rachel or listening to her weep and wail. For years after the war, whenever he left on a trip she was certain he would be killed or never come back and she would be abandoned, without protection. Her scenes were notorious in Nashville. Another husband might have stayed home, or kept her out of the public eye. But Jackson wanted to be President. That was all you could say.

"Aunt Rachel would be a great liability in the President's House," Hamilton said, with a lawyer's instinct for the flintiest, most impersonal word. *Liability.*

"Emily Donelson and some of the other girls can handle her just fine if need be."

"No. She needs a man's touch to reassure her," Hamilton said firmly, and Coffee looked up at him in surprise, because he was, of course, exactly right.

"You never wrote that other little memorandum about Jackson and Aaron Burr for me," Hamilton said after a moment. "You promised you were going to do that down in New Orleans."

Coffee added a second measure of plum brandy to his cup and inhaled the aroma. Like pouring hot silk down your throat, he thought. The first raindrops clattered on the gravel outside, spattering the windowsill, and the storm raised its voice off on the horizon.

"I meant to write that for you," Coffee said, "and I sat down once or twice to try. But I never got anywhere. And now the General says ignore the Burr rumors, as you heard."

Hamilton had faded in the lamplight to a pale oval face, a glint of china, a spot of reflection on polished brown boots. "Yes, and he says to forget the anti-Masons, too, because that's not going to be an issue. The people won't care."

"He's usually right, about the people."

"He is," Hamilton said brusquely, and put down his cup. "He knows what the people feel because he doesn't have any blood relations of his own. I think in most ways he's all alone in the world, except for 'the people.' "

"Except for Rachel."

"They are the kind of couple," Hamilton said, and Coffee could just hear him now over the raindrops and the clink of dishes, the sound of women's voices in the kitchen, "the kind of couple, when you find them together you shake your head and ask yourself, what in God's name does he *see* in her? But there it is." Hamilton scraped back his chair with the air of a man who has to deal with bigger mysteries. "Marriage. I'm going up to Kentucky next week, and while I'm there I want to ask a little more about that Peyton Short we talked about, just to be thorough."

Coffee felt a small thrill of alarm, a shiver in his back, but couldn't say why. He had never seen Peyton Short in his life. He didn't know anything more than his name.

In his symmetrical, thorough way Hamilton, now standing, lined up his cup and saucer along the edge of the study table. "Now I need to ask you something else as well, General," he said, looking down and making an infinitesimal adjustment to his spoon. "Van Buren has heard in a roundabout way that back in 1824 some documents—some letters and possibly a diary, to be precise—were offered to Jackson."

"Concerning Rachel."

"Concerning Rachel, of course."

"I never heard of that."

"A man named Charles Tutt, lived in Virginia?"

"No." Coffee shook his head.

"They were to be used against him in the election, but a friend of Jackson's suppressed them, and now they've disappeared."

"If they ever existed," Coffee said. "For as long as I can remember, people have talked about Rachel. There's never been anything to it."

Hamilton cocked his dark little head. "Bluff, blunt John Coffee," he said, and Coffee couldn't tell whether his tone was mocking or not. "Not a disloyal bone in your body. I call you Enobarbus to Jackson's Antony, you know. The Tennessee Enobarbus."

Coffee felt more and more ignorant and backwoods every day. He grunted and stood up himself and resolved, as soon as James A. Hamilton, Esquire, was gone, he would take down the family books and look up Enobarbus.

"Meanwhile," Hamilton said, "we also have James Monroe stirring up feelings about the Battle of New Orleans, and since Jackson *did* agree that might be an issue, I would take it as a real favor if you would write me something about the Creek Wars and the War of 1812, which you were a hero in, so I could pass it along back East."

"Oh, I wasn't a hero," Coffee said, and spat. "I just happened to be there."

Hamilton smiled. "Start it in 1812," he said, "and go straight like a shot to New Orleans."

Outside the window the rain was making a kind of moving grille of water. A chestnut tree seemed to shake its head in a puff of smoke. "You shall have it," Coffee promised, thinking he wasn't bluff and blunt, but was loyal, thinking of poor old Rachel. "You shall have it before you leave for Kentucky."

C H A P T E R

11

John Coffee's Personal Narrative

THE FIRST THING I REMEMBER FROM THE WAR OF 1812 IS THE SAD, WET lamb.

It was early March of that year, 1812, and we were in the middle of one of those hard, sleet-fat Tennessee storms that jump down from the mountains and soak the fields to a swamp, just like today. For some reason now forgotten I was visiting at the Hermitage, waiting it out in the downstairs room with General Jackson and his little two-year-old adopted son, Andrew Jackson Junior. There were just the three of us, and one scrawny, bedraggled white lamb that Andrew Junior had seen out in the rain and begged his father to bring inside, and so Jackson and I had gone out and chased it down in the mud and grass. And then we had pulled up our chairs in front of the fire to get dry, and I recall very well how the General was sitting in an old pine rocker holding the lamb in his lap and reciting "Mary Had a Little Lamb," which was a new poem then, only changing the name to "Andrew Had a Little Lamb."

And then the war stuck its fist through the door.

The transformation is what I have never forgotten. One minute Jackson was resting in his rocking chair holding a lamb and reciting a poem, the next minute young Thomas Hart Benton came crashing into the room like a six-foot, wet-headed rocket.

"WAR! WAR!"

The wind slung the fire up the chimney; Benton careened off the walls, staggered over the rug, thrust a rolled-up paper in my hands, and the next thing I knew the lamb was gone and Benton and Jackson and Andrew Junior himself were running wild around the floor, shouting and swearing death to the British, and Jackson had on that fierce, pale warrior face that all the Scotch-Irish men I have ever known are born with, war-babies every one.

And meanwhile I was standing by the window reading the damp paper, which was President Madison's proclamation of war and call for fifty thousand volunteers. And Benton, who had ridden thirty miles up from Franklin in the driving rain to tell us, had already worked out a plan in his head—Tennessee would expand the militia to three divisions, Jackson would be General of the West, Benton would be Colonel, I would be Colonel number two, and God knows what Andrew Junior and the lamb would be, but long before Benton could finish shouting, Jackson had lunged at his desk and grabbed a pen and started scribbling a counter-proclamation of his own. I have it right here before me, as re-spelled and corrected by John Eaton.

V o l u n t e e r s   t o   A r m s !

Citizens! Your government has at last yielded to the impulse of the nation. Your impatience is no longer restrained. The hour of national vengeance is now at hand. The eternal enemies of american prosperity are again to be taught to respect your rights, after having been compelled to feel, once more, the power of your arms. . . .

Who are we? and for what are we going to fight? are we the titled Slaves of George the third? the military conscripts of Napoleon the great? or the frozen peasants of the Russian Czar? No—we are the free born sons of america; the citizens of the only republick now existing in the world; and the only people on earth who possess rights, liberties, and property which they dare call their own. . . .

Oh, it was splendid, stirring stuff, and Jackson read it at full oratorical volume, as if the three of us in that wet little room (counting the boy) were a whole brigade of soldiers, set to charge.

And I stood watching, absolutely flabbergasted. Because not two days before, the same man, the very same *thundering* Andrew Jackson had been sunk in the grip of the only serious depression of spirits I ever saw affect him—the megrim, the hyp, hypos, spleen: I am trying to remember the old-fashioned eighteenth-century words my Virginia mother used to have for the days when a person could hardly budge, hardly get up out of bed and live. *The black dog who sits at your feet and barks.*

He had been barking at Jackson for almost a year. This happens to men when they are forty-five or so, as Jackson was. Life flattens out. Ambitions sour. Pleasures fail. Brightness, the poet says, falls from the air. But Jackson's case was worse; he was angrier, flatter than other men—he would sit by his fireplace all day and drink, or ride in his fields, rain or shine, not looking up or down, just staring ahead and working his Scotch-Irish jaw; and I would ride with him.

By 1812 so gloomy and protracted was his state of mind, he was actually meditating a move from Nashville west into the Arkansas territory. He had offered the Hermitage for sale, and a horse breeder scoundrel named Wade Thompson made him a bid just high enough to be tempting, so Jackson had started the escrow and written a friend in Congress, begging a job as a territorial judge at a paltry thousand dollars a year, and the week before Benton came through the door he had sent out one of his Donelson nephews to find him a place to settle.

What reasons for the black dog?

Rachel, of course, first. By 1812 all the sad old talk about Rachel and Lewis Robards had been revived. Nashville was growing into a proper little city, with a theater, a music academy, three schools and a college, and twenty-six different kinds of eastern pretensions. An old-time frontier character like Rachel looked more and more out of place, "Aunt Rachel" with her corncob pipes and cigars and her shapeless farm-waddle dresses, and her unfashionable down-on-her-knees religion. The new well-bred ladies on Charlotte Avenue would smooth out their crinolines and raise their teacups and whisper and mock, and though Jackson could call out a *man* and challenge him, there was precious little he could do about a woman. He wrote a few letters, he blustered, but there it was.

And money, second. Jackson and money. Years before, when he first came to Nashville, he had signed on as a guarantor of the debts of a man named David Allison. Allison had promptly gone bankrupt, and Jackson had worried and worked himself sick to pay it off. In 1811 he was just on the verge of doing it when the lands that were in question turned out to have flawed titles, and it looked as if he would have to start all over again. Anybody else would have kept his mouth shut—*he* went to see the smartest lawyer in Tennessee, Felix Grundy, and Grundy advised him to do just that—but Jackson is a man who would rather die than take advice. All by himself he made a long, dangerous horseback journey through Creek territory down to Georgia—Rachel's scene at parting was surpassing, even for her—and found Allison's heirs living in Fort Moultrie and worked out a settlement consistent, he told me, "with his Honor." But it had nearly wrecked him to do it. And her.

And reason third for the barking black dog of depression, that same damned "Honor."

Because you have to remember that twenty years ago Andrew Jackson was known far and wide, not as a Senator or would-be President, but as a bad, wild bully, the wickedest man in Tennessee. He was the man who had murdered poor Charles Dickinson in an unfair duel, who had stolen another man's wife, who would just as soon draw his pistol as spit, and while that may be one kind of reputation for a boy of twenty, for a man of forty and more it's worse than disgrace, it's close to being a joke; and Jackson knew it and he couldn't do a thing about it. He was going to leave Nashville for the same reason he left Salisbury, North Carolina: People were starting to laugh.

Now there is a kind of Tennessee wildflower that only blossoms in the heat of a forest fire, when the flames pass over the seed, and it probably ought to be named after Jackson.

From the moment he put down his lamb and wrote his proclamation, he was a different, red, white, and blue fire-blossoming man. Arkansas was forgotten, the black dog was forgotten. Day and night he did nothing but organize and drill and march and hone his soldiers to a fine, sharp fighting edge. And wait.

And wait.

Back in Washington City, where Nobody Forgets, Jackson enjoyed still another kind of reputation: He was the hotheaded friend of Aaron Burr, the traitor. And old James Madison, who lived his whole life under

Thomas Jefferson's thumb, wasn't about to order Aaron Burr's friend into the war. (On the one hand, he might turn out to be a traitor too; on the other hand, which was worse, he might turn out to be a hero.) Jackson wrote letter after letter pleading for duty, and President Madison ignored them every one. He simply let us twist and turn in the wind, completely idle, while the British drove our army back from Canada and the whole nasty war slippered and frittered away.

Not until mid-December, when the British made a sudden feint toward New Orleans, did Madison break down and order us to move out—west toward Natchez, where we could reinforce New Orleans—and even then he sent the order to the governor instead of Jackson and never once referred to Jackson by name.

But more than twenty-five hundred men assembled as fast as they could in Nashville, just before Christmas. They came in bitter weather, when the Cumberland was frozen from bank to bank for the first time in memory, and snow was fallen a foot deep on the ground. Jackson had provided a thousand cords of wood, which was to last for three weeks, but the troops burned every stick of it the first day. And he and I spent the next night, from sunset to dawn, walking together among the tents, trying to care for the men and animals, seeing that the drunken men were brought within reach of a fire and that no sentinel, out in the dark by himself, froze to death.

About six in the morning (here is a Jackson story for you, Mr. Hamilton), after a night of tramping in the snow and cold, Jackson and I entered the Nashville Inn and immediately met a man in the bar, who had passed the night comfortably in his bed. He saw our officer's insignia and started to mock us to his friends—officers who called together such a mass of troops, then stayed indoors while the poor soldiers went without shelter.

My God, Jackson's temper! "You d——d infernal scoundrel!" he roared. "Sowing disaffection among the troops. Why, Colonel Coffee and I have been up all night long seeing to the men. Let me hear one more word and I'm d——d if I don't ram that red-hot andiron down your throat!"

Andrew had a little lamb!

We set out a week later in flat-boats and keel boats, down the river. Thirty-nine days and two thousand miles over grinding ice floes and snow to Natchez, where Jackson established us in bivouac outside the town and waited for orders from General Wilkinson a hundred miles away in New Orleans.

And waited and waited again. Six full weeks, no orders, no plans, nothing except an occasional testy letter telling us to stay right where we were.

The men grew bored, then sick. Jackson was sick himself briefly. I remember well his writing Rachel a tender, untruthful letter, telling her he was healthy and Providence would surely bring him home. His eyes were inflamed or infected at the time, so I had to read her reply out loud. I kept a copy, the first of many Rachel notes I have read, not the least eloquent:

> *Do not My beloved Husband let the love of Country fame and honour make you forgit you have me Without you I would think them all empty shadows You will say this is not the Language of a patriot, but it is the Language of a faithful wife our little Andrew is the most affectionate Little Darling on Earth often dos he ask me in bed not to cry, Sweet pappa will Come home to you again. I feel my Cheeks to know if I am shedding Tears.*

You have seen Jackson's hair—straight as bristles on a brush. I thought it would spring off his head the next week when we finally received our orders: *Dismiss the men and send them home!*

He fairly ripped the paper out of my hands to read it again—dismiss twenty-five hundred American volunteers five hundred miles from home—without pay, horses, supplies! As if they were so much black nigger chattel!

Who are we? and for what are we going to fight? Free-born sons of America!

He roared and cursed till they must have heard him in New Orleans, and he sat down and wrote such an answer as few commanders in chief have ever received from a general.

Then he mustered the men and clenched his teeth and set about disobeying the order.

In the first place he gave his own personal note of credit to half the merchants in Natchez for shoes, clothing, and food. He had come south with three fine horses for himself, and these he turned over to the sick bay. And when finally we started off there was Major-General Jackson marching on foot with his men, and there was Jackson tending the sick, holding up their heads, strapping them onto the wagons—and there was Jackson on his haunches by the fire, eating the same brown slop the soldiers ate and sleeping on the same brown dirt. We averaged eighteen miles a day for a month, through a miserable, trackless forest, and Andrew Jackson walked every mud mile of it rather than take a horse, as was his right, and set himself over his men.

After a week or so, some plodding young soldier—blessed by the political muse—observed that Jackson was "tough." Somebody else said he was "tough as hickory." Then he was *called* Hickory, behind his back. By the end of the month, as we came in sight of Nashville, he was "Old Hickory" forever.

No more megrim, hypos, or spleen—we paraded straight up the steps of the State House, covered in glory.

And then not two months later Jackson and I together did the stupidest thing in our lives and ruined it all.

CHAPTER
12

H e's going to cause himself a stroke," Mrs. John Quincy Adams declared, and Emma Colden, assigned an actual writing commission for the first time in her life, blinked and leaned forward, pencil in hand, to be sure she had heard correctly.

"Standing out in that broiling sun," Mrs. Adams added. "The very idea." The President's wife made what Emma could only describe as a nervous flounce, from head to toe, and hitched her chair a few inches closer to the wooden railing that separated the ladies from the overwhelmingly masculine scene before them.

"When you write about it," her father had told her as she left that morning, "forget about the politics, look for *contrast*. The secret of writing is conflict, contrast; every paragraph," he had said, waving his pen with mock ferocity, "a *battleground*."

"He is going to have a paralytic stroke," Mrs. Adams repeated. "In a black wool suit on the Fourth of July, standing under that *awful* sun. The President of the United States."

And the first and most obvious contrast, Emma agreed, was the spectacle of several dozen distinguished politicians and businessmen in their dark frock coats and tall beaver hats standing in a wide, bare field of baked clay and dead grass, under a *fierce* Maryland sun, listening to each other make speeches.

Around them—second contrast—hundreds of ordinary working men, dressed in lighter, sensible clothes, many of them carrying banners and patriotic signboards and flags (and a few "Jackson and Reform" signboards as well—you could hardly step out a door without seeing a Jackson poster now).

"You must come farther into the shade," Mrs. Adams said with motherly impatience, and made more room for her under the striped canvas awning that protected the ladies from the sun. Only, Emma thought, looking about as she moved her chair, there were almost no other ladies to speak of—on Mrs. Adams's right there was Mrs. Southard, wife of the secretary of the navy, then Mrs. Senator Clay and two unidentified young girls no older than thirteen or fourteen, and that was all. There was certainly no other female journalist on their platform or anywhere else in sight, though the *male* journalists (a *fundamental* contrast) were thick as locusts on the ground in front of the politicians.

"That is General Mercer," said Mrs. Adams, Emma's new friend. "With the enormous red face, coming to the podium. President of the Chesapeake and Ohio Company."

Emma took out her notebook and added the name to her list of speakers. General Mercer's voice, high and thin but full of military vigor, carried easily over the fifty yards between them. She wrote a few key shorthand phrases as he talked—another of her father's tricks: *the most pow.ful repub. on earth . . . the Amer. Plan for internal improvements . . . perpetual Union.* And while she wrote she also glanced at her earlier notes. *7 A.M. Tilley's, Pot., swans, canal*—politicians and journalists had met at Tilley's Hotel in Georgetown at seven that morning, she translated, set out in a series of steamboats and barges up the Potomac to a point on the Maryland border, then taken another fleet of boats up an old canal (covered with lovely drifting swans, thick as lilies) till they arrived, just at noon, at this desolate field where the great new Chesapeake and Ohio Canal would begin.

"Dear heaven," muttered Mrs. Adams.

Emma looked up in time to see General Mercer hand a bright new metal spade to John Quincy Adams.

Contrast: the tall, tomato-faced general, ramrod straight; the short, squat figure of the President, whose face, as if by perverse defiance and will, was not red like everybody else's, but granite white.

"This humble instrument of rural labor," General Mercer declared, "is a symbol of the favorite occupation of our countrymen. I now present it to our chief magistrate, on a spot where, little more than a century ago, the painted savage held his nightly orgies. May its use today contribute to our diversified arts and industries."

Emma scribbled two quick lines. Beside her Mrs. Adams snapped open a Chinese fan and began to work it furiously. A military band broke into a tune. In the middle of the field John Quincy Adams appeared to test the handle of the spade by holding it at an angle, like a fishing pole; after a moment's hesitation he thrust the blade into the dirt and pushed hard with one foot.

Emma paused in her writing. Adams lifted the spade and thrust again, harder.

"A root," Mrs. Adams announced.

The President thrust once more, then threw down the spade. In a single blurred, decisive motion he pulled off his heavy frock coat (revealing a white shirt and black suspenders), picked up the spade again, and *drove* the blade down with an audible grunt.

There was one tree still standing in the field, and from its branches hung a number of boys and men. These now began to cheer the President, who was driving the spade repeatedly into the ground and after each stroke (and grunt) prying the root higher. All over the field spectators were joining the cheer. Adams thrust, *dug;* the crowd roared. General Mercer backed out of the way of flying dirt. From the rear of the politicians' group somebody trundled forward with a wheelbarrow, and at practically the same moment Adams made one last determined plunge with his spade and abruptly lifted the root, clods and all, into the air. He swung it high over his head like a trophy, and then as the crowd went wild with noise he tumbled it over into the barrow.

From that point on the day was his. He took up his coat and hat again and made a speech in which (Emma counted) he quoted Latin twice, the Scriptures once, the philosopher George Berkeley three times, but nothing (not even Latin) could dampen the enthusiasm of his audience. As Adams walked back to the canal boats after the ceremonies were finished, men of every description and class surrounded him, grinning, shaking his hand, shouting some word over the general roar of sustained approval.

Trailing behind and walking toward the ladies' boat, Emma desperately tried to write down her impressions. *President/shirtsleeved farmer, bare landscape/future glorious canal, Latin erudition/democratic fervor*—but it was left to Mrs. Adams, marching at her side, to make the essential contrast.

"General Jackson," she said scornfully, watching her husband, "would have turned every last man of them into a *vote.*"

On the trip back to Washington City, Emma sat in the stern with Mrs. Adams and discussed, to her surprise, not politics, not Jackson versus Adams or East versus West, but the plight of women. In particular the plight of women whose children were grown and living apart and whose husbands showed no awareness whatsoever that they were alive and had needs. In particular, Emma wrote, then erased, the plight of Louisa Catherine Adams.

Their boat docked at the Georgetown wharves shortly before two o'clock. Ahead of them the President's steamboat had already landed and its party gone ashore. On the dock Mrs. Adams took Emma's hand in a gesture of supplication as much as command and invited her to come for tea that very moment at the President's mansion.

"You would not believe," Mrs. Adams said twenty minutes later, leading her into the East Room where Emma, not many weeks before had attended a President's Evening, "the expense of keeping it up."

"No."

"In this room," Mrs. Adams said, indicating vaguely the ornate wallpaper, the gas-lamp fixtures, the tall gilded curtains, "my mother-in-law, Abigail Adams, used to hang her wash to dry. In the old version of the house," Louisa added, "before the British burned it. Mr. Jefferson kept it cleared for his books."

"Upstairs," Emma the journalist ventured.

"Upstairs is the famous billiard table and our apartments," Mrs. Adams said. "The President's room, my room, guest rooms for our sons when they can bring themselves to visit. Mr. Adams's office is there"—she pointed toward a closed door at the end of a narrow corridor. "He's undoubtedly in it now, seeing visitors or writing." From a hovering servant she took a brass tray of teacups, pots, biscuit dishes, and lemons and set it on a table. "Lemon? Sugar?" She poured, stirring briskly, efficiently with a thin silver spoon—Emma thought (without smiling) of her husband attacking the root with his spade. "I, too, spend hours writing," Mrs. Adams said, keeping her eyes fixed on the tea tray.

In retrospect, Emma thought, she should have guessed. One of her father's favorite poems was Pope's "Epistle to Dr. Arbuthnot," which described (in his hilarious recitation) the unceasing assault of would-be writers on the poor published poet in his country house—"The Dog-Star rages! Nay, 'tis past a doubt, / All *Bedlam* or Parnassus is let out!" ("I meditate a book in my retirement," her father liked to say, "about the modern thirst for *fame* by means of publication; I would leave it unpublished, of course.")

"I am really a very obscure and unpracticed writer," Emma murmured. In a gesture she recognized as fleeing Parnassus, she pushed her chair back from the table. "I've written articles for several Washington newspapers, but never with my name actually printed. Always 'Our Correspondent' or nothing at all."

"Because you are a woman." Mrs. Adams spoke with something of her husband's decisiveness.

Emma could not deny it. Yet—cautiously—she formed a distinction. In America a woman could write something, could work somewhere. Compared to Europe, America was a land of female opportunity. There was Sarah Hale in Boston, a novelist and editor of a magazine. Or Frances Wright, author of books and plays, speaker that very day at a Fourth of July celebration in the West.

"Europe," repeated Mrs. Adams. Emma was still holding her teacup, although Mrs. Adams had put hers aside, scarcely touched, and begun to nibble little shells of chocolate from a crystal bowl on the tray. But *nibble* hardly did justice to the speed and intensity with which she ate. "I lived in Europe for many years. Some of my happiest days were spent at St. Petersburg, when my husband was ambassador to the Czar's court. I spoke nothing but French, I hardly minded the winters because the Czar was so kind, his court was so"—she picked up three chocolate shells at once—"*élégant*. I would like you to see what I have written."

In a matter of moments she had hurried from the room and returned with a thick black leather portfolio of papers, some bound with ribbons, others loose or held at one corner by a pin.

She moved the tea tray to another table and spread out her writings. A tiny woman, Emma thought, watching her bustle, despite the chocolate. An upturned nose, a high forehead, thin, brownish hair whose curls had wilted hours ago in the heat; by contrast, below the rather full, rather pretty face her figure was flat and sticklike, as if she were a puppet's head on a body of wires. For some reason Emma suddenly thought of her mother.

"This is a translation from the French. I made it two years ago." Mrs. Adams extended a dozen sheets of paper tied with two green ribbons.

" 'Lamartine, *La Mort de Socrate,* ' " Emma read aloud. " 'The Death of Socrates.' " On the bottom of the first page was a date, July 11, 1826, and a dedication: "To my husband—John Quincy Adams."

"A great poet," Emma said, scanning the first lines (and meaning Lamartine).

"Here is another version." One after another Mrs. Adams passed her papers across the table. Poems of her own evidently exchanged with her sons in Boston: "The Silken Knot," "The Last Request." Two one-act plays about life in the President's mansion. A memoir of her two years in Europe entitled "Record of a Life, or, My Story."

Once or twice she started to pass over a set of papers, stopped, frowned, and put them aside. Emma glanced at each offering, not sure what to say or do, but murmuring politenesses or exclamations, occasionally reading a few lines aloud, then looking up and smiling.

Mrs. Adams seemed content at first ("All any writer wants," Emma's father said, "is absolute, unquestioning approval"), but as the stack of papers shrank she grew obviously nervous. The bowl of chocolates was refilled, emptied. Mrs. Adams drummed her foot.

"These are my most recent." She straightened a final bundle against the edge of the table. "They are . . . different."

At first glance, however, they were not. The topmost item was another play, this time called "The Metropolitan Kaleidoscope, or Vanities of Winter Etchings" by the archly pseudonymous "Rachel Barb." Emma read more slowly than before. Lord and Lady Sharply lived with their three sons in a great English mansion. The sons were negligent, indifferent. Lord Sharply was pompous, talented, cold; he ignored his wife. "He was full of good qualities," the introduction explained, "but *ambition* absorbed every thought of his soul."

Involuntarily Emma looked up. Mrs. Adams ate chocolates and studied the wall. Lady Sharply, by contrast, possessed a "heart perhaps too warm.

She was a woman of strong affections and cold dislikes, of pride and gentleness, of playfulness and hauteur." She enjoyed her feminine impulses. But her mind had been "deformed" by the oppressive world of men in which she was forced to live, she was not free.

"This last," Mrs. Adams said quickly, "concerns an event I read about in the newspapers." She gave Emma a clipping from *Niles' Weekly Register* of a few months past, then a two-page poem of her own. The clipping told the story of a poor Irish servant girl who had been seduced by her master, but later abandoned for a rich bride; the Irish girl, pregnant and heartbroken, had committed suicide by swallowing quicksilver.

The death in the poem was histrionic in the extreme:

The parching thirst, excruciat pain
Seize on the chaos of the brain
till Nature spent exhausted lies
Pants, rolls in agony, and dies!!!

But Emma turned back to read again the speech before death, which seemed so deep a cry of anguish that Lady Sharply/Adams herself might have uttered it.

Am I then doom'd she wildly cried
    Illusive hopes no more return
He revels with his lovely bride
    While I a wretch am left to mourn——
Forlorn, deserted, lost, beguil'd,
    In torment must I weep?
Become alas sad misery's child
    Thro' sorrows paths to creep?

"This is very powerful." She replaced the poem slowly on the portfolio. "You should write more, you should publish."

"The rights of women in this country," Mrs. Adams began, "scarcely exist. If I tried to publish—" Then she stopped. Her dark eyes opened wider in belated surprise. "You have been here before, at the President's *levées.* I've seen you with Senator Sellers."

"Yes."

"I've only just now realized it."

"You must see hundreds of new people every week."

"Senator Sellers is a widower. He comes to argue with my husband against the slave trade."

"He's in Ohio now."

Mrs. Adams leaned forward to touch Emma's hand, and with her gesture Emma thought of her mother a second time, a memory released by the faint scent of lemon verbena that Mrs. Adams used as perfume, or else by the actual physical touch of one woman's hand on hers. She had lived so long with the huge Falstaffian presence of her father, she was devoted to her father . . .

"You are very lovely, my dear," Mrs. Adams said. "Think of it. A published writer and lovely as well."

"Thank you."

"The point of my poem is that we are all like servants to men. They are all masters. A woman is no better than a slave."

"I am not sure," Emma said carefully—she was in the President's mansion, she thought, speaking intimately to the President's wife; America was the most amazing country on earth. "I'm not sure I quite agree."

Mrs. Adams patted her hand again. "Like slaves," she repeated. Tears filled the dark eyes. A sad, small woman, pinched by life, defeated by life, dreaming of Europe and her youth, unwilling to *act*. She scraped her fingers around the empty bowl of chocolates. The contrast, Emma thought, was not between the literate, aristocratic Mrs. Adams and poor Rachel Jackson, as she had imagined, but between Louisa Adams and herself.

CHAPTER

13

John Coffee's Personal Narrative

FOR ONCE IT WASN'T RACHEL.

No, we did the stupidest thing in our lives all by ourselves, with just a little help, as most of Tennessee knows, from the Bentons.

I start with Jackson and money, what my old Virginia mother used to call that well-known root, branch, and tree of all evil.

Now to put it bluntly, Jackson is a man who likes his money and hates to be cheated of it. The moment our division arrived in Nashville from Natchez, Jackson sent Colonel Thomas Hart Benton galloping straight on to Washington City; purpose: to shame the War Department into reimbursing him for the personal funds he had spent on the march home.

Meanwhile his brigade auditor, a Pennsylvania transplant named Billy Carroll, who had been a singularly unpopular man out in the field, continued to pester the officers for their accounts in Nashville. I have never known a *popular* auditor anywhere, of course, but Billy Carroll compounded his normal disadvantages, first by being efficient—a Yankee trait that we do not always love in the South—and second by being delicate, fair; effeminate, to tell the truth.

Jackson has and has always had the remarkable capacity to look past a man's appearance—how else could he put up with that feathered dandy Sam Houston?—and he paid no attention whatever to Carroll's manners. He thought Carroll was a splendid young man of great intellect, that was all, and he showed him every possible interest and favor, which naturally made Carroll more unpopular than ever.

At some point on the march Carroll and a second lieutenant named Littleton Johnston quarreled; nobody remembers the subject. But Johnston, itching for trouble, challenged him to a duel. Haughty, sneering, Carroll drew himself up straight and dusted off his shoulders with one delicate hand and then the other and simply refused to accept the challenge, on the profoundly insulting grounds that Johnston was no gentleman. (True.) Whereupon, Johnston ripped and spat and roared and finally persuaded one of the hotheads looking on to carry the challenge for him.

Jesse Benton, younger brother of Thomas Hart Benton, is notable for having no sense. Johnston wrote out a new challenge, Jesse delivered it to Carroll's house, and Carroll once again refused to bother with it. And this time, having worked himself into a froth about honor and debts and goddamned Yankee auditors, Jesse challenged Carroll on his own. Which Carroll, given the Bentons' social standing in Nashville, had to accept.

Not one of the junior officers would serve as Carroll's second. Nobody in Nashville would. So, baffled now and almost disgraced, Billy Carroll rode out to the Hermitage (like the bold Yankee he was) and asked General Jackson himself to do that honor.

I was there—for a long part of my life, it seems, I was always there—and I sat in a corner and listened. Those were my "diary days," and I wrote down exactly what Jackson said. He said, "Why Captain Carroll, I'm not the man for you. I'm forty-six years old. Years ago I would have gone out with pleasure to help you, but at my time of life it would be extremely injudicious. You must get a man nearer your own age."

And he ran his hand through his bristle-brush hair and showed his gray teeth in a Scotch-Irish smile, as if to say he remembered those years, and not unfondly.

He was right about Billy Carroll's shrewdness. Another man would have given up on the spot, because Jackson's "no" is about as firm as the language permits. But Carroll stood there—Jackson was sitting in his old pine rocker, newspaper on his lap—and, deliberately or not, he imitated the General's manner by running *his* hand through his hair, and finally he spoke the magic word.

"General, this is not an ordinary quarrel, you know. This is a *conspiracy*. They want my commission and they want to run me out of the country."

At the word *conspiracy* Jackson threw down his paper and jumped straight up, quivering. Jackson believes in Fate and he believes in Conspiracy—they may be the very same thing, you will say—how else could he account for society's behavior toward Rachel? (I have brought her in after all, I guess.) How else could he account for the way the administration had left him to dangle, idle in the middle of war? Or Jefferson's persecution of Burr?

He kicked the rocker aside and jammed his thumbs in his vest. "Billy Carroll," he said, "make your mind easy on *one* point. Nobody will run you out of the country as long as Andrew Jackson lives in it. I'll ride with you to Nashville right this minute."

All three of us rode, and in the annals of diplomacy Jackson's efforts that day would take an honorable place. The General called Johnston and Benton and all his junior officers in, bought them drinks at the Nashville Inn, and charmed and calmed everybody's temper down off the boil. When we left, the young men were shaking hands at the bar and drinking toasts to each other.

But when we woke up next morning, there was Billy Carroll again, with a *second* hung-over challenge from Jesse Benton, and this time Jackson was so disgusted he agreed to serve as Carroll's second.

More than that, since Carroll was the challenged party, he had the right to choose the distance, and Jackson, alternately grim and laughing, had him write back that they would start back-to-back and draw their pistols at ten feet—ten feet is an *amazing* short distance for a gunfight, you have only to stand by a wall or a door yourself and walk three paces and turn to see the effect.

Jesse grumbled, but he agreed. This was on a Friday, and the duel was set for Monday. The next two days Jackson did nothing but coach Billy Carroll on what to do. According to the rules, he said, there were three approved ways to wheel when you started from a back-to-back, and we went down into a hollow of trees behind the Hermitage and watched Billy practice all of them. He could place his left heel in the arch of his right foot, he could stand with his feet close together, or (best) stand with his feet apart and wheel in either direction. Jackson, forty-six years old, in his shirtsleeves and red suspenders, stood with his back to a sapling and demonstrated each one, then made Billy drill over and over, with live ammunition. Two full days of this—the blacks would lean on their hoes or just stretch out flat on the ground and watch us, grinning—until Sunday night Jackson grunted and clapped Billy's shoulder and said it would do.

Six o'clock the next morning we met in a field near Clover Bottom. It was one of those sublime Tennessee dawns when mist floats up in little white ropes over the Stones River and the big oaks and elms on the banks are lit green-gold at the top and sleepy black down on their trunks, and the ducks and birds are starting to rise and dry their wings and the clouds in the east look like sweet burning stubble.

Sublime above, comic below.

Billy and Jesse took their positions back-to-back in the grass. John Armstrong, Jesse's second, held up his hand and paused.

"Prepare!" he said.

Both of them cocked their pistols.

"Fire!"

Jesse took his three steps almost running, wheeled quick—and *squatted*! One loud shot, and Billy jerked his left thumb up with a curse. But there was Jesse still squatting, and like every one of the Benton men I ever saw he filled out the backside of his trousers substantially, and something more, and Billy, off-balance because of his thumb, fired once and sent his bullet raking straight across poor Jesse's big exposed posterior.

I was laughing (Armstrong was laughing), but Jackson was outraged and stomped all over the dawn, saying you had to wheel and stay *erect* and Jesse's conduct was a *disgrace* and he hoped he was *mortally wounded*.

Which he wasn't, of course. He stayed in bed for a week (facedown), while Nashville had its laugh, but then he was up again and ready for trouble.

In hindsight, so to speak, we should have seen that Thomas Hart Benton was a much more formidable man than Jesse, and Thomas was just then returning from Washington City to Tennessee in a bloody-minded mood. He had got Jackson's money all right, but just barely, and people in Washington had treated him rudely and kept him waiting because he was only militia and not regular army, and Jackson's militia at that. So instead of coming all the way home he had stopped for a while in Knoxville where he could put a little distance between himself and Jackson and maybe apply for a regular army commission. But in Knoxville Thomas kept running into Jesse and Jesse's friends and all those Jackson enemies from the past, who had been silenced by the great march home from Natchez. Thomas was as hot-tempered as his brother. He paced the taverns and gnashed his teeth and made outrageous sputtering threats. But he kept away from Nashville.

Somebody foreign—you will probably know the quotation, Mr. Hamilton—has said that all our troubles come about because we can't just sit still in a room and be quiet. Benton wasn't quiet. Jackson wasn't quiet. The General heard reports of Benton's language, and in his usual clear-the-decks manner wrote and demanded to know if Benton meant to challenge him to a duel.

Benton wrote straight back, and he must have been proud of his answer because he had it printed three days running in the Nashville *Register* as a full-page advertisement. He had four specific complaints:

1. That it was very poor business in a man of your age and standing to be conducting a duel about nothing between young men who had no harm against each other, and that you would have done yourself more honor by advising them to reserve their courage for the public enemy.
2. That it was mean in you to draw a challenge from my brother by carrying him a bullying note from Mr. C. dictated by your self, and which left him no alternative but a duel or disgrace.
3. That if you could not have prevented a duel you ought at least to have conducted it in the usual mode, and on terms equal to both parties..
4. That on the contrary you conducted it in a savage, unequal, unfair, and base manner.

Mostly correct, I guess. But Jackson brushed it aside. Had Benton said he would challenge him? That was all that counted. Benton replied he had not.

But nobody stayed in their rooms. Benton continued to mutter about

the unfair back-to-back "French" way of dueling, and his friends continued to pick away at Jackson's reputation (skirting close to Rachel's Sacred
Name again), and Jackson, infuriated, began to see all his newly won
honor and fame crumbling away.

He called me and his nephew Stockley Hays into the front room of the
Hermitage. "I have a good mind to punish Benton," he told us, and drew
his horsewhip out and cracked it the length of the rug. And we both knew
what he meant.

It was September third or fourth by then. The Bentons had just ridden
into Nashville and taken rooms in the City Hotel. Jackson and Stockley
and I went into town and took *our* rooms across the square at the Nashville Inn, where Jackson always stayed. Next morning Jackson and I came
outside and stood on the sidewalk and I proposed we walk to the post
office to get our mail.

The City Hotel burned down a few years back, but in those days the
two hotels sat at right angles to each other, not a hundred yards apart, on
the city square. The post office was just beyond the City Hotel. To reach it
we could either turn left and walk to the corner and turn right and walk
past the City Hotel, or we could cut diagonally across the square. We cut
across the square, and as we did Thomas Benton came to the doorway of
the City Hotel and looked daggers at us.

"Do you see that fellow?" I asked Jackson.

"Oh yes," Jackson said without turning his head. "I have my eye on
him."

We went into the post office and read our mail, not saying a word, then
we came outside, Jackson in the lead, carrying his riding whip in his right
hand, his left hand on the small sword that official gentlemen wore in
those days. And this time we started up the sidewalk, not across the
square, going straight in front of the City Hotel.

Both Bentons now waited at the door, scowling like Indians. As Jackson, still in front of me, came abreast of Thomas, he suddenly spun
around and raised his whip and cried, "Now, you damned rascal, defend
yourself!"

Thomas was fast. He dove in his pocket for a gun. Jackson was faster.
He dropped the whip and drew his own pistol while Benton's hand was
still in his coat. Benton took two steps backward. Jackson aimed at his
head and walked forward. Benton went back.

Not a sound now. Perfect silence up and down the street. Here and there a pale face watched from a door. Jackson advanced, gun in hand. Benton retreated, hand in pocket. Like two stage actors in a pantomime they marched this way down the long side porch of the hotel, past the open door of the bar, and I remember thinking—time holds its *breath* at such a moment—how the only thing we could any of us hear in the whole city square was the slow *thump-thump* of their boots on the wood.

Then the porch reached a corner. The bootsteps halted. Out of a side door lunged *Jesse* Benton with a yell, aiming his pistol and firing, and Jackson fired, and all three of them were gone in a cloud of smoke and noise.

I ran like a demon. When I rounded the corner Thomas was standing with his pistol drawn and Andrew Jackson was lying prostrate at his feet and his whole left shoulder was a pulp of blood. I must have yelled, but all I remember was springing toward Thomas Benton and firing my pistol and missing. I must have *roared* then, because I flipped my pistol around and made it a club and swung the butt at Benton's skull. He dodged my hand and slipped and fell down a set of stairs, head over heels.

With that I whirled and went to Jackson and pulled his bloody torso, just about lifeless, into my arms, and people have said I was weeping but I don't know.

All the while Jesse Benton, whose pistol it was that had wounded the General, was standing against a wall and trying to reload, until down the porch raced Stockley Hays. He saw at a glance that Jesse had shot his uncle, and he snatched from his sword cane a long, glittering blade, which he thrust at Jesse's very heart. If it had struck it would have pinned him to the wall like a rag, but it hit a big horn button on Jesse's coat and broke in half. In a paroxysm of fury Stockley flung him to the floor and pulled out a dagger.

I watched in a kind of stupor with Jackson in my arms. Stockley was astride Jesse Benton, holding him down with one hand. He raised the dirk to plunge it into his chest. Jesse frantically seized his coat sleeve and wrenched, and Stockley only managed to cut his arm and his hand, but the blood sprayed everywhere as they rolled and fought. Stockley tore his knife free and raised it again—I saw it flashing red and silver, high in the air—and he was about to *bury* it in Jesse when somebody grabbed his arm and somebody else pulled him off and Jesse rolled away screaming, though I never heard a sound.

The Bentons had loaded their pistols with two lead balls and a steel slug in each barrel. Jesse's slug had shattered Jackson's left shoulder. One of the lead balls had embedded itself in the bone of the left arm, where it still sits to this day. He was unconscious when we got him to his room in the Nashville Inn, bleeding so much he soaked through two mattresses before we could stanch it.

Every doctor in Nashville was soon in that room, and all but the youngest one of them recommended immediate amputation of the left arm.

We thought Jackson was passed out with the shock. The senior doctor whipped off his coat and called for a basin of hot water. Another one unpacked his saw from his bag. Just then Jackson opened his eyes and popped straight up from his pillow. "I'll keep my goddamned arm," he said. And by God he did.

The Bentons had recovered by this time. I went to the window and looked down in the square, where they had gathered an audience.

Thomas saw me at the curtain—I am not hard to spot—and shook his fist, which I ignored. Then he held up the General's dress sword and broke it over his knee, which I also ignored, because I knew that in those five minutes of pure, unadulterated stupidity Jackson and I had broken much worse than a little sword.

I looked at Old Hickory in the bloodstained bed surrounded by doctors and I looked at myself in the mirror behind them, and I thought, after all that hard-earned glory from Natchez, we were both diminished things.

C H A P T E R
14

John Coffee's Personal Narrative

THE OLDER I GROW, THE MORE INCLINED I AM TO CREDIT MR. JEFFERSON'S prophecy—the older I grow, the more inclined I am to credit Mr. Jefferson generally—that in the South at least the different races will never live together peacefully, not in my lifetime or yours or our children's, maybe not till the great convulsions of Apocalypse.

The Indian as I have known him out here in Tennessee is a savage and inhuman enemy, utterly without redeeming mercy (out here best keep your sentimental eastern fictions to yourself), and though I have now lived a decade or more in calm proximity to the Creeks and Cherokees of the Tennessee River country, I will remember to my grave the two red years of 1813 and 1814, when nothing passed between us except bullets and blood.

The War of 1812 was in part an Indian war, of course. The British paid them and gave them guns and turned them loose, and in an evil hour the redcoats found in Tennessee the most terrifying ally they could have possibly wanted, old Chief Tecumseh, a bloodthirsty Shawnee of enormous eloquence and anger, who reminded me then (I might as well say it) of Jackson. As soon as war was officially declared, Tecumseh roared up and down the West like a torch put to a map, raging from Fort Detroit all the way down to Pensacola, slaughtering whites by the hundreds for the sheer savage love of it. Our spies would come back and report his speeches, and the Nashville papers would print them over and over till almost everybody could repeat one from memory—"Let the white race perish!" he would screech, tom-tom rhythm. "They seize your land; they corrupt your women; they trample on the bones of your fathers. Burn their houses, destroy their towns, slay their wives and children! War now! War always! War on the living! War on the dead!"

(That last is pure Jackson, is it not?—*war on the dead!* Pure Scotch-Irish-Shawnee.)

But war on the living first. Not three days before our taproom brawl with the Bentons—for I have never been able to think of it any other way—not three days earlier Tecumseh's southernmost disciple, a ferocious half-breed named William Weatherford, led two or three hundred Creek warriors to the outskirts of a little wooden stockade near Mobile, Alabama, which the locals rather grandly called "Fort Mims."

By then the stockade was filled to bursting with anxious settlers who had abandoned their farms and scurried to safety out of Tecumseh's path. But after a few weeks of relative quiet they were becoming relaxed and careless. They left their gates open during the day. Children played outside. Women strolled down to the lake to do their wash. On the morning of August 30, 1813, Weatherford's scouts crept out of the woods and lay in the hot, muggy fields, invisible and motionless, Indian-fashion, until the dinner drum sounded at noon, and then just as the settlers put aside their rifles and sat down at their tables, the Creeks poured screaming through the two open gates, clubbing and shooting anything that moved. Twelve white men escaped. Every single white woman was killed and scalped ("war always!"); the pregnant ones Weatherford ordered cut open while they were still alive and the unborn babies trampled to death in the dirt. Every child, every white girl and boy, was killed outright. Most of them were seized by the ankles and whirled about and swung sideways hard against the fences, over and over and over till their brains were dashed into paste. Then the Creeks burned the fort to the ground and vanished.

When the first troops reached the scene four days later, the air was black with buzzards, and hundreds of dogs and coyotes were drawn from every part of the forest and were gnawing the bones and the bodies. The soldiers gagged and covered their mouths and buried what was left in two open pits.

We heard the news in Nashville a week after that. In New York and Boston it took a month more for the story to get in the newspapers, and even then hardly anybody noticed, because that very same week we won our first victory of the war—Admiral Perry in the Battle of Lake Erie—and at the same time over in Europe, where the northern states are always gazing like tranced cows through a fence, over there across the ocean Napoleon Bonaparte had just taken another giant step toward Elba. New York (never mind a few hundred Southern corpses) declared a month-long celebration.

Meanwhile, a thousand miles away in Nashville, Jackson lay helpless in his bed. His arm and shoulder were smashed and crippled. His features were gaunt and starch white from loss of blood. He worked his jaw and drank whiskey and brooded in Scotch-Irish silence. Nobody visited him, nobody declared a celebration. Nobody guessed, not even Andrew Jackson himself in his pride, that an obscure and unimportant little Indian massacre down by the Gulf of Mexico was about to make him as famous almost as Bonaparte. (I indulge in a rhetorical flourish.) History licked her finger and turned the page.

"IT is astonishing," said James A. Hamilton Jr. walking into Coffee's study with his thumbs in his vest and an unlit cigar in his teeth, "*absolutely* astonishing how instantly he can change from one Jackson to another."

Coffee put down his pen and turned over his sheet of paper. Hamilton sat down in the opposite chair. He took out the cigar and frowned at its stub, then carefully bit off the end and spat it out.

Coffee placed a volume of Shakespeare on top of the pen and suppressed the urge to spit himself.

"Faster than Janus," Hamilton said, working the cigar back and forth and showing his parrot profile. "We were driving back from Clover Bottom just now, and he was in front with the reins talking to Rachel, old gray heads together like a pair of Tennessee lovebirds. Then some hapless teamsters going the other way drove their wheel accidentally against our wheel and gave dear Rachel a bump. And you know, General Coffee, in less than a heartbeat Jackson was off his bench and down in the road and letting out such a horrible volley of language, I swear those poor teamsters actually blushed. They slunk away down the road like whipped dogs. I brought you a cigar."

Coffee took the cigar and pinched the end with his thumbnail instead of biting.

"They call these 'stogies' over in Nashville," Hamilton said. He struck a phosphorous match on his chair arm and leaned forward to light first his cigar, then Coffee's. "But I can't figure out why."

"Because Conestoga wagon drivers smoke them," Coffee said between puffs. "Stogies. Like the teamsters that bumped you probably."

"Something else," Hamilton said, and Coffee looked up from the cigar, unsurprised. By now he and Hamilton had evolved a style of communication in which Coffee explained away or managed Jackson's excesses—translated, Jackson's *temper*—and Hamilton relayed in his own oblique New York way what the money backers and eastern editors wanted of Old Hickory. It was modern politics, Coffee understood, but it left a blue film on your tongue like a stogie.

"Something else," Hamilton repeated. "I spent a week in Kentucky and Ohio, and I learned Lewis Robards is dead, for sure."

"Everybody thought so," Coffee said. He hadn't smoked a cigar in years. Filthy habit, worse than spitting. He took a last diplomatic puff for Jackson.

Hamilton patted his vest pocket. "Notarized death certificate. Now, you remember Peyton Short?"

"The boarder who lived with Robards and Rachel when they were first married, yes."

"Dead, too, apparently."

"Well, then—"

"Well, then, we were concerned, damnit," Hamilton said, and Coffee noticed with curiosity that both of them, in the same gesture at the same moment, held out their cigars to tap the ash. "I told you about those documents in 1824, the ones that never turned up. Some of us wondered. We said to ourselves Robards was a jealous man, Rachel was the Aphrodite of the Bluegrass. Add a young bachelor boarder like Peyton Short and count on trouble. . . . But it turns out Short was just a typical backwoods drifter. Left after two or three months and headed west."

Coffee asked the question that would never occur to a Yankee. "Family?"

"He had a sister in Frankfort—dead, too—and he got married there and ran a store. End of Short. The one I'm interested in now is a much more impressive man named Jack Jouett, who married Robards's sister."

Sometimes Coffee allowed himself the thought that America was the smallest country in the world, or else Providence took a special droll interest in it. He had been two words from writing about Jackson's belief in Providence when Hamilton had walked in. "Jack Jouett of Virginia?" he asked, and Hamilton nodded. "My mother knew Jack Jouett," Coffee said. "I knew him, too, when I was a boy."

Hamilton was busy rearranging items on the table beside his chair: pen, inkwell, a dirty glass the servants had overlooked. "Now, I never think of you as a Westerner, General Coffee," he said, peering up through a haze of smoke. "Nobody else out here ever asks me about France or New York or the theater. You have that old-fashioned Virginia air of *cultivation*, sir."

"Jack Jouett was the boy who rode fifty miles at night to warn Thomas Jefferson the redcoats were coming. He had scars on his face from where the branches and limbs whipped him, he was famous for years in Virginia."

Hamilton was no more interested in stories of Jefferson than of Aaron Burr.

"Well, he was famous as a ladies' man in Kentucky, so I would take as a personal favor . . ." the lawyer said, without needing to specify the favor. "Because the campaign has hit a new pitch of scandal back East—every day a different story, Rachel or Robards or some damned duel you people out here have conveniently forgotten to mention. Do you know there's a weekly paper that's just called the *Anti-Jackson Expositor*? And now John Q. has evidently decided to swallow his pride and make a pair of campaign speeches on his own behalf, in Baltimore and Philadelphia. His old father would spin in his grave, of course, but he's a powerful man, he's the *President* and people will listen. As Van Buren says, we can't afford to win the popular vote and lose the electoral college *again*, the way we did in '24. The country won't stand for it. What is that you've been reading?"

Coffee swiveled in his chair and held out the volume of Shakespeare for Hamilton to see. "I was curious who Enobarbus was."

"From *Antony and Cleopatra*," Hamilton said, puffing smoke, obviously puzzled.

"You said I was Jackson's Enobarbus," Coffee reminded him. "The Tennessee Enobarbus. So I looked him up. The blunt old Roman soldier, loyal to a fault. Only, I find at the end of the play he turns coat and betrays his hero Antony."

Hamilton puffed a moment longer, his sharp, calculating little profile caught in a pale shaft of light from the window. For an instant he looked exactly like his father's son. "Then Antony deserved it," he said.

Three Scenes from the Creek Wars.

Mr. Hamilton sees many Jacksons, I see one.

Scene number one.

You will hardly want a full history of all the blood we spilled that first year. When the news of Fort Mims finally reached Nashville, Jackson staggered out of his sickbed and wrote an untruthful announcement (*"The health of your general is restored"*) and set off with twenty-five hundred volunteers to track down the Creeks.

Now, western Tennessee is one kind of country, open, rolling, drained by fine, wide rivers, crested with tall, straight forests. Tennessee is like the top of a splendid table. But northern Alabama is another kind of place altogether, a wrinkled old bearskin rug of a country thrown anyhow in a corner, a smelly compactness of brown stick-pine forests and unhealthy creeks and ravines and mud canyons without end. We disappeared. We simply vanished into the stick-pines—an unsociable, arrogant tree I have come to hate—and nobody could find us anymore but Indians.

We had our skirmishes, we had our victories, but all the while we were drifting south like a thin line of smoke, and after two weeks not one of our suppliers in Tennessee could reach us. Twenty-five hundred men required ten wagonloads of food per day, a thousand barrels of grain per week, twenty tons of meat; but except for what we could forage or hunt in the pines we had not a peck, not a pound. By late October the men were grumbling, the horses were starving. By November men and horses were both starving.

I well remember (but this is not yet the scene) how Jackson, who could not squeeze his shattered left arm in his coat sleeve or even bear the weight of his little general's gold epaulette on his shoulder—Jackson, who weighed a hundred and ten pounds at most by then and had to lean on a sapling to cough out his orders, Jackson for three full days lived on uncooked tripe without bread or seasoning while his men ate the few skinny cattle we had brought from Nashville. Then those ran out, too. I was sitting under a tree with him one morning when a flat-bellied, woe-begone soldier approached us and begged for some food. "It has always been a rule with me," Jackson said, "never to turn away a hungry man. I will cheerfully divide with you what I have." He put his good hand in his pocket and drew out a few dry acorns. "This is my breakfast," he said.

The soldiers loved him—they called him "Father General," which delighted him—and they suffered through a good deal more than any of us had ever expected. But they were only volunteers, after all, and Washington had forgotten us, and the suppliers had forgotten us, and the Creeks were getting even harder to find than food. The volunteers began to grumble. They began to study their enlistment papers. The most malcontent among them started to claim that their term was up and they could leave for home whenever they wanted, with or without the Father General's permission.

By mid-November we had reached a state of open mutiny. Nothing was holding that army together except Jackson's will, and nothing was holding Jackson himself together except that same implacable will.

On November 17, 1813 (I have marked the day in my diary), one whole company of soldiers formed on their own and started to march up the road, north toward Tennessee. Jackson mounted his horse and galloped ahead. Half a mile on, I happened to be stationed with a few of my cavalry, inspecting our pickets. Jackson ordered us spread across the

road—five of us altogether—and told us to shoot any deserter who tried
to pass. Then he rode his horse twenty feet forward and stopped.

Up they came, not a company now, but a full regiment, four hundred
men.

In front of them, straight as a shaft, Jackson sat on his horse.

You read an expression sometimes—"his eyes flashed"—and you take
it as pure metaphor, an unreal figure of speech. Except that for once in
my life I saw it happen. Jackson suddenly stood up in his stirrups; his hair
bristled, his eyes flashed, and his voice roared till they heard him in
Tennessee. By the Eternal, he *ordered* them to stop!

They stopped. They shuffled. They looked around at each other.

He backed his horse toward mine and without looking or speaking
stretched his right arm back. One of my men handed him a musket. He
rode forward again; halted. Rested the musket on the neck of his horse
and aimed square at the mutineers. *By* the Eternal, he would shoot the
first man who took a step!

I rode up on his right, Major Reid on his left.

A minute passed. Two.

Somebody's horse stamped. Somebody coughed.

In the front ranks a man looked down at his shoes in the dirt. In the
back a few men started to retreat. More peeled away. More.

When they had all melted back to their posts and the road was as blank
and empty as the rest of Alabama, Jackson thrust the musket back to my
soldier, then spurred his horse and was gone.

Afterward, it turned out that the musket was broken and wouldn't have
fired. But I thought Jackson would have *willed* it to shoot.

Scene number two.

Much shorter.

Only two weeks before the mutiny, in the late afternoon of a cold,
foggy Alabama autumn, I was leading a detachment of a thousand men,
nearly half our army, down the black Coosa River. Jackson had been
forced to stay in camp, ill with the dysentery. On his orders we were
following a party of friendly Creeks—they wore white feathers and white

deers' tails to distinguish them from hostiles—toward an Indian settlement called Talluschatchee, where a certain body of warriors was thought to be hiding.

We arrived at the outskirts, still in the pine forests, just an hour before sunrise. I could hear their drums and war-screams—drums in the darkness, Mr. Hamilton, are one of the great devices of military *terror*—but I gave my orders anyway, just as Jackson had drawn them up for me. I scratched a few lines in the wet sand by the Coosa. Cavalry to the right, crossing over a swampy creek in front of the town. Infantry to the left, myself at their head, going through the forest double file to unite with the cavalry and encircle the town. As simple and direct and Jacksonian as two hands around a throat.

At the first rays of the sun we charged—straight ahead, firing, running so fast I thought we would beat our own bullets to the mark. But the Creeks jumped up and fought back, furious, absolutely savage. And for ten minutes it was anybody's battle, because their Prophet was on the roof of a house scampering back and forth and waving his Red Stick and yelling that they could crush us, and the Creeks fought like they believed him, till one of our men took aim with a pistol and brought that Indian tumbling down like a shot bird. In the end, we killed two hundred warriors and burned every house in the village, and I lost five men killed and forty-one wounded, mostly by arrows.

I am ashamed to say that some of their dead were women. (One old squaw killed two of my men, leaning back against her door and shooting her bow between her feet.) And worse yet, a pitifully slain young mother was found still embracing her child, a little boy not yet a year old. I ordered all the women and children sent back to Jackson's camp where they would be held safe till the end of the war, and this little child was brought in with the others.

When Jackson saw him, he was lying in his tent, almost crippled with pain. But he stood up and walked over somehow and looked at the baby and looked at the squaws and finally had the interpreter ask them to feed the child. They said, "No, all his family are dead, kill him too."

All his family are dead. You could see the General go literally stiff. You could see his mind and his will working. What other boy he knew about, thirty years ago, had been left an orphan by war, abandoned, as good as dead? Kill him too.

He turned that hard, long Scotch-Irish face to me. "Bring him to my tent," he said.

When I had washed the child up and carried him in, Jackson was down on his knees, rummaging through the pathetic little pile of stores he had. Then he came up with a paper sack of brown sugar, and this he mixed with warm water and took the baby on his lap. He sat there like Achilles in his tent, surrounded by rifles and bullets and swords, and he would dip the fingers of his good hand into the brown sugar and let the baby suck from his fingers.

Lyncoya he named him, and sent him home to Rachel, where they quietly adopted him.

Scene number three.

I have seen the slanderous and vilifying "coffin handbill." This is what really happened.

Our victories in 1813 brought no end to the mutinies. Sometimes, because the soldiers were flushed and full of themselves, winning only made things worse. Jackson labored like twenty men to bring us supplies, to keep our spirits up, to keep up *discipline*, but the truth is, those were dark days, our army was falling apart. One brigade disbanded when their enlistments legally expired; the second, and last, brigade would disband on January 14, 1814, and some of their troops were already slipping away. By early January our original army was down to a hundred and thirty miserable men, mostly officers, sitting inside an empty stockade on the Tombigbee River (worse than the Coosa). In a week or so more there would only be Jackson and me.

I have often thought that two things happened that winter. The first is that Jackson was seized, as great men often are, by a sense of his own Destiny, his own greatness. Those months he probably wrote more letters and made more speeches than ever before or since in his life—speech after speech to the troops, letter after letter to Washington, to the governor of Tennessee, to the U.S. commanding general in North Carolina. It was as if—to be very wise after the fact, Mr. Hamilton—he suddenly saw himself as an historical personage-to-be, and all these great, slow-moving

events, the settling of the west, the removal of the Indians, the final clash
with the British, all these were providential transformations, and Andrew
Jackson their instrument.

At the most desperate hour, as our first troops started out the gate for
home, we received a letter from Governor Blount of Tennessee ordering
us to retreat. Jackson wrote back instantly. "What retrograde under these
circumstances?" the General said. "I will *perish* first." Look to your reputation, he advised poor old Blount, think how the future will judge
you. "Save Mobile—save the Territory—save yr. frontier from becoming
drenched in blood. . . . You have only to act with a little energy. . . .
Give me a force for six months . . . and all may be safe. Withhold it,
and all is lost, and the reputation of the state and yrs. with it."

We had various ways to discipline the troops. Cowardly officers were
sentenced to wear a wooden sword. For desertion we would sentence a
soldier to ride a bucking wooden horse contraption with ten pounds of
weight attached to each leg, or else wear his coat inside out with half his
face blackened and the word *Deserter* sewn on the back.

None of it worked. Deserters leaked out like water. But Jackson's letters
stirred up the press and the people back home, and in February Governor
Blount finally sent us a whole new army. The trouble was, this one turned
out to be just as restless and unreliable as the first. To our amazement,
while the Creeks, rearmed by the British, were gathering for a spring
offensive, our new soldiers began grumbling and swaggering and poring
over their law books, exactly like the old ones. And so the second thing
happened. One rainy, flat February morning a new recruit named John
Woods, scarcely eighteen years old, was standing guard. Some passing
officer gave the boy permission to go to his tent for a blanket, and Woods
stopped on the way to grab his breakfast, which he had missed. Another
officer ordered him back to his post. Woods, sitting dry on a bench with
his hot food before him and the rain outside, refused to obey the order.
The officer tried to arrest him, and Woods kicked over the table and
grabbed his musket and swore he would shoot.

"Mutiny!" somebody yells.

Out of his tent storms Jackson—the very word must have struck him
like lightning. "Shoot him! Shoot him!" he cries. "Blow ten balls through
his d——d villain's body!"

We had seen such episodes every day, the army was accustomed to
shrug them off. But this time Jackson knew the Creeks were waiting,

knew History was building itself to a crest. He court-martialed Woods, and the court found him guilty, and although twenty officers one-by-one slunk up to him in private and asked for leniency for the boy, Jackson never yielded. They stood young John Woods up against a log and tied a black handkerchief over his eyes and aimed their rifles.

If you had glanced over across the muddy stockade at that moment, you would have seen Jackson a hundred yards away in his tent, the flaps open, sitting at his camp desk with his half-moon glasses on, writing another letter to History.

Major Reid raised his sword. The rifles cracked. The General never looked up.

If you could break Jackson open with an axe, break down all his doors and locks, you would find a vast landscape of jagged ice, with a small boy shipwrecked in the middle.

Many Jeffersons; one Jackson.

Noble Capitol dome on one side of the coin, eagle's claw on the other; same coin.

I am troubled by recalling these things and thinking these thoughts, and I will write no more.

The army performed magnificently; after we shot John Woods we killed a thousand Indians.

CHAPTER
15

The left one," Chase said, and propped himself up on his elbow. It was a July afternoon in Washington City, hot as the inside of a steamboat furnace, and exactly two weeks and one day since Emma Colden, like the muse of desire, had spelled out *Yes* on her printer's proof tray. Chase shuddered. Where in Jackson's green world did he come up with such atrociously bad phrases as "the muse of desire"?

Beside him, like the muse of real life, Emma sat cross-legged on the bed, completely naked, frowning down slightly at her left breast.

"Since you ask," Chase said, "the left one is bigger, but not by much, and it will be far more scientific—"

She slapped his hand away and cupped both breasts with her own hands. "Did you know," she said, still frowning and looking down, "that your friend William Short lived openly with a woman in Paris for three whole years in the 1790s? She was the widow of a French duke and wouldn't marry him. But they set up housekeeping together, as my father says, and came to be known as a right old scandal, even in Paris."

"We didn't move in the same circles, William Short and I," Chase told her. "But speaking of circles—"

This time she grinned and arched her back like a tawny blond cat, and Chase pulled her down to him, kicking away the tangled sheets and feeling the silky heat of her skin, breasts, nipples, belly glide against him; belly again, legs. On the pillow her face was red in streaks, her eyelids closed and dark. Her thighs moved softly apart. When he rose on his elbows and entered, her eyes flew suddenly open and her lips formed a silent red O.

For a moment they lay completely motionless on the bed. Outside the hotel window a wagon rattled by; a dog barked. The wind blew a watery ribbon of sunlight across the wall, over their heads.

"My father says," Emma said beneath him, hoarsely, beginning to move her hips, "that Lord Palmerston told him he and his wife . . . consummated nine times on their wedding night."

"Do not," Chase said. He was breathing heavily; he could hear his heart echo all over the room. "Do not quote your father . . . just now."

Emma giggled. "Are you doing sums in your head?" She twisted, squirmed, reached one hand down, under the flat muscles of his stomach. Chase groaned. "Nine times nine," she said, her own breath coming faster, her fingertips stroking, tips of flame. "Nine times—" Chase covered her lips with his mouth, braced on his knees. An invisible wave of light lifted them up and carried them forward, rising. In the long pulse of pleasure that burst through the light, he thought first, that she *was* the most beautiful woman he had ever seen; second, he would *never ever* let her go; third, eighty-one.

The little black boy dressed as an Indian brought them tea and cakes, and Emma hid behind the screen. When she sat down on the bed again she was still naked, but she carried a handful of Chase's notes and papers that she had taken from his table.

"You haven't written anything," she said, turning the pages. Her breasts jiggled, and Chase felt himself stir again. "Not really. Just notes and outlines and bits of summary. Nothing in fair copy." Her eyes strayed. "Stop that. You're not Lord Palmerston."

"*Noblesse oblige.* It's not only not in fair copy—" he shook his head at his double negatives; Emma balanced her teacup on his naked belly "—but what there is of it is terrible. Terrible writing."

"But you work all day."

"I *fidget* all day, I waste time. I go to the Congressional Library, I read newspapers, I interview editors, congressmen who know Jackson, I call on naked proofreaders at Gales and Seaton"—he gestured (carefully) at his notes and books—"I procrastinate. In Paris one year I wrote a weekly column for a paper. I called it 'Je Suis un Flâneur.' "

"*Flâneur* means 'walker.' "

"I've walked every inch of Washington, avoiding work."

"Short won't pay you."

"He hasn't. I have two hundred and three dollars in the hotel safe, my entire fortune."

She frowned and looked down at the disorderly sheets of paper.

" 'Who steals my purse steals trash,' " Chase said.

Still frowning, she placed the teacup and papers on a side table. "Emma."

She put one finger to her lips as if to shush him, just as she had done at the piano concert. Then she slowly leaned forward, smiled . . . and crossed her eyes.

Chase laughed out loud. "They'll get stuck that way."

"Shhh!" She stretched out beside him and drew his right hand up to her left breast. "My favorite," she murmured. "In Paris you had nine hundred times nine hundred lovers. Yes? No? Don't say." She brought his hand to her mouth, kissed his knuckles, replaced it on her breast. She smelled of sandalwood and sweat. Chase moved his palm gently in a circle and thought of numbers. Since that afternoon two weeks before, they had dined together three times, driven once to the Little Falls of the Potomac for a picnic, and sneaked into his hotel six times to make love, first at night, now more boldly in broad daylight. His two hundred and three dollars would run out in a week. He didn't give a damn.

"In Yorkshire," Emma said with her eyes closed, "when a woman holds out her hand in church to get married, she keeps one thumb free to show her independence."

"You're independent." He was puzzled; distracted; moved to the right. "You work for a living."

"I will never go back to Europe," she said, and her voice was solemn. But she turned and made the mattress ties creak, and she drew his hand lower; then lower. Then began to cry out in soft, unintelligible sounds, not solemn at all.

Afterward, Chase stood beside her trying clumsily to tie the ribbons and button the buttons that made up the back of her dress, but his fingers were mutton sticks, and Emma finally pushed him away and did it herself without looking.

"When I was a girl my father took me to see Chunee the Elephant in London. He could tie a ribbon with his trunk."

"Your father loves spectacles and shows." He tried to untie a ribbon with his teeth, Chunee in reverse.

"My father loves life. He loves me."

"Yesterday morning John Randolph sent me a note to meet him about Andrew Jackson, and then he didn't keep the appointment."

"John Randolph is a third-degree chthonian gargoyle," Emma said, and finished the last ribbon with a snap. And with the snap her mood seemed to change abruptly and for good. "I have to go." She straightened her skirt and reached for her bonnet.

"Stay a little longer."

"No. I have to go back to work. If William Short had any backbone, you know, he would simply *invent* a scandal about Andrew Jackson and *print* it. You write so well, people would believe it, whatever you wrote. But Short's too rich and cautious, and you're too poor and honest." Without looking at him she repeated herself to the mirror. "Much too deplorably honest."

It had almost the ring of a genuine criticism. "Well, stay for another half hour, reform old deplorable me." Chase placed his hands around her waist and kissed her neck, but she moved brusquely, decisively away. *Post coitum omne animal triste est*, he thought, shrugging. After love every animal is sad. What in the world did *chthonian* mean? Only a typesetter would know.

"People believe whatever they read," Emma said from the door, in her crispest English accent. "It is the most depressing fact in the modern world."

Outside, under a bruised July sky that now threatened rain, they squeezed their way along Pennsylvania Avenue, down the narrow sidewalk that was separated from the street (and the wagons and the horses and the pigs) by a single wooden rail. At the corner of Pennsylvania and Eighth, still in sight of the President's mansion, they ran into a crowd of dirty, boisterous men in shirtsleeves and floppy hats, spilling like a parade out of a saloon. The rail sagged and buckled under the crowd's weight, and they surged backward into the street, looking up and cheering as an enormous "Jackson and Reform" banner was unfurled from the second floor.

Buffeted by shoulders, dogs, flailing boots, Emma caught Chase's arm and shouted into his ear. "If you ever start to think well of democracy, my father says, just go to a Jackson rally!"

He nodded and steered her into the street. A water trough had been trampled to bits, mud and horses on the right, mud and men on the left. Such was the pace of presidential campaigning now; a rally like this was going on at some point in some city nearly every hour of the day. ("The patient is rallying," Gray had written sourly from Cambridge, "the outlook is hopeless.") From inside the saloon they could hear a jubilant "Jackson band" (drummer, banjo, trumpet) playing "The Hunters of Kentucky" while the audience whooped in chorus.

At the edge of the crowd somebody had set up a wooden booth to sell Hickory Hats and beer. Next to it, rocking with the music, a freckled boy was completely encased in the newest attention-getting device, two white cardboard placards that might have been giant slices of bread, strapped front and back over his shoulders and called "sandwiches." The placard that Chase could see had a black silhouette of Jackson and the simple, dazzling caption: OUR HERO. Over the din of the music the boy mouthed toothless words and shoved a miniature hickory broom at Emma.

"To sweep the rascals out!" It was Chase's turn to shout. He reached for her hand and pulled her single file after him, between two quivering teams of horses.

Inside the saloon the band staggered one at a time to a halt, like three drunken soldiers, and an instant later somebody with a megaphone began a chant—"Jackson and Reform! Jackson and Reform!" Emma pressed her hands over her ears and kept them there until they had turned the corner.

"I'm still too British," she began, white-faced, shaking her head. "*My* hero was William the Silent. My father said to tell you—" She paused and smiled with unexpected *tristesse.* Chase stubbornly reached for her hand again. He would wear a sandwich with her portrait, he would make a catalogue raisonné of her smiles: the Smile Direct, the Vanishing Cat, the Courtesan Chthonic. "It doesn't matter. My father said to tell you he's finally been well enough to read your last article."

"From the Spy in Washington?"

"He says he had no idea you were so funny."

"You would need a heart of stone not to be funny about American politics."

"No, he liked the joke about Washington food."

" 'God sends the meat,' " Chase grinned, quoting himself. " 'The Devil sends the cooks.' A Boston proverb, in fact, from the home of the bean and the cod." And as the chant of "Jackson and Reform" died away, he added impulsively, "Join me for dinner tonight at Gadsby's, devils optional. We'll spend the rest of Short's scandalous money."

In front of them Ninth Street ran straight and slightly uphill until, in the discouraged Washington manner, it simply ended flat on its back in a bare field. Emma shook her head and gave him the Smile *Désolé*. "I can't see you," she said, slipping out of his grip—thumb free, he noticed too late. "I meant to tell you. I really meant to be honest."

Chase stood where he was, feeling his heart and belly sink.

"I can't see you tonight," she said, and took a deep breath. "Or after. Senator Sellers gets back, this afternoon." She turned to move away, a swirl of blue, a dark blur against a backdrop of stunted trees and lost avenues.

"From Ohio?" Chase asked, on the whole the most thickheaded thing he had ever said.

And as if on cue, through the open windows of the saloon came a burst of sarcastic applause.

CHAPTER
16

Chthonian. Pertaining to spirits of the underworld. It was a phenomenon of Washington and nowhere else, David Chase thought (not drunk), that because the city had no streetlamps, almost the only lights visible after dark were the oil lanterns flying past on the sides of chthonian carriages.

He stumbled across the black expanse of what he thought was Tenth Street and bumped into a fence. In the distance two small orange lights winked left to right, then disappeared like meteors. An instant later two more appeared, streaking directly toward him six feet over the road.

Chase froze in his tracks (mud) and blinked two hundred times. The lights flew harmlessly past in a thunder of harnesses and wheels. He took a deep breath, sighed, and walked up a row of parked carriages to the door of the French ambassador's home.

"Cherchez la femme," he said to the butler who opened the door.

"Sir?"

"Et le sénateur. I'm Ambassador Chase, I've forgotten my invitation."

"Yes, sir."

"From Chthonia," Chase said, walking in. It was a second phenomenon of Washington that anyone of note who gave a reception or party listed it in advance in the *National Intelligencer* each week. He had already looked in at Gadsby's and the other two respectable restaurants in town; this was the only party or "squeeze," to use the Washington slang, listed. If Ephraim Sellers, he of the independent fortune and indeterminate politics, was going to turn up anyplace else, it would be here. With Emma.

Who would be chthonically glad to see him, Chase thought, lifting a drink from a passing table and launching himself like a raft into the party.

The French ambassador leased a typical two-story Washington frame house, which smelled of plaster and straw. The windows were shaded with muslin. Its moderate *grand salon* held no more than thirty or forty guests, mostly men, all talking loudly to make themselves heard over the strains of a chamber orchestra upstairs (in Washington, for chthonic reasons, you often danced on the second floor of a house). Chase was jostled by a congressman in high boots. He drifted past a shelf of books, a painting of the Loire Valley, an engraving of the Eglise St. Sulpice. He held the thought of Paris as a momentary stay against reality. The carpet was of delicate blue and white Savonnerie design, weighted down at the corners by brass spittoons.

He bowed to a distinguished-looking woman, who he decided (from her turban) was Mrs. Bayard Smith. Bowed and smiled to a western senator he had interviewed about Jackson's boyhood. Put down his glass and retreated into an alcove.

Through a doorway he could see another room, where tables were set up for cards along one wall. Opposite the doorway stood an elegant mahogany bar piled high with bottles and glasses. No women. American prudery decreed that women stay away from open bottles in public places. But men were lined up three deep around the bar, multiplying themselves in the mirror behind it. He listened to the orchestra for a moment, stiffened his shoulders, stepped out of the alcove, and came straight up against—inevitably, as he afterward thought—the smiling face of Charles Francis Adams.

"*Cher espion,*" said Adams, pink as a crayfish. "Come have a drink."

At the nearest table Chase could see Henry Clay, who was notorious for gambling, spread a deck of cards in a fan.

"Or several," Adams said unsteadily.

Nothing so sobering as a drunken Adams, Chase thought; Gadsby's whiskey sloshed inside his head like water in a bucket.

"Or several," Adams repeated, handing him a glass of champagne. "One here, then somewhere else, terrible squeeze."

"Wait by the door," Chase said, and elbowed his way to the foot of the stairs by the hall. Overhead the little orchestra had paused between pieces and he could hear the floorboards of the second story creak and groan under the feet of the dancers. He drank the champagne, then put the glass on a table by the railing—he would leave a trail of empty glasses behind him, like Hansel and Gretel—and mounted the stairs.

They were doing the waltz. Chase stood by the entrance to a long room that had been stripped of furniture except for paintings and six gas lamps on the walls. Thirty or forty more guests waited expectantly. At the far corner of the room the musicians struck up another tune, and one by one, slowly spinning, the figures began to dance. Chase squinted at shadows. She would be wearing a blue dress, of course. He could remember when the waltz was a scandalous dance, even in Paris. The first time he had ever seen it, at the Hôtel de Salm, the gentlemen all wore enormous dragoon spurs on their boots and the ladies hopped and skipped like dervishes to save their dresses.

"Mr. Chase."

He nodded at a side-whiskered man whose name he had forgotten, a Jacksonian politician likewise on Short's interview list. Where had he actually seen him before? What would he say or do if Emma *were* here? Sellers no, Chase yes, vote for Chase. Chase and Reform.

Two by two the dancers passed by. Skirts swirled like blossoms. For reasons of prudery, the men (American, not French) all carried handkerchiefs so that bare hands would be kept apart. No spurs. No Emma. No Sellers, no takers. On the stairway going down again he suddenly stopped and gripped the railing with one hand and came within an ace of laughing out loud. I am, he thought, grinning at somebody going up (not grinning), as obsessed as Andrew Jackson. That is the fact, that is the fact *du soir*. Emma is my Rachel, my obsession. No wonder I can't write a word. Next step, he thought, duel to the death: baguettes at twenty paces.

At the foot of the stairs he found himself backed into a corner while the man in front of him knelt and helped a young woman remove her dancing slippers and put on her outdoor shoes. A new Washington custom—who could have dreamed of it ten years ago?—intended, he had been told, to prevent the indecency of a servant touching the foot of a lady. Maybe there was a need after all for Jackson's brand of democracy. Chase leaned against the wall, inhaled perfume and sweat, and considered that he had fallen into America from another planet, out of the sky.

"Brilliant fine night, sir," said Henry Clay, going up the stairs and counting money.

Then Charles Francis Adams, still pink even in the dark, had his arm and they were back on the chthonian streets.

They walked for five minutes, less, under black, rustling trees, Adams chattering, Chase with his gaze fixed on a cluster of orange lights hovering in the air far ahead, on one of the avenues. When they had almost reached them, the lights unexpectedly flew apart, in three different directions, like fireflies. Moments later they were rounding a corner that Chase recognized as Pennsylvania and Sixth, and on their left was one of Gadsby's numerous hotel annexes, marked (in the absence of streetlamps) by a row of six flaming oil-soaked torches on poles.

"This is a place I never go," Adams said and pulled him in the other direction, down a hot alley, down a set of wobbling stairs, into a low-ceilinged basement.

The place he never went was named Patsy's, and Patsy herself was a giant mulatto woman with a great booming laugh and unsleeved arms like a pair of quivering golden hams. She led them through a card room and a kitchen and upstairs again to a narrow bar lined with wooden booths and tables and filled with tobacco smoke and—Chase permitted himself to think it—the acrid smell of Negroes.

"In New York last week," Adams said as they settled into a booth, "I had a disgraceful spree."

"Alone?" Chase wedged himself in the booth and took an academic interest in sprees.

"Thirty bumpers of champagne," Adams said, and added with the peculiar intensity of speech that made an Adams sound logical no matter what, "I am engaged to be married."

"You've told me that," Chase said. "She lives in Boston."

"And her father is rich, Mr. Peter Chardon Brooks. Look over there."

Chase made himself sit up straighter. The room tipped. A smaller, slenderer version of Patsy was just sitting down in the lap of a drunken white man, he dressed in yellow coat, green cravat, green trousers; she dressed apparently in smoke. Patsy's bulk interposed itself for a moment, depositing glass mugs of beer for each of them, and the girl leaned back into the darkness of the booth until only her bare legs were visible, kicking slowly.

The arrangement, Adams explained, was that you could go upstairs to a sitting room that was divided in four by curtains. That looked out onto a lounge where the girls of the house . . . lounged. When you saw one you fancied, you signaled Patsy and she would lead you upstairs to a private bedroom, though of course once in a while (he inclined his pink head wisely toward the wriggling booth) the girls wandered down.

"And the curtains?" In his skull the night tide of whiskey and champagne was steadily receding, leaving a white spot of pain behind each eye. "Why the curtains?" Could the Spy in Washington print any of this?

Adams drained half his mug, smirked, belched; a miracle of juvenile condescension. "Curtains," he said, "so the secretary of state doesn't sit down next to the secretary of war in the temple of Venus. This is a highly *moral* city, *vous savez.*"

Whiskey receded, beer advanced. Chase listened to Adams describe his spree, or at least focused his vision on Adams's moving lips while shadowy, aromatic forms came and went nearby. Outside it had been pleasantly warm and muggy; here, inside, the heat rose from the kitchen below their feet and the room expanded and contracted rhythmically, under the pressure of flesh and smoke.

"My father," Adams said (and for a giddy instant Chase looked up for him), "is actually an expert on drinking, more than me. I."

Chase raised an unseen eyebrow in the darkness.

"Last year at a party in Boston," Adams said, his pink face suddenly inches away, wreathed in smoke, "somebody served hock with oysters, champagne with the meats, and then Madeiras from covered bottles. My father correctly identified eleven of fourteen different Madeiras without ever seeing a label. Nobody else could name two. *In vino,* as they say at Harvard, *veritas.*"

"Your father the President?" *In vino stupiditas.* More beer had arrived. The booth behind Chase was gently rocking. He concentrated on Adams's face, pale on the jaws, pink on the cheeks. He looked like a burning snowball. Did everyone have trouble with his father? Emma was devoted to her father.

"My father fell in love when he was eighteen or nineteen, some girl in Newburyport"—Adams pronounced it 'gel' like an Englishman—"but he was only a poor student, of the law, which his parents promptly laid down. Too poor to marry, the gel unworthy, an Adams has his destiny." Adams giggled. "An Adams has his bit on the side. Before I was engaged, right here in Washington, thanks to Patsy—"

"I went to see John Randolph yesterday." Chase struggled to keep his head clear. He had not come out this evening to hear the Lamentations of Adams or plunge through the Dantesque circles of Washington, down to Patsy. "But I couldn't find him."

"My father hates John Randolph." Adams could change the subject instantly, Chase noted, without changing the subject at all. "My father writes lurid descriptions of him in Latin in his diary, then *I* have to copy the diary out. He mails the uplifting portions to my brother George in Boston, who is weak of character and not a true Adams, and of course George reads them and gets drunk."

Patsy, on cue, appeared with fresh beer. They were sitting, Chase decided, on the bottom of an ocean of gray smoke; light came and went in wavering, oceanic patches; voices were distorted, liquid; mermaids—

"He hates him," Chase said, trying hard to keep the subject on politics, not the Adams curse, "because of the 'corrupt bargain,' no?" And Charles Francis bobbed his head in watery agreement. As who in Washington would not? Chase thought. The present election of 1828—twenty politicians had told him the same thing—was little more than a ferocious vengeance-driven repetition of the election of 1824, the "corrupt bargain" that had sent John Quincy Adams to the President's mansion and Andrew Jackson boiling back to Nashville. In that election Jackson had actually won the popular vote by a large margin, but in the ridiculous electoral college dreamed up by James Madison to thwart pure democracy Jackson failed of a majority. So it had fallen to the House of Representatives to decide, and Henry Clay, out of the running but still desperate for higher office, had visited Adams one snowy morning and subsequently (no bargain, he cried, no bargain) thrown his influence to the New Englander. Adams's first presidential act, innocent, pure, suicidal, had been to name Clay his secretary of state.

Charles Francis Adams was dipping his finger in beer and drawing a diagram on the table. Chase leaned forward as if he could see it. "Here," Adams said, "is the Potomac. This is Virginia." He looked up, blinking. "I'm drawing the map of the duel between Clay and Randolph. You can put it in your column."

"I don't want to write a column."

"And also how do you write a whole *book*?" Adams asked, not listening, dipping his finger again, then licking it, then drawing a circle on the slick wood. "Capitol," he said. "Capitol, Capitol. Every Adams male has to write a book. My grandfather did, my father writes books while he's President—I don't know how writers do it. I can't draw a map. In the Capitol last year John Randolph made one of his most outrageous speeches, sir."

Chase found he was once again wedged into the corner of his booth (no longer rocking). Somewhere deep inside, the tiny gyroscopic creature that was himself, that did not wobble and waver, that stayed straight up—that self was watching, was thinking of Emma Colden, was upright, clear-headed, smart. The rest of him was knee-deep in beer and swirling smoke and rancid smells, while a sea of dizziness washed past him in dark alcoholic waves.

"Randolph was attacking the mission my father wanted to send to Panama," Adams said, indifferent to Chase's nausea. He actually had, Chase thought, gripping the table, considerable talent for telling a story, he should write a book. "He said it was, 'suh, a Kentucky cuckoo's egg laid in a Spanish-American nest,' and he took a glass of port from his Negro and slapped his leg with his whip and added in that filthy accent of his, 'And these were the same cuckoos by whom the great Jackson was defeated, horse, foot, and dragoons—cut up—and clean broken down, by the coalition of Blifil and Black George—by the combination, unheard of till then, suh, of the Puritan and the blackleg!'"

"*Tom Jones*," Chase muttered. "Blifil is from Fielding. You must be drunk, I see two of you."

"And so Clay challenged Randolph for the insult of 'blackleg' and they met *here*"—finger stabbed table—"Little Falls bridge, at four-thirty in the afternoon. Randolph chose Virginia because if he died he would fall, he declared, on sacred soil. Clay chose smooth-bore pistols, God knows why."

"Did they fire?"

"They fired at thirty paces and both of them missed. And then Thomas Hart Benton, who *should* know about gunfights" (Chase stirred at the name, a Jacksonian thought), "Benton tried to stop them, but Clay waved him off and demanded a second round. And this time Randolph raised his pistol and fired in the air. 'I do not fire at you, Mr. Clay,' he said and held out his hand, and Clay met him halfway and shook hands. Then Randolph said, 'You owe me a coat, Mr. Clay' and showed him a bullet hole right through the coattail, and Clay bowed in that absurd southern way and said, 'I'm glad the debt is no greater.' Come upstairs to the lounge, Mr. Chase. We need to console our beings."

But on the stairs, on the landing, in fact, beside the first of the curtained spaces, Chase stopped dead cold and shivered. Blacker shadows, sweeter smells. Adams tugged at his arm. Chase shook him off. Someone (not Adams) soft and yielding pressed against him and Chase thought of France and Emma and prayed he wouldn't get maudlin or, worse, get sick on the floor. Adams was still tugging. A round face, yellowish-brown with dark eyes and a twisted smile, was rising at his other shoulder, like a moon out of a lake.

He extended one arm, encountered a warm breast, not smoke, and excused himself, fighting his way clear of Adams's voice, Patsy's laugh. One of the curtains was pulled open as he passed and a man, buck naked except for his hat, looked out and lurched to his feet, saying, "Fine, fine."

Out on the street the night had suddenly turned windy, and as Chase walked past Gadsby's torches, whipped out by the wind like flags, drops of warm rain began to fall. Washington was a skillet, the streets were grease. He crossed a street, an alley. Distant lights resolved themselves more and more sharply into torches and carriages until Chase realized that he had somehow walked all the way home, but a block too far to the east, so that he now stood directly in front of Washington's one and only theater.

The play that night, according to the posters (barely legible under two flickering brass lanterns), was *Rip van Winkle,* featuring an actor he had never heard of. They could have come here; he hadn't thought of that, Emma and Sellers. He looked at his watch. A raindrop hit the crystal, grew fat and surprised, and disappeared. Rip van Winkle, he had told Francis Calley Gray in Boston, was an allegory of himself, returning after so many years in Europe. In fact, it was an allegory of the times, the country that went to sleep under Jefferson, woke up under Jackson. America must be drunk; he saw two of them.

The rain beat down harder. In the little theater of his mind, as he stood on the black street under the pelting drops, Emma walked out of the door on Sellers's arm, then rushed in splashing footsteps toward him. It was her warm breast he touched, her lips—Chase shivered again and turned up his collar and started to walk. Two blocks west would bring him to the Indian Queen and shelter, but in the wet, scudding darkness he must have taken a wrong turn again, because when he looked up he was crossing a bare field and the building before him, sixty feet away, was Hogwood's ramshackle boarding house, Emma's house. And he must have misread his watch or misunderstood the theater time, because the play was over and a carriage had just pulled up to the door, and in the orange glow of its little side lantern Emma was being handed out by a man in a tall hat, who was bending over her hand, lifting her hand.

The rain came down like drops of hot tar. Chase stood with his fists in his pockets. Tomorrow he would write. In the drifting black rain she appeared to raise her head and with her free hand sweep back her bonnet and fix her startled gaze, as wide-eyed as a deer's, on him.

When he reached his corridor at the Indian Queen, he fumbled with the candle, wet hands, and dropped the key. In the chthonian darkness of his room he deposited the candlestick on top of his papers and shook his arms dry and only then noticed the hat on the bed and, in the chair by the window, a quiet figure consulting his watch.

"I make it just past midnight, very late," said William Short.

CHAPTER

17

Hogwood was in a classical mood. Over luncheon he explained to Chase and Short that he had learned Latin at the age of eight from a violent and thoroughly effective master at Eton. "The first verb he taught us," Hogwood said, "was *tupto,* 'I thrash.' Not surprisingly, his hero was the deified emperor Tiberius, who was so warlike he used to eat off a shield instead of a plate." He rubbed his fat pink hands together, reached across the butter dish for another drumstick, and grinned mischievously up at Short. "He also passed an edict permitting citizens to break wind at the table."

"When in Rome," Short said sardonically but not unkindly. He held up his right hand and white-shirted waiters flocked around him like seagulls.

"Have an oyster." Hogwood extended a plate to Chase. "The thinking man's mollusk."

Chase spooned out two oysters and watched with something like awe as Hogwood, waving off the waiters, promptly slid the rest of them onto his own plate, where in the course of the last half hour he had built a little hecatomb of chicken bones, oyster shells, potato skins, bread crusts, and boiled carrots, which for some reason he took but never ate.

"Cooking," Hogwood said, cheeks bulging with oysters and chicken at once, "is the chemical process—" he paused to refill his wineglass himself—"the scientific arrangement by which man assimilates and subjects the universe to his own body."

Short looked at Chase and smiled thinly, and Hogwood, who in several senses missed nothing, aimed his drumstick like a gun. "He is about to tell us that the deified Thomas Jefferson ate nothing but vegetables and broth."

"In fact, he liked ice cream," Short said. "He was the first one to bring the recipe back to this country." Hogwood winked at Chase. "From Paris," Short added, not seeing the wink. "Did you know, David, that I made the acquaintance of our friend Mr. Hogwood in Paris? It was three years ago, and he was employed translating James Fenimore Cooper's novels into French."

"French and German," Hogwood muttered. "The Germans love him too."

"We went to the same bookseller—"

"On the Quai des Grands Augustins."

"—and used to end up talking at the same café."

"The Café du Parnasse, just by the Pont Neuf," Hogwood told him. "You probably know it."

Chase nodded and regretted it, as the brandy pain from last night hammered again at the back of his skull. He knew the Café du Parnasse very well. He could sketch the Parnasse from memory if he had to, the double casement door, the zinc counter, the coal fireplace shaped like a little Gothic arch, and the wooden cashbox stand by the kitchen where the old wife took your money and the young daughter took your order—you could look out the first row of windows and see the river and the red-roofed boats and the Quai des Orfèvres. He looked out the window now and saw a dirty yellow clapboard building across the street, two or three slaves in burlap trousers and straw hats, and a broken-off plank that said, with much precision and little poetry, THIRD STREET.

When he turned back, Hogwood had begun an oration on Cooper and the power of the written word. "If you print it," he said, sounding exactly like his daughter, "people believe it. That is a fact of modern life. Thanks to James Fenimore Cooper—and my humble translations, of course—

every literate European believes America is the promised land of milk and honey. Do you remember the chapter in *The Pioneers* when a whole village goes out to shoot pigeons?" He aimed the drumstick at the ceiling. "Millions and millions of pigeons! The air rains pigeons! Enough to feed the armies of Xerxes for a month, says Natty Bumppo. Little boys in Germany play 'Indian' now, you know; they walk 'Indian file' down the street and stick old crow feathers in their hair. Everybody in Europe wants to come to America and eat pigeons and live free. The trouble is—" Hogwood lowered the drumstick and took a bite "—no more pigeons. You've cut down your forests and slaughtered them all, and if Jackson has his way there won't be any more Indians either."

"We arrive at Jackson." Short pulled out his watch and pushed back his chair in the same motion. "Just as Mr. Chase and I must leave."

"They'll put it on your tombstone, you know. 'Checked My Watch, Had to Leave.' " Hogwood shook his head and remained in his chair, under a film of pink sweat. At the next table a man was looking curiously at them and dropping chicken bones into the brass spittoon at his feet. "Mind what I say. Andy Jackson is the Natty Bumppo of politics. He lives on the frontier, he slaughters Indians like pigeons. Nobody cares if Old Hickory can read or write because all the newspapers have made him into nature's nobleman. I'm glad we're friends again, Short. Where are you going?"

"My greetings to your charming daughter," Short said, handing money to a waiter. "I'll send the material we talked about."

On the sidewalk Short set off at a brisk pace. Chase followed, head pounding. "I've commissioned him to write a series of articles about his American travels, just as you asked," Short said over his shoulder.

"But you didn't tell him I asked?"

"She must be more charming even than I remember," Short said, and used the black malacca cane to steer them between a grocer's wagon and a horse trough. Tonkin's Oyster House, which Short had evidently chosen because it served men only, sat on one of the narrow, nondescript streets east of the Capitol, and he was taking them downhill toward a patch of muddy fields and tired-looking warehouses.

"About last night . . ." Chase began.

"You've stayed here far too long, Mr. Chase," Short said without even glancing at him. The cane rose and fell like a metronome. "As last night is evidence. I won't waste words criticizing you. I made my views perfectly known in New York. You're late with your book; you're lingering here when you should be in Nashville. As far as I can tell, for all practical purposes you've written nothing. Mrs. Hale needs at least three complete chapters by August and the whole book by September."

Chase concentrated on the uneven street, no longer possessed of a sidewalk, which was covered with puddles from last night's downpour. They were passing a redbrick building so porous and damp that it seemed to be made out of rust.

"Have you," Short asked in a slightly softer tone of voice, "heard anything of a rumor concerning Rachel Jackson and 'secret documents' in the campaign of 1824?"

"Nothing." But even as he spoke Chase found himself remembering a stray phrase of John Randolph's: *a dim recollection, my dear, of something in 1824.*

"I am told," Short said, without saying how he was told, "that in December of '24, when the election was about to be decided by the House of Representatives, a man named Charles Tutt wrote then-Senator Jackson and informed him that certain documents had been left in the hands of an individual in Alexandria, Virginia. They apparently concerned some new fact about Mrs. Jackson's past."

Chase was impatient. "Every possible stone in Rachel Jackson's past has been turned over twice for scandal." He started to add that he was in any case a serious writer, not a rumormonger about other men's wives, but this was hardly the time, he thought, to be praising his own writing.

"Tutt was a Jackson man," Short continued. "He was so disturbed by the nature of the documents that he refused even to describe them. Jackson merely wrote back that he regarded such attacks with contempt."

"So do I," Chase said.

Short stopped abruptly in the middle of the street. Behind them the Capitol appeared to tip its raffish black dome like a hat. In front of them, surrounded by high fences and the usual bare Washington fields, stood an ill-made two-story building covered with dirty yellow plaster and bearing a small sign over the door: WASHINGTON ROBEY TAVERN.

"Contempt or not, you've signed a contract, I remind you. You've accepted—and spent—a good deal of my money, and you are professionally committed to write a complete and well-researched biography of Jackson for me." Short pointed the cane. "Do you know who Washington Robey is?"

"He's a slave trader, one of two in the city. I can buy back my contract."

Short lowered the cane and pulled out his leather glasses case. "Hogwood was right," he murmured. "You do learn things with extraordinary quickness. Robey's doesn't advertise its business."

"And that's his slave pen," Chase said. Immediately next to the yellow tavern ran a line of wooden palings six or seven feet high, and just above it the slanted roof of a crude wooden shack. Through a gap in the fencing two black faces peered out silently. Slave trading, as northern reformers constantly pointed out, was not illegal even in the nation's capital; John Randolph himself had denounced it as a blot and disfigurement of government. In his six weeks of residence Chase had seen actual slave coffles, bound by chains at the wrists and ankles, shuffling down Pennsylvania Avenue, past the President's mansion.

"I'm to meet someone inside," Short said. "I must ask you to wait out here."

"I can buy back my contract," Chase repeated, "if you give me time. I'm making no progress at all. I've seen everybody on your list, I've read every book and article—I can't get started. I can't even write my first sentence."

With one hand on the brim of his hat Short lifted his cane and entered the tavern.

Chase turned on his heel, walked twenty feet, stopped across from the shack. Red, white, and blue "Jackson and Reform" posters fluttered from a linden tree on the other side of the street. He would *not* write a false, unfactual attack on Rachel Jackson. His temples were pounding, his eyes hurt; the white sky cupped the rooftops and hills of the city like the shell of an egg.

He turned again, stepped around a puddle the shape of France that he hadn't seen before, and walked into the tavern.

To his right was a conventional Washington taproom containing a long wooden bar, a spotted mirror behind a row of bottles, and two or three unfriendly, unshaven men studying him in it. He blinked at the darkness and then followed a hand-lettered sign on his left: SALES.

The next room, lit by a barred window, was a tiny office, decorated with more "Jackson and Reform" posters. Short stood in the doorway to the yard, talking to a man of fifty or so. He scarcely paused to glance around at Chase. The other man, toothless, bald as a kneecap, rubbed his scalp with one hand as a curious kind of acknowledgment. Then he grunted something unintelligible to Short and headed into the yard.

"I would wager my contract," Chase said, "that you're not here to buy a slave."

"You would lose," Short said, and began to follow the bald-headed man. Chase fell into step. "As you could have no reason to know, I'm an officer of the American Colonization Society. I have been for years. It is the one thing—" he corrected himself "—one of the two things I ever really disagreed with Jefferson about. The other was the French Revolution. We arrange for freed slaves to be taken away to the African country of Liberia, where they can begin a new life."

They had reached the center of the yard, halfway between the shack and the outside fence, which was blocked off here by a second, much lower fence, making a narrow, fetid enclosure some hundred or hundred and fifty feet square. It dawned on Chase that this was simply a holding pen, like a cattle yard, for male slaves. The bald man was unfastening a bolted gate. Around him, on the dirt, sat or sprawled fifteen or twenty black men of all ages, each one fettered at the ankles by a length of chain. A listless boy of ten or eleven, too small for chains, sat by himself on a stack of blankets.

"The women are kept on the other side of that building," Short said, "and I really must ask you to wait here. Mr. Robey's refined sense of propriety would be offended by an uninvited male among his ladies."

And before Chase could protest, he pushed open the gate with his cane and walked away into the shadows.

Chase jammed his hands in his coat pockets and squinted at the afternoon haze. Beyond the holding pen rose still another miserable shack, windows shuttered, grated iron door secured by a padlock. The night building, he guessed, where the men were locked at sundown to prevent escape. He paced to the bottom of the yard. Behind the tavern, through whose back windows drifted soft southern voices, black and white, he found a patch of tangled shrubs and upright boards; after a moment he recognized the upright boards as grave markers and the patch of ground as a pathetic little cemetery for slaves who had died in transit. In Paris his first editor had returned his first article with the brusque inscription, *D'abord voir, puis écrire.* First see, then write.

"The man is a scoundrel," Short said, coming up suddenly behind him. "I'll have to come back tomorrow. I'm trying to trace a female slave—the wife of a man we've already bought. Robey has probably already sold her off to the Richmond market, but he pretends he doesn't remember. For eight hundred dollars he thinks he can find her."

"And then you send them both to Liberia together?"

"It's the only solution, the best solution." Short was once again briskly leading the way, back toward Washington Robey's office. "Tomorrow morning," he said over his shoulder, "I've planned an excursion with Hogwood that should amuse you. Then tomorrow afternoon a stage ticket for Nashville—"

"You're wrong, you know," Chase interrupted. "You're completely mistaken."

Short whirled to face him, glasses flashing—a white-haired old snowman, Chase thought, being melted by the sun.

"Impertinent! *You* are *impertinent*, Mr. Chase! I have devoted my life to the antislave—"

"You're wrong about Thomas Jefferson liking Andrew Jackson. In Boston, when we were at the restaurant, you said that Jefferson 'rather liked Jackson' from their years in the Senate, which was why you wanted my book to be fair to him. I bit my tongue. But I was at Monticello the day Jackson won the Battle of New Orleans, or we heard he did, and I remember distinctly Jefferson turning to me and saying—he was almost your age then, he had pale red hair and gray eyes and he truly did look like nature's nobleman—he said, 'Andrew Jackson has terrible passions. Andrew Jackson is the most dangerous man in America.' He didn't like Jackson, he hated him."

There were three things to sort out at once—the vivid memory of Thomas Jefferson so unexpectedly aroused; the rank, heartrending smell of the slave pen behind him; the scaffolded profile of the Capitol dome rising splendidly over the roof of Robey's Tavern. *Voir, écrire.*

The pursed lips of Short's anger were yielding to a small, ironic, self-satisfied smile. "Let *that*," he said softly, "be the first sentence of your book, Mr. Chase."

CHAPTER
18

The excursion that would "amuse" him turned out to be, of all things, a picnic trip to Mount Vernon.

They set out on hired horses at exactly eight o'clock in the morning—Short snapped his watch shut on the hour—and threaded their way south, past the poultry and vegetable wagons coming from the other direction into the Washington Market. When they reached the open spaces of the Old Richmond Road, Short spurred his horse into a gentle trot. He had arranged for a guide at the mansion, he told Chase over his shoulder, and a catered lunch. They would be back in the city by three; his Nashville stage left at five. Chase covered a sleepy yawn with his hand and nodded. They lapsed into silence.

At the convergence of the Potomac and Anacostia Rivers, Chase began to look about with interest. He had ridden north into Maryland once or twice, past Kalorama, but this was the first time he had come south, truly south, since his long-ago trip to Monticello in 1815.

Things were clearly different now. For one thing, the countryside had a neater, trimmer look. In 1815 most of the rural houses he passed had been left unpainted and their windows were usually boarded up or else stuffed with rags, because paint was expensive, glass was expensive, and the South was poor. People had thrown their broken plates or pans straight out a window into a yard. Now the yards were clean. Some of the windows had not only glass but also the new wire-mesh screens that had been invented to let the air in and keep out bugs. Every house he had seen so far was painted, some of them two or even three colors.

His horse picked its way past a copper-brown cottage that sat on a grassy patch (no broken plates) fifty or so feet from the road.

And for another thing—the journalist began to assemble details—the general American craze for brushing teeth had obviously reached the South. Nobody that he could remember had brushed their teeth in 1815. Now he looked back to see a farmer standing at the door of the cottage scrubbing his mouth to a white froth.

"We turn just up ahead," Short informed him. Chase twisted forward again with more curiosity than he would have readily admitted. Mount Vernon was no longer inhabited and was closed to the general public. Short had clearly pulled strings. (Journalist's note: Compare Mount Vernon to *Jackson's* house when you finally see it.) On their left ran the wide, brown Potomac, dotted as always with sails. On their right, fenced off from the road, a long hill sloped gently upward, part open fields, part forest. In another two minutes the road split, just as Short had said, and they turned right into the forest.

It was a carriage road, well rutted and deeply shaded. Once or twice through the trees Chase caught an impressive glimpse of a vast rolling lawn and a distant roof and white columns, but for the most part they rode upward between thick galleries of pine. At the crest the road curved abruptly out of the trees. They trotted through an open gate. Chase rose in his stirrups. The river was a brown ribbon far below. But the long-awaited view of the house, now less than a hundred yards straight ahead, was blocked by the red walls of a barn, the level black roof of a phaeton, and the pink-faced pyramidical bulk of William Chester Hogwood, seated on a bench by himself.

"We have settled the presidential question," Hogwood said cheerfully as they dismounted. He grinned, wheezed, leaned forward to support himself on his stick. "On our ride over. If Jackson can keep his mouth shut he can win. If Adams can *open* his mouth *he* can win."

"Oh, I think," said Senator Sellers emerging from the barn, smiling as if at a private joke, "I think it still hinges on New York and Pennsylvania."

"My other guests," Short murmured to Chase. "I neglected to mention."

"Senator Sellers is always cautiously practical." Emma likewise emerged into the sunlight, on Sellers's arm.

Chase found himself still standing stiffly beside his horse, feeling his face burn. Sellers nodded to him, shook hands with Short. Emma passed behind them on her way to her father. She wore a light gray dress the color of smoke, no corset, and a wide-brimmed blue summer bonnet. "Mr. Chase," she said with perfect English politeness, but her face was lost in shadows as she spoke.

"David, please," he said; damned Short, damned Sellers, threw up a barricade of ironic French. *"Un plaisir de vous voir encore."*

"They came on ahead in the senator's carriage," Short said unnecessarily. "You all know each other, of course. Now, I've engaged a private guide." He looked first at his watch and then toward the white columns of George Washington's house, which showed no signs of life whatsoever. "He ought to be here by now."

"French," Hogwood said. He motioned to Chase to come closer. "Last week, I hear, Jackson's people distributed three thousand pamphlets in Pennsylvania written in *German.*"

"You can ride for days in Pennsylvania and Kentucky," Sellers agreed, "and never hear English. We call it the melting pot."

"And in Boston they claim that Adams is English, as everybody knows, but Jackson is really a true-born Irishman and every bog-trotting son of Eire should vote for him."

"That's how you win now, in America," Sellers said with the casual authority of someone who had won. "You court the voters."

Chase folded his arms across his chest. Senator Sellers was not a handsome man. He had thin, sandy hair flecked with gray and a weak chin. The first fleshy scoops of an old man's dewlap rested like folds of dough on his tight collar. According to Nicholas Trist, he was fifty-three years old, a widower, childless, and he had made at least a million dollars the way everybody made money out West, buying and selling land. He stared back at Chase with unfriendly black eyes, lifted one hand to adjust his cravat, then shifted his gaze to Emma.

" 'Court,' indeed," drawled Short. "Now perhaps if we go around to the front of the house—"

But before he could finish his sentence their guide appeared on the sloping lawn, an elderly black man in a tall straw hat, grinning broadly, and almost at once Short was herding them quickly along, even Hogwood, toward the shabbiest, most run-down shrine that Chase had ever seen.

Through the trees Mount Vernon had looked imposing, monumental. Close up, however, the white facade was peeling in fist-sized chunks, as if Time had strolled idly by swinging a hammer. The slanted roof had sprouted weeds and grass; the long two-story veranda that faced the lawn and that was Washington's own original architectural design appeared to be littered with shards of pottery and fragments of weathered gray tables and chairs. At one corner dirt and straw had simply been swept into a pile by the wind's lazy broom. If the rest of the country was looking fresher, neater, better-painted, Chase thought, then Mount Vernon belonged entirely to the past, like John Quincy Adams and Thomas Jefferson.

The guide was a former slave, not of George Washington but of his brother John. He informed them proudly that he had known the President very well and seen him almost every day of his life. He would show them the grounds first and the gardens, then they would go into the house and see all the rooms, and finally visit the tomb, which they were welcome, he added, to touch or to kiss.

Dutifully they wound past the house into the hot sunshine. Hogwood puffed. Emma took his arm and opened a parasol. They stopped to admire the window of the room where Washington had died; stepped onto the grass to look up at the glassed-in cupola on the roof, which Washington had copied from the governor's palace at Williamsburg.

"Monticello," Short said, falling back with Chase and fanning himself with his hat, "is in much worse condition today than this."

Chase looked at him sourly. A manipulative, secretive old man. Why else had he brought Emma and Sellers here together, except to demonstrate that Chase . . . ? Chase let the thought slide away. After paying his hotel, without a new advance from Short he would have exactly seventy-four dollars in his wallet. Ahead of him Emma's uncorseted hips swayed in her dress.

"Wasn't it always," he heard himself saying offensively, "a kind of monument to the great god Clutter?" An attack on Jefferson was an attack on Short. When he had seen it in 1815, the grounds around Monticello had been covered with piles of old bricks and lumber. There had been a row of wood-and-tarpaper slave shacks just beyond Jefferson's bedroom; a noisy, smelly nail-making factory was being built next to the lawn. It was only inside, where Jefferson's books and paintings and fine wines were found, that you escaped the South.

Short was bland. "When Jefferson died, in fact," he said, "he was totally bankrupt. Washington left one million dollars in his will, Jefferson left nothing. The creditors sold the house at auction and evicted his daughter and her children. Now a Jew named Levy has boarded up the windows and let the porch cave in."

"After he was President people came every week to stay a while with him." Their guide halted them before a greenhouse whose windows were all intact but whose roof was gone. "Trouble was, the President didn't care much for company. He used to get up at five in the morning and take his breakfast in his office so he wouldn't see them. Then he would ride off all day long to the fields, or sometimes to this little garden, we used to call it the West Indies, it gets so hot out here. He planted lemon trees right in that greenhouse, orange trees over there. He'd go back home about six o'clock and have tea and go right to bed. Never served his guests supper."

"At Monticello," Short said—Hogwood peered out from beneath Emma's parasol like a frog from a lily pad—"tourists would ride up the hill and stop and walk around at all hours of the day. I once sat on the porch and talked with Jefferson after dinner while half a dozen people simply strolled over from their carriage and stood on the steps and stared at us."

"Washington and Jefferson." Sellers cleared his throat with the warning intonation of a politician about to utter a cliché. "The two indispensable men—"

"Oh, the graveyards are full of indispensable men," Hogwood said, grinning.

At the end of the gardens they turned and marched back to the house, where Augustine, their guide, produced an old-fashioned wrought-iron key from his pocket and bowed them in.

Washington's office was first. Too small for the six of them, so Chase stood in the hallway and listened as Augustine proudly pointed out Washington's desk, his personal quill pen, his surprisingly large cabinet of books. On the wall, Washington's engraved portrait of Louis XVI of France seemed to blink myopically at the strange, alien landscape spreading out beneath the office window. Emma placed her hand on Senator Sellers's sleeve and frowned at the books.

In the main hall they stopped to see an authentic key to the Bastille, given to Washington by Napoleon Bonaparte, and Short and Hogwood began to dispute whether Napoleon had meant it as a gift or an insult. Augustine nodded, smiled, and steered them all into a musty parlor. Here, every stick of furniture had been removed, though tarnished silver sconces and cobwebbed paintings still hung on two of the walls (agricultural subjects: a plowman in a field, a boy mounting a horse, a milkmaid with fat Hogwoodian cheeks). The gigantic marble fireplace had been given to the President by Lafayette when he came to visit with Miss Frances Wright.

"You are a freed slave?" Hogwood suddenly interrupted with a wheeze.

Augustine hitched his pants over his hips and looked thoughtfully at the floor. "Yes, sir. The President freed all his slaves in his will. Mister John did, too, praise God."

"Now why did Thomas Jefferson," Hogwood asked, turning on Short, "*fail* to emancipate *his* slaves in his will? He had the theory right—all men are created equal—but he never put it into practice that I can see. Old Johnson defines theory as speculation by those unversed in practice." But Short only shrugged and left the room.

In a grove of sycamore trees near the garden, servants set out a table and chairs and unpacked two wicker baskets of food, supplied by Gadsby's own kitchen. Hogwood sat with his eyes closed, cherubic and happy, while Emma tied a napkin around his neck.

"Your life of Andrew Jackson hasn't appeared yet, Mr. Chase," Senator Sellers said, taking a seat beside Emma. "I looked in all the journals this month to find it. Or did I misunderstand why you were here in Washington?"

Behind them Short was supervising the laying out of the table, but as usual he seemed to hear everything. "Mr. Chase has had a literary explosion," he said, and Emma and Hogwood turned their heads to look at Chase. "Last night he wrote two full chapters about Jackson at the Battle of New Orleans. And he was up again at five this morning, writing more."

"Like Samuel Taylor Coleridge," said Hogwood, shaking his head as he poured himself a full glass of wine. "The human quill. Never stops writing. You set a terrible example for the rest of us, David. No one should be up, let alone writing, at five in the morning."

"I sent the chapters off to Boston by special messenger before we left," Short said. "They're quite brilliant."

"My daughter wrote an article for the *National Intelligencer.*" Hogwood smacked his lips and drank off half his glass in one gulp. "About John Quincy Adams on the Fourth of July. Also brilliant, of course. I forgive you, Short, for un-hiring me, but you should have hired her. Them."

Emma spooned out ham and potatoes for her father and gave Short the Smile *Tolérant.* "I'm listed as 'Our Special Correspondent,' not a real name," she told him sweetly, "being only a woman." Another spoonful of gravy. "In this heat," she announced, straightening and wiping her brow with the back of her hand, "I need to stroll a moment first, before I take a bite." To no one in particular she said very slowly, *"Je suis une flâneuse."*

The four men watched in silence as she walked past the table and down the row of green sycamores. Sellers and Short accepted their plates from a servant. Hogwood mopped his red face and poured himself a new glass of wine. "In fact, I rather like old Coleridge," he said. "He's almost as fat as I am. I used to see him often in Bath," he added, comically pronouncing the name with a flat American *a*, "a city he always referred to as 'the place where I had the misfortune to meet my wife.' "

Short laughed, Sellers snorted. Chase suddenly rose to his feet. He put down his plate and hurried after Emma. Past the cluttered veranda of Mount Vernon he turned to the left and walked halfway down the carriage path until he found her, leaning against a tree, gazing downhill toward the river.

"Should I be pleased for your literary explosion?" she asked without looking around.

"I went by Gales and Seaton yesterday. I left a message."

"I know."

"I almost came to your rooms, twenty times, but I was afraid to disturb your father. He isn't well."

"My father likes you."

"Is it because Sellers is rich and I'm poor—is it that simple?"

Emma shook her head. "Nothing could be that simple. My father needs . . . I won't blame my father."

"I leave for Nashville this afternoon."

She turned quickly to face him, and with one part of his mind he thought, They call it *falling in love,* admiring as always the wisdom of the language. Not stumbling in love, not walking, striding, jumping, bouncing, crawling in love. You *fall* in love, straight forward like a chopped tree, straight down like a rock from a cliff: gravity, earth, concussion. Chase took a step toward her.

"Your father and William Short are diagnosing the election," said Ephraim Sellers as he materialized on the other side of the tree, one hand in his coat pocket, one hand adjusting his cravat. "Your father, Emma, says the great unspoken issue of the day is slavery, and Short says no, not yet."

Emma pulled away at once from the tree and started to walk again, over the lawn. "And you say?"

"I say it's democracy," Sellers told her, a little too loudly. "I say John Quincy Adams and his people belong to the old politics, when a privileged group of aristocrats told the people what to think."

"You're a Westerner." Chase claimed his place on Emma's left, matching Sellers step for step.

"I own ten thousand acres in Ohio," Sellers replied. "I belong to the West, yes. I'm also old enough to remember what it was like." He gestured toward the decaying white house. "In my youth, in Virginia, farmers would take off their hats and tug their forelocks when they spoke to gentlemen. People deferred to wealth, rank. I met George Washington myself once—the old black man is right, he was more like a king than anything else. He had no time for the common people. The real issue of this election is whether we finally get a democracy or not, and all the vulgarity and excess that goes with it, or stay with a ruling eastern elite."

"Then I guess you're for Jackson and Reform," Chase said. "Unless I misunderstand."

"My father will want me," Emma murmured, and slipped from between them. "I should go see to him."

The two men stood on either side of an empty space of parched grass, studying each other.

"Are we rivals, Mr. Chase?" Sellers asked after a moment, blinking in the hot sun, baring his teeth.

Chase squinted toward the sycamores. Emma was a silver gray blur.

"Because I suppose," said Sellers, and took a step to block his view, "if we were in Old Hickory country I would have to challenge you to a duel."

"I have no idea what country we're in," Chase said, and turned on his heel.

When they reached the table again Hogwood was breathing heavily, his eyes closed. Emma sat beside him cutting the meat on his plate.

"Young Short has been telling me all about Thomas Jefferson's last years," Hogwood wheezed. He opened his eyes to a slit and sought out Emma. "In his last years, apparently he was ready to despair of the great American people. He had believed that once they cast off wicked old Albion every American farmer would read Homer and Locke and every American voter would think rationally, like himself, a little nation of Jeffersonian geniuses." Hogwood's voice was a low grumble, thick with phlegm. Emma's fork hovered at his lips. "He never imagined the people would prefer marching bands and barbecues and bedroom scandals. The people, silly old things, would rather be entertained."

He stopped and coughed.

"You exaggerate shamelessly," Short said, sitting down beside him.

Hogwood ignored him. He rubbed his big red moon of a face with a handkerchief and winked at Chase. "Jackson," he said, "is the price you pay for having Jefferson." Then he gripped Chase's sleeve and pulled him closer. "Save a chapter for John Randolph," he whispered, "speaking of entertainment. He left for Nashville last night in a boiling huff."

PART

3

August–September 1828

CHAPTER
1

The Life of Andrew Jackson, by David Chase

Chapter Six

SEEN FROM ABOVE, AS IF ON A MAP, NEW ORLEANS LIES ONE HUNDRED AND five miles up the Mississippi River from the Gulf of Mexico, a bright French ladybug caught in a vast green spider's web of bayous, creeks, and canals.

If you spin a globe and run your finger two hundred miles to the east, you reach Mobile, Alabama, perched on a deep crescent bay of the Gulf. There, in the last grim months of 1814, while British troops marched whistling away from the smoldering ruins of Washington City, Andrew Jackson sat with his bedraggled army looking west toward a swamp-flat horizon and reading his brand-new orders.

Now this is the part I know nothing about.

I am thirty-four years old, I have grown up between wars, no soldier, and lived for years at a time in European cities so remote and alien from my native American landscape that I sometimes seem to have sailed away to a different planet. What I know about war I have learned from books. But as far as I can see, the next few months of my narrative touch the nearest thing to Homeric epic the modern world can unfold.

By a literary coincidence, in fact, Andrew Jackson has a protégé, a young crony named Sam Houston, who ran away from home when he was fourteen and spent several years living with Indians. Houston has a grim temper, an Indian code of revenge, and an effeminate weakness for wearing bizarre costumes of painted feathers and silver jewelry. When he lived with the Indians he carried only one book with him, a stolen copy of Pope's translation of Homer, which he read till the pages fell out, but by then he had committed it all to memory. (A mistake, to underestimate the molding power of books on personality.)

But on reflection, everyone in Jackson's world seems to have memorized Homer and decided to act out an epic life. There is Houston, of course, who was second over the ramparts at the bloody Battle of Horseshoe Bend and who snatched a tomahawk out of a charging warrior's hands and laid about bloodily like Achilles. There is a buckskinned Thersites named Davy Crockett, a foul-mouthed, tall-tale-telling character who was third or fourth over those same ramparts and who afterward hacked himself out a belt of scalps. There is big, gentle John Coffee, whose nickname among the troops is Ajax. About to emerge on the scene is the handsome Creole pirate Jean Lafitte, master of his own private island. Above all there is Jackson himself, slipping down at nightfall to the warm Gulf beaches and climbing into a little six-man sloop for his first voyage ever on salt water. He wraps himself from head to foot in an old blue Spanish cloak and sits like Odysseus in the bow. His men splash through the waves and clamber aboard. Far to the north in Nashville—a plump, cigar-smoking Penelope—Rachel waits by a window. Down the beach, behind a stand of whispering palmettos, a British spy lights a signal fire.

Let them stand where they are for a moment. Spin the globe a little farther. Press your thumb down on the whitewashed clapboard river city of Hartford, Connecticut. When I returned to America this year, after my nine years' absence, I was astonished to find the newspapers filled with reports that the Federal Union was in dire and immediate danger of falling apart. The South was breathing—and still does breathe—fiery talk of secession over the twin issues of slavery and tariffs, and the North in return fumes and grumbles that the sacred Union of 1789 can never be broken. It was formerly the other way round. During that bleak winter of 1814, while Jackson and his men slipped through the gray, leafless forests of Alabama in search of Indians, in Hartford a convention of Federalist politicians were secretly meeting to consider secession. Their goal: a whole new nation, to be called New England, and a separate peace with Great Britain. Like many another loyalist, my stubbornly patriotic father used to call them "Blue-Light Federalists," because they would treasonously signal British ships in Long Island Sound by planting blue lanterns along the shore. In 1814, of course, Jackson has never heard of them. Nor has he heard much more than rumors about the negotiations half a world away, on the other side of the Atlantic, in the Belgian city of Ghent, where a delegation headed by John Quincy Adams and Henry Clay meets daily with their British counterparts to patch out a peace.

Peace is the last thing on Old Hickory's mind. He has boarded his schooner and set out in the darkness to plan a diversionary attack on British ships anchored farther west along the coast at Fort Bowyer, near Mobile. In his pocket is an official letter from President James Madison appointing him a Major General in the regular army and giving him full military responsibility for the southern half of the country. Another letter, from Secretary of War John C. Calhoun, reminds him (but Jackson hardly needed reminding) that for all practical purposes the southern half of the country is now New Orleans.

How has it come about that Jackson is marching west, two stars on his shoulder, in command of a regular army? Not quite one year ago he was lying in bed with multiple wounds from a tavern brawl, a laughingstock if not worse all over Tennessee, a man known chiefly for his hairtrigger temper and violent, sloppy passions.

It is probably fair to say that leading his militia volunteers south to avenge the Fort Mims massacre had truly changed him. Actual combat, military hardship, *leadership* had opened his character up and revealed new strengths, new beds of ore. It is probably also fair to say that, in politics as in everything else, victory possesses an unanswerable logic.

In the cold, wet spring of 1814, after quashing yet again a mutiny in his troops, Jackson's militia had fought two major Indian battles in rapid succession. The first, hardly a battle, more like a massacre, was an attack by John Coffee's men on a Creek village near the Coosa River, a morning of sheer leisurely slaughter after which Coffee, who had obediently murdered every Indian male he found, burned the houses and took the women and children prisoner. The slain warriors' bodies were left for the buzzards to tear apart and eat. (*"Coffee executed my orders in an elegant stile,"* Jackson reported to Washington City; Davy Crockett was blunter: *"We shot them down like dogs."*)

For the next two weeks Jackson's men terrorized the Indians. They burned villages and crops and herded survivors into guarded camps, where they would remain till the end of the war. But this was no test of generalship. And it was no true revenge either for the massacre at Fort Mims that had started the whole bloody campaign.

On March 27, 1814, when dawn broke the color of mud over the black rushing waters of the Tallapoosa River, Jackson finally had a chance to show his skill. The Indians considered the land by the Tallapoosa sacred; no white could violate it. In a final stand they gathered their army, some eight hundred warriors strong, at a place on the river called Horseshoe Bend, behind a daunting eight-foot-high breastwork of logs and brush, lined with double portholes for their guns. Major General Jackson planned his assault meticulously. He placed his two cannons on a small bluff. He sent Coffee's cavalry along one side of the river to feint attack; he ordered scouts to swim in the darkness and cut loose any canoes they found behind the fort; in absolute agony with dysentery, he wrote out his orders, drew his diagrams, and inspected every soldier himself, on foot. And at ten-thirty in the morning he started to shoot.

Over *seven hundred* Indians died at Horseshoe Bend—to keep track, the Americans counted the tips of noses cut from corpses—and Jackson lost only forty-nine men. From the smoking ashes of the breastwork he picked up a bow and a quiver as souvenirs for his little boy in Nashville. When the surgeons brought a wounded Creek to have his leg bandaged, the brave looked up at Jackson's fierce, angular face, recognized his essence, and said simply, "Cure 'im, kill 'im *again*?"

And thus the Creek nation was destroyed as a force in the South, Jackson wrote the next day to Washington City; he added without noticeable regret, *"The carnage was dreadfull."*

To make the victory complete, a few weeks later Chief William Weatherford, the notorious author of the Fort Mims massacre himself, came at dusk to Jackson's tent and personally surrendered.

Jackson's soldiers wanted to string the Indian up then and there on the spot, but Jackson held up his hand for silence. Weatherford was naked to the waist, scarred with battle wounds. He had on only buckskin breeches and badly worn moccasins. He carried no weapon. He had come on foot. "General Jackson," he said, "I'm not afraid of you. I fear no man, because I am a Creek warrior. You can go ahead and kill me if you want to. But I have come to ask for food and shelter for the women and children of my people, who are starving in the woods. There was a time when I could animate my warriors to battle. But the war is over. I cannot animate the dead."

I cannot animate the dead. A phrase that must have gone to the core of Jackson's nature. He was born of a dead father himself. He had lost his mother and brothers and all his Scotch-Irish world to the same inexplicable, unbending fact of human existence, the one force before which even his fierce Jacksonian will was powerless. He nodded. As his soldiers' jaws dropped, he pulled back the flap of his tent and invited Bill Weatherford in, a conference of men at home with the unanimated dead.

Paradox. Earlier Jackson was much hated by his soldiers in the Creek campaign, yet nonetheless they now flocked to join his army. His military discipline was notorious—he allowed no whiskey in his camp (an outrage in Tennessee) and set up guards to confiscate it. He ordered every soldier to be out of bed by three-thirty A.M., and his officers out of bed by three. When he had a young boy shot for mutiny, the whole army was forced to watch. But he won battles, which no other American general could say in 1814, and he killed Indians and captured land. The troops still called him Old Hickory, the Creeks called him "Sharp Knife." How could he ruthlessly kill so many Indians? a visitor asked the governor of Tennessee. "Because he knows how," Blount said, shrugging in the face of a phenomenon. To the haughty Spanish commandant at Pensacola, who was harboring Creeks, Jackson sent a terse demand for surrender that delighted his army: "An Eye for an Eye, Tooth for a Tooth, *Scalp for a Scalp.*"

After the capture of Bill Weatherford, Jackson did two things quickly—in this amazing year he seems to have done everything with the speed of a man possessed—first he called the Creek chiefs together and demanded in reparation twenty million acres of their land. I repeat: twenty million acres. A tract three hundred miles wide from Georgia to the Mississippi River. At a stroke he thus opened the whole vast country south of the Tennessee River to white settlement. Nobody except Thomas Jefferson and his Louisiana Purchase—with a stroke of the pen, characteristically, not the sword—has ever expanded the American nation so far,

244 / Max Byrd

so fast. And second, not content with the Creek millions, Jackson marched without the President's permission straight into Spanish Florida and seized yet more land, because it was there, because he wanted it, because the Spanish (since the days of Aaron Burr) made him angry. Then he whirled about, glared west, and set off for New Orleans.

I am exhausted simply to write it. But I am no Homer.

To inspect potential British landing places Jackson gave himself twelve days for the one-hundred-fifty-mile trek from Mobile to New Orleans, during eight of which he was so sick and debilitated he never ate a crumb, but subsisted entirely on doses of white powdered calomel and julep leaves. Behind him marched an army of not quite two thousand soldiers.

Ahead of him, sailing toward the mouth of the Mississippi was a veritable British armada, sixty ships, fourteen thousand troops.

CHAPTER
2

The Life of Andrew Jackson, by David Chase

Chapter Seven

JACKSON HAD NO IDEA OF THE APPROACHING BRITISH STRENGTH. HE COULD barely sit in the saddle. He crossed the eastern swamps of Louisiana with a small advance guard, slowed his horse to a walk, and on the chill, foggy morning of December 1, 1814, climbed up onto a muddy road made of broken seashells, which ran beside the Bayou St. John, exactly four miles north of New Orleans.

In an old Spanish-style villa just ahead, a Creole lady of considerable fashion and *ton* was at that moment standing with her hands on her hips in the dining room of one J. Kilty Smith, an American merchant with long-standing ties to Tennessee. Smith was a bachelor and thought himself deficient in the entertaining graces, so the day before he had called on his wealthy neighbor's wife and begged her to take charge of the breakfast welcome he intended to give the Hero of Natchez and Horseshoe Bend, *"le grand et impressionnant Général Jackson."*

Mr. Smith's neighbor had done herself proud. The table was set for a dozen, in the best French style, with engraved silverware (borrowed from her own cabinets), white damask cloth and napkins, crystal vases of flowers, and an extraordinarily delicate green and gold placing of Sèvres china. In the kitchen three cooks hired specially for the occasion were bent over their stoves, putting the final touches on a rich and savory Creole breakfast that featured six separate entrées and a marvelous *plat* of fish. Mr. Smith's neighbor had lived in France, she had seen great officers in Napoleon's army; she knew exactly what elegance to expect of a *Général,* and exactly what elegance to offer.

The bayou twisted alongside the road like a huge dark green serpent. The watchers peered through the fog. At half past eight, as the gray mists finally began to lift and the tops of the cypresses came into view, the first members of Jackson's party appeared. They clattered over a narrow wooden bridge and into Smith's courtyard and dismounted. The nearest of them tossed their reins to some grinning Negro boys, and then they all walked to the high porch, which even a Spanish villa requires in the Louisiana swamps.

These were young men, one or two of them very handsome, all of them cheerful, excited, gay. Smith and his hostess stepped forward to shake their hands and help pull off their heavy traveling coats, and his neighbor was gratified to see that underneath the coats they all wore crisp (or as crisp as the fog would allow) dress uniforms complete with swords and gold epaulettes. Then, arms full of coats, they both turned to observe the last man off his horse.

Jackson wore no dress uniform. As he came trudging across the courtyard, he had on a faded blue coat, nearly threadbare, a small-brimmed cap made out of cracked leather, and a short brown Spanish cloak splattered with mud. Unlike his young officers, who wore short boots and curved spurs, he wore high dragoon working boots, long innocent of polish or blacking, which reached to his knees. There was no visible insignia of rank. Nearer, Jackson's face was gaunt and yellow with illness; his body was shockingly thin and emaciated, and he moved with evident pain.

In the elegant dining room, while the young men sat down, shook out their damask napkins, and did full justice to the meal, Jackson explained that his digestion would only permit him to eat a few things these days.

Did they happen to have anywhere in the house a bowl of boiled hominy grits?

Smith's hostess called him sweetly into the next room and, once behind closed doors, threw down her apron and stamped her foot with Gallic disgust. "Such a trick! Such a miserable *truc*! You said a great *Général—un héros*! I worked myself almost to death to make your house *comme il faut*, I commanded a *splendide petit déjeuner*"—here her French broke down, and nothing would do but English—"and all for an ugly old Kaintuck flat-boatman!"

If Jackson heard any of that in the dining room he gave no sign of it. He took a single silver spoonful of hominy grits, pushed away the bowl, and spread out on the cloth in front of him a dirty, much-folded navigator's map of the Louisiana coast.

The historian, always in search of patterns and parallels, is pleased to record that two months earlier, on the island of Grande Terre in Barataria Bay, some seventy miles south of New Orleans, an almost precisely similar comedy had unfolded.

There, on the same kind of gray and overcast Louisiana morning, a British warship with the charmingly un-warlike name of H.M.S. *Sophie* had sailed in very close on a narrow strait of water that ran between Grand Terre and a lesser island to the west.

From the foredeck the British could see a steep bluff commanding the strait, and on top of the bluff a small red-bricked fortress ringed with exotic palm trees. One six-pounder cannon was clearly visible; others were undoubtedly hidden. The little fort had neither flagpole nor flag.

The *Sophie* anchored as close to the island as she could maneuver and fired two quick signal shots from her bow gun. In a few moments the officers on deck observed a boat containing five more or less nondescript men push out from the sandy beach at the foot of the bluff. The *Sophie* sent out its gig to meet them. When they were side by side, rocking in the light swell, Captain Charles Lockyer of the 52nd Devonshire Lights braced his arm on the gunwale, stood up, and introduced himself and his attendant, a marine captain named McWilliams. They were looking, Lockyer said in English, for the "privateer" (and visibly smirked at the word) Jean Lafitte. Could any of the gentlemen in the boat be of help? All of the gentlemen wore dirty looks, dirty canvas trousers, and grubby white shirts open at the throat. One of them leaned over his oar, wiped his mustache with his sleeve, and replied in guttural French that maybe they could, maybe they couldn't, but if Lockyer really wanted to find Lafitte, he would have to come ashore to see him.

Now this was not so easy as it appeared. In years past the British navy in its role as self-appointed policeman of the seas had done a good deal of damage, one way and another, to the "privateer" business in the Gulf of Mexico, and the mob of barefooted men now watching on the beach had finally recognized the hated flag of His Majesty's service. As the gig put ashore they came rushing forward, shouting, cursing, pounding tumultuously on its sides. Lockyer reached for his pistol. McWilliams pulled out a dirk. From the other boat their mustached guide splashed through the water to them and shouted back at the mob in a rapid-fire French. Whatever he said was not well received and he repeated it, louder, and drove them backward a little with his arms and his feet. Somebody cursed the British navy in Spanish, somebody else drew a cutlass and stabbed it hilt-deep into the sand directly in front of Captain McWilliams. After a tense five minutes of negotiations, standing all the while up to their knees in the warm Gulf surf, the two officers were allowed to pass between two rows of the muttering pirates and onto the beach. They walked for another five minutes uphill, passing several large, well-constructed brick warehouses, some tin-roofed dormitories, a kitchen, what evidently was a private saloon and brothel, and finally arrived at a windswept porch on the bluff, overlooking Barataria Bay. Below them the mob had regathered and was staring up in glowering silence. The white sails of the *Sophie* looked far away.

Their mustached guide strolled across the porch, hooked a wicker chair with one bare foot, dragged it forward, and sat.

"*Bon. Vous cherchez Lafitte. Puis-je vous demander pour quelle raison?*"

Lockyer had the usual British accent that sounds to French ears like a woodchuck gnawing a sausage, but seeing nobody else on the porch, he searched his memory for serviceable phrases and managed to answer that he had come seeking Lafitte on a military mission, a *peaceful* mission, with a personal message for the pirate leader.

"*Paisible?*" the guide asked doubtfully.

"*Paisible.*" Completely peaceful.

The guide crossed his legs and pressed his fingertips together under his chin. "*Alors, asseyez-vous, messieurs.* I am in fact myself Lafitte."

If Captain Lockyer was as surprised as J. Kilty Smith's Creole hostess, he concealed it better (but he was British, after all, not French). He bowed and took a chair as requested and then produced ceremoniously out of his coat pocket a small oilskin package addressed in a large flowing hand simply to "M. Lafitte."

"Ah, pleasure first," Lafitte said, putting the package on the nearest table without so much as a glance. "Business *après*."

Both officers long remembered the meal that followed—"pleasure" in Louisiana as in France being always linked (but not limited) to food. At a clap of Lafitte's hands, a stream of barefooted servants came out of nowhere and began to lay out an elegant table of fish, game, rich Bordeaux wine, fruit from the West Indies, Arabica coffee, brandy, aromatic Cuban cigars. Lafitte the Pirate chatted urbanely, sometimes in French, sometimes in English; smoked his cigar; regaled his guests with seafaring jokes and stories (most of them secondhand—it had been many years indeed since Lafitte himself had put out to sea on business).

Eventually the oilskin package resurfaced. Lafitte knocked cigar ash onto the floor and unwrapped it and held up, one after the other, three separate documents. The first was a royal proclamation to the Citizens of Louisiana, calling on them to assist and welcome their British liberators. The second was a personal letter from Colonel Edward Nicholls of His Majesty's Life Guards, offering Lafitte prosperity, security, and the rank of Captain in the British navy (Lafitte smiled and kissed it and put it aside). The last, from Sir William Percy, commander of the naval forces in the Gulf, informed Lafitte rather brusquely that he and all his men and ships must be either England's friend or enemy in the coming battle for New Orleans. In either case, since the battle was almost at hand, Sir William required an immediate answer.

Lafitte lit a second cigar. From the beach, angry shouts could now be heard again. This was a flattering offer, Lafitte told the two Britons, and he was utterly unworthy of it; but he was delighted to accept it anyway, gratefully, and become a part of England's inevitable victory over the Americans. He would very much enjoy having the run of New Orleans. Here he paused to listen to the shouts, now louder than ever. But he would naturally have to persuade some of his more unruly men that such a decision was in their best interest, and this, as they could judge for themselves, would take time. Captain Lockyer studied Lafitte's thin, confident smile and found himself remembering the most recent report he had read from British Naval Intelligence. Several months ago, apparently in a surprise attack just before midnight, a rebellious mob like the one below had rushed to the very door of this very house, intent on dethroning their captain, and Lafitte, eating an apple at the time, had said not a word, but calmly stepped out onto the porch with the apple in one hand and a pistol in the other, and shot the nearest rebel straight through the head. An undoubtedly persuasive leader.

In exactly two weeks, Lafitte now said, he would bring them his formal letter of acceptance in person—he stood, smiled, offered his hand— along, of course, with his financial terms.

(These things really happened, dear Reader. Sitting quietly in my room, writing, encased in an ordinary and modest obscurity, I slowly come to accept that some lives are actually led like this, like Lafitte's and Jackson's—grand, sweeping, fiery, totally *theatrical* lives.)

Afterward, Lafitte waved from the beach until the two officers had safely regained the *Sophie;* then he turned around, grinning, and promptly set about to betray them.

CHAPTER
3

The Life of Andrew Jackson, by David Chase

Chapter Eight

BACK IN NEW ORLEANS ON THE MORNING OF DECEMBER 1, AS THE SKY darkened and raindrops started to fall, Jackson left J. Kilty Smith's breakfast table and climbed into a waiting coach, which carried him briskly down the Bayou St. John and into the city.

And as if he had been split in half by a thunderbolt, he promptly became another person.

The first had been, of course, the nearly crippled old Kaintuck flat-boatman who sat down sallow-faced and weary to his little invalid's bowl of boiled hominy. The second, by all accounts, at noon precisely stepped out onto a balcony overlooking the Carré St. Louis, looked down at the hundreds of assembled citizens who were squinting up at him through the drizzle, and raised his arms high like Julius Caesar. The effect was electrifying. This Jackson had a fierce glare in his eyes, his gray hair stood up straight and savage. He began to speak. A presumptuous, cowardly, underhanded *Enemy* menaced their City, he announced to the people, and he, Andrew Jackson, was come to save them. They were, from that moment on, by his express order to cease all quarrels and divisions among themselves. They were to rally around his command. *He* would protect the city, he said—and he gripped the balcony rail with both hands and thrust himself forward dramatically—*he* would drive their enemies back into the sea or else he would *perish himself* in the effort.

A lawyer named Edward Livingston began to translate his speech into correct and tepid French, but the visceral message had already been received: The crowd was applauding and cheering wildly—*"Vive Jackson! Vive le Grand Général!"* Jackson wiped his pale brow and stepped back out of the rain.

That night his metamorphosis continued. Livingston had arranged for him a welcoming supper of some dozen or more of New Orleans's most elegant and socially prominent couples. But Madame Livingston, Creole herself, had already talked with Kilty Smith's neighbor, and she, too, stamped her foot in indignant Gallic protest—she would *not* have "that wild Indian fighter" in her drawing room.

Her husband was wearily amused. "He will capture *you* at first sight," he drawled.

And indeed somehow between his arrival speech and the Livingston dinner, while he was at the same time establishing his command post at 106 Royal Street and sending out a furious stream of letters and orders, Jackson managed to change into a genuine full-dress major general's uniform—peacock blue frock coat with buff facings, enormous gold epaulettes, a spotless white waistcoat, skintight yellow buckskin breeches, polished boots. The transformation startled Livingston; it *amazed* his wife. As Jackson entered the room, he stopped at the door, looked around and smiled, and bowed to all of the ladies present, who silently rose in awe. Speechless, Madame Livingston held out her hand. Gallantly, Major General Jackson took it and led her back to her sofa, where he sat down beside her and began to speak with cultivated enthusiasm of the beauty of the city and the exquisite taste of her house. When some of the Creole ladies expressed their fear of the British—whose slogan for New Orleans was reportedly "Beauty and Booty"—Jackson turned and gently reassured them that he would personally repel any invasion, any attack whatsoever. To Edward Livingston, at the table, he held up his glass of Madeira, inspected its color, and suavely remarked that he had not tasted anything like it since a dinner at Aaron Burr's house in Philadelphia in 1797.

I have no way whatsoever to account for human nature.

The next morning, however, Jackson doffed his gallantry and his glamour and reverted to the task at hand. His first action was to establish an official line of defense for the city (though he wrote in disgust to Coffee that nobody except the pirates seemed to have accurate maps). Despite a return of his dysentery and fever he rode out three days in a row to inspect emplacements and bridges. Then he sent detachments of engineers to cut down trees and obstruct the most likely roads and bayous that the British could use as approaches.

At this point he had fewer than two thousand troops on hand and was desperately short of ammunition. As usual, he called on Coffee. In a second letter he ordered that intrepid soldier posthaste from Tennessee to the city. Meanwhile he organized six or seven hundred New Orleans citizens into militias, hastily dressed them up in improvised uniforms, and set them to drilling in front of the St. Louis cathedral. And about this time, clearing his throat discreetly, Edward Livingston, who was by one of history's nice coincidences also Jean Lafitte's personal lawyer, came to Royal Street. He asked for a few moments of Jackson's time. Then he spread out on Jackson's desk the oilskin packet and the three British letters that Lafitte had received from Captain Lockyer.

Lafitte, he explained, had decided to make amends for his past misconduct. He wished very much to join Jackson's army, not the British.

Jackson swept the papers to the floor.

Why, by the Eternal, should he trust these "hellish banditti" (his very words), these worse-than-thieving goddamn *pirates*?

Taken aback, Livingston tried to lay out three lawyerlike reasons.

First, Lafitte was French-born and hated the British with the kind of tribal instinct that Jackson could understand.

Second, he had well over one million dollars' worth of pirated goods sitting in his Grand Terre warehouses. The Americans, especially the easygoing merchants of New Orleans, tended to wink and overlook the matter of import duties. The British (and most of Lafitte's stolen goods were British) were not likely to be so flexible.

And third, though nobody else in the world ever found him remotely lovable, Lafitte's swarthy and ill-formed brother (who went by the *nom de pirate* of Dominique You) was at that very moment languishing in a

New Orleans jail, arrested by the local authorities in one of their periodic fits of law and order. The merchants had remonstrated and offered to pay Dominique's bail, since Dominique was an extremely useful supplier of goods, but the governor was uncharacteristically firm (*cherchez la femme:* his wife was said to have been jilted once by Jean); he offered a reward of $5000 for the capture of Jean as well, to which the jaunty pirate had replied with an offer himself of $30,000 for the capture of the governor.

Jackson, not on record anywhere as enjoying this kind of joke, listened in silence. Lafitte's offer was rejected.

Rejected and scorned, that is, until the morning of December 16, one week later, when the British abruptly sank every American gunboat on the Gulf inlet of Lake Borgne, some fifteen miles southeast of the city, and all of New Orleans woke up to the news in a state of hand-wringing panic. Lafitte controlled dozens of ships, hundreds of men—no one knew the coast like Lafitte. A committee rushed to the federal judge and petitioned for amnesty, granted on the spot. Within an hour, Dominique was walking out of the Cabildo, rubbing his unshackled wrists and waving to his friends; meanwhile his brother Jean, unannounced, unarmed, uninvited, simply strolled down Royal Street, climbed up one flight of stairs, and knocked on General Jackson's door.

What the two old lions said to each other has gone unrecorded. For once Jackson was completely alone, reading his maps and drinking his poisonous calomel medicine. Apparently Lafitte brought news that was shrewdly intended to infuriate him—the British had on board their ships a number of printing presses with which they planned to print the new, *British* laws of Louisiana; after the invasion, Lafitte added, their commander would be dubbed the Earl of New Orleans—and clearly Jackson responded by changing his mind (not often on record for *that* either). While Livingston scratched his head and pondered the mysteries of life, the two men appeared on the street arm in arm, chatting like cronies; then Lafitte hurried off to join his pirates.

Now the king-making drama begins, the reason Andrew Jackson stands today on the threshold of the President's mansion.

The main bayou leading from Lake Borgne toward the city crosses over the plantation of one Major Gabriel Villeré, eight or nine miles to the south of the New Orleans docks. On his first inspection Jackson had ordered the bayou obstructed with logjams and a company of guards stationed constantly on its bank. For some reason the obstructions were never laid down, and the guard consisted of no more than a dozen sleepy, untrained militia huddled in an abandoned fisherman's shack on Villeré's property. At dawn on December 23 a convoy of British barges crept five miles up the bayou. They captured the dozing pickets, and continued on to the very edge of Villeré's yard, where Villeré himself happened to be sitting on his porch in front of the Mississippi, smoking a smuggled cigar and watching his brother clean a rifle. When he ground out his cigar and looked up, he was a prisoner.

The British escorted him quickly inside the house. On the bayou Villeré could now see barge after barge floating up out of the swamps. Each was jammed with soldiers and black cannon. He sighed, pretended to dust off his trousers, and leaped straight through the nearest window. In the yard he bowled over a sentry and jumped a fence, then disappeared into the cypress swamp running like a deer.

At half past noon that same day a guard rapped once at Jackson's headquarters door and calmly announced "three Creole gentlemen with news," whereupon in rushed Villeré and two of his neighbors, by no means calm but breathless and spattered from head to foot in red bayou mud.

Jackson was ill as usual, impatient as usual. He could barely stand or speak. "All right, damnit, what news?"

"Important! Highly important! The British—" Villeré was drowned out by the other two, who danced around him shouting in French.

"Here?" Jackson demanded, his hand to his ear. "Now?"

"Yes, yes, all over my farm—redcoats! They landed this morning, thousands!"

Then Jackson, according to all three witnesses, struck the table with his clenched fist and made an instantaneous and momentous decision: "By the Eternal, they shall not sleep on our soil! We fight them tonight!"

And by three o'clock that same afternoon he had in fact galvanized every troop in his command—Coffee's Tennessee cavalry, a ragtag group of men in dingy hunting shirts and coonskin hats, galloped past in a fury. The *Carolina*, Jackson's sole warship, lifted anchor at the Bourbon Street docks and started downriver; his two companies of blacks and mulattoes marched out double-time—every man and boy in New Orleans was apparently on the road. And yet by the strange mathematics of war, they were still only about two thousand strong, and by now the British had landed almost four thousand soldiers; another *ten thousand* waited on board their ships for the transport barges to return.

Ten thousand men. Jackson gathered his maps and sword and set out himself at a gallop.

By then it was five o'clock and the late December sun was sinking over the black treetops and the great humped levees on the opposite bank of the river. At Villeré's plantation the British had settled into an open camp that stretched from the Mississippi half a mile eastward to the edge of the impenetrable cypress swamps, a wide grassy plain crisscrossed by small canals and dotted with long patches of cane stubble. Hundreds of small campfires began to spring up where the troops, having scavenged the plantation, were cooking their meals. In the Villeré house a British major named Thornton was unrolling his maps and trying to convince his commanding general that the troops should push on to the city and surprise it and *take* it. (Thornton had a Jacksonian nature.) General Keane was cautious, correct; he made war by the book, as the book had been written in London; he intended to marshal his forces and wait until dawn.

As the two men paced Villeré's porch, arguing in low voices, six hundred yards to the north a squadron of soldiers on horseback, perhaps a hundred in number, came trotting boldly down the New Orleans road. At the first British outposts they suddenly widened their front and, scattering over the field, charged recklessly forward up to the nearest ditch. There they halted and their commander coolly stood in his stirrups and surveyed the camp; then he wheeled his squadron and cantered away, under a volley of gunfire.

Silence returned. Darkness gathered over the camp. The British soldiers returned to their meal.

At seven o'clock a shadowy vessel could be seen drifting downriver. The British sentries assumed it was one of their own warships and hailed it. The officers assumed it was a freighter making for the Gulf and safety. The ship moved slowly with the current until all at once it sheered directly toward the shore on the left flank of the British. In the blackness her anchor could be heard going down with a splash. Lighted matches moved eerily over the deck. And then as the British uneasily stood or sat, illuminated against the darkness by their brilliant campfires, without any warning at all the *Carolina* fired a perfect tornado of cannonballs and grapeshot and the British camp flew apart like glass under a hammer.

She fired steadily for ten full merciless minutes, raking the unprotected field from left to right. It was so dark that, apart from the flashes of cannon and spiraling geysers of coals blown skyward out of the campfires, no one could see, no one could make out an object more than an arm's length away. All over the black fields the wounded were shrieking or crawling for shelter. At each new thundering broadside their bodies were knocked and tossed into the air like flying logs. For ten full merciless minutes the shocked British army huddled on its knees in the mud.

And then, at an unheard signal the ship's cruel barrage began to slacken. Major Thornton hesitated for no more than an instant; he ran forward, crouching, to assemble his men and regroup, only to hear, to his amazement, far to the right at the edge of the swamps, isolated reports of rifle fire, growing louder and louder every moment.

In Thucydides's *History* the armies of Athens and Syracuse clash once, and once only, by night. So chaotic, so terrible is the black swirling confusion of that battle that unknowing brother slays brother, unseeing friend slaughters friend; demonic spears thrown by invisible hands seem to whir suddenly out of the sky; whole troops of men disappear screaming into the darkness. What Thornton heard that night was the charge of General Coffee's eight hundred Tennessee hunters, dismounted now, roaring up out of the swamps with their rifles blazing. In a matter of minutes, the two armies had run headlong blindly into each other's arms. History, always unoriginal, began to repeat itself. No one could tell friend from foe at much more than a saber's length. Both Americans and British shouted commands and counter-commands in English. Tomahawks and bayonets hacked at sheer nothing, pistols and rifles fired point-blank mindlessly into the night. Coffee himself stormed through the battle like the Ajax he was, huge and unhurt, somehow leading his troops by his voice alone. They struck, retreated to the right, struck again.

And Jackson, meanwhile, Ajax's hero?

From a command post high on a levee Major General Jackson could see little but shapes and shadows and the constant flash of muzzles. He ordered his infantry forward. He rolled a battery of six-pounder cannons to the edge of the levee and started firing just as the *Carolina* slackened. When the artillery horses reared in panic, he jumped down among them and dressed the lines himself.

At a stake-and-rail fence that guarded a shallow canal, his soldiers started to stumble and fall. Thornton's marines charged out of nowhere. Jackson drew his own sword and pistol—"Save the goddamn guns!" The two lines seesawed back and forth in the thick mud and thicker darkness.

For the first five minutes it appeared that Jackson's daring assault would carry him all the way forward to the Villeré house. But the British troops were the best of Wellington's veterans. These were soldiers who had fought the Spanish in the bloody Peninsular Wars and Bonaparte up and down Flanders (six months later some of the Tennessee horses captured this night would figure at Waterloo); they regarded the American army with scorn, thanks to its disgraceful flight from Washington City. Thornton rallied his men. Jackson's thin line wavered, fell back. Coffee fell back. At half past eight a thick fog blew in from the river and covered the fields. All artillery ceased. By nine o'clock the two invisible armies lay in the wet grass and mud exactly where they had started, six hundred yards apart.

There are two stories told about Jackson's conduct during Coffee's raid.

In the first, some weeks later a Louisiana belle compliments the *Général* on his most graceful and elegant bow, which would ornament the court of a king, and Jackson smiles his best drawing-room smile and says that he learned the art on the night of the twenty-third, when he spent the whole evening bowing politely to the British bullets as they passed over his head.

In the second, which is verified by Coffee, when dawn finally did break on Christmas Eve Jackson was surrounded by a committee of frightened New Orleans legislators who had ridden out to tell him that the Legislature was frightened by the size of the British army and wished to surrender at once. *Surrender* is not a Jacksonian word, and this was not the drawing room Jackson. He threw his hat violently into the mud. He glared about him. The committee began to edge backward, out of his range. "Tell the goddamned cowardly Legislature," he bellowed, "I intend to *smash* the British or die. If they say one more word, I shall close them down first and then *blow them up!*" And at the nearest of them he pointed his finger and roared, "And by the Almighty God, if you don't send me balls and powder instantly, I shall chop off your head and have it rammed into a cannon."

They scattered like rabbits.

C H A P T E R

4

Well, I would make one *small* correction of fact," John Coffee said.

He handed the chapter back to Chase and stretched his right heel out to the very edge of the new Persian rug that the Nashville Inn had recently and recklessly installed in the lobby. A grizzled old Cumberland farmer in mudboots paused six feet away, worked his jaw like a rusty gate, then spat a dribble of golden-brown tobacco juice in the general direction of a brass spittoon. Missed by a foot.

"I only had about *seven* hundred men with me on the night raid of the twenty-third," Coffee said, scratching his knee and watching the juice spread over the delicate red wool. Filthy habit. Filthy taste. He cleared his dry throat. "Not eight hundred, the way you say. When we dismounted by the cypress swamp I had to leave a hundred men back to take care of the horses."

"O.K.," Chase said, making a note, and then he looked up and flushed right to the roots of his hair.

Coffee grinned. "Everybody says that out here," he told him. "*Oke.* It's Cherokee for 'that's right.' Now you're looking all red and embarrassed because back East they credit General Jackson's illiterate bad spelling—'orl keerect' or some such, am I right? Seven hundred men."

"Seven hundred." Chase wrote something else in the miniature notebook he carried, made out of leather so finely tooled that Coffee assumed it was French, or foreign at least. "Any other corrections?"

"As far as I know," Coffee said, "the rest is fine. The Creek War is fine, Horseshoe Bend is fine, the Revolution, the General's boyhood. You've done a pile of reading and interviewing, Mr. Chase." Coffee leaned his big body forward a little to scratch the other knee and get a better look at Chase's face. "I would say that you start out pretty neutral about the General, in those early chapters, and in the newest ones you're starting to make him out to be a hero. Which he was."

Chase had—Coffee searched for the word—an *expressive* face. As he scribbled another note, the flush gave way to a boyish twist of the lips, an eyebrow lifted. The young man wrote very well indeed, Coffee thought. And it was a skill Coffee admired and envied. He tugged at his ear, the agreed-on signal, and James A. Hamilton Jr. detached himself from the bar.

"This is David Chase," Coffee said as Hamilton reached them. "The writer."

"The writer." Hamilton sat down just as Chase stood up, so that they looked for a moment to Coffee like a set of human pistons shaking hands.

"Mr. Chase is writing a book about General Jackson," Coffee said, as if Hamilton didn't know, and Hamilton crossed his legs and cocked his head to show that this was important news. "He brought a letter of introduction from the editor of the New York *Post* and he wants to come on out and meet the General."

"I know the owner of the *Post*," Hamilton said, and added with perfect sincerity, "a very rich man."

"*And* a letter from General Lafayette in France."

"Impressive." Hamilton nodded briskly. "Most impressive. I've been away in Kentucky and hadn't heard about this, but the fact is, General Coffee, I've actually read two or three of Mr. Chase's articles, he's a very well-known writer, quite well-known, positively."

"The letter from Lafayette was the publisher's idea," David Chase said with a rather dogged honesty that made Coffee wonder how he could write about politics. "I'm afraid I've never met Lafayette in my life."

"I met him once," Coffee said. "The biggest teeth I ever saw on a man.

He looked like a redheaded pineapple. He came out here in 1820 when he was the Guest of the Nation, on his famous tour, and he stayed at the Hermitage two or three days and General Jackson gave him a banquet and a sword."

"Colorful days," Hamilton said with one of his two-second New York smiles.

"And a few years later," Coffee said, because he felt for some reason irritable or mischievous or both, "his friend Frances Wright turned up at the Hermitage with a letter from Lafayette, too, and she wanted the General to advise her in buying some property."

"I don't think the General has any connection with Fanny Wright," Hamilton said quite sharply.

"No." Coffee cleared his throat.

"You're one of his campaign managers," Chase remarked, and Hamilton nodded, pleased at the title, and sawed at the point in his collar where his silk cravat should have been. But over the past three months Hamilton had gradually transformed himself, in dress at least, from a New York fop to a Tennessee dandy. Coffee observed the new Stetson hat by the side of his chair, of course; and the buck trousers and shiny high-top boots (today with a set of silver spurs) and now a beautifully tanned deerskin jacket with half a mile of fringe over the chest and sleeves. If you saw him loose in the woods, Coffee thought, you'd have to shoot him.

But the new clothes hadn't made him any less shrewd or political. "I'm sorry you came all this way," Hamilton was saying now, "just to interview the General. The truth is, we've had so much trouble with books and writers—you have that awful 'coffin handbill,' and the unspeakable newspaper attacks on poor Mrs. Jackson, and now Davy Crockett is writing slanders about the General at the Battle of New Orleans. What else?"

"Land fraud," Coffee said.

"Land fraud *accusations*," Hamilton snorted. "From the Florida campaign, when General Jackson added twenty million new acres to the country, out of the sheer goodness of his heart and patriotic vision, and not a square inch for himself—utterly baseless. The General makes very few public appearances, if any, because of misquotation and slander like that. I'm sorry to disappoint you, Mr. Chase, and the New York *Post* too."

Coffee shifted in his chair and let his mind drift. John Eaton walked through the bar on his way upstairs. Two more farmers paused to spit. Outside the front window of the inn you could see the brand-new First

Presbyterian Church of Nashville, a great redbrick emblem of prosperity that lay alongside the street like a ship pulled up at a quay. Chase had accepted his correction of fact (and language) in good spirit; in his last chapter he had begun to see Jackson as the hero he really was. But what kind of hero hid from the press?

Hamilton had come to a halt with his usual smiling offer of an interview (perhaps) after the General was elected in November, and now he was sitting in his chair, hands crossed stiffly over his lap as if no letter or finely tooled notebook in the world would make him change his mind. Which was the point, of course. And after that the writer was supposed to shake his head in frustration and gather his pencils and just slink away, "handled." But Chase stayed right where he was. He looked at Hamilton and then at Coffee and then said something that made Coffee completely revise his opinion of him.

"Who actually makes the decision?" Chase asked, and in the abrupt silence that followed, Hamilton looked like a man who'd been kicked by a mule.

"I do," Coffee said, and started to rise. "Let's go out for a ride, Mr. Chase."

CHAPTER

5

The Life of Andrew Jackson, by David Chase

Chapter Nine

DECEMBER 24, THE DAY AFTER COFFEE'S RAID, DAWNED PALE AND FOGGY AND sullen, no one but an Englishman's idea of Christmas Eve.

For nearly an hour after sunrise neither side's sentries could report anything better to their watch commanders than darkness visible. But by seven o'clock, as a new shift of guards took up their stations for Jackson, a faint white oval sun was groping its way through the gray air. In another ten minutes the long carpet of muddy brown stubble that lay between the two armies gradually began to expose its wreckage. Across the no-man's-land of the center a few blackening bodies caught the light. Closer to the river splintered beams and shafts of wood poked up into the fog like the spars of a ghostly shipwreck. When the sentries crept farther into the field, they could see half-wheels of shattered wagons buried in mud, overturned cannons, charred and smoldering wood, dead horses, and up and down in every direction patches of darkening red where the drying grass slowly licked at the blood.

In the heat of battle the Americans had taken up more or less blindly a position six hundred yards north of the British line, behind an abandoned mill-race. Under the bleak but growing sunlight the streambed now turned out to be little more than a shallow ditch, ten or fifteen feet wide, three or four feet deep; it ran due west from the black cypress swamps on Jackson's left straight into the soft, treeless levees that separated the fields from the Mississippi River. The locals, Jackson was informed, called it the Rodriguez Canal.

Jackson's first impulse was to cross the canal and advance closer to the British sentinels; but by mid-morning, with the whole scene before him, he had taken the advice of his engineers—odd to write, but he had: The furious and independent Jackson had taken somebody else's advice—he had listened to their recommendations and ordered his troops to dig deeper and construct a defensive mud rampart behind the canal.

Now this is terrible country to dig in, a vast blanket of porous soil spread only four or five inches thick over oozing water. Walk a few feet anywhere along the Mississippi Delta and you feel its pulpy mush giving way like sponge under your heels, a trembling, quivering green-and-black gumbo that is Louisiana's bizarre version of *terra firma*. By contrast, Tennessee is a hard, muscular country where earth and water stay obedi-ently apart. (In New Orleans Jackson had been visibly shaken by the sight of the famous cemeteries of St. Charles's parish, whose coffins and crypts are all elevated on stilts or carved pillars five feet above the pasty earth, to be out of the reach of the water; he wrote Rachel that it was as if the living and the dead had changed places.) When his Tennessee soldiers tried to deepen the ditch, they found they were shoveling as much water as dirt, and before many minutes passed they stood in it waist-high or more, cursing.

Meanwhile Jackson, possessed by his mood, was everywhere at once. He paced the growing ramparts and shouted instructions. Wrapped in his old Spanish cape, he rode ceaselessly back and forth between his front lines and New Orleans, commandeering horses and mules and every kind of wagon or sledge from the increasingly nervous city. He sent convoy after creaking convoy of tools and food to his army. He filled the jails with slackers and deserters.

When night came the work went on. One detachment would fall back to its blankets and fires—there were no tents—and another would climb down into the mud. Jackson stayed on his horse, in sight of the troops. By Major Eaton's count he went three full days without closing his eyes. From time to time an aide would hand him up a bowl of cold rice, which he ate in the saddle.

This, Dear Reader, is the superhuman quality that friends and enemies alike call the *Iron Jacksonian Will.* Unleashed, whether in war or politics, it seems to carry everything before it, like a cold, furious tide of calculated anger. (I have no idea yet whether it is virtue or vice.)

Toward the end of the first day Jean Lafitte joined him to inspect the mud ramparts, and for the second time in twenty-four hours Jackson bent that Will to someone else's advice. Lafitte, jack-of-all-piratical-trades, had at one time studied the art of military entrenching, from French engineers stationed in Haiti. To his eye Jackson had stopped his defensive ramparts fifty perilous yards too short, just before a stand of woods bordering the impenetrable swamp. "If you leave it open," Lafitte diplomatically observed, "not that it is likely, but still it is *possible* that a lucky English charge could get past the canal and turn your flank. If, on the other hand, the ditch were extended all the way to the swamp . . ." Within an hour, Coffee's Dirty Shirts had dragged their shovels into place, and even more mud was flying.

On Christmas morning Jackson's troops awoke to the sound of guns in the British camp, which their spies soon reported were salvos in honor of a brand-new commander-in-chief, who had arrived in the night to replace General Kean.

Who was it?

History—the Muse of Coincidence—was having her usual chuckle. Lieutenant General Sir Edward Pakenham had been born thirty-nine years earlier in County Antrim, Ireland, the very place where Jackson's parents were born, and he had gone on to college in Dublin with one Dr. Redmond Dillon, a military enthusiast who subsequently emigrated to middle Tennessee, where he and his wife counted among their very best friends General and Mrs. Jackson. From Redmond Dillon, Jackson had already heard more than a belly-full of stories about the classmate Pakenham's soldierly prowess, especially his series of brilliant, reckless victories in the late Napoleonic Wars. (Jean Lafitte told him another: In 1803 a Creole privateer had shot Pakenham in the neck, a wound that had the effect of permanently tilting his head to one side; six years later at the capture of Martinique he was shot in the neck again, and this wound restored his head to its original upright position. As a younger man I once contemplated writing fiction instead of history, but how could mere fiction compete?)

This valorous and formidable and once-again straight-necked Pakenham took a single glance at the British position and with Jacksonian decisiveness ordered a battery of heavy cannon to be hauled in from his warships on Lake Borgne. For the *Carolina*, still anchored in the river and firing broadsides, had now been joined upstream by a second gunboat, the *Louisiana*, and until they were both silenced Pakenham's huge, unwieldy army was in effect trapped on its narrow plain, tied down like Gulliver by a pest of rag-tag Lilliputians.

In the porous Louisiana soil, it is no easy thing, however, to haul nine field pieces, two howitzers, one mortar, and a two-ton cast-iron furnace for heating cannon balls—these last needed to set fire to the wooden ships—no easy thing to pull such great iron burdens sixty miles through sucking mud and shivering swamp and then, by torchlight at night, install them in wooden emplacements opposite the American ships.

Meanwhile, as the caissons inched and groaned toward the river, the Americans began to engage in a type of warfare that infuriated the British. When they were not digging their ditch, Coffee's Dirty Shirts now amused themselves by creeping, on their bellies, day and night, through the dark cane stubble and firing single, deadly accurate rifle shots into the British camp. "Snipers," the British contemptuously called them—a newly coined word—in Europe no *gentleman* fought this way. Pakenham lifted his nose and sniffed and sent a small delegation under a truce flag to protest. Jackson refused to see them. Coffee walked over, looked the delegation up and down, and calmly remarked that troops who invaded other men's country hadn't much right to complain when people shot back. Then lowered his head and spat.

On the morning of December 27 Jackson climbed as usual to the second floor of his farmhouse headquarters some one hundred yards behind the canal, ready to survey his lines. An old Frenchman had lent him a telescope mounted on a tripod. Eaton carried him rice and a tin cup of spiced coffee. He sipped and ate. And then as the first beams of sunlight struck the tops of the cypress trees, Pakenham's new battery of cannon suddenly erupted down by the levees. An absolutely thunderous roar brought every sleeping soldier to his feet, every sailor on the *Carolina* scurrying for cover.

Red-hot cannon balls shot like meteors across the sky. Some fell hissing into the river. Others burned rings in the canvas sails, blasted the deck into spinning fragments.

Jackson peered through his telescope, suddenly jubilant, and sent two brisk orders *subito*—abandon the *Carolina,* tow the *Louisiana* upstream.

Because the brilliant and reckless Pakenham had made an inexplicable mistake.

Had he attacked the *Louisiana* first and afterward the *Carolina,* he might have blocked one with the sunken hulk of the other and disposed of them both. Instead, for nearly half an hour his guns concentrated on the poor *Carolina* alone, whose ropes were now burning, her upper deck, her masts and branching spars, every bone and rigging: a black skeleton in scarlet flames. The crew clambered over the sides into their skiffs. Wind rose, fire crackled; everything paused, even the guns, for a long moment. Then the flames reached the powder stores in her belly and the *Carolina* glowed yellow-red for an instant and went up in a massive explosion that shook the unsteady earth for miles around and threw smoking arcs of debris as far as Jackson's farmhouse.

Through the drifting haze came the cheers of Pakenham's soldiers. Unharmed, un-noticed, the *Louisiana* crept half a mile north, just out of range.

For the rest of the day Pakenham busily arranged his troops into two formal assault brigades. By nightfall Jackson's sentinels could peer over their mud ramparts, across the intervening black fields, and count hundreds and hundreds of low campfires bunched now on each flank. In the darkness they could hear horses moving, muffled orders. From time to time, next to a fire, a silver bayonet glinted.

On the same day, December 27, 1814, some four thousand miles to the east it was raining gray sheets of water in the already unspeakably gray and monotonous city of Ghent, Belgium. In their chambers in the Hôtel des Pays-Bas, on the ancient flag-draped Place d'Armes, the five American commissioners sent to negotiate a peace with Great Britain filed to their chairs, ordered their coffee, and sat down. On the table in front of them lay the final, official copy of the treaty they had just concluded, after six months of dreary meetings. A treaty that would bring an instant halt to hostilities as soon as it was signed in Washington. The commissioners picked it up with a general sigh of satisfaction, and then, just as they had done every day for the past six months, John Quincy Adams and Henry Clay quickly burst into a flaming row.

There was no problem with the treaty itself. Adams, however, was chairman of the commission, and he began by asserting that it was therefore his privilege to keep the official document with him at all times and indeed to carry it with him in his personal case when he set sail for New York. Clay, whose late nights and incessant gambling had set Adams's New England teeth on edge, instantly smacked his palm onto the table and demanded that *he,* as a former member of Congress, be allowed to carry the papers in *his* official baggage. Adams refused. Clay jumped up and paced the room, shouting. And for the next half hour they snapped and quarreled and heckled each other childishly, without mercy, until old, weary Albert Gallatin, Thomas Jefferson's friend, proposed some now forgotten but tactful compromise. The day passed westward over them, setting its face steadily toward New Orleans.

CHAPTER

6

There had been a delay at the hotel stables where Chase had to hire a horse, and then another delay at Clover Bottom when two racing Conestoga wagons sideswiped each other and overturned in a fine billowing confusion of chickens and canvas and flying axles that took nearly half an hour to untangle. It was almost five o'clock in the afternoon before Coffee and Chase finally turned off the Lebanon Turnpike, twelve miles east of Nashville, and started up the road to Jackson's property.

"One more mile," Coffee said, twisting in the saddle and looking back at Chase. The sun was brutally hot, Tennessee hot, out in the open on the dusty road, and poor Chase's face was cherry red and dripping with sweat. The hair on his bare head was plastered flat, coated with dust. He managed to grin anyway and hold up a thumb like a Roman emperor.

Coffee nodded, satisfied, and turned back to contemplate the depressing scrub pine forest that lined the road and gave next to nothing by way of shade. It was a silly thing to say, but he disliked pine trees, and always had. Forty years ago, when he had first come out to middle Tennessee, there were no pines at all down in the old-growth forests, which was one of the reasons he had wanted to stay. It was hickories mainly then, and red oaks and hollies and canopy elms, but most of those were hardwoods, of course, and they had long ago been cut down for building.

He let his eye follow the pines as they rolled downhill to the left in a gray scraggly wave, following the slope toward the Stones River. In the old days the virgin forests hadn't been half so close and overgrown, either. The trees had stood far apart—a man could walk out in the woods and take a shovel and throw it sixty or seventy feet and not hit a tree—and the forest solitude had a certain feeling of luxurious space about it. Now . . .

"Those would be General Jackson's cotton fields," Chase said, trotting up next to him. Side by side their sweating horses slowed and fell into a syncopated *clop-clop* that was about as peaceful a sound and rhythm as Coffee knew.

"Over beyond the pines," he agreed. "You look hot," he said. "Maybe you should have waited to ride out with Hamilton in his carriage."

Chase shook his head. "I came this far, I waited two days in the hotel for you to see me. I'm ready. Besides, Mr. Hamilton didn't seem all that happy about your decision."

Coffee chuckled. No, he hadn't.

"On the trip from Washington City," Chase said, craning his head now and looking about, too, "past the Cumberland Gap the stagecoach would pass whole fields of nothing but dead stumps, where somebody had cut down every single tree and hauled them away for timber. Acres and acres of nothing but stumps."

"Sometimes," Coffee told him, "a lazy farmer will strip off a ring of bark first, so the tree just dies on its own and he can chop it down later if he feels like it. You can kill off a square mile a day like that. Used to be different. When I came out in 1793 you always carried your axe or your tomahawk into the woods, of course, and people opened up their cropland to plant, but you didn't have this massive, endless clearing for profit."

And after another moment he surprised himself by adding, "We had herds of buffalo out here too. All gone now. The first spring I lived in Nashville the General and I watched a man shoot a buffalo—it wasn't a mile from this road—shot him right in the forehead, and the buffalo's skull was so thick the bullet just flattened against it. He chased all three of us up a thorn tree. That's the Hermitage there."

Chase rose in his stirrups. He peered toward the two whitewashed brick gateposts that marked the driveway, and Coffee leaned over and allowed himself one last spit before he entered Rachel's house, on the condition that he would indulge himself in no more old-man's reminiscences about the past, when everything was bigger and better. The good old past was a boneyard, a clear-cut field full of rotting stumps, and everything good about it was probably just a nostalgic fiction. He looked up at the slate gray roofs behind the trees where Jackson lived. Well, no, not everything.

✷ ✷ ✷

RACHEL was sitting on the porch smoking a Spanish cigar when they rode up and dismounted, and Coffee made it a point to linger by his horse and let Chase get out a few steps in front of him. Because, he thought as he loosened a cinch, you always liked to study somebody else's face who was meeting Rachel for the very first time.

"Well, there you are, John Coffee," she announced, struggling up from her chair. She was dressed as usual in a shapeless calico housedress without a collar—Lord, how the fine ladies in New Orleans had grimaced—and her old-woman's belly poked out like a shelf. She waddled to the edge of the porch with the cigar in one hand and her apron full of beans in the other. How tall was she now? Five feet? And five feet wide around? Thirty-five years ago she had been taller and thinner—well, who hadn't been?—but age had treated Rachel far more cruelly than the other women in her family. He remembered a snatch of Shakespeare about Time's injurious claws, Time's scythe, Time that gave beauty did his gift confound.

"I believe," Rachel said, "the General kicked off all the kivers last night and I'm afraid, saints prevent it, he's coming down with a summer cold. But now you, look at you, you're *hot,* young man!" She was puffing and wheezing asthmatically by now, but she beamed up at Chase as though she were his oldest friend in the world and then fussed over at one of the black girls to bring them some cold water.

"*Ice* water," she called, "*plenty* of ice," and took Chase by the elbow. "The General made me the best icehouse in Tennessee; you'll have to see it down by Alfred's cabin. I'm Rachel Jackson."

Chase performed a courtly little bow, just as if he had been introduced to a Parisian belle, which made Coffee like him even better, and Rachel, still holding the shelled beans in one corner of her apron, smiled in pure delight and said, "My!"

"This is Mr. David Chase from Boston," Coffee told her. "He's come to meet the General."

"Well, he can stay for supper too," Rachel said. To Chase: "He's in his lib'ry with his books, and John Coffee surely knows the way. We'll send your ice water there."

In the hallway they shook off their dust and scraped their shoes on China-reed matting, and Coffee watched Chase register with surprise the elegant red and white silk wallpaper depicting Calypso and Telemachus, which the General had picked out himself in a catalogue and ordered from France. "Now down the hall and to the right," he said, "second door."

If it was interesting to see someone (an Easterner especially) meet Rachel for the first time, it was a revelation, always, to see a stranger meet Jackson. Coffee had never laid eyes in his life on George Washington, but he had heard older people in Virginia talk about the actual, physical shock of Washington's presence—like a Greek statue come to life, like a personal *force* or an *aura,* they would say, groping for words. And it was the same way with Jackson, he guessed, except that Washington was by all accounts really a splendid manly specimen, tall and muscular and heavy, and Jackson had a surprisingly skinny, high-shouldered beanpole of a body, and a long, nearly lantern-jawed face that nobody would ever mistake for handsome. But men (and women) usually reacted as if they had received an electric shock. Thomas Jefferson had been taller and stronger, but *his* electricity evidently only worked through pen and ink.

"Mr. David Chase," Coffee said as they walked in, "General Jackson."

Jackson was standing by the window holding a newspaper in his hand. He turned around slowly and looked first at Chase and then at Coffee with flat, unfriendly eyes.

Chase bowed and took an instinctive step backward, Coffee observed. Force.

"The young man who's writing a book?" The General's voice was stern and curt. So far in this summer of 1828 Jackson had no cause to love writers.

"I took it on myself to bring Mr. Chase around," Coffee said. "He's come all the way from Washington City. He's written some very nice pages on New Orleans." Meaning not a word so far about Rachel.

Jackson studied Coffee for a long, thoughtful moment. No cause to love writers, but no reason to affront them either. Courtesy, when it could be managed, was Jackson's code.

"Well, I'm glad to see you, Mr. Chase," Jackson said. He relaxed his clenched mouth just a fraction.

"He wants to spend a little time around the Hermitage—I'm going to find him a room over at the Fountain of Health—and maybe talk about early times, for the first part of his book. And he'd like to ask some questions about the election campaign."

Jackson nodded. "As for the campaign, you can just take a look at what arrived in the mail today, Mr. Chase. Not twenty minutes ago. You can include it in your book under 'The Beauties of Politics.'" He put down the newspaper and produced from a chaotic stack of envelopes and boxes on his table a huge, foot-long tortoiseshell ladies' comb, trimmed with colored feathers and crowned with a six-inch oval portrait of Jackson himself (looking for all the world, Coffee thought, handing it back, like the poet Lord Byron).

"I have waistcoats with my portrait," Jackson said, "and hand towels and badges and beer mugs and ugly china plates, and now a ladies' hair comb. When a Jackson commode arrives in the mail, I shall retire in glory."

Chase laughed, and Jackson indicated a leather chair by the single glass-front bookcase that made this room the "lib'ry." "Have a seat, Mr. Chase."

"This is part of the book he's writing," Coffee said. He handed him the set of page proofs Chase had brought along as his *bona fides*. Jackson looked at them warily for a moment. Then he sat down himself in his own leather chair by the round newspaper table and crossed his legs. "General Coffee mentioned Washington City," he said, "but I see this is being printed in a Boston magazine?"

"Yes, sir." (Ice water appeared with a giggle—two shy black girls distributing clay mugs from a tray.)

"I can't say that I enjoy tremendous popularity in Boston," Jackson remarked. His eyes lingered on Chase's obviously eastern coat and fashionable white collar. "I'm told when they want to frighten little children in Boston, they say Andy Jackson is coming to get them."

Coffee had taken his usual place on the horsehair couch by the window. "Mr. Chase was doing most of his research in Washington City," he said, to steer them away from Boston. "He came out by the Cumberland Gap and the National Road, and steamboat from Cincinnati."

"Nine days on the road altogether," Chase said. "In Kentucky, I told General Coffee, I saw some of the most beautiful country in the world and stayed in the worst taverns in my life."

"Oh, the pampered younger generation," Jackson said, but without any real sting in his voice. He turned over a few pages in his lap. "People have different ideas about early times. When General Coffee and I were coming out, back in 1788, we used to say it was like traveling backward in time to come out West—you left the cities and the streetlamps and the nice hotels, and pretty soon you were going through villages with nothing but a country store and half a dozen frame houses, then farms, then nothing but forests. Once you crossed the Cumberland Gap you didn't even see money. Do you remember that, John? People would cut a dollar bill into triangles and use them for quarters, because there weren't any coins."

"They would indeed."

"No chamber pots," Jackson said. "I was a young, delicate boy somewhere around Knoxville and I asked for the chamber pot where I was staying, and the innkeeper didn't even look up. He said, 'There's a broken pane in the window.' Which there was."

"Don't use that in your book," Coffee said, and sipped his water and wondered if he had made a mistake after all in bringing young Chase around. Jackson flipped another page in his lap. When he glanced Coffee's way, the eyes were as hard and remote as ever.

Despite his vow about old-men's reminiscences, Coffee said something else, just to be talking. "You wouldn't believe it back East, Mr. Chase, but out here we were so poor and crude we used to put maple sugar chunks in our tea instead of real sugar. To sweeten it. We'd break a chunk right off the tree with our fingers. I don't think there was a sugar bowl in Tennessee. Farther west, people didn't even know what to do with tea. I stopped with a family in Arkansas that boiled the leaves in a pot and ate them like stamp-porridge. Another man spread his tea leaves on his bread and butter. He told me he once ate half a pound at a meal.

"I have sometimes wondered," Coffee added, "what it would have been like if the country had been settled west to east, instead of the other way around."

"Oh, then I would be the sophisticate and the writer," Jackson drawled, "and Mr. Chase would be coming to us from the remote fishing village of Boston."

And this time, if you were looking for it, there was sting.

"But you wouldn't be the Hero of New Orleans," Chase said pleasantly, looking straight back at him, "or the next President." And as Jackson slowly nodded and smiled, Coffee realized that for the second time that day, misled by the writer's youthful face and mild voice, he had underestimated Mr. Chase.

☆　　☆　　☆

CHASE had made out a list of factual questions about the Battle of New Orleans, and since Hamilton had finally arrived to monitor the interview, Coffee left them together while he walked down to inspect the fields. It was something he did anyway from time to time, for both of them. Rachel was a very bad manager, and Jackson himself was too distracted by other things—this had been true since 1813—to pay close attention to his crops. If he had wanted it, Jackson could have been a rich man by now—John Eaton was, Coffee himself was—but the truth was, no matter how much he moaned and complained, Jackson was a public man, a politician, and the only crop he cared about was votes.

Coffee shook his head at his own figure of speech. Talking too much to writers. He crossed a pretty little tree-ringed hollow where two abandoned log cabins still stood, unoccupied for years, the very first places Jackson had lived when he was building the Hermitage for Rachel. He wondered if Jackson knew that *Hermitage* was the name Jefferson had originally used for Monticello. Probably not. It was stranger and stranger how Jackson was looking only to the future, to the election, to Washington City and the President's House, and he, Coffee, just about the same age but not the same temperament at all, was looking more and more to the past.

The trail he was following, for example, was an old Indian path originally—most trails in Tennessee were. Sometimes they were worn a good two feet below land level by centuries of use. He noticed such things every day now. The West looked unspoiled and young, but it was an old country, truly. In the fertile plains south of Nashville he had watched farmers dig up ancient burial mounds and plow old pottery and jewelry and even stone-lined graves out of the soil. And long before the Indians, people said, other white men had lived first in this landscape, a lost tribe of whites who spoke Welsh and were wiped out by the savage Chickasaws drifting down from the north. It was a fact some Indians had been found in Ohio who spoke a kind of Welsh.

Or maybe it wasn't a fact. Coffee had trouble trusting anything lately except his own memory, and at his age, he thought, memory made up most of a man's life. A man's life was like an iceberg by now, nine tenths of it memory, frozen and out of sight.

He passed through a grove of mixed hickories and pines and entered one of Jackson's cotton fields, where a party of blacks worked under the broiling afternoon sun, stooped and almost motionless till they caught sight of him and started to shuffle their feet a little. Miserable life. Clouds of dust. Bleeding fingers. Hard, speckled blue sky, like the inside of an enameled cooking pan.

At a shady confluence of mossy gray rock and spring-fed creek, though he wasn't in the least bit tired, Coffee sat down and wiped sweat from his forehead and neck. He scowled at a pine. If he thought of the woods as they had been in his youth, he remembered ringing axes, sweating men and horses, deadened trees, the smell of newly cut wood or freshly killed venison steak on charcoal fires, even the occasional crackling red-hot forge of an itinerant blacksmith who had left the East, where Jackson wanted to govern, and traveled westward in time, onto the rolling green sea of the wilderness, God knows why. When Coffee's father had died, he and his mother had made their first move west, just the two of them. They'd carried seeds in a wagon, in a string of gourds. Sometimes he could still hear the clicking sound they made when he shook them like a rattle, and his mother's soft voice from the front of the wagon telling him to shush.

Oh, the past was dangerous. The past could close around you like a fist.

The most vivid memory he had of the wars wasn't from New Orleans. It was at Enotachopco Creek, before the Battle of Horseshoe Bend, when Jackson's front regiment broke under the rush of an Indian assault and started to retreat in a wild, screaming panic. Coffee had been wounded three days before—shot in five different places—and he was lying on a horse-drawn litter far in the rear. But when he saw the troops running, he somehow staggered up from the litter and mounted a horse, swaying in the saddle, pale as chalk, clinging to the saddle horn with one white bandaged fist, and recklessly spurred the horse forward, toward Jackson, his leader, his past and his present. And when Jackson saw him, he cried out in his fierce Jacksonian glee (the reason he *would* be President)—"Now we're going to whip them, men! The *dead* themselves have risen to help us!"

Coffee looked at the sun overhead and figured he ought to head back to the house and help out with the interview and the campaign. But he sat where he was on the rock and dipped his fingers in the cool springwater by his feet. The Indians used to say that if you sat in the woods and listened long enough (say, half a lifetime), the murmur of the streams and the leaves would finally begin to sound like human voices, barely distinguishable, no more than a fleeting whisper, but saying something, sending a message.

He was no Indian. He was too ordinary and earthbound and commonsensical to fall into trances or listen to visions. And yet he made no move to stand up. He closed his eyes and listened instead to the whole tremendous future that was coming toward them like the roar of the wind.

CHAPTER

7

Chase left the Hermitage after supper carrying two thick folders of notes and papers, and John Coffee rode a few miles with him down the Knoxville Road, where he thought there might be a room in an inn called "The Fountain of Health."

Jackson watched them canter off into the twilight and then took his evening coffee back into the library, alone. The round oak table in the center of the room—he had bought that table, he suddenly thought, on Bourbon Street in New Orleans thirteen years ago—that table was still covered with a dozen more hard brown accordion folders spread out in a careless fan, just as he had left them, because nobody, not even old Alfred, had permission to touch his papers.

He would have sat down, but he had been sitting all day. Instead, he put his coffee cup beside the oil lamp on the table and braced both hands flat, leaning forward to take his weight off his back. He looked down at his spread hands, two pale fish in a little white pond of oily light. One of his sergeants in Florida—name long ago forgotten—had had the unconscious habit of picking at the hairs on his left hand, then putting the crook of his thumb right up to his nose to sniff it. Jackson let his own nose wrinkle at the memory. The last time he had seriously studied his corruptible flesh had been in the year 1814, when he discovered one day, during a bout of excruciating bowel pain, that three or four razor-thin chips of bone had actually come loose from his upper arm and were sticking straight out of the skin, like tiny white sharks' fins cruising across his body.

Thomas Hart Benton's bullet had done that, the doctors said. It was nothing but splintered bone from the bullet that was working itself up to the surface. Jackson had pulled them out one by one with a pair of tweezers and saved them in a deerskin pouch, which later he gave to Rachel, God knows why; *flesh of my flesh, bone of my bone.* That pouch was probably somewhere in the library at that very moment.

Not in these campaign folders, however. He picked up the nearest one. Chase was a clever young man; he could see why Coffee liked him. From fifty questions about the Battle of New Orleans—and by the Eternal, the boy had read everything, the boy was a patriot—they had moved by stages to the Florida Wars, the "corrupt bargain," the slanderous attacks on Mrs. Jackson. When Coffee had gone out for his walk, Jackson had taken down the set of confidential folders Hamilton had started (and which everybody foolishly thought Rachel never saw; they didn't understand her, or him).

He closed his eyes to let a little grimace of pain wrinkle across his chest, left to right. His mind drifted in the darkness, not quite dreaming. They didn't understand because they didn't see Rachel now the way he did, or remember how brave she had been in the days of her youth. When he had carried her off in "elopement" to her sister's house that July of 1790, he was understood to be her special protector, but Rachel was scrupulous and modest, still a legally married woman, and there was never a question with her of anything more. Sometimes they would walk in the fields together, or make an excursion to Clover Bottom, two boiling pots . . . Then the next spring Robards had set about making such ugly threats and coming down to Nashville and *haunting* the Donelsons so, Rachel had simply stood up one day and said she was going away to Natchez on Captain Stark's boat, to spare them and save everybody's peace. And when her mother said she'd never survive such a journey, Rachel reminded old lady Donelson that she had come down the Cumberland as a little girl with Indian arrows singing in her ears, and she wasn't about to be fearful *now.*

What could be braver than that?

Jackson had gone along as extra protection, of course, in pure inno-cence. When he let her off and got back to Nashville, Overton told him Lewis Robards had filed for divorce. Ten days later Jackson was back in Mississippi, on his knees in front of her, and they were married that August in the curtainless parlor of Thomas Green's riverside house, by a justice of the peace. They were both twenty-four years old.

For the next two months he had rented a little log cabin at Bayou Pierre, on a cleared bluff above the river, and at dusk Rachel would nestle under his arm and they would sit on the porch and watch the copper moon and the silk stars floating by on the dark water far below. Later, in the hot, sweltering Mississippi night, she would come to his bed, a pure and lovely young bride, and smile at him in the moonlight and cross her arms and slowly reach both hands down to the hem of her gown.

Jackson blinked himself straight, felt the crease of the confidential fold-ers in his hands.

Why had he brought them out? he wondered. He rubbed his throat where the locket hung. He had brought them out to show young Chase, he remembered now. To show young Chase what his enemies were like—to show the *persecution* saintly Rachel endured—he had passed over to Chase a sample of clippings. He wet his thumb and turned a page. This one, for example, from a Cincinnati newspaper: "Gen. Jackson had ad-mitted that he boarded at the house of old Mrs. Donelson, and that Robards became jealous of him, but he omits the cause of that jealousy: that one day Robards surprised Gen. Jackson and his wife exchanging most delicious kisses."

This one: "When Rachel Robards voyaged to Natchez on Colonel Stark's flat-boat, the Gen. omitted to tell they slept under the same blan-ket."

This one, from *The Anti-Jackson Expositor:* "Ought a convicted adulter-ess and her paramour husband to be placed in the highest offices of this free and Christian land?"

And this one, two weeks ago: "Simply put, she is a fallen female." Van Buren had written a hasty note from New York clipped to it: "Do not respond. Our people do not like to see publications from candidates."

Our people do not like, our people do not like—Jackson closed the folder with a snap, feeling his heart begin to tremble. What else was coming loose inside him? He stood up straight, as if to back away and sit down, but on their own his treacherous fingers turned over another folder and picked up the "coffin handbill," as even he called it, a foot-long sheet of paper with six ink-black coffins over the printed names of the six soldiers he had ordered shot in Mobile in 1815. He hadn't been there . . . he had signed the execution papers 150 miles away in New Orleans. Under the "coffin handbill" was a pamphlet called "Jackson and a Standing Army," which declared the people's dread of his military tyranny. "Jackson a Negro Trader," filled with viperous lies about his slaves—a man never treated his slaves better, he had *never* in his life engaged in the slave trade. More about Rachel, a list of his duels, a letter about Charles Dickinson. Be careful, John Coffee had told him over and over; show self-control, be *silent.* Don't let them draw you out, even when they mention the Sacred Name. A would-be President cannot, *cannot* fight a duel.

Jackson lowered himself into his chair, rigid—rigid, he thought, as splintering bone. It had been a mistake to talk to young Chase, to look at these things again. His treacherous fingers picked up something that had dropped to the floor, one of the latest, a broadside cartoon suitable for framing. He held it to the light. A portrait of himself entitled "Richard III" in which his hat was a soldier's tent, his hat plume was a gun barrel billowing smoke, and his coat collars were formed out of army cannons. His face was composed entirely of naked corpses. His nose, chin, eyes, every feature composed of twisting corpses. Under the title was a line from the play: *Methought the souls of all that I had murder'd, came to my tent.*

He had only done his duty, he had only fought to show that the people could govern themselves. Stuck to the cartoon somehow was one more clipping, and despite everything, against his vaunted Will, his fingers picked it up, too, and spread it on his knees.

The door opened and Rachel came into the room.

He was Old Hickory, he had killed a thousand men, he was famous for Will and Strength and Fury. But at this moment, looking up and seeing her soft round face, blurred as if it came from another time and place, at this moment, for her alone, his strength failed.

"What's the matter?" Rachel asked.

"Myself I can defend," Jackson said. "You I can defend. But when they attack the memory of my mother—"

With a looping gesture of despair he handed her the paper. At the top of the left-hand column, a neatly drawn little hand pointed to the opening paragraph, which Rachel had already read weeks ago in a state of horrified amazement: *General Jackson's mother was a* COMMON PROSTITUTE, it said, *brought to this country by British soldiers!!! She afterward married a* MULATTO MAN, *with whom she had several children, of which number General* JACKSON IS ONE!

She sat on the arm of the chair and stroked his stiff gray hair, so much like the bristles of an old brush. She pulled his bone-hard, sixty-year-old face against her breast and lifted her gaze to the window, where the sun was just going down in a pure blaze of light, God's promise. "My sweet baby, my sweet baby," Rachel murmured over and over, wife to husband, while Jackson rocked in the chair and sobbed, his hot tears scalding her hand.

8

The Life of Andrew Jackson, by David Chase

Chapter Ten

AT NEW ORLEANS THE MORNING OF DECEMBER 28, 1814, BEGAN, NOT DAMP and foggy for once, but bright, balmy, almost hot. In the stubble fields between the two waiting armies, rice birds set up a noisy racket. Mockingbirds echoed from the cypress swamps. Four different diarists remember it as a glorious southern dawn, bliss to be alive.

From the first moment of sunrise Jackson was at his post on the upper floor of the Macarté house, studying the British lines through his old black telescope. Those nearest him observed that, although he moved about with his usual brisk, fearless confidence, from time to time the General stopped and frowned anxiously (for him) northward, where the New Orleans road crossed a stagnant canal.

A little past seven, even as the two British columns were beginning to advance, Jackson turned and put down his telescope to watch a straggling band of red-shirted bewhiskered men hurrying, out of breath, from the New Orleans road.

"Devils," Jackson's aide murmured, shaking his head.

"Pirates," Jackson said with satisfaction, and turned back. This was in fact Dominique You, Jean Lafitte's grimy, rather desperate-looking brother, a cross-eyed, slightly hunchbacked man who had run half the night from the other side of New Orleans, on Jackson's express order. Because somewhere in his hundreds of conversations and reports over the past two days, Jackson had learned that Dominique You was considered (by those who had seen him on the high seas) a master artilleryman, an *artiste* of the cannon and mortar, and Jackson liked anything superlatively destructive. As he trotted past, Dominique glanced up with a gap-toothed grin. Jackson grinned back and lit a cigar. *Twin spirits,* the aide wrote in his diary.

In five minutes more Dominique had taken up his position at the central cannon on the mud ramparts and started to shout orders in French up and down the line. And then, as the sun climbed higher, making the stubble fields into a silver carpet half a mile wide, even the Frenchman grew silent.

No one knows to this date what Pakenham's intentions were. He outnumbered Jackson on the ground eight thousand infantry to three thousand, he had sunk the *Carolina* and cleared his flank—now he sent one column in parade formation straight up his left, parallel to the river, while his right-hand column marched parallel to the swamp. The British go to war in style, of course, in fashion. This morning the men had donned their brightest dress uniforms—red, gray, green, vivid tartan—as if they were marching down Piccadilly. Muskets and bayonets were polished to a glittering luster; parade drums rattled and whirred, here and there a trumpet sounded quick golden notes. An actual assault? A mere show of sumptuary force to intimidate the Dirty Shirts?

Seven hundred yards from the mud ramparts, at eight twenty-five precisely, Pakenham dropped his sword in a signal.

Instantly the air shook with the high-pitched scream of Congreve rockets.

I am so little a soldier myself that, until I reached this page in my story, I had no idea what a Congreve rocket is. General Coffee, who has kept a collection of military curiosities from that war, has now taken me out in the fields near Clover Bottom, Nashville, and fired six of them in demonstration—they made their American debut, he says, in the Battle of Lundy's Lane near Niagara Falls, July 1814, where they drove the Americans back in wild disorder. And it was Congreve rockets that Francis Scott Key was observing at Fort McHenry a month later when he wrote of "the rockets' red glare" and saw "bombs bursting in air."

In appearance it has a cylindrical body and a pointed iron head about a foot long, attached to an eight-foot-long stick that serves as a guiding tail in flight. They take off with a roaring *swoosh* and, from the other side, seem to be aiming personally at a watching soldier, making him shake in his boots, the General says, and his knees turn to water: a most terrifying weapon. Sometimes it explodes overhead, raining sharp, hot metal fragments down. (*Shrapnel,* to use the new word.) Most of the time it strikes the ground and writhes smoking and sputtering through the grass, like a burning serpent, till a time fuse reaches its black powder charge and the iron head explodes in crimson smoke.

Pakenham launched almost a thousand rockets, ten at a time, ripping the dawn to bloody shreds.

On the mud ramparts the Americans squatted, dove for cover, scrambled away in panic—and then out of the smoke and noise, striding through it like a Scotch-Irish cigar-smoking Achilles, came Andrew Jackson. He stomped on one rocket with his boot and broke it apart, batted another out of range with his sword. "*Goddamnit,*" every witness agrees he shouted—"Goddamnit, boys, pay no attention, these are just *toys!*"

("I *love* Andrew Jackson," General Coffee says.)

As always, the men turn in the direction of Jackson's voice. The sharpshooters flatten themselves on the ramparts, level their guns, and watch the two great columns come into focus.

Jackson had arranged his own signal for his cannons. As the British columns passed a set of abandoned houses along the river Jackson's batteries opened up. The houses, which he had ordered stocked with explosives, blew apart in a ball of flame. Simultaneously the *Louisiana*'s guns began to roar. Dominique You poured round after merciless round into the British troops, now only about six hundred yards away. Their bright uniforms vanished into the mud of the nearest ditches.

For a time the British artillery fought back, but though the field cannons on each side were closely matched in numbers, the Americans had the advantage of position, especially on the *Louisiana,* and of lethal accuracy. By ten o'clock most of the British batteries were disabled or silenced; most of their troops had assumed what is called in military English a *supine* position. For five hours longer the American artillery fired almost at will as the broken British columns rallied, scattered, scampered south in retreat. So accurate and artistic was Dominique You that one twenty-four-pound shot, by all accounts, killed fifteen British soldiers at once. When a British captain—six hundred yards away—climbed up from a ditch to call his men, Dominique squinted and aimed and a single nine-pound ball struck his head and knocked it off his shoulders.

By nightfall the British had slunk back to their tents, and Pakenham was writing in his official report that the day's action had been only "a reconnaissance in force."

Behind the Rodriguez Canal, Jackson watched as his men interviewed a captured British officer. Would the prisoner like a fresh change of linen, someone kindly asked, to replace his muddy uniform? With infinite and inimitable British hauteur he drew himself up: He would change his clothes in New Orleans, he said, where his bags would arrive in a few days with the rest of the army.

The Americans held their breath. Every face turned toward Jackson.

In the flickering light of the fire his countenance darkened and scowled. Did he think, at this moment, of himself forty years before, the Brave Boy of the Waxhaws, struck down by a haughty redcoat's sword? Did he finger the white scar on his brow?

Coffee cleared his throat and spat into the fire.

Jackson wrapped his rusty old Spanish cloak tighter around his shoulders. In the South there is a code to strangle every unworthy impulse. "Treat him with great courtesy," Jackson told his men and disappeared into the darkness.

In that same darkness two miles below the Rodriguez Canal Pakenham huddled in a damp, three-sided slave shack with his chief strategists. If the *reconnaissance in force* had failed because of Jackson's artillery, he announced, then Jackson's artillery must be blasted aside. Admiral Cochrane, still an advocate of naval power, grumbled; a few infantry colonels hesitated. But Pakenham folded his maps decisively (tilted his head) and sat back, and long before dawn orders had gone out to the ships waiting in Lake Borgne—the great thirty-two-pound cannons lying idle on their decks, each battery capable of hurling three hundred and fifty pounds of lead at a time, these must be ferried ashore and dragged up the soft, miry road that stretched along Bayou Bienvenu. Once in place beside the other, smaller cannons, they would obliterate the American guns in a matter of hours.

Dramatically, the changeable Louisiana weather joined in the plan. For the next three days a thick, roiling fog lowered over the two encamped armies, obscuring them completely from each other. From their mud ramparts the Americans could hear constant hammering on the British side; scouts in the cypress swamp occasionally sighted construction crews on the move and, odder still, hogsheads of sugar stacked on wagons. In the fog, nothing else could be discerned.

For his part Jackson used the time to sweep tirelessly once more through the city of New Orleans for recruits; on Jean Lafitte's advice he began a second defensive ditch a mile behind the first. Warned by a tip from a deserter, he had his men dismantle and transport four of the *Louisiana*'s guns to the western shore of the Mississippi, where they lined them up, in the fog, at what they guessed was the British front. At one point, impulsively, he confiscated several hundred bales of cotton from an excitable merchant named Vincent Nolte. He placed them, covered with mud, as improvised bulwarks in front of his weakest batteries. At night he wrote furious letters to Washington City requesting more men, more guns. On the third day, to boost the morale of the troops, he ordered a full-scale parade and review behind his lines, and invited the sulking and tremulous legislators to come out from the city and enjoy it.

Thus it happened that at the dawn of the year 1815, as Jackson rested on his sofa in the Macarté house, a gay pageant was gathered several hundred yards to the rear: soldiers, banners, flags, military bands, ladies in bonnets, fashionable carriages, all were preparing, despite the fog, for a gala morning of New Orleans–style festivity. Through the damp air floated female laughter and the first strains of "Yankee Doodle." A Creole band tuned its instruments for the "Marseillaise."

And then, exactly at ten o'clock, just as dramatically as it had appeared, the gray curtain of fog blew away. There, revealed in bright sunshine seven hundred yards to the south, stood a series of newly constructed British batteries.

Thirty huge British cannons to Jackson's fifteen.

For a long moment Jackson's sentries simply stared in disbelief. Pakenham's signal rocket went up, burst. A horrendous, screaming barrage of rockets and shells streaked toward the parading soldiers.

In the Macarté house, targeted by two different British batteries, walls and windows shattered, plaster fell in billowing clouds. Outside, ladies and carriages raced round and round in terrified circles; legislators leaped for their horses. By the time Jackson pulled himself free of the Macarté house—afterward his men counted more than a hundred separate balls, rockets, and cannon shells in the house's rubble—the *Louisiana*'s land batteries had begun to return the British fire.

As if by instinct Jackson hurried to Dominique You's Number 3 battery, in the center of the line.

"Goddamnit, Dominique!" Jackson shouted. "Shoot back!"

"Goddamnit, Général!" At which instant a British cannonball sailing past scorched Dominique's left arm as if with a red-hot poker. He cursed in French and Portuguese and jammed his barrel with chain links and ponderous ship's canister. His first shot knocked the nearest British cannon off its platform and blew the hogsheads of sugar in front of it fifty yards high in a sweet white geyser.

Jackson nodded and strode away, to the next emplacement.

"By the Eternal, Colonel Butler," he cried over the cannon fire, "I thought you were dead!"

"Only bumped over, General." Colonel Robert Butler, Jackson's favorite aide, was covered from head to foot with dust and splinters, but in one of war's little miracles he drew from his breast pocket a pair of undamaged Spanish cigars. Jackson took one and strode on.

General Coffee is a modest man, but shrewd with words (shrewder, in fact, with everything than he lets on). He has asked me to sit down and imagine: nearly fifty pieces of large-caliber artillery, each one firing from once to three times a minute. Often three or four of them thundering almost at the same second. After ten minutes the earth shaking, the stubble fields, the trees, the very air itself so densely covered with brown and yellow smoke pierced from moment to moment by flaring red rockets that the gunners aim from memory and have no idea what, if anything, they hit.

On Jackson's lines the cotton bales have caught fire despite the mud, and a party of volunteers is pushing them into the canal, where they will smoke and smolder for hours. On Pakenham's line the infamous hogsheads of sugar, which the British general thought would somehow protect his guns, have been blown to pieces almost at once. Now sugar coats the guns, men, and ground with bizarre, sticky white crystals that transform the landscape into a scene like a snowy winter in Hades.

Through it all Jackson paces from gun to gun, shouting encouragement and defiance. For nearly two hours the battle hangs in furious and equal balance, and then at noon the British fire abruptly slackens; at quarter past it stops altogether. Jackson's guns now fire at will, unanswered, and in the fields and ditches Pakenham's beautifully dressed infantry, poised since ten o'clock for attack, scramble once more into the supine position and wait on their bellies in the mud for dark. At five o'clock rain begins to fall. The last cannons cough and grow silent.

In the smoky dusk, while the Macarté house was being repaired, Jackson found a makeshift desk under a tent and by candlelight wrote more letters. Most were formal reports on the day's action, regiment by regiment. One, provoked by exhaustion and anger perhaps, was a miniature exercise of Jacksonian Will. For among his units, as I have already mentioned, were some troops of Choctaw Indians and two battalions of free men of color, recruited from New Orleans and stationed along the mud ramparts with the other soldiers, and that morning long ago, before either parade or battle had started, his paymaster had left him a note of complaint about handing over good American money to "niggers." The haggard general now stabbed his pen in an inkwell and scribbled with his own dirty and soot-covered hand a terse, Jacksonian reply:

> *Be pleased to keep to yourself your Opinions upon the policy of making payments to particular Corps. It is enough for you to receive my order for the payment of the troops without inquiring whether the color of the troops is white, Black, or Tea.*
>
> *A. Jackson, Commanding General*

Then he paused, alone for once, and listened to the drum of rain on the tent. He had not trained in the king's army under Wellington, as Pakenham had, nor had he campaigned in the great tactical school of the Napoleonic Wars. But he was a soldier and he knew without a doubt the conclusion that Pakenham must now have reached. Two attacks had failed. His artillery was beaten. The river was blocked. No way was left to take New Orleans—and his earldom—except by a frontal assault of infantry, man to man, bayonet to bayonet, over and through the American lines.

The only question that still hung in the cold, wet air was when.

CHAPTER
9

John Randolph of Roanoke eased himself out of his saddle with slow, shivery, long-legged motions; a black spider dismounting a gray horse.

He stood in the heat of the road and squinted at the signboard, which, remarkably enough, was half in English, half in German; then he handed the bridle to a waiting boy, black or white, Randolph scarcely glanced down to notice. He coughed consumptively into his left hand and disappeared into the tavern.

Two hours later James A. Hamilton Jr. wearing his new brown Stetson hat and a tricolored vest he had borrowed from Sam Houston, rode up on the Nashville road. He, too, dismounted in front of the tavern and stood in the dust, under the hot August sun. From the vest he pulled out an ingenious silver French repeater watch that his father had bequeathed him, which told the year and day as well as the time. It was August 23, 1828, 2:41 in the afternoon. In Nashville over the past ten days they had received no fewer than six separate messages from Randolph—he was on his way, he had been detained, he would meet them in secret, he had stopped at Bizarre to sell a horse. The only reason Hamilton had finally decided to come—and from Nashville to Knoxville was a miserably hard ninety miles, in the hottest month of the year—the *only* reason was Randolph's value as a congressional ally, as an unparalleled attacker of John Quincy Adams.

Hamilton paused, one booted foot on the tavern step, and allowed himself the rare and exquisite sensation of total political honesty. In fact, John Randolph was an unparalleled ass and madman, and nobody outside the halls of Congress put the slightest value on his ravings. Hamilton had come all this way for one reason and one reason only: the last three words of Randolph's note, an uncharacteristically terse document containing no more than the name of the tavern outside Knoxville, the date and time they should meet, and in slightly fainter script, as if Randolph had hesitated before writing . . . With a shake of his head Hamilton dismissed the thought and the memory. The presidential balloting would begin in less than two months. There was not a chance in the world, not the slightest, remotest scintilla of a possibility that Andrew Jackson had anything at all to fear.

10

The Life of Andrew Jackson, by David Chase

Chapter Eleven

FOR FIVE DAYS, FROM THE SECOND TO THE SEVENTH OF JANUARY, THE BRITISH camp echoed morning and night with unceasing commotion.

Out of the inexhaustible warships on Lake Borgne, to the steady crack of military drums, marched two more divisions of veteran infantry, fourteen hundred fresh, bustling reinforcements. A regiment of Highlanders unpacked their bagpipes. From the edge of the cypress swamp came the thump of hammers and axes as a new wooden redoubt was constructed, and more artillery batteries erected to replace those Jackson's guns had shattered and sunk in the mire on January first. When the fog blew aside, as it did only once or twice a day, Jackson's spies, creeping on their hands and knees through the silvery cane stubble, could discern elaborate maneuvers and training marches going on, but little more. A full-dress review of the new arrivals insultingly turned their backs and rumps toward the American line.

Even the British sentinels broke silence, fascinated apparently by a gang of Choctaw squaws who had pitched camp behind their huts and went about naked all day except for a short cotton petticoat; the unmarried girls wore nothing at all, and squatted beside their fires in a state of nature. The goggle-eyed British noted that the white ashes stuck to their skin like soft, delicate feathers.

On January third Lieutenant General Pakenham himself was spotted, halfway up a pine tree like a squirrel, peering through a telescope at Jackson's lines.

If Jackson peered back, there is no record. Once again he had embarked on a desperate whirlwind sweep through New Orleans for weapons and men—he found no men, and only a few hundred rusty Spanish fowling pieces called *escopetas*—once again his aides marveled at his ability to go without food or sleep and to galvanize mysteriously every fiber of the rag-tag, dirty-shirted army, which visibly stiffened and came alive in his gaunt presence. Those closest to him marveled as well at his vocabulary of imprecation. Guns and powder had been promised him by steamboat from Kentucky, but day after day brought no sign of them. In the fog-shrouded mornings Jackson paced the docks at New Orleans, just below Bourbon Street, and in richly sulfurous language described the ancestry and physical appearance of the steamboat captain and the utter certainty that once the guns were delivered the captain would spend the next two eternities locked in irons. Each evening he walked down the mud ramparts to the edge of the swamp where Coffee's regiment was stationed, and where the Louisiana version of soil was close enough to liquid that the soldiers literally walked about knee-deep in mud and slept, when they slept, on floating logs.

On the fourth of January a division of Kentucky volunteers arrived as reinforcements, but so ragged and scantily clad that they covered their bodies in shame as they marched through the city. And worse yet, completely unarmed.

"I don't believe it!" Jackson shouted when he heard the news. "I have never in my *life* seen a Kentuckian without a gun and a pack of cards and a bottle of whiskey!"

On the morning of January seventh, as the signed treaty of peace was being unfolded and filed away in London, and its duplicate rested in John Quincy Adams's trunk somewhere west of the Azores, on that same morning Jackson's total strength had reached just over four thousand men, about a quarter of them unarmed. In front of him, suddenly motionless and silent, covering the plain of Chalmette, as the field was called, from one end to the other stood a fresh British army of well over eight thousand soldiers.

Late that night a courier arrived at the Macarté house. He stumbled and fumbled through the dark and entered the hallway, where he whispered hurriedly to the sentry on duty.

Jackson was asleep on a sofa in the next room. On the bare floor around him slept four of his aides, all still in uniform except for their sword belts, which were unbuckled, and their pistols, which lay side by side on a desk.

Jackson was sitting up straight before the sentry could call him.

"Who's there?"

The courier came in with a candle and a note from the commander of the detachment across the river defending the battery of guns. About an hour ago a large party of British soldiers had been seen clambering out of the mist and into boats on the eastern shore. Obviously they were preparing to cross and attack up the west bank, a flanking maneuver. Jackson's officer begged for reinforcements at once.

"Tell him," Jackson said quietly, "that I have no men to spare. And tell him that he's mistaken. The main attack will be here, on this side."

Then he glanced at his pocket watch and saw that it was just past one o'clock, so the date was January 8, 1815. History twirled her skirts.

"Gentlemen," he said, throwing off his blankets, "we have slept enough."

The group passed out into the chilly darkness. Jackson led them first toward the levee, but the fog was too thick to see much, and the only sound beside the occasional stamp of a horse and the rustle and clink of soldiers' gear was the swift, unending ripple of the Mississippi current.

On the way back he stopped to inspect a half-moon redoubt that the younger engineers had talked him into constructing. Jackson shook his head in mistrust and lingered for a moment with the rifle company that manned it.

Then he lifted his nose and sniffed. From down the line floated an unmistakable aroma. Jackson walked along the top of the rampart until he reached Battery Number Three, and there he found the bright and misshapen little Dominique You making spicy coffee in the ritualistic French manner that baffled Americans. He had a special drip pot of tin-coated iron, and he had just lowered it into a kettle of simmering water, which he kept heated while he carefully ladled spoonfuls of water onto the grounds.

Jackson rubbed his chin and watched. "That smells like better coffee than we get," he said finally. Dominique ladled another spoonful. "Maybe you smuggled it in?" Jackson said.

"Maybe so, Général." Dominique tilted his head and flashed a crazy lopsided grin, and poured him a tin cup full to the brim.

It was amazing to Jackson's aides how many of the soldiers he knew by name. The General proceeded slowly down the rampart, coffee in hand, and every few yards paused to exchange a word with somebody. At the stubby cypress woods he and his aides entered Coffee's sector and proceeded along a log walkway into the swamp. Here the men actually left their posts and crowded around him. No fires burned in the mud and slime, but Jackson appeared to recognize names by the sounds of voices, and he called out greeting after greeting despite the utter darkness. Then he returned to the rampart and stood by himself watching the gray wall of fog as it drifted and billowed, opaque as stone.

Just before six o'clock, thin milky traces of light appeared in the east above the cypress trees. Jackson sent a man for his old black telescope. But with it or without it he could see little more than thirty or so yards ahead, and a new breeze was stirring the smoke from his smoldering campfires and thickening the haze.

A Major Latour approached with the information that his pickets reported movement behind the British lines. Jackson nodded. The fog would scale back in about an hour, Latour added. He was a Louisianan and knew the country. Off to their left, two rifle shots rang out, then nothing.

"Some of my Choctaws," Jackson said laconically. "That's about where they ought to be."

In fact, in another ten minutes the breeze shifted abruptly to the south, and the fog lifted all at once into the sunrise. Across two thirds of the silvery stubble plain, standing in complete silence, the dark British ranks became visible. Suddenly a rocket flashed into the sky to the left and broke apart in a shower of blue sparks. An instant later, from the riverbank, a second rocket rose and burst.

"That is their signal for advance, I believe," said Andrew Jackson calmly, as if he were the Brave Boy of the Waxhaws once more and the previous forty-seven years had been merely prologue to this moment.

They came forward still in eerie silence. From Jackson's vantage point the first troops now seemed no more than six hundred yards away. The cane-stubble field that lay before the ramparts was coated with heavy white frost. Across it, from swamp to river, stretched an endless line of bright red tunics. Over their belts their white ammunition straps formed an X, and above their helmets, like a moving hedgework of steel, flashed a thousand fixed bayonets.

Jackson shouted his order: "Hold your fire! Aim above the cross plates!"

On they marched through the rising fog.

At five hundred yards a young American artilleryman named Spotts could wait no longer. He fired his twelve-pounder into the closest scarlet ranks, then watched as the line wavered and re-formed and marched inexorably forward, stepping over the fallen bodies.

A moment later every American cannon started to fire, and out of the distant haze the British batteries lit up in answer, and the uncanny silence of the first minute was replaced by a thunderous series of roars. From the mud ramparts the flashes of British cannon fire looked as if they were coming out of the bowels of the earth. The reverberations from the woods redoubled the sound. The sky itself seemed to be cracking and falling apart.

After the third salvo Coffee sent word that the smoke from the cannons was obscuring his riflemen's view. Jackson ordered his batteries to halt, and the smoke slowly and majestically rolled in clouds across the field. And then out of the smoke, dark shadows of men coming at a silent run.

Somewhere in the cypress trees on the British side a lone bugler sounded a charge. Just behind Dominique You's Number Three Battery a band began to play "Yankee Doodle Dandy."

At three hundred yards Jackson spoke softly to his aides. "They're near enough now, gentlemen. Fire when ready."

He had ordered four ranks of riflemen on the ramparts. The first rank stood with cheeks pressed against their rifle stocks, beads fixed on the white crosses.

"*Fire!*"

It was as if a single sheet of flame had erupted. The charging British went down in reeling crimson waves. The first rank stepped back, reloading. The second rank stood up.

"Fire!"

The second rank stepped back; forward the third.

"Fire!"

The huge British army bent like grain in the wind. The American fire was virtually continuous, accurate beyond belief. At the lowest point of the mud ramparts, where the cypress swamp began, redcoats were running forward, some carrying ladders for scaling, others the tall bundles of cane called fascines, which would fill the canal for the troops to cross. But none could reach the canal, few carried enough fascines. Coffee's marksmen brought them down dozens at a time, bodies spinning.

Out of the smoke rode Pakenham himself, and a burst of fire shattered his arm and killed his horse. Almost before Jackson's eyes the British general swung onto another black pony and waved his good arm in a signal.

From the far left, by the river, the fresh, tartan-clad Highlanders answered his call. They began to dash forward, nine hundred strong, every man in the ranks at least six feet tall. Running beside them, their bagpipers played the fierce regimental charge "Monymusk." But they were going at an oblique, through treacherous wet cane stubble, over ditches and puddles, and their entire left flank was exposed to Jackson's ramparts.

"Fire!"

The front of the line buckled and fell, stood and charged.

"Reload, Aim, Fire!"

A solid blaze of orange and red, an indescribable pulp of carnage. "Hurrah, brave Highlanders!" shouted Pakenham, his last words on earth. The black pony reared and pawed the air. A dozen Kentucky rifles swung to the right—*"Fire!"*—and pony and rider went crashing down in a storm of bullets. The Highlanders staggered, rose, closed to a hundred yards, and then broke apart forever. More than five hundred lay on the ground when even the bagpipers turned and fled.

At Jackson's little redoubt a British assault troop had reached the top and begun fighting hand-to-hand, but Americans swarmed around them after a few moments, they too fell away like the Highlanders. The next in command on the field, General Gibbs, rode back and forth screeching at his men, beating at their backs with the flat of his sword. When they rushed past him to the rear, he wheeled his horse around and galloped in a mad charge, all alone, toward the American line. A stupendous hail of fire raked him, tumbling him from the saddle.

And as quickly as it had begun, almost in an anticlimax, the battle was over. Highlanders, veterans, royal marines—the whole enormous British army was turning and running.

Jackson's men began to break ranks themselves and clamber to the top of the mud ramparts. A young Tennessee volunteer sprang over and into the canal, waving a tomahawk and crying, "Follow me, boys!"

Behind him Jackson snatched a pistol from his belt—"Stop!" He stood with the pistol cocked, a tall, thin silhouette fixed in history. "I'll shoot the first man who goes with him! We *shall* have *discipline* here!"

No man moved.

By eight-thirty, just half an hour after the first British charge, he ordered his rifles down. His cannons continued to fire methodically at the retreating army. Across the river new cannon fire briefly sounded, then grew sporadic and faded away; twenty minutes later the first gasping messengers reported that the British had breached the American lines along the western bank, halted inexplicably, and likewise fled in retreat to their boats.

At the news, the Tennessee troops along the ramparts lifted their hats and cheered for Jackson, and the regimental band, which had never stopped playing for an instant, broke out into "Hail, Columbia!"

And then at last even the cannon fire ceased. An awestruck hush settled onto the battlefield. Jackson stood on his rampart, arms straight at his side like a statue. His soldiers glanced up at him and slowly, one by one, began to walk forward in silence.

What They Saw.

The ground directly in front of the ramparts was everywhere covered with dead and dying men. The cane stubble was soaked red with their blood; the filthy drainage water ran crimson. In the canal just below Jackson's feet stretched a crooked line of more than forty dead British soldiers and, sprawled among them, over a hundred more wounded. And this was only a small corner of the battle. Beyond them in every direction bodies were piled or stacked on other bodies, in places three or four deep, as if they had been tossed out at random from passing wagons. You could walk on corpses for half a mile and never touch ground. Many of the wounded writhed or coughed in agony. A few tried to crawl. Here and there a man screamed. To Jackson's left, perhaps fifty yards into the field of slaughter, a Highlander lay on his back with his face shot away, but his right arm still rose and fell mechanically, convulsively. Someone collected severed limbs in a basket.

At the end many of the British survivors had actually hidden themselves from the American barrage behind the piles of their own dead. Now, in a sight like some vast apocalyptic canvas come to life, they started to stand up all over the plain. As far as the eye could see, hundreds and hundreds of them emerged as if from the ground, rising slowly up to their feet and coming silently forward with their arms held high in ghostly surrender.

On his parapet Jackson seemed stunned. He stared out over the plain as if he were mesmerized by a vision. He lifted his hand; he slowly took off his hat.

Was he saluting the generous intervention of Fate, as Major Eaton later thought, the goddess of all successful commanders? Or did he believe for a moment that the whole cycle of advance and attack and retreat was beginning all over again, as it always had for as long as he could remember? He fingered the rough scar on his brow. He watched his prisoners shuffling toward him out of drifting blue-gray eddies of smoke and sunlight. I never had so grand and awful an idea of the Coming Day of Resurrection, Jackson thought, suddenly breathless; whose whole life had been spent in the valley of the shadow of death.

British casualties that day were two thousand, thirty-seven soldiers. Jackson's losses were thirteen dead and thirty-nine wounded.

Under the white dome of Monticello nine hundred miles to the northeast, Thomas Jefferson groaned and turned in his sleep.

W hat has turned up," John Randolph said—"what has been *resurrected,* so to speak, is Peyton Short."

"Peyton Short is dead." Hamilton found the inside of the tavern far hotter than the outside. And worse yet, like some arachnid creature of the tropics, Randolph actually seemed to thrive on the heat. He had already insisted on shutting the windows. Hamilton wiped his brow with a red silk handkerchief (Houston's) and wondered if the man was now about to order a fire.

But Randolph had entered a new phase of eccentricity and affectation that had nothing to do with the heat. In a series of exquisitely sensitive rearrangements and adjustments, he sat down in a straight-backed chair beside the fireplace and crossed one long spindly leg over the other. He closed his eyes. His pale white face appeared to levitate gently above the stiff collar and the buttoned coat; the pink tip of his tongue slid slowly left to right like a snake's.

"Henry Clay says the General has engaged in the slave trade," Randolph murmured. Eyes popped open exophthalmically for a moment, closed again. "Now, I have little or no regard for Henry Clay—when I die

I want to be buried facing west, to keep an eye on Henry Clay—but in large matters such as this he is veracious."

"You called me here about Peyton Short."

"I have made a number of speeches denouncing the slave trade," Randolph said, waving the objection aside with one limp hand. "I once made a motion in the House that the slave trade in the District of Columbia should be abolished—abolished, sir. It is a scandal that the most disgraceful and infernal traffic that has ever stained the annals of the human race should take place in the very streets of our nation's capital. The *institution* of slavery I accept. It was established by our fathers, which is enough for me. But the actual trade for profit in human souls—no, I spent long enough at the knees of St. Thomas of Cantingbury to absorb his one great prophecy. 'I tremble for my country,' Jefferson used to say, 'when I reflect that God is just.' "

"Peyton Short."

"Is the General engaged in the trade of slaves?"

"No."

"Never?"

"Never at all."

"Then Clay is wrong." Randolph slouched in the chair, squeezed his eyes shut, and slung one long, weightless leg over its arm.

Had he entered into a trance, or simply one of those interminable southern pauses? All Southerners were excruciatingly slow, but in Hamilton's experience Randolph set new standards. He watched while a skeletal white hand toyed with the pewter mug of whatever he was drinking. Worm's blood. In Washington City, Hamilton knew, behind his back they called him Jackson's handler—just as they called Van Buren the Little Magician—because it was his job to keep the General out of the fray, safe from the prying, unscrupulous press; safe from the thousand and one impostors, pests, and pious well-wishers who would otherwise flock to Jackson like demented moths to a bonfire. And if there were ever such a moth, it was Randolph.

"Peyton Short is dead," Hamilton repeated, calculating precisely how much impatience he could put into his voice. "I've seen the death certificate myself. I hope you haven't called me here—"

"Do you know what Peyton Short *actually* did?" Randolph opened his lazy eyes halfway. He took a sip from the mug. "Before he so tactfully passed over that bourn from which no traveler returns?"

"I am aware," Hamilton said, aware in the oppressive combination of heat and fatigue that he sounded almost as stiff and pompous as Randolph sounded eccentric, "that he boarded in Lewis Robards's house when Robards and Rachel Donelson were first married and that Robards was insanely jealous of everything in long pants in that part of Kentucky. In any case, Short had moved to the Missouri Territories before the General even appeared on the scene. We're very thorough, Mr. Randolph. We've investigated every *soupçon* of gossip. I would add for myself—" Hamilton cleared his throat, as always in preparation for an untruth "—I would add that I regard the General's marriage to Mrs. Jackson as one of the greatest romances in American history. We've proposed to several journals in the East that they write about it from *that* point of view instead of this present dwelling on scandal. I might even write it myself. They are an utterly *devoted* couple."

Hamilton stopped, blinked uselessly at the unbearable heat, and sipped from his own pewter mug. Lukewarm beer that tasted like soap, except that in his experience there was very little soap in Tennessee. The truth was, the utterly devoted couple was utterly ridiculous to anyone except other Southerners. He would never efface from his memory the sight of them dancing in New Orleans last winter, at the commemorative banquet, the General tall and haggard, with limbs like a starved stork, and Madame La Générale a short, fat, hoop-skirted dumpling, the two of them bobbing opposite each other like half-drunken Indians, to the wild melody of "Possum Up De Gum Tree"—Hamilton shuddered and shook his head. "So if Peyton Short is your only concern . . ." he said to Randolph's immobile face.

"A man named Henry Banks," Randolph said, "lives in Frankfort, Kentucky."

"I've met him." (A moth.) "He wants to be postmaster of Frankfort when the General is elected."

"Henry Banks knew Peyton Short very well." Randolph cocked his head at the door. Outside, two men were now shouting (Hamilton would never understand the South) in German. "He *claims* that Short kept a collection of letters between himself and young Rachel. He saw them in 1824."

Hamilton wiped his brow, which was suddenly dry. "Go on."

"And he *fears* that they are about to reappear now."

"And they are scandalous?"

Randolph smiled his ghastly smile, slouched his skeletal slouch.

"The election takes place in five weeks, Mr. Randolph," Hamilton said, which was true; voting would begin in the western states at the end of September, but it would go on intermittently across the country until early November. "They would need to be very scandalous indeed to make a difference now." When Randolph said nothing, Hamilton put down his mug and leaned forward intently, rallied instinctively by the complex, improbable algebra of politics. "Jackson has the complete support of the West and South, sir. He has swept aside all reports that he is a Mason, he has maintained a judicious silence on the question of tariffs. And now, this week, John Quincy Adams has once again put his foot in his mouth—did you read his speech, sir? He said, he actually said out loud, that Congress must not be 'palsied by the will of its constituents'! Imagine how foolishly—"

"Peyton Short asked Rachel Robards to elope with him, and she agreed."

Hamilton stopped, opened his mouth, closed it again.

"He wrote her love letters, *billets doux*"—Randolph cackled at some unthinkable memory—"which she dutifully answered in her own passionate and inimitable style. I know the good lady, Mr. Hamilton, *have* known her for years. Those letters, like no true southern gentleman, Peyton Short evidently kept secreted away in what we used to call a budget."

"She answered." Hamilton scarcely heard his own voice. "In her own writing."

"God has punished her for her sins," Randolph drawled, "by making her a saint."

"Do you know where the letters are?"

"Would the General pledge, in *his* own writing, that he would end the trade of slaves for profit in Washington City?"

"Yes, of course he would." Hamilton had no idea what the General would do. He was already on his feet, opening the lid of his father's watch. Going full speed it would take a courier twelve hours at least to reach John Coffee.

Randolph stayed precisely where he was, one tightly trousered leg still slung over the arm of his chair. His long white face floated like a mote of dust. In a burning slant of sunlight from the window he showed yellow-orange teeth, tar-black eyes. "Then I will endeavor to find them for you," he said, with such extraordinary mildness that he might have been speaking only to himself. But Hamilton had been a politician long enough to know the sound of a second barrel being cocked when he heard it. He stopped in mid-pace, mid-calculation, and looked up, frowning.

"Did your thorough investigations—" Randolph came suddenly, effortlessly to his feet, his face drifting supernaturally toward the ceiling "—reveal anything at all about Peyton Short's family?"

Hamilton dabbed his brow with Sam Houston's handkerchief. John Coffee had asked the very same question. "It's a common name in the South," he replied. "He was a migrant passing through Kentucky, a would-be attorney. No one had heard of him before. We never thought to inquire . . ." His words scratched to a halt.

There was an old poem somebody had written about his father, a taunting, mocking, painful thing to hear. Randolph suddenly burst into high-pitched singsong quotation. " 'Burr, Burr, what hast thou done?' " He whirled and flung the pewter mug, bouncing and clanging, into the empty fireplace. " 'Thou has shooted dead great Hamilton!' " He swung around again and leered. "Peyton Short's brother"—the horrible tongue hissed, the white face burned—"his *brother*, you insufferable Yankee *fool*, is an antislavery Judas named William Short!"

CHAPTER
12

True to his word, Coffee had indeed found Chase a room at the intriguingly named Fountain of Health. It turned out to be in fact a combination rural post office, general store, and hot springs health resort situated in a muddy pine hollow six miles east of Jackson's Hermitage.

Not that Chase had much time to "resort" to its pleasures, as the owner (postmaster, clerk) expressed it. For the first three days of his stay he sat like a monk in his narrow little bedroom overlooking the hot springs and went methodically, steadily through a huge stack of pasted albums and letters and military records that one or another of Jackson's nephews brought him each morning, apparently every slip and scrap of paper about the Battle of New Orleans that the General's staff historians had ever collected.

In the late afternoons he rode over to the Hermitage and took his dinner with the more or less official house family, never alone with Jackson, but never excluded either.

The first night he sat beside an irritable half-shaven man his own age, introduced to him by Coffee as Colonel Henry Lee, who had come out from Virginia in January, Chase gathered, to write Jackson's New Orleans celebration speech for him and had simply stayed on and on to see what orts might fall from the table. Next to him, and far pleasanter, was plump, sleek John Eaton, the senior senator from Tennessee, not remarkable for intelligence, on the contrary somewhat slow, but good-natured and friendly. Eaton, too, had once been a writer, he amiably confessed; he had published a little campaign biography of Jackson, in pamphlet form, for the election of 1824, and he promised to find a copy for Chase and bring it over to the Fountain of Health one morning.

Meanwhile, from time to time Jackson himself would glance down the long and crowded table and address some courteous, rather courtly remark to Chase, usually about Boston or Paris. (*AJ often mispronounces words,* Chase wrote in his notebook, *and when he does he seems to speak the word in question very loudly, as if he knows exactly what he's doing and defies you to correct him—"soo-blime Paree"*). To everybody else he talked politics—the treachery of Henry Clay, the arrogance of Adams—or horses, except to Rachel, whose conversation ran chiefly to farm news and the comings and goings of itinerant preachers in Nashville. At any point in the meal one of the numerous political hangers-on might suddenly spring to his feet, hat still on his head, chewing and snorting, struck by an idea; off he would hurry to Jackson's study or the upstairs parlor, now commandeered as a campaign office, to return five minutes later with an urgent paper or letter that he would silently deposit next to Jackson's plate. Invariably Jackson would look down and regard it for a moment with his stern, impassive gaze, then slip it in his coat pocket unread and turn back to Rachel. (*AJ almost* hovers *over her,* Chase wrote in the notebook, *tall, skinny, bristle-haired Jackson; stout, butter-faced little Rachel. The Ancient Mariner and Mrs. Humpty-Dumpty, as opposite as night and day. He pats her hand, he strokes her dowdy gray hair; he listens with perfect attention to every rambling, inconsequential thing she says. Let me not to the marriage of true minds . . .*)

On the third night, when Jackson had retreated temporarily into his study with Coffee and Eaton and his other advisors, Chase strolled out into the clearing behind the house that served as a backyard. It was eight o'clock in the evening, still twilight, still brutally hot. He wandered past a few dusty chickens scratching at the dry clay; past a locked smokehouse that smelled of ham; past a broken-down landau with only three wheels, and found himself eventually at the gate to the little white-fenced garden

Rachel worked herself. And just on the other side, on her knees, flower basket in hand, Rachel looked up and gave him her broadest, shyest smile.

"Well, I thought you'd be inside with the men, Mr. Chase."

Chase opened the gate and helped her to her feet. "I think they're talking campaign business, which isn't any business of mine."

Rachel wiped her hands on her apron and wrinkled her brow at the garden. "Well, there isn't much to see out here, not in August when the ground gets so parched. My roses are all right, but everything else of the vegetable kind looks mournful."

"It's a beautiful garden."

"Now I suppose Paris must get pretty hot in August, too, where you're from?"

"Not quite so hot, but it stays light in summer till almost midnight, especially in August."

"Come on down to my bench," Rachel said kindly, and Chase followed her short, waddling figure along a gravel path between two banks of pale yellow roses. She sat on a whitewashed stone bench under a beech tree and dusted a little space for Chase with her apron. "Are there lots of white people in Paris?" she inquired.

Chase paused in utter surprise. He looked down at her earnest, well-meaning face. Time and sun (and southern food) had done their work on her brown complexion. There was a faint dark mustache across her upper lip, a band of rolled-up fat where her dress pinched her neck, and many a reasonable man would have said that in old age she had become a genuinely homely woman. But the eyes that she now shaded with one pudgy hand were soft and vulnerable as a doe's. For an instant, beneath the wrinkles, he imagined he saw the smiling young belle of Nashville who had so captivated Andy Jackson back in 1789, back in the eighteenth century, before politics turned into scandal.

"I ask," Rachel continued, "because we lived in Pensacola while Mr. Jackson was governor of Florida. We had a beautiful Spanish house right on the Gulf of Mexico. Pride-of-China trees in the yard. Mimosa trees, orange trees. Purple-blue hyacinths. On the beach the sand was so soft it squeaked under your shoe. Oh, the gardens were lovely. But there were Jamaicans and mulattoes and Spanish and Indians everywhere. Whites were the least there."

"Paris is mostly white," Chase said, sitting beside her. "You would enjoy the gardens."

"Well, I didn't mind the other races," Rachel said. "We're all God's children. I loved little Lyncoya like my own baby, that we adopted, and he was pure Creek. A sweet child." She looked down at the flower basket beside her foot and nudged it, pointlessly, a little farther into the shade. "That boy used to stick turkey feathers in his hair and scare the other children from the bushes, you know, just like a real Indian I'd say to Mr. Jackson, and he would laugh and say, 'Well, sure enough, Rachel, because he *is* one!' Lyncoya died this summer, the first of July. The doctor said it was consumption."

"I'm sorry."

"Mr. Jackson always says he hopes to meet everyone in heaven, white and black, all the same." She kept her dark eyes fixed on the basket. "But he only says it to me. He says other people might not understand."

Chase nodded, unable to think of a response.

"Don't write that in your book," Rachel said.

"No, I won't."

"You look sad, Mr. Chase," she said after a moment, her beautiful eyes on his, "sometimes, when you think nobody's watching." And then in a gesture remarkably like her husband's she gently patted the back of his hand. "Whatever it is," she said, "the Lord's Will be done."

✳   ✳   ✳

THE next morning, along with his usual quota of books and albums, Jackson's nephew *du jour* brought Chase a plain white envelope bound with a purple-blue ribbon. Inside it Chase found a note from Rachel and six or seven faded sheets of old writing paper.

My respected friend, she said in her note, *here ar some letters I rote from new Orleans after Mr Jacksons battle for yr book.*

The first and longest by far was an account to someone in Nashville—the name was indecipherable—of her arrival in New Orleans for the victory celebrations of March 1815.

> *To give you a disscription is beyond the power of my pen, the splendor of the brilliant assembleage the magnificence of the supper and orniments of the room. I was placed opposite a banner with the Motto Jackson and victory ar one, on the table a most Ellegent Piramid of ices, on the top was vive Jackson in Large Letters, on the*

*other side the Immortal Washington. ther was a gold
ham on the table.*

*it is the finest Country for the Eye of a stranger but
after a little while he tires of the Dissipation of the place,
so much amusement Balls Concerts Theaters, but we
dont attend the half of them.*

*I have given you some of the flowers now the thorns.
Major Read tells me more than a hundred men have
died of the fevr. Doctore Fore is gone. genl Coffee had
him decently interred in the burying ground. Mr Webb
our near neighbor is dead.*

When John Eaton appeared about an hour later, he recognized the
handwriting instantly. "One of Rachel's letters for sure," he told Chase.
"For somebody who can't spell or parse an English sentence, that woman
does love to write letters." He glanced in a possessive, senatorial way over
Chase's shoulder. "New Orleans. Telling you all about the gold ham on
the table, I bet. She's never forgotten that ham or the wicked French
ladies in their low-cut dresses."

"She thought I might use some of the details in my book, I guess."

"Well, here's *my* book." Eaton handed Chase a little gray-covered pamphlet of thirty or forty pages. "Guaranteed to parse. Every fact O.K. Now
don't you want to forget literature for a while, Mr. Chase, and come on
down out of this hot-box of a hotel room? We can have a healthful drink
of whiskey over by the Fountain."

As it turned out, Eaton's idea of a drink included stripping down
behind the men's partition at the hotel springs and stretching out naked
on his back like a bear in the tepid, mildly sulfurous water. Chase shook
his head at the idea of immersing himself in warm water while the sun
was already blazing down through the trees in ruthless Tennessee fashion.
But after five minutes soaking with a glass of whiskey in hand (brought
by a small black boy who also rented towels), he began to relax and enjoy
himself. Eaton was good company, the water was pleasantly enervating;
the whiskey was as good as gold ham.

"You put anything about Henry Clay in your book?" Eaton splashed
water on his hairy chest and contemplated his white penis as it floated
limply on the green water. He splashed water on it too.

"I haven't gotten to the election of 1824 yet," Chase said.

"Fought a duel with John Randolph, you know."

"Yes."

"Told me Randolph was so skinny it was like trying to shoot a pair of fire tongs. I don't trust Henry Clay as far as I can throw that hotel over there, but he's a funny son of a bitch."

"Never met him. He wouldn't see me in Washington."

"Once sang me a song he said he wrote, called 'The Extinction of the British Fire.' Said it was inspired by a congressman friend of his who put the British ambassador's fireplace to an unorthodox personal use. That was in 1812, just before the war." Eaton rolled over lazily. He motioned the black boy to bring them both another whiskey. "You won't find that kind of detail in Rachel's letters."

"Not likely."

"I would adore to be in Paris, where you are, one of these days," Eaton said. "For the French women. New Orleans was just a taste. You know American women, Washington women, are so strict and virtuous, we have a saying—'American women divide the body into two parts: from the top to the waist is the stomach; from there to the bottom is the limbs.' Now France must be different."

Chase nodded and grinned what he hoped was a knowing, masculine grin. He had heard of Eaton's reputation as a womanizer in Washington, where he was rumored to carry on a liaison with a barkeeper's married daughter. Eaton was the kind of man, he would guess, who was divided into one part.

"If we were to go around to the other side of that partition"—Eaton rolled over again and pointed his glass at the thick wooden screen that ran across the pool—"which is the women's side, why that would be the end of me. Even if it's perfectly innocent."

"Why does Jackson have all those busts and statuettes of Napoleon in his office?" Chase asked to change the subject, thinking at the same time that Eaton had a curiously self-destructive imagination. "I noticed them right away and I counted five books about Napoleon in his bookcase."

"He beat the British," Eaton said concisely. "Napoleon whipped the red British ass." He cocked an interested eye. "Now is that the kind of detail you mean to put in your book? You need to be careful if it is. People might say why is a great Democrat admiring a Dictator like Napoleon?"

"I was puzzled about it myself."

"So you need to remind them that Thomas Jefferson had a big bust of Napoleon in his house too. I remember seeing it in the library."

Chase closed his eyes and smelled the faintly sulfurous fumes of the Fountain of Health, a smell that seemed to him for some reason like the color dark orange, and tried to recall if Jefferson had really had such a bust.

"I remember Jefferson," Eaton said, "telling Madison one day how the British were the only nation on earth that required to be kicked into common good manners."

"That sounds like Jefferson," Chase said, and found himself yawning and closing his eyes again in the warm pool.

"People's censorious attitude," Eaton told him, in what was apparently a complete non sequitur, "is what causes these attacks on poor Aunt Rachel."

Only later, as he lay on his bed upstairs, groggy from the whiskey and the heat, did it occur to Chase that it was not a non sequitur at all. He was being as carefully observed by Jackson's friends as a matchbox next to a powder keg. He sat up and walked over to his writing table and discovered that slow, sensual John Eaton had nonetheless managed to carry away Rachel's little envelope of letters. He lay down again and made a wry face at the ceiling. Whose idea had it been, he wondered, to send Eaton around with his pamphlet and his patter? Coffee's, or Henry Lee's, or Hamilton's?

He watched the shadows ride from the top of the window across the wall, only to ripple and vanish into a mirror. He yawned and pictured a white crescent of sunrise slowly rising up the black rim of the Atlantic, light striking the roofs and domes of Washington City, where Emma and her father and Ephraim Sellers were. It couldn't have been Hamilton, he suddenly thought. Two days ago Hamilton had put on an oversized Stetson hat and a spangled leather vest and ridden away on an errand, somewhere to the east.

He stretched out his legs and closed his eyes. His thoughts drifted, darkened. Hogwood had said that John Randolph, the fire-tongs man, had also gotten on his horse and ridden away from the great Serbonian bog of Washington, toward Tennessee.

Whatever for?

CHAPTER

13

He almost didn't tell us."

Coffee folded his arms over his chest and moved his head an inch or so to the left until he could see through the half-open door into the parlor, where David Chase was visible, sitting next to Rachel, who was talking (so it appeared) to one of Jackson's knees. Satisfied that all was well, he looked back at Hamilton.

"The son of a bitch," Hamilton repeated slowly, distinctly, furiously, "*almost* didn't tell us at all. He said he's known about Peyton Short's letters for months—he very nearly blurted it out to somebody else back in April. He only told *me* in the end because I promised him Jackson would outlaw the slave trade in Washington City."

"The General won't make any such pledge," Coffee said. Through the open door Jackson's hand slapped Jackson's knee.

"I know that. Randolph is a *fool.*"

Coffee nodded. They could sort out later who was a fool. There seemed to be limitless choices just at the moment.

"And as for William Short . . ." Hamilton snorted.

"Now you remember I don't know about William Short," Coffee reminded him. He moved his head back the other way. Hamilton's hat was much too large for him and was covered, like the rest of Hamilton, with a day's worth of dust from the Knoxville road. Under the hallway lamp he had taken on something of a powdery white glow.

"William Short was Peyton Short's brother," Hamilton told him, and instantly corrected himself. "His *estranged* brother that died. They hadn't seen each other for twenty years, apparently. William Short was Thomas Jefferson's protégé in France; he's an antislavery man, a millionaire, a political meddler—" Coffee refolded his arms the other way, scarcely hearing, registering only key words. Jefferson again. It was amazing to him how far the shadows of old men like Jefferson and Washington still reached, and Alexander Hamilton, too, for that matter, the giants before the Flood. Washington had died in 1799. Jefferson had retired from office in 1809, nineteen years ago exactly, but politicians still latched onto their ghostly coattails. "Jefferson and Jackson" was one of John Eaton's better campaign slogans.

"And let me tell you one other goddamned thing," Hamilton said, suddenly clear as a bell, commanding Coffee's complete attention. He pointed one dusty finger. "About your big-toothed smiling young writer in there."

✳   ✳   ✳

FROM his chair in the parlor Chase could hear Hamilton and Coffee talking out in the hall, their voices low and intense, and he could just make out the shadowy bulk of Coffee's shoulder against the door frame, but whatever they were saying was lost in the rising medley of voices on either side of him.

"Predestination, yes," repeated the Reverend Marston Ashe. "Yes. The invaluable doctrine of our Protestant founders, which explains the present and future state of our immortal souls."

Chase turned back to the parlor and strangled the impulse to strangle the Reverend Ashe.

"Predestination," echoed Rachel doubtfully. She sat on Chase's left, clad as usual in a shapeless blue calico dress and a white apron, and turned a ring of house keys over and over in her lap, the picture of unhappiness. "I don't really understand it, you know, such a *hard* word."

"Well," Chase began, not sure how to break in.

"Very simple word," declared the Reverend Ashe, who nodded offi-
ciously and looked sideways at Jackson, but Jackson was staring blankly
out the window, pipe between his teeth, apparently lost in thought. "Very
simple indeed. Predestination is the Calvinist conviction that every soul
born into this vale of tears is already destined by our Creator, from the
first, as either saved or damned to hell, begging your pardon. It makes no
difference and it does no good to work for our own salvation. We are
either saved or not; the whole thing was decided long ago before we were
born."

"We could sin terribly and still be saved," Rachel said, more doubtfully
than ever.

"We could do endless good works and still be damned," said the Reverend Ashe with great satisfaction. "No matter how hard we try, if we are
already damned, nothing we do can redeem us. No amount of repentance
will help. Christ has no use for us in that case. *He* sends us away, eter-
nally."

"My blessed Redeemer," Rachel said, and her round face looked close
to tears.

"He drives us from His bosom," said Ashe.

The keys dropped with a clatter from Rachel's apron. She turned in her
chair, in mute appeal to Jackson, and though Chase would have sworn
that the old man hadn't heard a word they had been saying, he nonetheless glanced up quickly. He removed his pipe from his mouth and leaned
forward.

"Do you contend, sir, that when my Savior said, 'Come unto me *all* ye
that labor and are heavy-laden,' He didn't mean what He said?"

The Reverend Ashe opened his mouth, then closed it.

"Mrs. Jackson is sleepy, I think," Jackson said, firmly. He came to his
feet, and Rachel stood up at almost the same instant, nodding and
smoothing her apron. "Mr. Chase," Jackson added as he led her to the
door, "perhaps you can take a turn with me in the evening air in five
minutes' time? Good night, Reverend. You know which is your room."

It was closer to ten minutes than five before Jackson reappeared at the
back door of the Hermitage. Coffee and Hamilton had long since vanished into the house. He motioned to Chase and proceeded to stroll out,
pipe clenched once again between his teeth, into the soft Tennessee night.

"The Reverend Ashe is from Virginia," he said as they passed the kitchen, a detached building just behind the back steps. "He grew up in Accomac County, which was the home of Mrs. Jackson's mother. Until last month he was minister of the very church she attended as a girl."

"And now?" Chase found himself wondering less at the reason for the Reverend Ashe's presence than at the astonishing pervasiveness of Virginia in American life.

"Now he's on his way to Cincinnati, along with dozens of other outraged ministers, all of them running as fast as they can to denounce the terrible Miss Frances Wright." Jackson chuckled. "Between myself and Fanny Wright, you know, the East is hard-pressed to keep up. Me, of course, they regard as little better than an illiterate Indian fighter, with a knife in one hand and a scalp in the other, ready to knock down the first man who differs from my opinion. Fanny they regard as the 'priestess of Beelzebub' because of her radical ideas."

"I would have thought her radical ideas very different from yours," Chase said. They were just now alongside the first of several slave cabins rising on the grassy slope behind the house; the night breeze brought a rich mixture of smells and voices that suddenly seemed to Chase as exotic as Paris.

Jackson paused to knock his pipe against his palm, scattering a little bird's wing of glowing sparks into the darkness. "Her ideas will undoubtedly have their day," he said, with unexpected gravity. "I mean her ideas on slavery and property. But not now."

"No."

"Don't repeat that in your book."

"No, sir."

"I've read your New Orleans chapters," Jackson added after a moment. "Very good, full of sublime facts, due credit to Providence. That's why I thought we might talk a little, just the two of us."

By this point they had reached a high, flat ridge behind the house, which was the crest on which the Hermitage should have been built. Despite the example of the Reverend Ashe, Chase was emboldened. Time, he guessed, was running out. Seize the soo-blime moment. He took a breath and ventured into the Jacksonian minefield.

"Would you object to a political question, General? Not biographical?"

"Speak, Mr. Chase."

"The election is still in the balance, sir—I've wondered from time to time, these last few days, if you don't intend to go out on the campaign trail yourself and make a speech, like Fanny Wright?"

Under the pale starlight Jackson took a step sideways to cough into his fist, a loud hacking cough that reminded Chase of how sick, how literally ill he could look sometimes. By rights, John Coffee had said, counting on his fingers Jackson's chronic ailments from dysentery to spitting blood, by all rights he ought to be dead about six times over.

Jackson cleared his throat violently, and then turned his usual grave, impassive face back to Chase. "I'm not a candidate for President by my *own* volition, Mr. Chase, but by the selection of the people. Mr. Adams was chosen by an elite caucus of his party. I was nominated by the people themselves, through their state legislatures. I will *not* abandon principle by entering upon a pandering electioneering campaign, as Mr. Adams has. Keep to principle, Mr. Chase. Never lower yourself."

"You have that much faith in the people?"

"Yes, sir, I do. I have great confidence in the virtue of a great majority of the people. They have the all-powerful constitutional corrective in their hands, the right of suffrage, which I would like to see extended even further. When this is used with calmness and deliberation—not distracted by base slanders and wars against women—why then, the people can perpetuate their liberties, the republic is safe."

"Jeffersonian principles, in other words."

"For elegance of writing style, Mr. Chase, as you are a literary man, I will say I always preferred Madison. But for faith in the people's virtue I am a pure Jeffersonian."

Jackson stopped to cough again, but this time he finished with a rasping sound somewhere between choking and a chuckle. "To tell the truth, Mr. Chase," he said, recovering, "I might be more tempted to make a speech if my goddamn false teeth didn't keep falling out."

Chase joined in the chuckle, then ventured another step. "There was an article in one of the Boston newspapers linking you with Aaron Burr's conspiracy, back in 1807."

"One reason I have ever been reluctant to stand for President, Mr. Chase, is that I foresaw that every little error and indiscretion of life would be magnified into crimes of deepest dye."

Chase ventured as far as he could. "The stories concerning yourself and Lewis Robards—"

But if Jackson heard the question he gave no sign of it. Before Chase had finished his sentence he was already six feet away, peering into the shadows. Chase cocked his head and listened. Nothing but the hoot of an owl, a peal of laughter from a cabin. Jackson held out his arm and said, "John Coffee, you're as loud as a bear."

"I followed your pipe, General." Coffee appeared, walking (to Chase's ears) in complete silence, and moments later came the sharp, blustery little profile of James A. Hamilton Jr.

"You can almost see Nashville from here," Jackson said. He swept his pipe along the horizon, where a few tiny lamps blinked in the deep hollow of Clover Bottom. "I was just about to point it out to Mr. Chase, who told me the other day he's never been this far west before in his life."

"It's all changed since we came out," Coffee said. "There wasn't anything then except the river and the Indians."

"I remember," Jackson said, "the first doctor in Nashville."

"John Sappington," Coffee said. As if by unspoken agreement all four men had slowly turned in a circle, until they were facing downhill again, where the roof of the Hermitage rose a darker black against the shivering outline of summer trees. Far to the right the Cumberland River gleamed like an unsheathed sword.

"John Sappington," Jackson told Chase, "used to sell a patent medicine called Sappington's Pills—good for any ailment whatsoever—I've taken them myself. He had an office next door to the old Nashville Inn, and so small was our little town then, Mr. Chase, that at a certain hour each morning Dr. Sappington would step outside on his porch and ring a cowbell to let his patients know it was time to take their pills."

But under Coffee's and Jackson's booming, good-natured laughter, Chase heard or imagined he heard Hamilton's clipped and angry mutter: "Mr. Chase ought to think about his own damn health."

Back at the Hermitage, Jackson shook hands with him, wished him good night, and disappeared into his ground-floor bedroom.

"He is an enigmatic man," Coffee said, walking with Chase into the main hallway next to the stairs.

Chase glanced at him and wondered at Coffee's choice of word—*enigmatic* was far too subtle and tentative for someone so decisive as Jackson. Wondered, too, at his tone of voice. Wary, cautious, with the faint edge of a warning as well. What had he and Hamilton been talking so long about? *Enigmatic* was a far better choice for loyal, deep-thinking, far-seeing John Coffee himself.

"Well, I like him," Chase heard himself saying fatuously. "Very much. I confess, General Coffee, I had not expected to like him. After all the stories you hear in the East . . . But I begin to see why men followed him into battle in the war, I might do it myself." He tried for a joke. "Even his political evasions are forthright."

Coffee crossed his big arms over his chest and said nothing. Down the hall, at the other end of the house, Hamilton's voice rose petulantly, calling for brandy. A slave carrying a lantern hurried past.

"And Mrs. Jackson," Chase added, feeling more and more awkward in the face of Coffee's silence. "I like her too. Very much."

Coffee was well over six feet tall and even now, in his late fifties, was a thick-set, imposing mass of muscle. He had a sharp, prominent nose. His silver-black hair was tied at the back in a queue, an old-fashioned eighteenth-century style, *démodé*, which Chase hadn't seen since his boyhood. Hamilton was still calling loudly down the hall, but somehow Coffee contrived to place himself in front of Chase as if to block out the sound.

"I understand you spent part of the afternoon with her, Mr. Chase."

"She took me along to some of the slave cabins where she was visiting the sick. They do all seem to love her, all the slaves. Then the Reverend Ashe got her upset tonight with his theology."

"Rachel Jackson," Coffee said softly, "is a person, Mr. Chase, who has never quite known how to fit herself into the world. She has, in fact, striven against it for thirty years, ever since her marriage, but the ways of people other than children and slaves—the ways of ambitious people or cruel people, these utterly baffle her. Outside her house, I think she feels that everything she sees is quite alien to her."

Chase nodded, impressed, even moved. He looked around and realized that Coffee had imperceptibly drawn him down the hall, past the red and white Telemachus wallpaper, to the front door of the house. Now he pulled it open and brought them both onto the porch.

"You were asking him questions up there, Mr. Chase, before we arrived."

"General questions about politics, biographical questions."

Coffee steered him to the very edge of the porch, where a single oil lantern hung on a square white column. Beyond its flickering beam the lawn curved up and away from the house like a bowl. The warm night slipped down its sides in silky black waves of heat. A chorus of crickets started up in a field. Oddly enough, Chase's horse appeared at the corner of the house, uncalled-for, led by a yawning stableboy.

"The General is a great man," Coffee said.

Chase watched for a moment, perplexed, as the boy walked the horse toward them. Then he surprised himself by saying, "I think he is too." And surprised himself even more by adding, "To tell the truth, General Coffee, I've been away so long, I'm like Mrs. Jackson—everything I see is alien to me now. But this country seems to be whirling out of control, like a dervish. It needs a *center*. I used to think it needed somebody like Thomas Jefferson again. But Jefferson's day is over, the eighteenth century is over. What it needs is somebody like Jackson."

Coffee took the reins from the boy and handed them to Chase. "Mr. Hamilton wants me to stop you from finishing your book," he said.

CHAPTER
14

John Quincy Adams detested the American political custom of toasts. He looked down at the empty glass in front of him, up at the blurred and sweltering mob of diners crowded fifteen or twenty deep beyond his own head table. A waiter poured viscous red liquid into his glass, which Adams knew for a fact was bad Rhône wine that had been badly shipped and badly stored and had undoubtedly stood in an overheated bung-stopped barrel for two full days before the banquet. Baltimore. What could you expect of Barnum's Tavern in Baltimore?

"I give you," said the Governor of Maryland four chairs away, standing and raising his glass. All over the hall men stood or tottered or outright staggered to their feet, likewise raising their glasses. With what he hoped was a cordial smile of respect and interest (but feared was the reverse), Adams, too, came to his feet and held up the glass of liquid.

"I give you, my friends," said the governor, "Charles Carroll of Carrollton, last surviving signer of our glorious Declaration of Independence. Glory to our patriot fathers!"

"I knew *your* father, sir," said the man on Adams's left as they all sat down again in a rumble of scraping chairs and boots. A platoon of white-sleeved waiters spread out among the tables with the next course. Beef ribs, the President noted as the armloads of plates began to drop into place; burned to a crisp.

"Did you indeed know him?" Adams watched a slab of coal-black meat slide onto the plate before him.

"I visited him in Quincy, in your own family home. He showed me enormous piles of manure in the garden, of which he was inordinately proud."

Adams nodded tightly. His late father had in fact often boasted of the quality of his manure.

"I am the mayor of Hagerstown," the man told him confidentially. "If you did not remember, sir."

"Of course I remember, Mr. . . . . Slidell." In ancient Rome, Adams thought, snapping open his napkin and tying it around his neck, candidates for office employed a nomenclator, who would stand next to them and whisper a voter's name. Without doubt Andrew Jackson had such a person. Without doubt Andrew Jackson by now would have had his arm wrapped in instant and undying friendship around Mr. Slidell's scrawny shoulders. The noise of the banquet rose to an intolerable level of clacking dishes and silver. Adams leaned closer to his neighbor and showed, as his wife would say, an interest.

"I see that you are proposing a toast tonight." The President nodded toward the sheet of paper folded beside Slidell's glass. It was the practice on these occasions to have half a dozen scheduled toasts, then open the floor to "volunteers."

"The great founders: Washington, Jefferson, Franklin," said Slidell proudly, with no sense, obviously, that the son of John Adams might be offended by his omission.

"The great untouchables," Adams said with asperity, and turned to his burned meat.

"I look forward to *your* toast, sir," Slidell added, but Adams only grunted and lowered his head. At the other tables the sixty or seventy guests—invited to see and hear a living President, but in fact doing their best to ignore him—the whole tavernful of them were chattering and tearing at their food with democratic gusto. Adams pushed a bit of dark beef through a swamp of redeye gravy. His mind flickered, as it so often did, to the days of his bachelorhood, when he had been the American minister to The Hague and lived alone, without regard for voters, elections, toasts. In those halcyon days he would rise about five, read Tacitus or Ovid for an hour, take his cold breakfast in his parlor, then study Italian. At eleven he would translate from the Dutch until lunch. Write letters, walk, dine at five, read Shakespeare or some other light author while he smoked his evening cigar. To anyone else, he thought with grim pride, this would have seemed like too much reading and solitude. But I was not formed to shine in company, Adams reminded himself, staring out at a sea of red faces and champing teeth, nor to be delighted with it.

"I give you, gentlemen," announced Charles Carroll of Carrollton, seated in white-haired splendor next to the governor, "the United States of America—may other countries learn from her the easy access of the people to their rulers!"

The mob rose in a cheering mass, glasses flashing. Adams bowed, smiled. To his unspeakable disgust, through the open windows came the sound of a marching band and the strains of "The Hunters of Kentucky."

"You will be next, dear sir," said an egg-shaped man on his right, whose name Adams had not been told. The waiters spread out again, bottles of wine poised in each hand. In Philadelphia his wife had begged him to speak German to a delegation of voters, but the most he could bring himself to do was shake their leaders' hands and murmur (in English) "God bless you" to perfect strangers. Adams pursed his lips at the brassy taste of the truly dreadful wine. Every compromise with principle was a knot in the soul, ashes in the throat. But there was no American in history, he thought, so well prepared for his country's highest office.

An anonymous man two seats to his right leaned behind the chairs and seized his free hand. "I'm opposed to you, sir," he sputtered, "*politically* speaking." Drunk. "But friend to friend I'm mighty glad to see you well."

"We are all friends *here*," said the President frigidly. Felt his hand released.

"Your toast, Mr. Adams," called the Governor from down the table, loudly enough to stop the buzzing of conversation. Slowly, all around the vast tavern, voices came to a halt. Waiters scurried between tables with their bottles. Silver clinked against china. The gas lamps on the wall hissed for silence. Even the rival Jackson band in the street apparently paused for breath.

Adams came all the way to his feet. The thought stabbed across his mind that he was not a tall man and would not be fully visible, behind the rostrum, to many of the diners. He placed his left hand behind his back, under the tails of his frock coat. With his right hand he raised the glass of undrinkable wine.

"Gentlemen, I propose ebony and topaz—General Ross's coat of arms and the republican militiamen who gave it!"

Even before the glass reached his lips he knew that something was wrong, but he had no idea at all of what it might be. His audience was standing, some were drinking, others turning to their neighbors and whispering. A feeble cheer went up from the back of the room, then men on all sides began to sit down and mutter.

The Governor of Maryland twisted in his chair and regarded Adams blankly. " 'Ebony and topaz,' Mr. Adams? I don't understand, I fear." He gestured toward the tables, where to Adams it appeared that every man had now turned his back. "What are 'ebony and topaz'?"

"I allude, sir, to Voltaire's tale *Le blanc et le noir.* My meaning was that whenever the spirit of evil, which Voltaire represents as ebony, should invade our country, the spirit of good—topaz—should repel it."

"And General Ross?"

"The British general, sir, shot dead by a militiaman in this very city of Baltimore during the War of 1812. His sovereign rewarded his grieving family with a coat of arms."

The governor drained his glass and sat back. The man on Adams's left wiped his sleeve across his mouth. "Who the devil is *Voltaire*?"

✳   ✳   ✳

TWO days later, as he sat at his desk in the President's mansion, Adams heard a second interpretation of his toast.

"They say, sir," his son Charles Francis Adams explained. He stopped and gave a significant glance in the direction of the hired portrait painter who waited ten feet away, daubing absentmindedly at his canvas.

"You may speak freely in front of Mr. Sully," Adams said.

Charles looked doubtful, stood on one leg, and rubbed the calf of his trousers with his shoe. "They say in New York, sir, that you meant by *ebony* and *topaz* to personify the slave and free states."

"Nonsense," said Adams. He looked down at the budget of letters on his desk. Applications for places, army reports, newspaper clippings; a manuscript copy of an anti-Jackson article written (anonymously) by Henry Clay, with the marginal notation in Clay's distinctively large handwriting: "To be printed in tomorrow's *National Journal.*" Adams placed it under the blotter, where he kept the loose pages of his diary and also a single sheet of paper with the heading, in his own distinctively small handwriting, *Enemies.*

"Nonsense," he repeated, and looked at his daily calendar.

"I've asked that no visitors be admitted till afternoon." Charles waved his hand vaguely in the direction of the President's desk. "So that you can catch up, sir."

"Thank you," Adams said. After a moment's hesitation Charles nodded briskly, once, and left the room.

Sully put down his brushes and took up a charcoal pencil. Out of the corner of his eye Adams watched him as he worked, but made a point of not trying to see what the artist had so far done. He knew very well what he looked like, inside and out. He wrote *John Quincy Adams* across the bottom of a letter. He looked like his son.

"You knew Mr. Jefferson intimately, sir," said Sully at length, in a conversational tone. "Or so I understand."

Adams read the first paragraph of a new letter slowly and deliberately, then raised his eyes. "I knew Mr. Jefferson in Paris, of course, yes, when he was the American minister and I was a boy." He tried to recall what else Sully had painted; remembered a vast historical canvas, *Washington Crossing the Delaware,* which had proved too large to hang in the Capitol.

"I painted a portrait of him too," Sully said. "In his old age."

"I saw Mr. Jefferson once or twice in this city when he was President. I never saw him afterward."

"An elusive man," Sully observed. "Very ethereal. I felt I was painting an idea more than a face. Talked about everything under the sun while he sat."

Adams read a second paragraph. The letter was from a political acquaintance in New York who warned that one Dr. A. Todson, a disappointed office-seeker, had announced he was coming to Washington City to assassinate him. Adams put it aside. He received such threats all the time. Last month a traveler from North Carolina had walked into his office and demanded a loan of ten dollars to see him home again, and when Adams refused the man had actually brandished his stick. Gracious God, what a life—Jackson was welcome to it!

"Jefferson was much given to exaggeration," he remarked to Sully after a pause. "Once at a dinner party he claimed in my presence to have learned the Spanish language in nineteen days." The painter seemed unoffended. Adams tried again. "He told my wife that in Paris he had seen Fahrenheit's thermometer at twenty degrees below zero for six straight weeks. 'Never once,' said he, 'even so high as zero, which is fifty degrees below the freezing point.' "

Sully made a sympathetic clucking noise and reached for a sponging cloth.

"Fahrenheit's zero is not fifty degrees below freezing," Adams told him. "It is *thirty-two*."

The painter scratched his ear and erased a line. Adams looked out the window toward the south lawn. Gray August sky, threatening rain. Brown, uneven stalks of grass. At the edge of the lawn he could just see the roof of his personal gardening shed. When he had returned the previous day from Baltimore he had rushed down to observe the little cork oaks he had recently planted there and had been deeply chagrined to find so few of them surviving the summer's heat and the repeated assaults of insects and vermin. *The infancy of plants,* he had written in his journal, *seems to be as delicate as that of animals.* He had forborne to make a cheap and obvious analogy between his horticultural and political fortunes. Instead, he had limited himself to two neutral observations: one, that self-planted seeds thrive the most vigorously; two, that the plants he most cherished were the most apt to disappoint him and die.

At five, despite the threatening sky, he set off on his afternoon walk from the President's mansion to Capitol Square and back, a total distance of four and three-quarter miles. He had just stepped into the house to record the time in his journal when his wife emerged from the garden, and behind her a strikingly attractive young woman whom he had seen before, somewhere. Behind *her,* never very far from youthful female beauty, his son Charles.

"You have met Mr. Adams, I believe," his wife said. "Miss Emma Colden."

"Well, I have passed down the receiving line when you were 'at home,' " said the young woman in the clear, quick kind of English accent for which the President knew he had a great weakness.

"With—Senator Ephraim Sellers," he replied, rising on his toes and permitting his mouth to form the white O of a smile. He could no longer read Horace or Virgil without a dictionary, but the names of the most obscure acquaintances leaped to his mind in a flash. Did this not prove he was a politician?

"Miss Colden is a journalist," said his wife.

"Ah." Adams felt his mouth grow smaller, tighter. "The only female journalist I know is Anne Royall, who is . . . eccentric."

"Crazy, you mean," muttered Charles.

Louisa pretended not to hear him. "Miss Colden is very kind. Her father went to Oxford. She has lived in Paris, London."

"Are you here, Miss Colden"—Adams strained to be jocular—"professionally?"

"Mrs. Adams invited me for tea," she said. "We've just been admiring your plantings."

"Write a story about them," Charles suggested brainlessly. "Get the gardeners' vote."

Adams looked his son into silence. Emma Colden wore a cool linen dress with a low-cut neck, revealing the soft curve of her bosom; she had removed her bonnet as she came in, and her blond hair, cut shorter than most American women's hair, curled charmingly around her neck (Adams quoted Milton to himself: *in wanton tendrils*).

"I have sometimes thought an article about the President's visitors would be of interest to the public," he said. "Only last week I had a woman call on me, a perfect stranger, dressed entirely in men's clothing. She demanded that I give her money. When I refused, she accused me of prejudice against her manner of dress."

"And you replied, sir?"

"I replied that it was perfectly true."

"My father says that when you were secretary of state you so admired General Jackson that you proposed appointing him to a foreign post."

Adams cleared his throat. His wife had stepped to one side, as if to straighten something on a table. Charles had adopted his one-legged stork posture again and was gaping. Louisa knew very well that he made it a policy not to grant interviews to journalists. A polite question or two, a sober answer; yes. Nothing more. There is a difference between courting the people, she had hissed, and *shunning* them.

"He said," Emma Colden persisted, though blushing slightly, "that you supported the General's violent invasion of Florida after the War of 1812 and then wanted to reward him with the ambassadorship to Russia."

"It is true," Adams said, because it was true. "I believe General Jackson had the legal authority to march into Florida. The Spanish were inciting the Indians to war again; they were secretly harboring British agents. I believed it was right for the nation."

"And the matter of Russia?"

But Adams was not ever to be pestered or bullied—by a woman, no matter how handsome—beyond the strict limits of discretion. She was correct, of course. He had supported the General entirely then. President Monroe, however, unconvinced, had made the pilgrimage to Monticello to seek Jefferson's opinion. According to Monroe, Jefferson had come to his feet in horror. "Jackson ambassador to Russia—why, good God! He would breed you a quarrel before he had been there a month!" But it would be wrong, contrary to all duty and principle, to reveal such a confidential fact, to reveal it casually to a female journalist. He would be reelected honestly, or he would . . . fail.

"It was so long ago," the President said, bowing stiffly.

✳ ✳ ✳

THAT night as they prepared for bed his wife came across the hall and into his room, where he was, as always, writing.

"She is a most attractive young woman," Louisa Adams said. "Emma Colden is."

"Most." Adams put down his pen. Courteously.

"You would like me to be as slender and attractive."

Adams sighed and held up both hands in mute, weary protest. What could one answer?

"Well, she's leaving tomorrow for Cincinnati," said his wife. She prowled from desk to table to window. "Traveling by herself, free."

"Is she going to interview General Jackson?" Though he affected not to be aware of him, Adams now kept a tense watch on Jackson's reported travels and the ceaseless political forays of his henchmen Sam Houston and John Eaton. In forty-three days exactly balloting would begin. "I understood Jackson was still in his lair in Nashville."

"She is going to write a series of articles about Frances Wright, for the *United States Telegraph*." His wife had always believed (and perhaps correctly) that Adams's mother, Abigail, had despised her and deplored their marriage. Now she stopped in front of the small oval portrait of her that hung above the bookcase. "The priestess of Beelzebub," she said. Adams looked up sharply. "That is what the newspapers call Frances Wright," she said.

"Yes." He could think of nothing further to say. Forty-three days. There were disgraceful chocolate smears on his wife's fingers. Her small, birdlike face was terribly sad. She passed from his room without a sound.

The Life of Andrew Jackson, by David Chase

Chapter Twelve

TWO MONTHS AFTER THE BATTLE OF NEW ORLEANS, JACKSON WAS PLACED
under arrest for contempt of court.

In so little time did his sublime and bloody victory on the battlefield pass into ordinary low political comedy.

The facts were these:

In the three days following the stupendous victory of January 8, the
British army requested a brief truce in order to bury their dead. Wagonloads of bodies passed from the American ramparts back across the stubble field and into the devastated British camp. Jackson sent doctors and
nurses from his own ranks to aid the enemy wounded, a humanitarian
gesture. Inspecting the lines below his ditch himself, the General passed
corpses in every possible stage of decay and mutilation. In the British
hospital tents the surgeons cut, amputated, sliced with flashing knives;
whole baskets of legs and arms lay by their tables as they worked.

At the end of the week, under cover of night, the remains of the British army slunk away so silently that in the morning the American sentinels still had no idea they were gone.

Where, in fact, had they disappeared?

Jackson soon knew.

They had retreated across the alligator-infested, frost-covered, black-water swamps and bayous back to their waiting boats on Lake Borgne, and from there they had skulked and sailed eastward, fuming with re-criminations, along the Gulf of Mexico to Mobile. But at Mobile, with distance, their courage had returned, and according to Jackson's spies the whole enormous fleet was now drawn up in menacing and snarling for-mation just outside Fort Bowyer on the outskirts of the city. They looked, the spies said nervously, as if they were preparing for a siege.

In New Orleans, meantime, having given Jackson and his troops the most elaborate, carnival-like celebration the Creole race could devise, the citizens of that city assumed they could therefore disband their militias and return to their lives. The Legislature called itself into assembly for that purpose. The merchants re-opened their warehouses and shops, the octoroon ladies began to ride to and fro in their elegant carriages, while the lawyers and swells took up their places again at the no less elegant tables of the city's coffeehouses and saloons. New Orleans, in a word, smoothed her skirts, tossed her hair.

Jackson took one look around and tersely informed the city that as long as the British fleet was in the Gulf, threatening his troops, martial law still prevailed. The lawyers and gents, he said, could go straight back to their regiments, the ladies could go back into their houses during curfew, and the Legislature could go back to the devil. Dissenters would be jailed, deserters would be shot. The river, the city, the whole g——d——d state itself, he said mildly, was under his sole and complete authority.

Into this tense and unexpected confrontation sailed the good ship Ru-mor.

The war was already over, Rumor declared. *A treaty had already been signed in Ghent. The British fleet had gone straight past Mobile, was on its way full-sail back to London.*

Jackson folded his arms across his chest. The Hero glowered left, right. Until he received—until he held in his own two Jacksonian hands—a certified, official announcement of peace, martial law would continue. Six

American soldiers in Alabama had been found guilty of desertion. He signed the orders for their execution. A New Orleans dry-goods merchant had written a letter to a local newspaper inciting disloyalty and disobedience. Jackson sent ten armed guards to Maspero's Exchange Coffee House and had the man arrested in broad daylight, as he sipped his *café au lait*.

With a single, massive surge of disgust, New Orleans turned on her savior.

And meanwhile? Meanwhile in Mobile, in Washington, in Ghent?

Here at last your historian can speak with personal knowledge. Not of Mobile, though the army records are clear enough. Jackson's Draconian orders there *were* read, carried out; six mutinous soldiers executed. The British fleet crowded closer and closer to the Alabama shore.

Nor of Ghent, either, for John Quincy Adams and Henry Clay had long since settled their childish dispute and the official American copy of the treaty was in a clerk's strongbox, nearing (but slowly) the snowswept coast of New England.

But in those days, fresh from college, filled with patriotic fervor, I was about to travel north toward Boston, after an extended visit in Virginia. So slow and cumbersome was transportation then, we knew almost nothing of what was passing in the West. The very day of the great battle, January eighth, was the first day that the eastern newspapers printed the news that the British army had just landed at New Orleans. On January twenty-first we learned of Coffee's night battle of December twenty-third. After that, thanks to a winter storm of unparalleled fury and duration, we heard nothing. Silence. The whole great western range of the country beyond the Alleghenies was lost behind an impenetrable curtain of weather.

I have been asked by European friends to account for General Jackson's astonishing popularity among his countrymen, a popularity that duels, scandals, the bitterest kind of personal attacks seem hardly to touch. One answer, which I only begin to perceive myself, is that Jackson, like all great heroes, has been recast by the people and given the virtues they hope to see in themselves: he is an American; he is therefore brave, iron-willed, independent, self-made; unlearned in books but learned in nature; quick to anger and vengeance, swift to tears of kindness.

But a less fanciful, more historical answer is this: If you were to choose the gloomiest, most despairing days of the new American nation, from the signing of the Constitution to the present moment, you would surely choose without hesitation the dark winter of 1814–15. In the north, at Hartford, a convention of radical Federalists (some not so radical) was meeting to consider actual secession from the Union, dissolution of the young republic as a failed experiment. In the South and East, disbanded soldiers were straggling home, miserably beaten. At Washington City the ruined Capitol and President's mansion sat under a film of snow and muddy ashes. President Madison was said to be close to nervous collapse. The British navy pecked and raided wherever it wished, up and down the Chesapeake shore. The country hung its collective head and awaited news from the West of a final, crushing defeat.

And then, in two great successive thunderclaps, Victory and Peace—on February fourth the first riders came bursting over the mountains, saddlebags stuffed with Jackson's reports. The country went into a paroxysm of delight—every paper published its "extra," every tongue repeated Andrew Jackson's victorious name over and over, every word of his eloquent dispatch (written in fact by Edward Livingston) was printed in giant type and plastered on walls, fences, churches. On February tenth I was passing through Philadelphia, where a local patriot named John Riggs had ordered theatrical scene-painters to cover his house with enormous posters showing Jackson on horseback in pursuit of the British, Jackson with sword raised, Jackson wrapped in the swaddling clothes of a bright American flag!

Thunderclap number two. On February eleventh I was in New York, on my way to Boston. It was about eight o'clock, a Saturday evening, when the ship carrying the treaty slipped quietly into its dockside berth. Half an hour later Broadway was one living sea of shouting, rejoicing people: "Peace! Peace! Peace!" Somebody came with a torch; the idea passed into a thousand brains. In a few minutes thousands and tens of thousands of people were marching about with candles, lamps, torches—making the jubilant street appear like a gay and gorgeous procession. We were all, in Jefferson's famous words, all republicans, all federalists! I moved about for hours in the ebbing and flowing tide of people, not being aware that I had opened my lips. The next morning I found that I was hoarse as a frog from having joined all night in the exulting cry of "Peace! Peace!" And after "Peace!" of course, "Jackson! Jackson!"

Who knew nothing of it, not a word.

In New Orleans, on the basis of the rumors of peace, the unfortunate dry-goods merchant whom the General had arrested now sued for a writ of *habeas corpus*. The judge, named Dominick Hall, born in England and perhaps because of it more fiercely aware of American rights than anyone, ordered Jackson to release his prisoner at once. Jackson replied by arresting the judge.

The Legislature foamed and raged. They passed a resolution of thanks to the army and mentioned every single officer by name, except for Jackson, to whom they made no reference at all.

Boys who dared it mocked his carriage in the streets. Militiamen skulked to the French consul's office to register as foreign citizens, supposedly exempt from service and therefore entitled to discharge, until Jackson ordered all foreigners transported a hundred miles up the river, and that put a stop to the consul's business.

As long as the British army stood a day's voyage from New Orleans, he said, he would not yield a step.

As long as he had received no *official* word of peace, martial law ruled, Jackson's iron will ruled.

Edward Livingston came back from a prisoner exchange with General Lambert bearing copies of the London newspapers, which had already, weeks ago, announced the treaty—but somehow when he went to bring them out and show them, he had lost his luggage!

On March sixth, the day after Jackson clapped a furious Judge Hall into prison, a State Department courier arrived out of breath from Washington City. In those days it was a trip that normally took a full month on horseback. The courier made it in nineteen days, and he galloped up Bourbon Street the last half mile to the General's headquarters waving his bag and whooping at the top of his lungs (like a long-delayed echo from Ghent), "Peace! Peace!"

But when *he* opened his packet, there was no word of peace at all, only some old letters from the Department of War, written months earlier. In his haste to depart from Washington, it turned out the poor man had grabbed the wrong bag!

During the reign of Queen Elizabeth the players at the Globe Theatre sometimes amused themselves by presenting a play one night as a tragedy, and then the next night the very same play again as comedy.

Some such thing had happened to Jackson's fortunes. All of his virtues, his fearless, vigilant, indomitable Scotch-Irish warrior virtues, had overnight turned into their opposites, into defects.

On March thirteenth, at last, another courier arrived from Washington bringing the certified documents of peace, and within the hour Jackson proclaimed his martial law at an end.

One last scene remained to be played, however.

Judge Hall, released from confinement, stormed into his courthouse and instantly wrote out a writ for Jackson's arrest (though no one could be found who would actually attempt to take the General into custody). The charge: contempt of court.

On March twenty-fourth Jackson's lawyer, the ubiquitous Livingston, appeared in court for his client. He began to read a scholarly defense, which said in effect that the necessity had existed for continuing martial law, and in such an emergency martial law took precedence over civil. Judge Hall banged his gavel before Livingston finished his first paragraph. He ruled against Jackson and his decision, he said, was "absolute." The defendant must appear in person to be sentenced, one week from the day.

And so it happened that on the cool, windy morning of March thirty-first, while half a continent away his portrait hung in triumph over public buildings, a crowd gathered at the door of the little red-tiled Spanish courthouse on Royal Street to see him sentenced. Jackson, never in his life unaware of the force of symbols, arrived alone, on foot, modestly dressed, not in his glittering, gold-epauletted Major General's uniform, but in an ordinary gray civilian suit.

The crowd followed him in, a boisterous, angry throng made up mostly of Baratarian pirates, Jackson's old "hellish banditti," themselves dressed for action in red shirts, white trousers, and buccaneer sashes. When the judge entered the courtroom they erupted into shouts and whistles, and for a moment it looked as though Dominick Hall would turn and flee. But the General stood, looked around, and silenced the room with a single sweeping gesture.

Judge Hall sat down. He put on his spectacles. He nodded to his clerk. "The United States versus Andrew Jackson."

Jackson rose. Without Livingston, without Coffee, without any help whatsoever he quietly told the judge that because he had not been permitted to offer his defense in court one week before, he appeared now only to hear the court's judgment. "Nonetheless," he could not resist adding, "since no opportunity has been furnished me to explain my conduct, I expect that censure will form no part of that punishment which Your Honor may imagine it your duty to perform."

Judge Hall took off his spectacles and wiped them. Restored them.

Studied the stern, bristle-haired soldier standing straight as a rod before him. It was impossible to forget the defendant's important services to his country, the judge observed in his brisk English accent, which must have sounded bitterly ironic to the Brave Boy of the Waxhaws; and so the court would not sentence him to imprisonment. Instead, the court found him guilty of contempt, and ordered him to pay a fine of one thousand American dollars. "The only question in this whole affair," Judge Hall said, for some reason needing once more to look down and clean his glasses, "was whether the Law should bend to the General, or the General to the Law."

NEVER a question at all, snorted Andrew Jackson, putting aside the last pages of Chase's chapter. Never a goddamn question at all, by the Eternal. Outside the New Orleans courtroom the Baratarian pirates had raged and howled and carried on like madmen until he stood up on a carriage seat and told them he would pay the fine at once, from his own pocket, and what was more, he wanted them all to see that this was how a citizen behaved; this was the American way, to obey the law.

Jackson glanced up from his reading chair. On their bed, under a light coverlet knitted by one of John Coffee's daughters, Rachel stirred; snored once. He stood, noiseless as a cat, and pulled the coverlet straight. And then, because his arm hurt and his lungs hurt and his entire body from head to toe hurt, he stepped outside into the hallway.

Old Alfred rose on his elbow from his pallet by the wall, but Jackson waved him back down. He walked toward the center of the house, past his study on the left, where somebody he didn't know was sleeping on the horsehair couch; walked into the dining room, set for breakfast; walked out on the front porch, where the stars were so thick and bright they seemed to be roosting on the branches of the trees, among the dark leaves, like thousands and thousands of twinkling silver birds.

Jackson hooked a chair with one foot and pulled it to the edge of the porch. David Chase. He had really only skimmed the chapter at the end. He trusted Coffee's judgment that it could all be published without any harm, though he had watched curiously from the window while Coffee and Chase engaged in what looked like a tense, whispered discussion, right on this very spot. He trusted John Coffee, he thought again; not necessarily Hamilton.

Jackson leaned back in the chair until he achieved a comfortable position, or as comfortable as he was likely to get that night; any night. A strong breeze began to rustle through the trees. In another moment, he thought, all the lights would go flying up from the branches flashing and blinking, a whole flock of flying stars scared from their perches.

Jackson yawned. Young Chase had gotten his facts right, the facts were there, but it was remarkable to think how little of reality you put down in words, after all. The army surgeons, for example, working at their wooden tables under a brown tent, with wicker baskets of amputated limbs by their feet . . . Chase couldn't have known that while they operated—hacked and sawed, to be precise, all splattered with blood and unspeakable pulpy gore in their hair—they had a regimental fiddler in uniform walking between the tables and playing music. Marches, dances, anything; "Greensleeves," he remembered hearing over the screams of the men on the tables, "When Daffodils Begin to Peer."

Jackson rubbed his eyes and stared grimly straight ahead. A mistake to read about New Orleans again. Rachel believed in a loving God, most of the time, but that was probably because in Jackson's experience people tended to make out God in their own image and Rachel was ever a loving person.

In front of him the linden trees puffed in a sudden gust of wind and shook dozens of angry stars from their heads.

Something else David Chase had not known, not written. When the militiamen were executed in Alabama, six empty coffins were placed in a row, several feet apart, in a flat clearing near the city of Mobile. The troops were drawn up in formation. The prisoners were driven up on a wagon, taken out. Each one was led to a position next to a coffin. Then they were blindfolded and helped to kneel on their coffins. And while they knelt and the troops watched, the signal to fire was given. American soldiers. By his order. Bending to the Law.

Jackson opened and closed his eyes, unsure whether he was awake or dreaming, some nights it made no difference. After the Battle of New Orleans the British had dug their graves too shallow in the wet, mushy Louisiana soil, and a day or so later, when the rains started to fall, one by one the bodies slowly rose to the surface again. Legs, arms, heads poking up out of the muddy ground like a vast field of sprouting corpses, like the Day of Resurrection as dreamed by a careless God.

PART

4

September–October 1828

CHAPTER

1

At 8:14 in the evening, according to Chase's watch, the curtains went up on the bare stage of the Cincinnati Opera House, located at Main and Sycamore Streets in the Queen City of the West and filled to the absolute rafters with a grim-faced audience of men and women.

The curtains went up and nothing happened.

Two minutes passed. Shoes scraped on the floor. Skirts rustled. Five hundred hand-held fans stirred hot air from one sweltering corner to another. A single gas chandelier swayed gently over the center of the stage, like a giant teardrop of light against a backdrop of shadows.

Behind the balcony, brown dusk filtered in through a row of open windows. Outside in the street a wagon rattled slowly by. Then the sound of whispering voices drifted in from the wings on the left, and the entire theater seemed to hold its breath and lean forward on the edge of its chairs. Chase wiped his eyes. He gripped the balcony rail and scanned the seats below.

Another minute.

"Too damn skeered to show up," said the man on Chase's right, and spat on the floor, and precisely at that moment six young women in white mobcaps and shapeless gray Quaker dresses marched onto the stage in single file. Each one carried a light straw-bottomed chair. They halted center stage and lowered the chairs to the floor together, without a word, as if in a military drill.

Silence. The ticking of a theater clock somewhere.

The fans resumed. Stopped.

From the opposite wing now entered a short, thickset man in parson's black, holding a wooden lectern in one hand and a chair in the other. He placed the lectern in front of the row of Quaker ladies and took his chair to the end of the line. And before its legs had touched the floor, out of the left-hand wings like a shell-burst of color, swept the tall, theatrical figure of Fanny Wright.

She was dressed despite the heat in a silk-lined crimson cape that reached to her heels, a cap, a white Queen Mary ruff at her throat, a gorgeous spencer jacket, and a dress of iridescent blue. A gold brooch gleamed on her breast. As one of the Quaker ladies stepped forward to take her cloak, she lifted her right hand and flung off the cap in a swift dramatic gesture. Red hair, ringlets.

"Ladies and gentlemen," said Fanny Wright, "George Washington was not a Christian!"

Uproar, pandemonium! Chase's neighbor shot to his feet—others were already shouting, waving their fists. Someone threw a tomato; someone else hurled a book, which tumbled over and over and fluttered to the stage at Fanny Wright's feet like a wounded bird. Slowly, unevenly, the shouts subsided to a grumble.

From somewhere in her costume Fanny Wright produced a set of pages, her lecture notes, and spread them out on the lectern. She looked left; right; waited. Then raised her clear, quite beautiful voice a second time.

"Nor was *Thomas Jefferson* a Christian!"

Uproar again, pandemonium *redivivus*. Chase's neighbor flailed at the air like a madman. Men in the audience below whistled and stamped their feet, though to Chase's ear the protest this time was markedly less energetic. "Radical Tom" had a mixed reputation west of Virginia.

"This country," Fanny Wright persisted over the whistles and taunts, "was not founded as a religious state. Yet you are foolishly allowing religion—and one form of religion only, the least educated, the most narrowly vulgar—to poison all your institutions. In your schools religion diseases the infant mind with superstitious terrors. In your colleges religion stifles the breath of your teachers of science and entangles simple facts with the dreams of theology. In your legislatures religion dictates unconstitutional ordinances. I refer, of course, to the so-called 'Christian Party in Politics!' "

Chase smelled the smoke an instant before he saw it—from an aisle to the left of the stage, a billowing black cloud roiling toward Fanny Wright.

He had just enough time to pick out the barrel top covered with chips and rags that was the source and to breathe the turpentine laced in the smoke. Then the whole theater was on its feet and screaming and Fanny Wright was spreading her arms and calling for calm. Somebody jumped through a window. Dozens followed. The rising smoke cut off his view, and he spun, pushing toward the stairs. When he reached the lobby, the air was oily black and he was buffeted sideways and into a post by a great rushing tide of spectators and smoke pouring out of the doors. He lowered his head and plunged back into the theater.

For a minute at least, probably more, he lost all sense of direction. He staggered straight ahead, bounced off a wall. Turned and dove, bounced off the same wall. His hat was gone. His eyes burned. Bonnets, shoulders, elbows floated in smoke. Chase put down one hand and began to follow the rows of seats. At the edge of the stage he glanced up to find the chandelier, then turned to the right, which was the last place he had seen her, and forced his way through a knot of coughing, flapping men until he found the corner next to the curtains and stretched out his hand.

"Always one arm for the fair," he told Emma Colden, gasping.

☆　　☆　　☆

IN the streets they walked rapidly away from the Opera House, scarcely noticing what direction they took. Behind them a crowd, hacking and coughing, still milled around the front steps and a red fire brigade wagon, just arrived, was filling its buckets, but it was plain that Fanny Wright's lecture was over for the evening.

"In Kentucky," Emma said, still coughing, "somebody put out the gas lights. Last Sunday they clanged a Christian cowbell every time she spoke. But to set off smoke and fire—this is the worst, far and away the worst. I can't believe you're here."

"They finally used your name." Chase matched her cough for cough.

" 'Report of Miss Frances Wright's Lecture Tour, by Our Correspondent E. Colden.' " He took her arm, unnecessarily now, and drew her to the left, down the first street he saw. "When I saw it, I came like a house afire."

"Mr. and Mrs. Raccoon," she said as they paused in front of a storefront window. Two black-and-white faces, ringed around the eyes, stared solemnly back.

"Your dress is ruined."

"No, just soap and water will clean it." Emma shook her hair, now as short as Fanny Wright's, and began to walk again.

Chase coughed convulsively; cursed turpentine and smoke. "When I read your first report," he said—and stopped in midsentence and lifted his head. "Good Lord!"

Emma followed his eyes and laughed. The last turn of the street had brought them around a ramshackle corner and then, without warning, onto the sloping planks of the city docks. Before them, lined up one after the other in the fading light, Alp upon Alp, sat seven enormous white steamboats at anchor. The nearest rose some sixty feet into the air at its smokestack and stretched almost two hundred feet down the wharf.

The others were just as large, and all their decks were jammed with smaller mountains of barrels and crates, stacks of iron bars, racks of lumber. Chase picked his way down the planks between creaking ropes and cleats and looked about him with his mouth (he knew) agape.

The docks seemed to run for a mile or more along the muddy riverbank, blocked off from the rest of the city, as if in a canyon, by a row of new brick warehouses, three and four stories tall. Across the Ohio River—which appeared to be twice as wide as the Cumberland at Nashville—was a series of treeless black hills. A few straggling freight wagons climbed down a switchback road, bugs on a log. At the base of the road, on the Kentucky bank, more steamboats, flatboats, keelboats, wagons, gangplanks, shacks.

"I came down from the north," he said slowly, "by stage. I had no idea it was so enormous."

"You should see it in the mornings," Emma told him, "when the city traders are here and they're loading the cargo. Yesterday they filled half a steamboat with ginseng and beeswax, then drove on five hundred pigs at least, bound for New Orleans."

"Porkopolis," Chase said.

If Emma heard him she gave no sign of it. She was lifting her skirts and crossing a filthy ditch that ran from a warehouse into the river. A party of sailors hooted. Somewhere down the dock a crate fell to a deck with a splintering crash. When he caught up, she was gazing at the far bank of the river, where the western sun was now raking the hills. Here and there, in a distant house, glass windows glimmered and burst into flame. The black hills flared. The brown river rushed splashing by them, swift and disorderly, bound for New Orleans.

"You like it here," he said. Even in the fading light the exhilaration in her face was unmistakable.

"Oh, I love it here," Emma said. "No matter what they've done to Fanny."

And for an instant Chase felt his own face sink and fall. He frowned at the water, the chaotic docks, worse than Boston. Emma's blond hair was so short that he almost hadn't known her.

"Did Senator Sellers come with you?"

She raised her eyes to him boldly, clear and direct despite the smears of greasy smoke on her cheeks and nose.

"He stayed in Washington," she said.

☆   ☆   ☆

FANNY Wright had installed herself in the cavernous and famous six-story Burnet Hotel in the very center of Cincinnati. Her three adjoining chambers were on the top floor and looked straight across the now black Ohio River toward Kentucky. "A slave state," she explained to Chase, leading him to the window and gesturing as if she were still on the platform before an audience of thousands. "I took these rooms to remind myself daily of the greatest single blot on this free nation."

Since the interrupted lecture she had changed her stage costume for a simple white muslin dress, which was pinched at the waist and clung to her hips and breasts like a Grecian tunic. The other members of her party—three or four of the gray Quaker ladies, an unexplained and unintroduced man with a sketch pad, a severe-looking Englishwoman—all sat or lounged about the room in still-smoky clothes, watching her every motion.

"Mr. Chase is a journalist." Emma emerged from another room, scrubbed and radiant, as un-Quaker and unsevere as it was possible to be. "You met him in Washington City."

"At Gales and Seaton." Fanny Wright smiled at her own excellent memory. "You were writing a book about General Jackson."

"Yes."

"I adore General Jackson. His wife is the most maligned woman in America."

"Well, you might have a certain claim to that yourself," Chase suggested wryly, "after tonight."

Fanny Wright possessed the rich, insistent physical presence of a great politician. She placed her hand—large as a man's, ribbed with dark blue veins—on Chase's arm. "I gave my same set of lectures once before in this city, in July, before the unspeakable camp meetings and revivals began. *Then* they met with great success; the courthouse where I spoke was packed, attentive, rapt. But now—"

"But *now* they come just to mock you." The severe-looking English-woman materialized next to Emma, teacup in hand, sniffing. "*Now* you're seeing America as she truly is."

"Mrs. Frances Trollope," murmured Emma. "Mr. Chase."

Chase smiled and bowed. Mrs. Trollope held on to the teacup and extended her little finger for him to shake.

"Mr. Chase is a writer," Fanny Wright told her.

"Mr. Chase is an American man who doesn't chew tobacco or spit on the floor," Mrs. Trollope corrected her sardonically. "I have been observing. *Quel grand plaisir.*" She handed her teacup to Emma. "I'm keeping a journal of notes on America, Mr. Chase," she said. "The spitting, for example. It would require the pen of a Jonathan Swift to describe the filth of spitting, don't you agree? Your countrymen spit on the carpets, the streets, the stagecoach floors. It's a wonder they don't spit themselves inside out. I don't know how Fanny dares to wear a white dress. I would infinitely prefer sharing a cabin with a party of well-trained pigs to living in an American house with an American man."

"There are pigs sufficient in Cincinnati," said Fanny Wright mildly.

"Study the language," Mrs. Trollope instructed Chase. "Copy it down—'right clever,' 'I reckon,' 'I swan'—this is *not* English." She shook her head.

"No."

"They read nothing but newspapers here," Mrs. Trollope said. "I met an American man last week who declared to me—chew, spit—that

'Shakespeare, madam, is obscene.' Chew. 'And thank God we are suffi-ciently *advanced* in Ohio to have found it out.' Spit."

In the lobby downstairs Chase paid seventy-five cents for a room and registered in a leather-bound book where guests wrote not only their names but also political slogans. The man before him had put *Adams for ever* under the box for comments. Above him somebody else had scrawled *Jackson and Reform, Jackson and New Orleans* across the top of the page. Chase wrote *Shakespeare for ever,* then followed a black servant with a candle through a labyrinthine series of yawning halls and stairways until they reached his room, two floors below Fanny Wright's, also facing the river.

At midnight he got up from the bed, still fully clothed, and unlatched the door.

Ten minutes later Emma slipped in.

CHAPTER

2

If he were William Short the Damned, Chase thought, he would doubtless check his watch to confirm that it was nearly dawn. Instead, he rolled onto his side, kissed Emma's forehead, and tried to peep under the sheets.

"Stop that," she whispered, and pushed away his hands. "Stop. Stop, you promised to tell me about General Coffee."

He groaned and rolled completely over onto his stomach, so that they were side by side. The hotel shifted its weight and creaked like a ship. Somewhere between the river and the street an owl screeched, making him think, oddly enough, of Boston.

"General Coffee," she said.

Chase fumbled for the champagne bottle he had left on the floor by the bed. "General Coffee," he said, "on the fourth day I was there, just announced out of the blue that James Hamilton wanted to tear up my book, rip off my head, and clap whatever was left of me into the Nashville jail, legal charges to be thought up later. James Hamilton," Chase explained, "is a lawyer, so his first impulse is naturally to dodge the law."

"But Coffee wouldn't let him?"

Chase tilted the champagne bottle to his lips. Through the open shutters of his window the distant Kentucky hills were just beginning to glow rosy white along their crest. There was a western word for hills like that. *Hogback.* Very un-Bostonian. He swallowed champagne and pictured the Hermitage beginning to catch the same sunlight on the tips of its dark trees, its hogback hills. Jackson would be looking out his own bedroom window, gaunt, hollow-cheeked, the famous gray hair as stiff as bristles, the famous blue eyes as flat and cold as . . . Chase had no idea how to finish the comparison. Future generations were going to wonder what Jackson's secret was, he thought, why men as strong as Coffee and Sam Houston leaped to attention at his bidding.

"Coffee said he wasn't going to interfere with my book—*or* clap me in jail—but he *was* going to see that I didn't come to the Hermitage anymore. He wanted me, he said in his calm, straightforward Coffee way, to stay away from General Jackson."

"In the South everybody's a general," Emma murmured.

Chase nodded. Mrs. Trollope had told a story of sitting down at the dinner table on a Mississippi River steamboat. When the waiter said, "More chicken, General?" twenty-five of the thirty men present said yes.

He twisted onto his back and touched her hair in the dark with his left hand.

"And all this," she said sleepily, "because William Short is Jackson's political enemy?"

"No. Because William Short had a brother named Peyton, whom he hadn't seen or written in twenty years. But Peyton was the first boarder at Lewis Robards's house in Kentucky. Over there—" Chase pointed at the window "—and he evidently fell madly in love with Rachel."

"I want to meet Rachel."

"And so they think Short sent me out to write an unfair, slanted attack in my book, which is, of course, exactly what he hopes I'll do, but Short's got too much Jeffersonian scruple to say so out loud."

"And you have too much scruple to write it."

Chase took another swallow of warm champagne. "So far."

To his profound delight she picked up his hand and kissed his fingers gently one by one, then drew them down beneath the sheet. "There must be more to it than that," she said, turning.

★   ★   ★

AT breakfast in the hotel dining room they met as simple acquaintances again (fully clothed), fellow journalists bobbing in the wake of Fanny Wright's great crusading armada.

That armada had been augmented overnight by more and grimmer Quaker ladies, rushed to her aid because of the smoking barrel, and since there were now twenty of them and one of him, Chase found himself banished to a distant table. There he nodded and smiled politely at the company from behind a vast stack of buckwheat cakes and pure cane syrup. "The 'gol-darn'd' finest in the world," Mrs. Trollope assured him with mocking sarcasm as she passed to her own table.

In the lobby she invited him to join them in a visit to the local museum, where she had devised an artistic and cultural waxworks exhibit—appropriate to the Ohio summer, she explained—of "Dante's Inferno."

Obediently they strolled in a party down Cincinnati's dusty Main Street, between piles of bricks and timber, through bustling crowds of riverfront traders in shirtsleeves and black hats, parked freight wagons, staring stevedores, loose pigs, and barking dogs, all as democratically chaotic as Emma had promised.

"You have completed your book, Mr. Chase?" Fanny Wright was indifferent to the spectacle she and her female Quaker escorts created. She drew back to Chase's side and matched him stride for stride.

"Well, I've sent everything to Boston to be printed," he told her, "except the final chapter, which I mean to write by the end of the week—the first states vote in less than a month."

"And then?" They were mounting the wooden steps to a ramshackle three-story clapboard building whose sagging porch supported a large black-and-white sign—WESTERN MUSEUM OF CINCINNATI—and a smaller poster by the door: SEE THE TWO-HEADED PIG. Ahead of them Emma's trim figure, all in blue, made a vivid contrast with Quaker gray. She glanced back over her shoulder at them—luminous eyes; wide, full mouth, made for kissing; long, slender throat like a swan's—at least the lover's clichés came tumbling on. Her dress today was cut high, all the way to the base of her throat; his imagination proceeded downward, on its own.

"And then back to Paris, or straight on west, or even back to Boston—I have no idea."

A steamboat whistle was screaming at full pitch three blocks away, shaking the air. Fanny Wright leaned so close to him that their faces almost touched. "The freedom of modern life," she said, "is *paralyzing*, is it not? We are the first generation, male and female, able to come and go as we like, to *construct* and *conduct* our lives as we wish, without regard to society's hypocrisy, Mr. Chase. My next lecture will be on the subject of the condom. I hope you will stay to hear it."

"Turn to the right." Mrs. Trollope grasped each of them by an arm. "Up the stairs. 'Abandon all hope, ye who enter Cincinnati.'" And with a flurry of sleeves and bonnets the party followed a set of painted red arrows past a single row of glass-topped display cases and up to the second-floor landing, which was hung with black crepe and lit only by a dirty skylight.

"Two at a time, my dears," Mrs. Trollope instructed. Chase contrived to wait and go in with Emma, just behind Fanny Wright. The door behind them banged shut. Directly in front of the party, illuminated by an unseen lantern, sat a colossal wax figure of Minos, the Judge of Hell, holding a two-pronged scepter that looked like a pitchfork. One of the ladies gasped and cried out for Fanny. Beneath Minos's right hand was a frozen lake from which protruded the heads and torsos of various wax sinners, including Dante's cannibal Ugolino, who gnawed like a dog at the faceless skull of an enemy. Minos himself wore a golden crown and a long beard made of horses' tails. As the ladies (and gentleman) crowded closer, he nodded his head and rolled his glaring eyeballs.

At the far end of the room a transparent canvas sheet depicted Purgatory's great winding mountain, but before it, much larger in scale, rose a wriggling landscape of glass icicles, rotating red lights, dancing skeletons. Mechanical groans and shrieks began to issue from the Inferno; steam hissed through tiny jets in the floor beneath Minos's throne. Chase and Emma were pushed and carried to the front, where a flame-colored sign on an iron grille warned spectators not to touch the exhibit. One of the Quakers stretched out her hand and received (with a shriek of her own) a visible electric shock.

Of course there was more to it, Chase suddenly thought—the exit from Hell led past another transparent canvas, this time angels in flight above Paradise—*of course* William Short had hoped he would uncover some new Jacksonian scandal, any Jacksonian scandal. That had been clear from the start. "We need an *honest* biography, do we not?" Short had murmured in Boston, transparent himself, far too devious and manipulative to say straight out what he wanted, far too hobbled by Jeffersonian notions of honor . . .

"This way," said Mrs. Trollope gaily. "Downstairs for the other wax figures—Washington, Chief Tecumseh, Andrew Jackson riding a stuffed horse."

Chase walked without seeing: narrow stairs, window, another dark, musty room. His mind was turning and tugging, slowly working an idea loose like the buried stump of a tree.

"Through here," Mrs. Trollope said. He felt Emma's hand brush his in the dark. The chronology was this: Peyton Short had lived with the Robards family in Kentucky long before Rachel left her jealous husband and ran away to Nashville in 1788. Jackson came onto the scene only there, much later.

"This is Chief Tecumseh." Mrs. Trollope halted them before a sad little wax model of an Indian brave.

What had Short told him about 1824?

"And that is Andrew Jackson," said Fanny Wright doubtfully. She walked past the brooding chief to the last model in the room. "It's been five years since I saw him. Is it like, Mr. Chase?"

Chase glanced up, focusing.

"What is Jackson *like*, Mr. Chase?" repeated Frances Trollope briskly.

In front of him, astride a white horse, was a too-short, too-pale wax figure in a general's uniform, hatless. The hair was black, not gray, and lay in handsome Byronic ringlets across the forehead, not iron-stiff bristles. The eyes were large and almost cheerful. He could have been a cobbler, a baker, a clerk in the Hotel Burnet. A writer should come up with similes, metaphors—what was Jackson *like?* He owns five books on Napoleon, Chase thought, and has eyes like Minos the Judge. He's as fierce as Tecumseh, as aloof as Washington. He doesn't believe the earth is round. I started out six months ago thinking he was a backwoods savage. And if I'd stayed another week I would probably follow him into the mouth of a cannon.

On the porch Mrs. Trollope proposed a look at the picture gallery next door, but Fanny Wright held up one hand and shook her head. She and all her friends were moving that afternoon from the hotel to a rented house. And afterward she needed to work on the next week's lecture, her correspondence, her thousand and one good deeds.

"She is disbanding Nashoba," Emma whispered to Chase. "A terrible failure—the freed slaves don't work, won't go to school. Her unmarried sister is having a baby." A few steps later: "I'm tempted to publish it all."

Chase gave her a crooked smile.

In the hotel lobby, while the ladies retired upstairs, he stood by a window and watched the endless wagons churning up and down Main Street. The upper deck of a steamboat glided eerily above the rooftops across the way. He turned the question around—forget William Short; *why* had John Coffee sent him away?—but got no further.

The Burnet Hotel was so large that it issued its own five-dollar banknotes, accepted as legal tender throughout the West, and kept a veritable library of newspapers for its guests. Chase walked from table to table. *The Anti-Jackson Expositor.* The Cincinnati *Liberty Hall and Gazette.* He found an old copy of the New York *Post* and read two stale paragraphs of the "Spy in Washington." More up-to-date, the *Liberty Hall and Gazette* reported that Congressman John Randolph had just that week returned to Washington after a short election trip to Knoxville.

Chase put it down; picked it up again. He was almost out of money, as usual. Who knew if Short would actually publish his bland, nonscandalous Jackson chapters, much less pay for them? Could you spend Burnet banknotes in Paris? He carried the newspaper to a cracked leather chair surrounded by four overflowing spittoons. Hogwood had told him Randolph was going to Tennessee; he had told him that at Mount Vernon, the last day. But Randolph hadn't shown up at the Hermitage, then or later, so why else travel to Tennessee? Chase looked at the dates of Randolph's trip and closed his eyes. James Hamilton had disappeared from Nashville for two full days, unexplained. Chase opened his eyes and looked at the maps of Kentucky, Tennessee, and Ohio that the newspaper printed in its top left corner. Nashville to Knoxville; Nashville again. Walking to Robey's Tavern, Short had said that in Washington City in 1824 people had heard rumors of "secret" documents about Rachel's misdoings, seen by a tipsy and unreliable Virginian named Tutt; but nothing had come of it, nobody else had ever seen them. Either the documents had never existed—one more electioneering whisper—or else . . .

Or else why had John Randolph gone to Tennessee?

A Conestoga wagon thundered past the hotel window, inches from the sidewalk, scattering boys, dogs, spraying impenetrable clouds of dust. Chase folded the newspaper and let it drop.

His mind pried three questions loose.

What had Short's brother done, exactly?

What had *Rachel* done?

Under the baking September sun the street seemed slowly to come to a halt, every grain of dust suspended in air, motionless, every wagon silent, at a standstill.

Where were the papers that would tell him?

Henry Banks has them," James Hamilton said for the third time that morning. Hamilton was a lawyer, Coffee thought, and tended to confuse repetition with logic.

"Henry Banks is a pure, loyal Jackson man," John Eaton said, also for the third time, also a lawyer.

"But he was Peyton Short's best friend, was he not? He *saw* the actual letters. He *wrote* John Randolph about them." During the first half of their impromptu little meeting, Hamilton had sat tilted back in his cane-bottom chair with his Stetson at his feet and his short, fat parrot legs perched on the rung while Eaton paced the floor; now, on some unspoken cue, the two men got up and changed places, as if they were in a courtroom instead of Jackson's overhot and overcrowded Nashville office, and it was Eaton's turn to take the stand. In an easy chair under the "Jackson and Reform" banner, just returned that very morning from Philadelphia, sat toothless old Judge John Overton, who wore a red bandanna over his bald head to keep off the heat and who had the unenviable distinction of heading the Nashville committee to protect Rachel's good name. One judge and two lawyers, Coffee thought, wishing he could chew tobacco and spit; which left him, he supposed, the jury.

Overton cleared his wobbly throat. Dislike for Hamilton made him smoothly polite. "As a matter of fact, Mr. Hamilton, Henry Banks wrote *me* about this matter too."

Hamilton stopped in midstride. He had a new silver belt buckle, which he hitched with both hands like a gunman.

"Twice," Overton said. "I wish I'd been here to tell you. I wish I'd been anywhere but Philadelphia. I filed his letters over there"—one hand wagged at a locked desk in the corner—"where I keep all the other windbag letters."

"You didn't believe him." Hamilton folded his arms and cocked his head in a neat little pose Coffee mentally labeled "New York Suspicion."

"Presidential politics," said Overton, unaffected by pose or state, "works on some people like a full moon on a hound, sir. I have certificates and testimonials in that desk there, Mr. Hamilton, from people who knew Rachel back when she was a wicked and immoral baby and showing promise of things to come, people who used to see her down in a black brothel in Natchez, people who claim she's their long-lost Irish mother or the Queen of England or a Choctaw princess. Your fellow Henry Banks has written my committee two or three dozen unsolicited letters—which is nowhere near the record, by the way—on everything under the sun. When he wrote last year about this Peyton Short business, I looked into it quietly myself."

Overton paused to adjust his bandanna and sip ice water from a Jackson mug.

"Henry Banks hardly knew Peyton Short," he said, and wiped his gums. "Henry Banks is a well-known liar and work of flatulence in Kentucky who would like to have a postmastership or two when the General is elected, as a reward for his campaign services, real or imagined."

"So you don't believe him." Hamilton joined disgust to suspicion.

"I doubt it sincerely," Overton said. The room fell silent. Overton's teeth were so completely absent from his mouth that his nose and chin almost collided when he talked. In profile he looked like the Witch of Endor with a wattle, Coffee thought. But the judge had gone over every document in the Rachel case a dozen times, he knew every date and fact; nobody in Tennessee approached his practical knowledge.

Hamilton put on his hat and walked to the window. He glowered down at something in Demonbruin Street, then came back and planted himself in front of the judge. "What about the rumors of 1824?"

Overton shrugged.

"Jack Jouett?" Hamilton said.

"Jack Jouett sponsored Robards's bill of divorce. He was married to Robards's sister Sallie and possessed a family interest in clearing his brother-in-law's name, and he never once mentioned Peyton Short, in court or out." Overton also had the distinction of being the first man in Nashville to learn about the actual delayed decree of divorce in 1793. He smacked his gums and recited the legal jargon, which still, after thirty-five years, Coffee thought, stung. " 'Thereupon came a jury to say that the defendant Rachel Robards hath deserted the plaintiff Lewis Robards and hath, and doth still, live in adultery with another man.' That's Jackson, not Short."

"He's dead anyway," Eaton said. "Jack Jouett died six years ago. His wife died before that. His only son died last year."

Hamilton was admirably stubborn, Coffee considered, in the face of so much western mortality. "Peyton Short had two wives," he said.

"Two wives," Overton agreed. "One dead. Other one lives with their only son."

Hamilton studied a sheet of paper in his hand, presumably one of John Randolph's daily reports of unsuccess. "This is the son that teaches at Transylvania College in Lexington."

"Charles Short," said Overton. "He collects plants and herbs. He's not a political person, he's a professor, poor as a mouse. We talked to him, we talked to them both. We're not all fools out here, sir. We know what's at stake."

"The goddamn *election* is at stake," Hamilton said suddenly, briefly furious.

"We're not fools." Like everybody else, Overton was reduced to repetition.

"General Coffee believes there *are* letters that Rachel wrote," Hamilton said, now looking straight at Coffee. "Don't you, General?"

Coffee raised his eyes to Hamilton and after a moment slowly nodded, yes. Yes, he did. And at precisely the same moment his mind made a strange intuitive jump. It had been a goddamn stupid mistake, he thought, to send David Chase away.

"Here comes Jackson," Eaton said at the window.

☆   ☆   ☆

NOBODY had yet had the nerve to tell Jackson about Peyton Short and Rachel—if there *was* anything to tell—or John Randolph's flying visit to Knoxville.

By the time the General reached the outer office Eaton had managed to pack his satchel with papers, ready to leave, and Judge Overton was sitting with his boots on a chair and his hands on his paunch, complacently peeling an apple.

"John Eaton!" Jackson said as he took off his hat and strode into the room.

"General?"

"Did you write this?" Jackson thrust a printed flyer into Eaton's hands, and Coffee and Hamilton looked over his shoulder to read it:

WANTED FOR COOL AND DELIBERATE MURDER

Andrew Jackson

Jackson coolly and deliberately put to death upwards of fifteen hundred British troops on the 8th of January, 1815, on the plains below New Orleans, for no other offense than that they wished to sup in the city that night.

Eaton flushed and handed it back. "I wrote it. I get so sick of it, that goddamn coffin poster."

"Well, it's a soo-blime answer," Jackson said, grinning and drawing out the word to mock himself good-humoredly. "I want you to print up ten thousand more and send them off to Van Buren."

"I heard a story about you, Andrew, over in Philadelphia." Overton finished peeling the apple and stuck it in his pocket. "Sunday school teacher asked who it was killed Abel in the Bible. Little girl answers, 'General Jackson.' "

Jackson held his grin, Coffee thought, just long enough to let the room know he was not much amused.

"Well, you set them straight, John, I'm sure," he said.

"Fourteen electoral votes," Overton told him enigmatically, and stood up. "I'm tired as hell."

Outside in the street Coffee and Jackson walked first to Jackson's bank, passing without comment, as always, the spot on the square where they had rolled and brawled in the dirt with the Bentons. Inside the bank, dark and cool as the bottom of a well, Coffee paid nine hundred dollars into Jackson's account, and Jackson gave him a discounted personal note for half that sum, which they were silently agreed constituted a campaign loan.

Then they walked to the other end of the square and paid a duty visit to the sickbed of an ancient freed black named "Major" Lockelier, who had served as a soldier in Jackson's New Orleans army long ago and who sat up straight and started talking, with an old man's abruptness, the minute the two generals entered his room.

"Do you remember them oranges, General Coffee?"

"The oranges we brought back from New Orleans?" Lockelier was eighty years old at least, and wrinkled as a raisin. His house looked out on the Cumberland River. He was lying full length on a plain, clean cotton-covered pallet, his married daughter was sitting by his pillow with a straw fan in the shape of a heart, and he was calmly, visibly dying, at a good, stately Christian pace.

"We cut those oranges *long*," the old man told Jackson, "and stuck the stems in red potatoes. Put 'em on a boat. Still *alive* when they reached Nashville."

Coffee remembered. Oranges were such a rarity in Nashville back then, his wife had given a party for their neighbors and friends to eat them. Now they came up twice a week on the steamboats, common as sugar.

"I knew a senator back in Washington City," Jackson said, and sat down by the cotton pallet and took the old man's wrinkled hand in both of his. "He used to suck on oranges while he was making a speech, and he kept his top hat on his desk full of them up to the brim, sliced in two." And everybody laughed at Jackson's pleasantness.

But back in the private drinking room of the Nashville Inn, Jackson was serious and solemn, as Coffee knew he would be after smelling fresh death, close at hand. He took off his jacket and glowered at the walls, then sat stiffly in his chair and ordered a full bottle of Tennessee whiskey just for the two of them. Coffee tried to distract him with a little talk about cotton—prices were low, the banks were calling in mortgages every-where—but Jackson only shook his head and unfolded his newspaper.

"I see they're eating parts of Egyptian mummies for medicinal food, over in Europe," he commented grimly while Coffee paid the waiter and poured them each a short glass. Coffee glanced at the paper. A damn subtle way to bring up death and dying.

"Now, you don't believe what you read in the papers, General," Coffee said, and Jackson gave him a quick, thin, unhappy smile.

"No, I don't. Not unless John Eaton writes it."

Neither Coffee nor Jackson had ever been to Europe, in fact, where people ate parts of dead mummies and men and women talked foreign languages like French and Dutch. Hamilton had been to Paris. John Quincy Adams had been to Russia and Paris. Coffee's mind drifted again to David Chase . . . He watched Jackson turn his page and rub his upper teeth, which were looser and yellower every day from all the poisonous calomel he had dosed himself with since 1812.

"I remember when old Lockelier built himself a house," Coffee said, "after the war, out by the Stones River. Made the whole house out of wood, even the chimney. Of course, everybody did the same thing then." As a boy, Coffee remembered putting out a fire in a wooden chimney with snowballs.

"He also built a secret trapdoor in the floor," Jackson said brusquely and gave the newspaper an angry-sounding snap. "To hide from the goddamn Indians when they got their liquor up. He came out here the year they killed old Donelson. There's another story about *her* in there."

Coffee nodded. He had seen it.

"I tell myself," Jackson said, "we're all instruments of Providence." Coffee nodded again. Jackson believed deeply that Providence governed his life, his fate; it was what, in Coffee's opinion, gave him his amazing self-confidence and self-assurance. "But this is hard," Jackson said, "you know it's hard, and if it's going to be hard for nothing . . ."

Coffee studied the brown liquor in his glass and listened to voices murmuring on the hot stairs, on the streets of Nashville outside, in the calm, quiet back places of his memory where he was a boy.

"I should have shot Henry Clay," Jackson said.

Coffee watched him stand up and pour another unwise glass, a gaunt, powerful presence even if you had known him for forty years and seen his hair grow gray and his teeth go yellow and bad and his moods go so black on certain days, and not just in the war, that he sometimes literally trembled and shook with unstated and unslaked anger. After forty years he could read Jackson's mind almost as well as Rachel, and he knew without asking exactly what he meant by referring to Henry Clay. Coffee held out his own glass, because you might as well drink with him in those moods, and Jackson poured it full, brown to the brim. He meant he should have shot Henry Clay because Clay had literally robbed him of the presidency four years ago, and the people of their vote, and would do it again tomorrow if he could. Two instruments of Fate in providential collision.

"Van Rensselaer," Coffee said, to show he understood, and Jackson grunted and drained his glass.

In 1824 Jackson had won a majority of the popular votes for President, but not a majority of electoral votes, and so the election had to be decided in the House of Representatives, just the same as in 1800, when Jefferson and Burr were tied. Each state had one vote. New York was key, as usual: If New York went for Adams, it was clear that despite the people's sentiment Clay could maneuver the western states to follow; but right up until the morning of the vote, as it happened, the New York delegation was divided precisely in half between Jackson and Adams. General Stephen Van Rensselaer was a doddering old patroon from Albany who was always convinced by the last person he spoke with. He promised Van Buren he would vote for Jackson. Then he promised Clay he would vote for Adams. Then he wandered around the floor of the House muttering to himself while the other states voted, and when New York's turn came the old man was so confused he sat down at his desk and lowered his head and prayed for guidance. And as he finished and leaned back and wiped his eyes, the first thing he saw was a discarded ballot for Adams on the floor, which he took to be a providential answer to his prayer, so he picked it up and dropped it like a burning match into the box. (Coffee had heard the story from Jackson himself.) Adams was elected, thirteen states to seven.

Five days later Clay was named secretary of state and collected his thirty pieces of silver.

Privately Jackson bellowed and raged like a madman—Coffee had never seen him so *furious,* before or since—the people had been *cheated* of their vote, the people could bid farewell to their freedom, *bartered* away for *corrupt* promises of office. Publicly, however, he shook Adams's hand

and went about his business with iron self-control. No canings, no duels. He went to the theater with Rachel. He gave an elegant party at the Indian Queen Hotel for twenty-two of his loyal supporters, with apple toddy, punch, wine, brandy, whiskey, cider, and champagne. It cost $86.25, and Coffee paid the bill.

Peyton Short and Rachel. John Randolph.

Coffee looked up to find Jackson back in his chair, long legs crossed, cold blue eyes staring straight at his face. Old Hickory.

"Something's wrong," Jackson said flatly. "In the campaign."

Coffee gave the correct and reassuring answer, as he always did, because Providence had assigned him a role as well. "No, sir. Everything is fine, just fine."

What was at stake—James Hamilton had been perfectly right—was the whole democratic American election, stolen from Jackson once before, stolen from the people by Clay.

In the evening Coffee told his wife he might be gone on a trip for two or three days.

CHAPTER

4

They were harder to find now, thought John Quincy Adams, because people liked the new metal tips, but old-fashioned quill writing pens could still be bought. They came in three standard sizes, from smallest to largest: goose quill size; swan quill size; condor quill size. Penholders cost extra and ranged in quality all the way from bone (the cheapest) to onyx, pearl, ivory, and even gold. With a politician's inherent desire to straddle the middle, though he much preferred the tightness of line of the goose quill size, Adams invariably bought the swan, with a plain bone holder.

He took a new one from his desk drawer, studied for inspiration the wavering beams of dusky light that passed through his half-closed curtains (a suitably poetic image, he thought), and dipped his pen once in the inkwell. He copied in Latin the fourth stanza of Horace's "Ode to Licinius":

Sperat infestis, metuit secundis
  Alteram sortem bene praeparatum

Pectus. Informes hyemes reducit
Jupiter; idem summovet.

Then he dipped the pen again and almost without a pause wrote out his translation:

In adverse fortune, *hope* will cheer,
   And joyous moments check with *fear,*
   The justly balanced mind.
'Tis the same Being good and wise
   The genial breeze of spring supplies,
   And winter's blasting wind.

He reread it with great pleasure—this was his sixth translated stanza in six days—and noted as always the great economy and force of Latin. Horace took only four lines to his six; the single word *Jupiter* he had to translate, for the sake of the antithesis, as "Being good and wise." But still, it was not bad; it was curiously satisfying.

He put the translation away in his desk drawer for his son Charles to copy out fair and with a sigh turned to his neglected stack of newspapers. Here there was need for "the justly balanced mind." Senator Ephraim Sellers of Ohio, an inconsequential man but still a senator, had come out for Jackson. Also in Ohio, Frances Wright's most recent radicalizing, atheistic lecture had been interrupted by a firebomb and threats of mob violence, and the Jackson forces, by a tortuous and invisible logic, were blaming Adams, either for her views or the firebomb, it was not clear which. In Georgia the latest in a string of demagogic, administration-baiting governors had just announced that, treaty or no treaty, President or no President, he was going to drive the Creek Indians forcibly from Georgia soil.

News from the East was better. It had now been widely established (Henry Clay's doing) that Jackson belonged to a secret lodge of the Masonic brotherhood, and the anti-Masonic parties of New York and Pennsylvania were hopping up and down in anger. Better still, for the third week in a row John Randolph's acid tongue had been uncharacteristically silent. Adams put down *Niles' Weekly Register* and opened the Richmond *Courier* and read, motionless and unblinking as a statue, the first lines of an article by one Thomas Arnold, an anti-Jackson candidate for Congress from Tennessee: *General Jackson,* said Arnold, *spent the prime of his life in gambling, in cock-fighting, in horse-racing, and to cap all his frailties he tore from a husband the wife of his bosom, to whom he had been for some years united in the holy state of matrimony. I heard one of the General's prominent friends boasting of it, as an act of gallantry, and said that* 'the General had driven Robards off like a dog and taken his wife.' *If Gen. Jackson should be elected President, what effect, think you, fellow-citizens, will it have upon American youth?*

It was Adams's policy not to comment on this, or any other electioneering matter. He put the newspapers in a stack for his son Charles to throw away.

It was hot in the room. He wiped his brow with a clean silk handkerchief and stuck the handkerchief in his shirt cuff, Parisian style. On the desk his favorite gold pocket watch ticked softly.

He had recently sat up most of the night reading *Macbeth* again, which was a play, he was well aware, about the usurpation of a throne by an unworthy man. In the margin of his notepad he now quickly adapted a quotation from it and permitted himself a small, thin smile, about the breadth and tightness, he supposed ironically, of a goose quill pen: *If chance will not have Jackson king, / Why chance may topple him, / Without my stir.*

CHAPTER
5

D r. Charles Wilkins Short began the eighth day of September with his usual faintly disapproving precision.

He tore off the last page of his calendar for the previous week and hung the new sheet on the peg to the left of his desk. He endorsed a note on the Lexington Agricultural Bank for the outrageous amount of his quarterly mortgage, sealed it in an envelope with a quarter-ounce dab of red wax, and placed the envelope in a worn leather satchel. He placed the satchel on top of a stack of books to be returned promptly that week to the library at Transylvania University, where he was professor of *materia medica* and medical botany but did not abuse his privileges.

Then he walked outside into the cool, watery semidarkness of the new dawn and entered the herb shed behind his house. This was his "green library," as he liked to tell his students, a roofless enclosure fenced off from deer and rabbits and containing more than four hundred specimens of local herbs—local from Kentucky, Tennessee, southern Ohio—which he had meticulously collected himself on his hands and knees, pious in scholarship. If the university ever granted him the money, he intended to install a movable glass roof over the shed and transform it into a hothouse for the winter.

As always, Dr. Short spent a full hour inspecting his plants and giving instructions to the two sleepy black gardeners who followed him about, yawning.

At half past seven he was back in his study, seated at his desk. Voices from the other side of the house came closer and resolved themselves into the Swedish cook and her clinging daughter, who was shyly allowed to hand him his cup of tea.

The rest of the morning ought to have been as systematic and unexceptional as the beginning. He prided himself on a love of accuracy, and so always wrote out completely the lectures he delivered to his students. There were two more of those to finish before his classes resumed in a week. He had recently agreed to edit a scholarly journal on medical botany, and the first issue would include his own catalogue of native phaenogamous plants and ferns of Kentucky, due at the printer's very soon. He glanced at his newly hung calendar. Due next Friday.

But instead of settling down to his work, Short turned in his swiveling chair and regarded Limehouse Road, outside his house. Emigrants' wagons were already rattling past, despite the early hour, piled to the sky with mattresses, chairs, children, stoves, on their way by the Shelbyville shortcut to Big Bone Lick on the Ohio; from there westward on keelboats and flat-bottomed barges down to the Mississippi; from there westward yet again, yet again.

He had on his desk an amusing letter from a former student now touring in England, who described the latest aristocratic craze of building grottoes and instant ruins on their country estates, instead of useful gardens; his student had visited a site in Hampshire where the sheep bells were tuned in thirds and fifths, and the flowering plants were all imported from China, especially the new purple-blossoming wisteria plant, which Short had never seen. He reread the letter and put it aside.

At nine o'clock he looked at his watch, a family habit, and went to the door of his study. At nine-forty-five, much later than he had said, the long-expected visitor arrived.

✭   ✭   ✭

ARRIVED, as it happened, in the brown wake of yet another emigrant wagon, riding a spavined mare and apologizing breathlessly as he hurried up the path. "Sorry to be late . . . couldn't hire a horse for the longest, the town's packed with people!" The visitor dismounted at the gate and gave his horse to a servant. "You must have been waiting for hours."

"No inconvenience, none at all," murmured Short, coming down the steps to meet him.

And David Chase extended his hand and simultaneously thought that between Cincinnati and Lexington he had somehow traveled thirty years backward in time. The tall, slightly stoop-shouldered man in front of him resembled perfectly, right down to the pale blue eyes blinking behind thick wire-rimmed glasses, some younger, milder, far less sardonic version of his worldly uncle William, Chase's employer. "Sorry," Chase said again, remembering to smile, "to be so late."

"You're alone?" Dr. Short asked. He craned to look back down the street.

"Just myself," Chase told him.

"I thought I saw . . . But come in, sit down. Can I bring you a cup of rosemary tea?"

Chase inwardly shuddered, politely said yes. When Short had vanished through a door to the main house, he ran a finger around his collar and looked about the little office. Shabby, poorly furnished; bare pine-wood floor except for a small machine-woven Persian rug between the desk and the door. A silent grandfather clock with the hour hand missing. He faced the mud-plaster walls behind the desk. Just what George Ticknor would have constructed for himself, he thought, if George Ticknor had lost all his money and turned Kentucky botanist. There were two battered cases of books, one on each side of the window; more books in piles on the floor; a cabinet of dried plant specimens under glass; a faded four-color print of Linnaeus's table of plant classification that must have been ordered years ago from Paris. Small spiky herbs grew like green whiskers in a wooden tub. Chase looked around the quiet room again. He closed his eyes for a moment and pinched the bridge of his nose with two fingers. Then he did what he had always done in a new room, for as long as he could remember, and started to inspect the books.

The case on the left was devoted entirely to scientific titles in Latin, French, and German, the professor's working library. The other case was framed by two miniature Doric columns and divided in half by an un-painted board. The top half contained sermons and biblical commentar-ies, with, inexplicably, a bound set of Sterne's novels. The lower half contained a few three-volume novels, the works of the poet Burns, and five or six dusty books about the natural history and geography of Virginia. The last was a small leather-bound copy of Thomas Jefferson's *Notes on Virginia.* Chase knelt and stretched out a finger—

"Those were my father's books," said Charles Short behind him.

"No secret letters in them, Mr. Chase," said another voice, far less pleasant. "You'll have to look someplace else."

Chase came to his feet quickly, wiping his hands against his trousers.

"My stepmother," Short said. "Mrs. Jane Short."

Chase accepted a mug of warm tea from a thin white-haired woman in country gingham. She studied him for a moment and then bowed formally like a man instead of shaking hands; like Sarah Hale of Boston, Chase wryly thought, returning the bow. Full circle.

"I took the liberty of showing her your letter," Dr. Short said, "since I think we agree it concerns her too." They backed into their chairs and formed a wary crescent around the Persian rug. Chase found himself by the desk looking up at a new angle of wall and an incongruous oil painting he had missed before.

"That was my late husband, Peyton, when he was a boy." The old woman followed his eye, then jerked her head at Charles. "*His* father."

William Short's younger brother stared over their heads, eyes fixed on the horizon. Peyton had been painted in his early twenties, against a backdrop of weeping willows and a distant but oddly familiar stone arch that Chase could not immediately place. His hair spilled in girlish curls down his brow. He wore the white ruffled neckpiece and high black velvet collar of a late eighteenth-century Virginia dandy, and a bland, handsome, irresolute expression that was the very opposite of Jacksonian bluntness. Peyton Short was altogether as unlikely a piece of political dynamite, Chase considered, as he had ever seen.

"You asked about letters, Rachel Jackson, all that disagreeable history." Charles Short cleared his throat of history. "I don't know what we have to tell you. Judge Overton came over here from Nashville last fall and asked me the very same questions—"

"Tried to swear Charles to 'political' secrecy," Mrs. Short interjected scornfully. "Whatever that is."

"—and there was nothing we could say, then or now. My father boarded with the Robards family as a young man. Lewis Robards accused him of attention to his wife."

"And her of starting it. Rachel Jackson was a flirt."

"But that was Robards's way; everybody in Kentucky knew it. He was a bitterly jealous man. My father was innocent and he didn't want to stay and cause trouble in the house, so he moved on after a few months and opened a dry-goods store here in Lexington. When my mother died, he married Mrs. Jane." Short glanced at his stepmother with an irresolute expression exactly like his father's in the painting. "We just don't involve ourselves in the politics."

"You were commissioned by William Short?" In the main house a child began to cry. The old woman ignored it. "To write a book?"

"Yes."

"We haven't seen or heard from William Short in twenty-six years. He and Peyton were very close. They thought of themselves as true Virginians, if you have any idea what that means, Mr. Chase, out to save the rest of the world. William sent him that book by Thomas Jefferson you were holding." She sat back in the chair, neck stiff, chin high. "They both thought Thomas Jefferson was the cleverest man in history, but then they quarreled about money," she said, "as brothers often do. Peyton had very little of it, God knows. He had to scrounge hard. William has a great deal, but from what I hear he spends it on niggers and art."

For five days, Chase had gone entirely on instinct. He had tracked down Lewis Robards's widowed sister on a farm near the Ohio River. Then the young widow of her son, three towns away. Then an old fool in the village of Frankfort named Henry Banks. Dry trails, dead ends. Common sense told him to get up and leave. Instinct told him to sit where he was and hold his tongue.

The handless grandfather clock made a single bizarre tick and fell silent again. Overhead a bird or squirrel tumbled heavily across the length of the roof.

"If documents existed," the old woman said, "somebody might pay money for them."

"Mother—"

"Overton said as much."

"Mother—"

"I told him there weren't any documents."

Chase sipped the tea he had been holding on his lap for hours. He listened to the scratching sounds overhead. He could promise money on William Short's behalf, he was certain he could, almost any sum, but money obviously hadn't worked before; money was not paramount in this room of books and malice. Instinct repeated its whisper. He sat where he was, held his tongue.

"Have you met Rachel Jackson?" the old woman asked.

"Yes."

"My husband's first wife was a decent, God-fearing woman. I knew her well. She died painfully from the consumption—I was already a widow myself—and when she died, Peyton and I married inside three months. That's the frontier way."

"Yes."

"When Peyton got sick you could see the hand of death on his face. He had to be nursed and fed like a baby. I wore myself out for him." She held up a withered white hand wormy with veins. "It done me no good. For the last six weeks of his life he never stopped talking, to me, about sweet-wonderful Rachel Jackson, Rachel Robards, that was—"

"I don't have to listen to this," Charles Short said abruptly, not to his stepmother but to Chase.

"Then leave," she said; but her stepson stayed rooted to his chair. "What you heard as rumor was true, Mr. Chase—it must run in the family, William Short lived in open adultery with that French woman, you know—Rachel Robards was a miserable, unhappy person and she saw Peyton as a way out. She was a flirt and a Jezebel, and when she got desperate enough, certain things . . . happened."

"What kind of things?" Chase asked, and for a moment thought that to speak at all had been a mistake. Jane Short lifted her chin and narrowed her eyes. In the main house the crying child had finished; two doors slammed, one after the other.

"In his mind," she said slowly, "Peyton was unfaithful to me, and to his first wife. Rachel was the one he preferred. 'Loved,' if you want to say it."

"You have been badly used," Chase said.

She nodded, not looking at him, looking at the window, the graceful green dome of a mulberry tree on the lawn, a narrow road running south. The stone arch in the portrait, Chase suddenly recalled, was the famous Natural Bridge of Virginia, forty miles from Monticello, where all roads lead. "I don't care about Jackson and Adams," Jane Short said. "'Adams Forever.' 'Jackson and Reform.' I'm too old to take any notice of that."

"You have the letters?"

She made no answer. She stared at the road.

"Where are they?"

"If I didn't give them to Judge Overton," she said, finally transferring her flat, implacable gaze to Chase, "why would I give them to you?"

And Chase gave the only answer that would do, that would matter, feeling himself sick at heart, feeling self-loathing rise sour in his mouth like bile as he spoke. "Because if they are disgraceful, Overton would suppress them," he said, and stopped.

Jane Short finished his answer for him. "But you would publish them," Peyton Short's widow said with a yellow smile, "every shameful word."

CHAPTER
6

The Life of Andrew Jackson, by David Chase

Chapter Thirteen (Draft)

RACHEL DONELSON—RACHEL JACKSON-TO-BE—WAS MARRIED IN NASHVILLE to Lewis Robards in the wet, late-blooming spring of 1785.

Shortly afterward, the couple took up residence in Harrodsburgh, Kentucky, where Robards's mother presided over an enormous blue-grass farm and a beautiful two-story stone mansion, the finest for miles around.

Rachel and her new mother-in-law became instant friends. The old lady was proud, well-connected, a lapsed Virginian. She liked her new daughter-in-law's vivacious ways, her Virginia history, and the considerable fortune in land and prestige a Donelson brought in that part of the world. The two of them spent hours at a time on the stone porch, dipping snuff (Mrs. Robards), smoking a pipe (Rachel), and planning the future.

Two boarders also lived in the house, apprentice lawyers. John Overton, who would keep his nose to the grindstone and someday be a judge, and

Peyton Short, a dreamy, fair-skinned, ineffectual young man who had graduated from the College of William and Mary (in Virginia, of course) and subsequently drifted west all by himself in the manner of younger sons in the eighteenth century, seeking "life."

I have found no word of warmth or praise on record anywhere for Robards. He was a big, barrel-chested man with a curiously flattened nose (result of a boyhood accident), physically imposing, physically brutal. Despite the fact that his wife was young (just eighteen) and by every account remarkably attractive—I string together a dozen descriptions: "gay, lively, beautiful, alluring, the best story-teller, the best dancer, the sprightliest companion, the most dashing horsewoman"—despite all this, or because of it, Robards was a notoriously tyrannical and un-tender husband. It was an open secret that he walked down late at night to the slave cabins and sometimes did not return till dawn. It was an immediate, tumultuous fact that Robards did not like Peyton Short, did not at all like Short's courteous manners toward Rachel, nor Rachel's lively response to Short's good manners. More than once he publicly called her "flirtatious," "wanton," "a slut-faced tease"—he raised his hand to her sometimes, reduced her to tears at the family table. In a secret note to Rachel—unpublished until this moment—Peyton Short wrote that "the gay light in your eyes has turned somber, the laughter is gone from your voice. I would do *anything* to change the world and bring back your happiness." And Rachel replied . . . in a similar vein.

More notes followed. More fiery glances from Robards, more hot tears. The judicious Overton removed himself temporarily to town, settling some business matters. Short was a handsome, pleasing contrast to the glowering Robards. In yet another secret note, left under his dinner plate on May 14, 1786 (Short kept every word that passed between them), Rachel asked Short to meet her on the porch after everyone was asleep, to talk about what was to be done. *Rachel* asked Short.

Now as best I can tell, from interviews, from documents never before used in a Jackson biography, this is what happened next:

Rachel and Peyton Short met on the moonlit porch. They talked. They whispered. At some point, in an evil hour as the Puritan poet says, they embraced.

And at that same point Lewis Robards walked onto the porch.

The subsequent uproar awakened every person in the house. Robards raged as never before—Rachel wept; old lady Robards took her daughter-in-law's side and cursed her son and her son's temper; Peyton Short vanished into the darkness.

He vanished as far as the tiny town of Crab Orchard, on the road back to Virginia. There he wrote a long, impassioned letter to Rachel, begging her to leave Robards and come away with him to the Spanish settlements across the Mississippi, where nobody knew them and they could start life over again, as man and wife. Peyton informed her he had seen from the start that she and Robards were miserable together, that a separation must inevitably occur—otherwise he would never have "cultivated an attachment for her" (his very words, the picket-fence abstractions of eighteenth-century prose). He was going to Virginia, he said, to convert his patrimonial property into ready money—he would do whatever she thought best, after that.

He left the letter at the Crab Orchard tavern and commissioned a friend to deliver it to her in Harrodsburgh. And he set out for the Chesapeake region where his older brother and he had been reared.

But like the long-mustachioed villain of the stage melodrama, like Lovelace to Rachel's Kentucky Clarissa, Lewis Robards somehow contrived to get possession of the letter—and Rachel's desperate, incriminating reply—and off he thundered down the Virginia road in pursuit of poor Short. He overtook him at Gault's Tavern in Richmond, where two of Short's friends, an officious young man named Henry Banks and someone else called Charles Tutt, literally held Robards back at the door. If blood was his object, Short called from inside the bar, pistol at his side, he was ready to meet Robards on the field of honor. But if some "compromise" could be achieved by the payment of money, that was possible, money could be paid.

Robards backed away from the door. Short took a shaky breath. After a time Henry Banks was dispatched for paper and pen. And late that night, beside a guttering candle on a tavern table, Peyton wrote a promissory note for a thousand dollars, and Robards folded it in half with a grin, leaned back, and stuck it in his pocket.

Such was the compromise; such was the price of Rachel's honor. About as un-Jacksonian an action as can be imagined: a promissory note instead of a pistol! Short never wrote her again, though he crept back to Kentucky some years later and settled into a quiet, unprofitable life some twenty miles from Harrodsburgh. Meanwhile Rachel returned to her mother's house in Nashville, there met Andrew Jackson, there, so to speak, reinvented her life.

Was she a victim? or a seductress? The reader can judge for himself. Here is the first of the notes Rachel Robards, a married woman, wrote to Peyton Short under her husband's roof . . .

DAVID Chase put down his pen and stared at the piece of paper in disgust. His third draft so far, each one worse than before, each one tawdrier, coarser. He tried to picture the sweet-natured elderly woman he knew at the Hermitage reading her own long-buried words; Jackson reading her words. He crumpled the paper in his fist.

"Aposiopesis," he said. "The rhetorical figure of breaking off a statement in the middle before you vomit." He walked around the table and picked up a book from a white nest of papers and notes. "Did I show you? This is what she put the letters in." He held out the book to Emma Colden. "Jefferson's *Notes on Virginia*. Jane Short came out to my horse and stuck it in the saddlebag and turned on her heel without a word."

"It's inscribed," Emma said, reading the flyleaf. " '*To Peyton from his loving brother William far away——Paris, March 1783.*' "

"Epanalepsis." Chase replaced the book on the table. "Repetition at the end of something from the beginning."

Emma smoothed his crumpled sheets of paper on the front of her dress and then took them to the window, through which he could still see the soft gray late-summer rain that had been falling all afternoon, more mist than rain.

Chase sat down and slipped Jane Short's eight "documents" back into the book. If he rewrote and copied till midnight, he could send a final chapter on the morning express to Boston, Sarah Hale could print at once, chapter or separate pamphlet, and the world could be reading it three weeks from now, if not sooner. And if he used his head for something besides staring mooncalf at Emma, he could no doubt extract a grateful, colossal, Paris-worthy bonus from William Short, his loving sponsor.

At the window Emma shifted her pose. She wore a dress of pale blue cotton; her breasts and hips curved in profile against the muted light of the window. Slender and voluptuous at once, he thought; an oxymoron.

Since they knew nobody at all in Lexington they had registered at the hotel as man and wife . . . He turned his gaze to the rumpled bed.

" 'The truth is mighty and will prevail,' " Short had quoted Jefferson in Boston. Tell the truth in your book, that was all he asked. But remember: Andrew Jackson is a demagogue, an illiterate frontier duelist, no Jefferson. Portray him as he *really* is and let the voters decide. Only this had nothing to do with Jackson, Jackson's politics, Jackson's character. This was all about Rachel, whom Jackson loved.

Whom Jackson had married.

From the window Emma looked up, frowning. "You've softened the story," she said. "Your next draft needs to be harder—Rachel as scheming, flirtatious, deliberately unfaithful with another man. Rachel's guilty conscience. You should *start* with a quotation from one of her letters—"

"I can't." Chase made a face at the empty fireplace; suppressed all conscious memory of Rachel's pathetic, half-literate love notes, a girl of nineteen or twenty, trapped in an unhappy marriage, un-free—his thoughts skittered, skipped, raindrops on glass. "I can't do that."

For no particular reason he picked up *Notes on Virginia* and put it in his jacket pocket. He stood. "I can't do that," he repeated.

Emma came to the table where he had been writing and sat down in his chair.

"The stronger your story," she said bluntly, "the more Short will pay."

"I know."

"I could write a first paragraph for you," she said, taking up one of his pens.

"No."

Emma kept her eyes fixed on the writing table as she shuffled papers into a stack. "I could even," she said, "write it for Gales and Seaton instead of for Short. They'd pay thousands to have it in the *National Intelligencer*, or Henry Clay's people would, Adams would."

"A bidding war."

She found something of absorbing interest in the first sheet on her stack. "I could publish it under my own name."

Chase was silent. He listened to the rain whispering against the window, indistinguishable noises from the hotel saloon below. He had spent the last six months listening to American hotels, riding American hotels westward like great square clipper ships of the future, borne on the rising American tide.

"In Europe," he said, shaking his head, "in France I started to write because I wanted—"

Emma sprang up, furious. "*Don't!*" she said. "*Don't* tell me you're a serious writer, God help us, you can't *lower* yourself to bloody Gales and Seaton, can't write *trash,* can't forget your 'standards.' I've grown up with standards; I've had standards for supper half my life; standards don't buy food—I'm a writer's daughter!"

"Your father—" Chase began.

"These are *true* documents." Emma was white with rage. "You can print them, you can write them into bloody Andrew Jackson's bloody life. You're not *betraying* anything."

Chase slammed the table with one hand. "What's at stake—" he said.

"What's at stake," Emma said, "is us."

He lifted his hand, surprised to find it damp with sweat. She turned, an electric crackle of blue skirt and anger, walked three steps, turned again. "If you write this, and write it *well,* David, you can earn more money than either of us has seen in years. You can claim a job with half the newspapers in Washington City. If Adams is reelected, who knows what else you can claim."

"We can just go, right now, to Paris."

"No. My father will never travel again. I will never—*never*—leave this country for Europe."

Chase stayed exactly where he was, leaning against the wall. Emma paced to the window, back to the table; spread her skirt and sat down. She started to read again.

After a moment he slipped open the door and stepped outside.

On the street the rain had stopped, leaving silver and copper puddles everywhere, like so many giant coins flung at random. Chase twisted his mouth into a smile at his metaphor. Money. He walked west along a set of wagon ruts toward the edge of Lexington's town square. Everywhere around him were the signs—familiar by now—of American progress. Wood-framed buildings going up in overgrown fields, new businesses and stores lining the square. Commercial posters fluttered on a fence, thick as leaves. Great-hipped wagons swayed in the mud like pachyderms. At a vacant lot he stopped and tried to picture Paris and found that no picture came to mind. He felt less and less American every day, yet what else was he?

At the hotel again he took a seat in the shadows on the porch outside the saloon. The sun was beginning to set behind a black hump of Kentucky hills. He moved his chair a few feet to watch the last flashing of colors. The air was sweet with wet, unharvested clover. The evening, as they used to say in Boston, darkened over.

From the other end of the porch a shadow detached itself and went into the saloon. In a minute or two it returned with a pair of glass beer mugs. Chase felt no sense of surprise whatsoever—*epanalepsis*—when it sat down in the chair beside him and placed a mug of beer at his elbow. They each took a sip.

"Well, how did you like Jane Short?" John Coffee asked.

I liked her fine," Chase said without turning his head.

"I was over at her house." Coffee stretched his legs companionably in the dark. "Just a couple of hours back. She wouldn't say two words to me. The professor either. Little black child told me a man pretty much like you had come on a visit this morning."

"Good-looking chap, noble profile, high moral character. That would be me, all right."

Coffee spat into an invisible spittoon. "I promised my wife I'd stop. Nasty habit." He took a sip of beer and shifted so that his big body made the wooden chair groan and his boot tips caught a gleam of light from the saloon. "John Overton saw her last year," Coffee said, as if he were now simply reflecting, reminiscing out loud. "He told us in Nashville that nobody had any letters, Rachel never wrote a single word in her life that would make her a bad example to American youth. If she had, it might tar the General just enough—it's not logical, I know, but it's politics—just enough to cost him two or three states."

"She's a harmless, well-meaning lady."

Coffee's shadow appeared to nod in agreement. "I've known Overton since back when he had teeth, and Rachel even longer. The judge wouldn't know how to talk to Jane Short."

"No."

"And Rachel used to be young and foolish, along with well-meaning. You want my opinion, Mr. Chase, I think she might have written a letter or two when she was married to Robards. And I think the General wasn't over-particular about legal niceties when he was boarding in the Donelson blockhouse, either, and Rachel was a damsel in distress. The General is not what you'd call a lust-driven man, but lightning strikes once for everybody." Coffee shifted the other way in his chair. "By and large," he said, "the General is an honorable man, otherwise I wouldn't be here."

"Did you follow me?" One part of Chase's mind was genuinely curious. Another part was contemplating the rich, massive complexity of John Coffee's character.

"I sat down and tried to figure what you would do, where you might go. Guessed wrong the first time and went to Jack Jouett's old place in Frankfort. Then I guessed right and came here." Coffee paused. "I didn't know you were married, by the way, until I looked in the hotel register."

Chase smiled wearily. Epanalepsis gives way to irony, he thought.

"Give me the letters, son," Coffee said.

CHAPTER
8

H e can't," said Emma Colden. "He can't and he won't."

She walked three steps down the porch and stopped in front of John Coffee's heavy boots, and she had never, Chase thought, looked more seductively beautiful. He rose and touched her arm with his left hand; with his right hand he felt the dead weight of Jefferson's book in his jacket pocket.

"You must be General Coffee," Emma said.

Coffee remained where he was in his chair, not rudely somehow, and smiled pleasantly up at her.

"Jackson's henchman," she added with a defiant edge to her voice.

Even seated, Coffee was an enormous figure, at least as heavy as Emma's father, but wide in the shoulders and powerfully muscular. Chase had long ago guessed that he deliberately kept all his motions slow and gentle, in order not to startle or frighten small creatures. Coffee stood up carefully now, hitching his belt. His head and shoulders actually blocked the light from the hotel lobby.

"And you are Mr. Chase's friend."

"Emma Colden," she said, not moving.

From the saloon door behind them three men stepped onto the porch.

"I think we might have a little more privacy inside," Coffee said, mild as ever.

It had long been Chase's idea to write an article about the institution of the American hotel—there was simply nothing like it in Europe, there had been nothing like it when he had left America ten years ago. In Europe you still stayed in taverns and inns and *relais,* little stations for food and rest on a traveler's route. Americans, on the other hand, apparently built hotels before they built anything else—they were magnets, palaces—in Washington he had admired the Indian Queen as a social center in a city that obviously lacked one. And out here in the West, in Tennessee, Kentucky, in every upstart town he had seen, the hotel was already there, hogging the best location, bigger than any other building, better furnished, more democratic. Americans lived in hotels. Americans sat down at hotel dining tables and rubbed elbows with perfect strangers. They mingled as equals and regarded it as natural. In hotels they were all transients, all migrants, drifting, on the move; American Adams checking into Eden.

The Kentuckian Hotel of Lexington had two hundred rooms and a public lobby that ran half the length of the building. To the left, under a row of moth-eaten buffalo heads, was the entrance to the saloon. To the right the clerk's desk and his wall of keys and bells. Beyond it the dining room, where black waiters were clearing dishes and a family still in dusty coats and overalls lingered over their supper. Directly in front of them were a semicircle of padded chairs and a stone fireplace next to a window. One of the waiters was on his knees laying out logs.

"He can't give you the letters," Emma said, "in the first place because they're upstairs in our room. In the second place because he won't."

Coffee pulled one of the chairs out of the semicircle and sat down. Chase and Emma remained standing. Chase fingered the book in his pocket. The waiter finished arranging the logs and applied a candle to the kindling. Nearby another waiter was lighting the whale-oil lamps that hung from polished scallop brackets attached to the walls.

"Unless," Emma said, and abruptly sat down herself, "you mean to offer us money for them."

Coffee was silent so long that, to an outside observer, he might in fact have been considering the idea, a "compromise," to use Peyton Short's prudent word, Chase thought. But Chase had no doubt at all.

"I don't think I can do that, Miss Colden," Coffee said at last.

Emma lifted her chin and stiffened. Her hair was golden, her profile white and sharp against the shadows. "They are worth a good deal."

"I know that." Coffee kept his impassive gaze on her. "But the General would never forgive me if I bought his wife's honor with money. Or his election either, for that matter."

"The General would never know."

Coffee leaned forward and delicately spat.

Chase looked past him to the window beside the fireplace. Outside, at the end of the street, an atmospheric phenomenon was making the sky suddenly flare up again and bathe the misty horizon in a brilliant red light, as if someone were blowing on a bed of coals. *Alpenglow* was the name for a much paler form of it in Europe. In America what was it called? All the western hills seemed ablaze. Such was the pace of American energy, American ambition, that time itself was in a hurry, time itself was in flames. The sun might have been a great ball of fire that had rushed across the sky full-speed American style, reached the end of the continent and started to bounce right back, doubling the American day.

"It's up to you," Coffee said to him.

What had he told Coffee back at the Hermitage? He and Rachel were alike, he had said; everything he saw here was alien to him. Jefferson's day was over. The center had shifted. He had no right to sacrifice Jackson, he knew it in his core. The people's choice. Much less did he have the right to sacrifice poor Rachel, with her baffled eyes and her timorous soul and her sad, parched flowers. To drag her out into the blazing American sun and publish every shameful, predestined, utterly forgivable and human word; not for money, not for anything else he might gain.

Emma stepped in front of him. "Choose me," she said.

But Chase shook his head and reached in his pocket, conscious as he did that she would now, in due course and entirely because of his cowardice, marry Ephraim Sellers.

When he looked up, the sun had set and she was gone.

PART

5

October 1828–March 1829

CHAPTER

1

John Coffee thought he had never seen anything so confused and chaotic as the presidential election of 1828. For sheer free-firing, lung-splitting hurly-burly, it almost rivaled a cavalry charge. And in fact three of the nine members of the Chillicothe, Ohio, Jackson committee were mounted that very moment on little white ponies, right in front of the polls, and galloping back and forth through the crowd like whooping Cossacks.

Not that the crowd seemed to notice. Coffee stepped up on the wooden sidewalk by the Chillicothe Hotel and watched a party of volunteers roll out yet another enormous keg of whiskey, stenciled, like the two others in the middle of the street, JACKSON AND REFORM. Down the block a similar party was tapping *its* keg—ADAMS FOREVER—and in between at least two or three hundred men were staggering, braying, cheering, vomiting, and otherwise exercising their democratic suffrage. Coffee counted twenty-six men still waiting in line to go into the courthouse and vote, but the line pushed and shoved and twisted back on itself so often, like a snake on a stove, it was hard to be certain how many really intended to vote.

"Two more hours," Hamilton shouted in his ear and held out his gold watch in pantomime.

Coffee nodded and waved to one of their salesmen down in the street. In Oxford, Ohio, where they had stayed last night, the voting was carried out in the local taverns by voice only: A man simply walked in, gave his name to a clerk, took a free drink in his hand from either the Jackson or the Adams side, and shouted out his vote. In Chillicothe each side had individual printed ballots already available, and squadrons of hired "salesmen" who wandered through the streets (and the barbecues and the marching bands and the galloping ponies) trying to pass them on to voters. Inside the courthouse there was no such thing as a secret ballot. You handed over either a Jackson or an Adams ticket and the whole room watched while the clerk called your name and read your vote. "The virtue of the people," Jackson had told him before they left Nashville, gazing solemnly off at the horizon. "I rest my fate in the virtue of the common man." The common man, as far up and down the street as Coffee could see, was drunk to his eyeballs.

"Did you place your bets?" Hamilton put away his watch, grabbed Coffee's arm, and started to steer him into the relative quiet of the hotel lobby. "Van Buren says to bet as high as we can the next two days."

Coffee grunted something unintelligible, which Hamilton took for affirmative. They stopped in front of a crowded, smoky makeshift bar—three planks on a pair of sawhorses—and Coffee signaled for whiskey while Hamilton patted his vest, patted his coat, finally came up with a much-folded letter. If he had pulled it out of his hat like a rabbit, Coffee wouldn't have been surprised. Back in Albany, New York, Governor Martin Van Buren was universally known as the Little Magician. Coffee and Hamilton had visited six Ohio towns so far, at Van Buren's request, as official Jackson "watchers." At every town there had been a new letter waiting, rooms in a hotel, local banknotes for betting on Jackson, local committeemen ready with posters and buttons and lists of Jackson supporters. When the Little Magician got down to work, people said, he could "Van Burenize" a whole state.

"Names of the vigilance committee." Hamilton flourished the letter and drank his whiskey, all in the same neat motion.

"Now, that's not the same as the old Friends of Jackson committee, is it? I don't always keep them straight."

If anything, Hamilton had grown brisker and more parrotlike over the past few weeks. Now he wiped his big beak of a nose with a blue silk handkerchief and shook his head. "Floaters," he said, using the Van Buren term for the wagonloads of men who were driven from district to district to vote, first copying names from the nearest cemetery. "The vigilance committee watches out for floaters. The Friends of Jackson take care of this"—he flicked his handkerchief toward a colorful array of posters and Jackson banners floating on the lobby walls.

"And *that*, too, I guess." Coffee tilted his head toward the door and the uproarious street outside.

"One-hundred-proof democracy," Hamilton said cheerfully, unfolding his list again.

Coffee spun two dimes onto the bar and took his own whiskey to a chair beside the staircase. He was fifty-eight years old and tired, tired certainly of traveling back and forth across southern Ohio; tired of the continuous noise and hubbub of the election, which had been going on in one state or another since late September. Even tired, if the truth be told, of the sacred Common Man himself, and Hamilton's ceaseless harping on the great theme of the Jacksonian people versus the Adams elite.

Somebody set off a string of firecrackers by the bar. Coffee closed his eyes and dreamed of Nashville. Why was he here, weary to his bones like some itinerant peddler, instead of back on his own front porch watching the sun go down on the Cumberland River? He knew why, of course. At the end of September the first state to report, Maine, had surprised the whole country by giving Jackson one of its nine electoral votes, when everybody swore New England was rock solid for Adams. Then in the first week of October returns had started to dribble in from Pennsylvania, which was supposed to be Adams country, too, and Jackson was actually taking the lead by an astonishing two to one margin, flattening and mauling Adams from one end of the state to the other. At which point it was decided at the highest levels to Van Burenize Ohio, right in Henry Clay's backyard. "You can do it without me," Coffee had said, backing away. "No, I can't," said Jackson, "I never can."

Coffee opened his eyes. At the bar Hamilton was mopping his brow with the blue silk handkerchief—a traveling present, strangely enough, from Rachel—and raising yet another glass of whiskey. The laws of chemistry seemed to be suspended during an election. Hamilton drank from morning to night, bucketfuls, barrelfuls, and hardly ever showed it. Coffee, on the other hand, took one or two sips late in the day, as now, and instantly felt his head start to spin. Hamilton was standing on his toes, calling him over. Three sleek, pork-faced men in heavy vests and black frock coats were waiting by the bar, as obviously mayor and judge and alderman as if they wore signs on their hats. Hamilton was practically bouncing, and despite the clatter of voices and glasses and the unending yawp from outside, Coffee knew exactly what he was saying: Come and meet the famous General Coffee, Jackson's right hand at New Orleans. Coffee groaned and got to his feet. "I never vote," a leather-skinned old farmer (the virtue of the Common Man) had told him in Oxford. "It just encourages y'all."

✯   ✯   ✯

COFFEE returned to Nashville, alone, toward the end of the third week in October.

He rode up to the Nashville Inn and climbed the stairs to the Central Committee's offices and made his reports and shook his hands, then sat down in a side room with Overton and pulled off his boots. Ohio was starting to come in, Overton told him, and the trip must have done some good, because Jackson had the lead, there, too, though not as great as in Pennsylvania.

"Send the news to New York," Coffee said, and scratched his foot and listened to himself with a wry grin. Two weeks with Hamilton had turned him into a strategist. According to their schedule, New York was the last of the eastern states to vote, and voters, as Hamilton liked to say, run with the pack. A big lead in Ohio would push New Yorkers Jackson's way.

"Thought of that." Overton scratched his own foot companionably. Somebody opened the door and handed him a sheaf of papers. "Van Buren says no, timing is everything, wait till the *exact week* before they vote."

"O.K."

"Eaton talked with the General. He's going to marry that girl."

Coffee stretched his long body to its fullest length and looked out the window. A single little cirrus cloud was stuck to the hot, flat sky like a piece of hammered tin, white on blue. October was as hot as August this year, which sometimes happened in Tennessee.

"Fact is, the General encouraged him," Overton said, and scrunched his jaw and his nose together in distaste. Plump John Eaton was not the brightest man in Jackson's entourage, or the most discreet. *That girl,* Coffee knew, was a bartender's daughter in Washington City named Peggy Timberlake, whose husband had been a purser in the navy until he mysteriously cut his throat that spring and left her a widow. During Timberlake's long and numerous absences at sea, Eaton had taken a fairly scandalous and open interest in Peggy, which everybody around them could see, except, predictably, Jackson.

Overton was now cracking pecans with one brown old claw. "The General said she's a fine young woman, he knows they'll be happy." He showed his gums in a mirthless smile. "Sam Houston says she's slept with twenty men."

"He thinks all women are like Rachel," Coffee said, not meaning Sam Houston.

"Like his *idea* of Rachel," Overton said, and cracked another pecan. He looked sideways at Coffee, shrewdly. "You ever going to tell me what you did in Kentucky?"

Coffee reached over and took a pecan from Overton's fist.

"Hamilton told me he thought you found some letters but didn't actually destroy them. He said you must be keeping them safe somewhere, just in case."

"That's how Hamilton thinks."

"She's worse than ever."

Coffee nodded. From midsummer on, Rachel had seemed to be sinking daily into greater and greater gloom. *Gloomth,* Coffee thought, which was his mother's funny old eighteenth-century Virginia word for melancholy spirits. It wasn't Rachel's health so much—though she was fatter than ever now and breathed with an audible wheeze—it was her strained, passive expression and her listless movements. She had rallied a little when young (and handsome) David Chase was visiting, but since then her mood had been bleaker and grimmer than ever. The toll of all that public abuse, Coffee guessed, that and the unbearable prospect of worse if she actually became the First Lady. Put yourself in Rachel's place, he thought—how would an uneducated little Tennessee farmwife, with her Spanish cigars and her corncob pipes and her notorious "adultery," stand up to the sophisticated eastern ladies who would come to her house to stare and whisper? Tomahawks and bullets were easier to dodge. And far less lethal.

"She claims she don't even want to move to Washington," Overton said, "if he wins."

Coffee nodded again. "I'll go see her," he said.

✯ ✯ ✯

BUT he didn't go, not for a good ten days. He was sick himself, of politics and ballots and hubbub. He stayed at home instead and supervised the workers who were baling his cotton—back when he had started farming you shipped your cotton to New Orleans in floppy burlap sacks that were irregular to weigh and awkward to carry; now somebody had invented a machine to compress it into clean white bales four feet square, perfect for stacking. The age of enterprise. In front of his wagons on the Lebanon Turnpike, waiting to be loaded, the bales looked like blocks of ice.

Coffee saw his cotton onto the wagons, and he wrote his factor in New Orleans and paid his overseer and repaired some rail fences and talked in the evenings with his soft, calm wife, and when he finally saddled up and rode over to the Hermitage it was to find that he had waited too long, and young Dr. Henry Lee Heiskell was sitting in her bedroom getting out his knife and cup to bleed her.

"I never understood the theory of that exactly," Coffee said as he followed Jackson into the study. Out in the hall a group of slave women, led by a black giantess named Hannah, hurried past carrying basins and clouts and chattering like sparrows. Jackson closed the door with his boot.

"The four humors of the blood," he said. "He drains away the malignant humors and strengthens the inner body."

"You would think," Coffee said, taking his usual place on the horsehair sofa, "it would do pretty well the opposite—make you weaker." Old Hannah boomed something that carried through two sets of walls. Just about now the doctor would be bending over the bed to slice open a vein in Rachel's fat forearm with one of his tiny blades, then he would watch a full measured pint of her blood spurt into a special copper cup he held under the arm. It looked like superstition to Coffee, it looked illogical.

"The theory is sound," Jackson said, with the gruff assurance of somebody who had been bled himself a hundred times. Coffee glanced around the room—on a hook was a canvas and leather contraption called Kelley's Consumption Jacket that Jackson occasionally wore to combat his breathing trouble. On the desk, by a plaster bust of Napoleon, was a vial of

W. W. Gray's Ointment, which Jackson had publicly endorsed in the newspapers as a treatment for dysentery, croup, and gum disease. In the bedroom, Coffee knew, next to the French mirror, was a whole personal pharmacy of Jackson's patent medicines. He kept calomel in big earthenware jars, the way some people kept candy. And something called the Matchless Sanative, and sugar of lead, too, which the army doctors had started giving him in 1813 to swab the ugly red bullet wound the Bentons had left in his arm. Never one to do things halfway, he sometimes both drank and bathed in the foul stuff, whenever the pain from his lungs or his arm or his stomach got to be too much. Once Coffee had found him actually squirting a dose of sugar of lead straight into his eyes to cure his blurry vision. How much of Jackson's white-hot anger came from his bad health? How could you ever know?

"Ohio's polled for us," Jackson said from his desk.

"I heard about that."

"You did a fine job, you and Hamilton." He looked at the closed door and they both listened to the silence. Jackson pulled out his watch. In one part of his brain, Coffee thought, he's probably already filed away and sorted the numbers from Ohio; in another part, separate and sealed off, he's counted exactly how long poor Rachel has been bleeding. Coffee had never been able to seal off parts of his brain that way; it was a gift (or a curse) that Jackson had. Jackson enjoyed a far more complex and powerful mind than any Easterner believed.

"Well," Coffee said, "the people in Ohio were already behind you. It didn't take much doing from us."

"The people and Providence," Jackson said, and snapped his watch shut.

At the door to Rachel's bedroom they looked in together, where the patient sat propped in her high canopied bed.

"You look fine now, Mother," Jackson told her, and Rachel gave him a feeble gray smile.

"Much, much better," said young Dr. Heiskell as he stood by a bloody basin putting away his instruments. "Next time I see my friend here, she'll be dancing in the President's House."

Rachel's eyes flickered open. She wore an old white mobcap down on her brow and a quilted green bed jacket that rose and fell with her wheezes, and she had never looked less like a dancer in her life. "I assure you, Doctor," she whispered, but loud enough for Coffee to hear, "I had rather be a doorkeeper in the house of God than live in that palace in Washington."

Jackson patted her hand and stared out the window at the bare November fields.

CHAPTER

2

eanwhile, the theory worked. Two days after she was bled of her "humors" Rachel left her bed and resumed her household routine, though nothing at the Hermitage seemed routine any longer. Every day brought a new mailbag of election returns, and every day made it clearer and clearer that straight across the country the Common Man had outnumbered, outvoted, out-Jacksoned the eastern coalition. Despite himself, Coffee became caught up in the calculation. Ohio went soundly for Jackson, all sixteen electoral votes. Pennsylvania gave him twenty-eight; New York split twenty for Jackson, sixteen for Adams. Virginia was for Jackson more than two to one. Louisiana, of course, voted for the Hero of New Orleans, but so did Mississippi, Indiana, Maryland. In the end, even next-door Kentucky, Henry Clay's home state, went for Jackson, too, giving him every one of its fourteen votes.

When the news of his final tally reached the Hermitage—178 electoral votes to John Quincy Adams's 83—it seemed almost anticlimactic. One of the Donelson boys came trotting in from the Fountain of Health post office in the late afternoon of December 6 and gave the official letter to Overton, who read it aloud in the dining room while Jackson smoked his pipe and a dozen or so neighbors and hangers-on lounged around the table and clapped. Rachel sat by the door with her sewing in her lap. Coffee bent over to wish her congratulations, but she kept her eye on her needle and simply murmured (a little wistfully, to Coffee's ear), "Well, for Mr. Jackson's sake, I'm glad. For myself, John Coffee, you know I never wished it."

In Nashville, the Friends of Jackson decided to hold a great celebration banquet on December 23, the anniversary of the night battle at New Orleans, and Mary Coffee, as the wife of that battle's leading general, was somehow deputized to put Rachel into "proper" dress. Rachel was to ride to Washington in a coach pulled by six white horses, after all, lent by a North Carolina senator. She was going to preside over an inaugural ball and a gala reception. She needed to have a new fitted wardrobe, suitable for the President's wife, and an up-to-date hairstyle and silk slippers, and she needed to start getting ready now. Rachel shook her head, looking profoundly miserable, and smoothed her old calico farm dress and wondered if it wouldn't be better for her to remain at home until the summer, and go over to Washington City then. A stern letter from John Eaton reminded her that the General's enemies would claim she was ashamed to show her face.

Long before the banquet Nashville had filled up to bursting with well-wishers and hungry office seekers. The Hermitage was like a bustling camp, readying itself for departures. On the morning of December 12 Mary Coffee escorted Rachel into town for a session with a seamstress, but by noon Rachel was so fatigued and unhappy that they let her go into a private parlor in the Nashville Inn and rest. In that parlor, by a cruel accident, somebody had accidentally left a copy of an old anti-Jackson, anti-"adultery" pamphlet, no worse than any of the others, but apparently new to Rachel. She picked it up and began to read. When the ladies entered the room, they found her crouching in a corner, terror-stricken and weeping hysterically. On the way back to the Hermitage they stopped by a creek and Mary Coffee helped her to wash her face and dry her tears, but when she reached home and Jackson came down the steps to greet her, Rachel burst into tears again.

Five days later Coffee was standing in a field not far from the house discussing with Jackson the dismal prospects for next year's cotton. Afterward he would remember the exact sentence he had just spoken: "You were elected by the people, General, but you're going to have to govern the banks." Jackson gave a lantern-jawed scowl and kicked at the frozen earth. A little crystal white puff of frost and sunlight rose from the toe of his shoe—and at that same moment a slave girl came tumbling and running full speed off the porch, screaming at a high, steady pitch.

By the time they reached the back door old Hannah had carried Rachel into her bed, and Rachel was clutching her heart and writhing and twisting the sheets in torment. The doctors bled her twice that day and again the next morning—three pints of blood in all—and once more the theory seemed to work. She sat in a chair by the fire and Emily Donelson read the Bible to her. She drank tea with sugar and was cheerful. Jackson never budged from her side. She gripped Coffee's hand when he stopped by to visit and told him she hadn't had so much of the General's company since the election started.

On December 22 she caught cold, and Dr. Heiskell, who was staying in the house by now, brewed her a sweating medicine to drink. Jackson poured the mixture himself and held the cup to her lips.

Around eight o'clock she yawned. The banquet was the following day in Nashville. She thought the General ought to go to sleep, off in another room, so he could be fresh for the celebration. The doctor agreed; after all, it was only a cold. Jackson hesitated. Hannah volunteered to sit by her mistress all night if it would make Jackson feel better. Slowly and reluctantly, he gathered his things and went to lie down on the sofa next door.

Twice after that Rachel got up from the bed and smoked her pipe a few minutes to clear her throat. At one point, out of the blue, she repeated her drowsy words to Hannah: "I'd rather be a doorkeeper in the house of God than live in that palace."

Just after ten o'clock she suddenly rolled to one side and stood up and cried in a loud voice, "I'm fainting!" And then she collapsed into Hannah's arms.

The slave's shrieks roused the whole house. Heiskell came first at a run, then Emily, then Jackson himself, struggling into his clothes. The two men picked Rachel up and carried her to the bed. The doctor grasped for a pulse, leaned over and listened for a heartbeat. The black December wind flung itself at the windowpanes and made the candles shake. He straightened and looked at Jackson.

"Bleed her!"

Heiskell bent and cut. No blood flowed from her arm. Hannah groaned.

"Try the temple!"

Heiskell bent once more with his scalpel. Two red drops appeared and stained the white cap. Then nothing.

The room by now was crowded with slaves and relatives, weeping and howling, and Jackson turned in a full, halting circle to see them. Somebody held a lamp over the bed. He turned back. "She's only fainted." Emily Donelson gave him a chair. "She's only fainted," he told her in a harsh whisper, and sat down and gripped Rachel's right hand in his.

Hours later he was still by her side. From time to time he would rise and peer into her face and grope for a pulse, then sit back. Quietly, Heiskell directed the servants to prepare a table where they could lay the corpse. Jackson lifted his head and watched them. "Spread four blankets on it," he told them. "If she does come to, she won't lie so hard on the table." Heiskell nodded.

Coffee arrived at dawn. He found Jackson sitting alone by the body with his head in his hands, his pale fingers thrust through his stiff gray hair. He looked utterly stricken, Coffee thought; numb, turned to stone, a statue of grief.

"Why don't you come in the other room, General, and take a little coffee or tea?"

"They can bring it in here," Jackson said, and stretched out one trembling hand to stroke Rachel's cold brow.

A servant girl brought a tray with a silver pot on it, and Coffee added a little milk and sugar to a cup and poured. "First time around it was tea that beat the British," Jackson said inconsequentially, looking at the motionless body. "Second time around it was Coffee."

"They used to say that." Coffee had no desire to drink or eat anything at all, but he poured a new cup for himself.

"She was sixty-one years old," Jackson said. "We were married thirty-seven years, from Natchez."

"Thirty-seven years."

"She's gone on a grand party of pleasure, I hope," Jackson said. "At one with her Redeemer."

After that he fell silent, and except when the women came in to dress the body, he never left the room. Coffee rode back to his house for a few hours at midafternoon, then spent the night at the Hermitage making funeral arrangements.

At nine o'clock the next morning, December 24, Christmas Eve, he dressed himself in the upstairs bedroom that sat over Jackson's study. The house had been strangely silent for hours. Now a low murmur seemed to be rising around it on all sides. Coffee pulled aside the heavy winter curtains and looked down on an amazing sight. For as far as he could see, out to the bleak, gray horizon, the ground was covered with wagons and carriages and coaches, every type of buggy and farm rig and conveyance he could imagine, all filled with men and women in mourning black. And where there were no wagons, there were saddle horses and draft horses, many holding two or three riders. And where there were no horses or wagons, there were people on foot, streaming across the fields and pastures and down the lawn. He learned afterward that the Nashville *Union* estimated ten thousand people, more than the population of Nashville itself, had made their way to the Hermitage that morning.

At one o'clock, under a damp and drizzly sky, Sam Houston opened the door at the northeast corner of the house. Half a mile away, a church bell started to toll. Houston led the pallbearers down a curving path to the open gravesite in the garden. Some of the slaves had laid out long patches of cotton for the procession to pass over, but from where he stood at the door Coffee could observe mud and water already seeping through. He took Jackson's right arm, Major Henry Rutledge, one of Jackson's former aides, took his left, and the three of them stepped out the door and slowly followed the coffin. Behind them came a long, weeping train of relatives and servants, winding out of the house.

Even though Coffee held his right arm, Jackson carried a long black cane in his fist, pointed straight ahead like a sword. When they stopped at the pile of clay by the grave, he rested its tip on the clods. At that moment old Hannah suddenly burst through the group standing around the pit and fell to her knees. She swung both legs over the edge of the grave and started to sob—"My mistress, my best friend, my love! I'm going *with* her!"

The sexton and Sam Houston pulled her back by the arms and tried to lift her, but Jackson quickly raised the point of his cane and said, "Let that faithful servant weep."

They put Hannah down, and she cried for a time until her daughter led her away.

Jackson, who had not shed a tear so far that anybody knew of, now looked around at the immense throng of people and said in a loud, clear voice, "She was worthy of our tears." Then he fell silent.

The minister was a young man named Hume whom Coffee had known since he was a boy. He walked to the head of the coffin and opened his Bible. Coffee listened to the text and the first few words of eulogy, but his mind drifted. He found himself wondering if Hume—or anybody else today—would dare to mention Rachel's scandals. He looked past Sam Houston's big shoulders to a row of long-necked Donelson boys in high collars and tight-fitting coats. He had thought he was protecting Rachel, and Jackson, and the country, too, when he had traveled to Kentucky in search of David Chase. He had done the best he could. But in the end . . . He stared at the crowd, and his mind, like a deep transparent bowl, filled up with images. Charles Dickinson and his brace of pistols. Tall, skinny Jackson and short, stout Rachel dancing in New Orleans. Rachel's cigar, six black coffins on a handbill. Rachel's girlish scrawl on a sheet of paper addressed to Peyton Short, which out of natural human curiosity he had read before he burned.

"She was the soul of charity," Hume said. "She had a heart to feel and a hand always ready to relieve the poor and needy. She was adorned with a meek and quiet spirit. By her kindness and sweetness, her husband was rendered more happy in his own family than in the midst of his triumphs."

The minister paused and looked down as if he were consulting his Bible. "Some, indeed, during the presidential struggle, with unfeeling hearts and unjustifiable motives, exerted all their powers to throw her numerous virtues into the shade." The whole crowd seemed to draw in a vast collective breath. The best I could, Coffee thought, and when I die the facts die with me. "We cannot doubt," Hume said, "but that now she dwells in the mansions of glory in company with the ransomed of the Lord."

And he, too, fell silent.

Nobody moved. Then a few sad drops of rain splattered on the coffin, and Jackson's iron control at last gave way. He wiped his cheeks, wiped them again, blindly grasped Coffee by the sleeve.

"It's all right, General," whispered Henry Rutledge, at his side.

"It's unmanly," Jackson said through his tears. "But she shed many a tear for me."

"Come inside, General," Rutledge said, because Coffee was likewise standing blindly, with his hat off, in the quickening rain. For some reason Rutledge added, "You're the President of the whole United States now."

But Jackson shook him off. He walked a few steps closer to the open grave, into which the workmen had started to lower the coffin. He stopped them with a gesture. Syllable by syllable the strength returned to his voice, and he could be heard as far away as the house, the open fields, the road. "In the presence of this dear saint," he said, "I can and do forgive my enemies." He paused. The wind blew a little gray gust of rain. "But those vile wretches who have slandered her must look to somebody else for their mercy."

Then he turned and felt with his cane for the path.

CHAPTER

3

On Sunday, January 18 of the new year 1829, nearly a month after Rachel's death, the steamboat *Pennsylvania* came to anchor at the little landing on the Cumberland where Jackson normally loaded his cotton. In an hour or two the President-elect sent down word that he preferred not to travel on the Sabbath.

The *Pennsylvania* waited. Next morning his carriage rolled up just at sunrise and, all in black, he stepped on board. A few curious neighbors and friends stood in the reeds and the thin, cold mist along the bank, shivering ghosts. A boy ran up the gangplank and installed two big new hickory brooms on either side of the bow. Jackson waved one hand in the pale sunlight, toward the bank, and the paddle wheels creaked and groaned and began their slow *slap-slap* against the cold brown water. In a few minutes, for the silent party on shore, the boat was lost to view.

When it rounded the bend at Cincinnati eight days later, having traveled down the Cumberland and up the Ohio, David Chase was among the thousands of spectators crowding the docks. From the hillside spot he had chosen at the edge of Flower Street, he could see over the wharfside jumble of smokestacks and cranes all the way to the tree-capped point of the bend. First came the boom of distant cannons, and he checked his watch: two o'clock. Then the heavy panting of steam engines. Then three majestic white steamboats sailing abreast, like three white gulls on the water.

Chase fumbled for his notebook and pencil. Editors paid for details. The white boats were trimmed with green paint. The roofs of all three boats were covered by crowds of dark-hatted men. Flags and banners hung from every spar and mast. (JACKSON FOREVER! PRESIDENT ANDY!) Other cannons were firing from the Kentucky side almost constantly now. The three great boats steamed past the cheering docks and proceeded about a quarter of a mile upriver; there they turned about in stately unison—Chase searched for a simile—like the spokes of a wheel, and came back toward the docks, so close together as to appear one single connected mass. When they reached the main dock cleared for their arrival, they swept around again in formation, and the two escorts fell back half a boat's length to let the *Pennsylvania* glide gracefully forward and land alone.

The gangplank dropped. The cheering people surged forward. Chase spotted one of Jackson's nephews and Henry Lee, the speechwriter, coming down the rails. A band almost pushed into the river by the crowd somehow struck up a march, Lee lifted a drooping banner, and a moment later, without warning or ceremony, Andrew Jackson was on the deck and walking toward the gangplank. Chase had just time enough to note his clothes—black suit, white shirt, black tie; tall beaver hat with mourning band and weeper—before the mob swarmed onto the boat itself and the President-elect vanished in a rolling, swaying, democratic tide of heads and shoulders.

Afterward Chase learned it had taken Jackson an hour and a half to walk the five blocks to his hotel, where he was intended to rest and receive distinguished visitors while the steamboat was refueled with wood. Chase himself got as far as the reception desk, left his name, was beaten back. At nightfall, evidently fearing for Jackson's safety in another such crush of welcome, his travel committee spirited him down to the docks in a disguised buggy, and before morning the President-elect was on the river again, bound for Pittsburgh.

"Well, I saw him," Mrs. Trollope announced triumphantly to Chase when they met in the street the next day. The sky behind her was bitterly cold, ash gray. A sulking wind kicked yesterday's litter sideways in little angry spirals. The ubiquitous Cincinnati pigs grunted in slow pursuit. Chase stamped his feet on the frozen mud and wished he were anywhere else in the world, wished he were in Paris, exactly one lifetime away.

"He is," Mrs. Trollope conceded, sniffing, "a distinguished-looking man."

"Presidential," Chase agreed, employing the latest newspaper word for Jackson. It was a word nobody had ever thought of applying to John Quincy Adams.

"But the *familiarity* of the people." She shook her head and stared at a pig. "Brutal. And to their ruler. I heard a dialogue—Miss Colden told me you were a writer—I jotted it down."

"Have you seen—" Chase began, but Mrs. Trollope had already extracted a paper from her coat and started to read.

"A greasy, *odorous* fellow, just outside the hotel. He accosted Jackson. I was standing six feet away, I heard every gruesome word.

" 'General Jackson, I guess?'

"The General bowed assent.

" 'Why, they told me you was dead.'

" 'No. Providence has hitherto preserved my life.'

" 'And is your wife alive, too?'

"Jackson signified the contrary, sadly.

" 'Aye, I thought it was one or t'other of ye.' "

Chase shook his head impatiently. "You've seen Emma Colden?"

Mrs. Trollope was busy refolding her sheet of paper. She signified the contrary, sadly; then placed her hand with surprising gentleness on Chase's arm. "Miss Colden likes it here. You and I, Mr. Chase," she said, not unkindly, "are both out of place."

The following morning Chase climbed into the overland coach, bound, like Jackson, for Pittsburgh. But at that city he changed again and in a series of slow, wintery stages made his way north to Boston. There he called on Sarah Hale, received a small check from her, a terse note of thanks and dismissal from William Short, and half a room full of unsold copies of *The Life of Andrew Jackson,* by David Chase. These he transferred to Gray's house on Chestnut Street, where he was staying, and when Ticknor came to visit, he gestured rather grandly toward them, stacked as they were almost to the ceiling, and remarked that now he, too, had a library of a thousand books, nine hundred of which he had written himself.

Ticknor was unamused. Ticknor was Ticknor. They had a second reunion dinner in Ticknor's room, flatter and duller than the first, and discussed the latest rumor that Jackson had died en route to Washington City.

"A sincerely democratic act if he has," Ticknor sneered, "to join the *silent majority*," using Homer's famous phrase for the dead gathered in the underworld.

All in Jackson's coffins, Chase oddly thought.

On the crisscross path back through Harvard Yard, Gray proposed that Chase write an account of their mutual trip fourteen years ago to Monticello. But Chase, who by this time, after two months of travel in the West, had exactly fifty-four dollars to his name, nonetheless demurred. "I'll save it for my memoirs," he said.

"Which I expect you will write in Paris, in French." Somewhat in the manner of Mrs. Trollope extracting dialogue, Gray stopped in the middle of a path and reached into his handsome fur-collared coat. Snowflakes drifted patiently in the beam of a new gas streetlamp. With a flourish, Gray's leather glove produced a ship's ticket for Le Havre, departing from Philadelphia the ninth of March, and a cashier's note on the Mechanics Bank of Boston for two hundred dollars. "I imagine if you hurry," he told Chase, "you can arrive in Washington City in time to witness the inauguration. I'm led to believe that with the exception of Ticknor, who is too snobbish, and myself, who am too fat, every other person in the United States plans to attend. Write an account, David, sell it in France, pay me back. Jackson," he added sardonically, pulling up the collar and waving away all thanks, "forever."

CHAPTER

4

On the morning of March 3, one day before the inauguration, Chase alighted on Pennsylvania Avenue from the same stagecoach he had ridden down eleven months before. Looked around at the same mud. Slapped (he swore) the same mosquito.

But everything else he saw was different. The once empty expanse of paved street in front of Gadsby's Hotel was thronged with tumultuous, uproarious traffic—foot, wagon, horse. Gadsby's lobby was a sea of agitation, and when he started to look for a room, every last tavern, hotel, boarding house, and mess in the city was already jammed to capacity with Jackson supporters.

"They sleep five to a bed," said Nicholas Trist, his friend from Henry Clay's office, who took pity and offered Chase the broken couch in his parlor, "or on the billiard tables, or the floor, or the street, or they just don't sleep at all, I guess. Half of them came to celebrate, the other half want Jackson to give them a job. Man at Gadsby's told me they're about to run out of whiskey."

"Serious," said Chase, pouring himself some of Trist's brandy.

"Fatal," said Trist, doing the same thing. "Barbarians invading Rome."

"This is not Rome." Chase peered through Trist's window at a field of mud and brown grass.

"Well," said Trist, "these are sure as hell barbarians."

And when Chase went back on the streets, on a certain errand, he saw precisely what Trist meant. Tennessee backwoodsmen still in their buckskins and moccasins, Irish immigrants with sacks of filthy clothes on their shoulders, lame, mutilated, grizzled army veterans, cardsharps, men with ropes, men with knives—an indefinable hostility and defiance sat on their brows. They were like an army of occupation in the city. They camped in the open fields between the far-flung Washington buildings. They roamed, shouted, quarreled in sudden explosions of noise and drunken fists. He crossed C Street and the same open ditch he had passed one year before, still unfilled. The druggist's shop had been replaced by a barber who advertised "Jackson-style" haircuts. The optician next door displayed a sample pair of "Jackson Reading Glasses" in his window, resting on a dusty copy of *The Life of Andrew Jackson* by David Chase.

Inside Recamier's Boarding House, the clerk behind the desk stared hard at Chase, and before he could speak recommended looking in Georgetown or Virginia for a room.

"I don't want a room. I was hoping Mr. Hogwood was in."

"Moved out," the clerk said, and spat.

"Moved out when?"

The clerk shrugged and squinted at the window, where a military band was marching down the muddy road, scattering pigs. Chase looked at the desktop, turned the registration book around and opened it. "Did he leave an address? Is he still in Washington?"

"Moved out three weeks ago," the clerk said and closed the book with a thump. "Just paid his bill and up and left." He hooked his thumbs under the armpits of his vest. "Now if it was *me*," he said, showing his teeth in a leer, "I'd be lookin' for the daughter."

But the daughter was not to be looked for, as Chase well knew, not by the clerk, not by Chase, not by anyone except Senator Ephraim A. Sellers, widower, investor, Jacksonian patriot, who, according to the infallible New York *Post*, had married her in Columbus, Ohio, January 10, in a quiet, private ceremony, and then returned with his bride to the capital.

If it was *me*, Chase thought; he stepped back outside and let the rest of the sentence drift away unfinished . . . me, me, me. He walked past Gales and Seaton's double building, closed for the celebration. He tramped up Capitol Hill, under siege by drunken sightseers, through narrow streets so jammed with people that it was almost impossible to pass. At the Gadsby's Hotel bar he unexpectedly encountered Senator John Eaton and learned, first, that Gadsby's was now called the Wigwam by Washington society because Jackson and his unrefined Jacksonians were staying there; second, that General Coffee had remained in Tennessee.

"Fact is, he's moving to Alabama next month," Eaton said loudly, over the constant Wigwam noise, clutching two bottles to his chest and himself moving away from Chase as fast as the crowded room would allow. "Tired of politics," he said over his shoulder. "The General was sad."

"Congratulations on your marriage."

Eaton colored and shook his head in a deprecating gesture that defied interpretation. On January first, as that same New York *Post* had reported, Eaton had married the barkeeper's widowed daughter, Peggy Timberlake. He took a confidential step back to Chase. "Your book wasn't half bad," he said as softly as he could. "Did no harm, anyway."

"The Hippocratic oath of authors."

But irony was wasted on newly married senators. "Come to the ball tomorrow night," Eaton said, pleased to show his power. "Closed to the public, but I'll leave your name at the door."

At the door of Gadsby's Hotel the next morning, Chase and Trist joined an impatient crowd that stretched the length of Pennsylvania Avenue, half a mile straight to the East Portico of the Capitol. The city fathers had planned to give Jackson a victory parade when he entered town three weeks earlier ("Jackson's Day"), but he had slipped in at nightfall before anyone knew, unheralded, escorted only by a handful of aides—*The General thus stole a march on his friends,* Chase scribbled in the draft of the article he had promised Gray, *just as he used to steal a march on his enemies.* (Not bad. Harmless.) But there was no escaping a parade this time.

At ten o'clock a thirteen-gun salute from the Navy Yard shook the city. Chase sketched a little map for his would-be readers in Paris or London or Mars. The President's mansion stood at one end of the broad, tree-lined street (poplars, planted by Thomas Jefferson; editors still paid for details); then the business district consisting of narrow two- and three-story frame buildings, fields, and mires; several impressive federal office buildings in the new Greek Revival style; the low black inverted washbowl of the unfinished Capitol dome, with its web of wooden scaffolds.

"Add mud and water," Trist suggested, peering over his shoulder as he drew, "eye of newt, hair of toad"—but in fact the day was hazy and warm, and the avenue in front of them was newtless and toadless and (for Washington City) almost dry.

At ten-thirty a group of veterans from the Revolutionary War marched up a side street to the door of Gadsby's. At eleven exactly the door swung open and Jackson himself appeared on the steps, and the mobbed street burst into prolonged, ecstatic, deafening cheers.

Afterward, writing as fast as he could before his ship set sail from Philadelphia, Chase ventured the opinion that Jackson's wildly memorable inauguration had been a Symbolic Moment in American history (editors paid for symbols, too), like the signing of the Declaration of Independence. It marked the great transition at last, in reality if not by the calendar, from the old wig-and-sword days of the eighteenth-century Jeffersonian republic to the new marching-band-and-billboard days of the People's Wigwam Democracy.

And Jackson, lover of theater, friend of actors, understood it from the start.

He would be, the newspapers had announced, the first President since Jefferson to *walk* to his inauguration. He waved his hand, fell in behind his escort; the crowds along both sides of the street roared again, and President and people set off together toward Capitol Hill.

From time to time, running among the poplars, Chase caught a glimpse of him in the middle of the street, hatless, dressed in black, Old Hickory striding vigorously along. Boys, men, slaves, women—a whole Dutch wagon full of cheering women, pulled by a pony—kept pace beside him. Trist vanished. Banners and flags flew from every window they passed. The cannons at the Navy Yard began to thunder again—for the sheer pleasure of it, evidently—and a company of Marine artillery by the river boomed in answer as if they would storm the city.

At the East Portico, out of breath, Chase looked back and down at the great procession coming up the avenue. He considered climbing a tree for a better view, settled instead for a place on a flat wagon parked fifty yards or so from the south steps and already filled with well-dressed spectators who had scorned to walk with the mob.

He jostled to the front, gripped an upright post. To his right the crowd poured toward the Senate entrance—he made a guess and tripled Cincinnati: *thirty thousand people*—and Jackson, still escorted by the veterans, disappeared inside.

"The swearing-in of Vice President Calhoun," the lady standing next to Chase explained. *"He* preferred a ceremony out of sight."

Chase sketched as fast as he could—Rotunda, scaffolding, Marine band, artillery companies, a ship's cable stretched across the steps to hold back the rising, rolling flood of bodies.

"They really seem to think," said the woman next to him, observing his notebook, "that the country has been rescued from some dreadful *danger*." (Chase wrote it down.)

"Beautiful! Sublime!" cried the man on her left. "The majesty of the people!" (Chase wrote again.)

The sun rose higher. The crowd slowly grew silent. Chase looked at his watch: high noon. Two marshals swung open the doors of the Rotunda, and a moment later through an expectant hush, the justices of the Supreme Court walked out onto the portico. The Marines snapped to attention. Senators, representatives, wives, filed onto the porch. Some took their seats on red plush chairs and sofas arranged in a semicircle for them, others stood on the steps alongside the taut line, just below a speaker's table covered with scarlet velvet and positioned between two white columns.

For an instant nothing happened. The immense crowd seemed to rise, strain its eyes, hold its breath. And then, with a dramatist's perfect timing, Jackson strode into view.

Met, Chase thought—he had no need to write down anybody else's impression—by the loudest single noise he had ever heard in his life.

The cheers split the air again and again, drowned out the cannons, the sweating band. Jackson stood alone before the table and simply stared back at the spectacle, hatless still, hands at his sides. Then, in a gesture too perfect to have been rehearsed or planned, too completely the expression of the moment, he bowed low to the majesty of the people.

When he had read his brief address, he turned to Chief Justice John Marshall and took the oath. Marshall shook his hand. Jackson raised the Bible high, held it to his lips, and, amid another stupendous eruption of cheers, reverently kissed it.

After which the Symbolic Moment flew apart like a bomb and Jackson's day disintegrated into chaos.

The crowd, unable to control itself any longer, charged forward in a single hysterical mass. The Marines and congressmen scattered. The restraining cable curved like a huge bow and snapped under their weight, and Jackson was suddenly, entirely surrounded. He retreated somehow into the Rotunda, emerged again on the west side of the Capitol before anyone could spot him, and mounted a white horse held for him by a soldier.

With another wave, another ovation, he started back up Pennsylvania Avenue, toward the President's House, followed now—Chase varied his image—not by a mass, but by a torrent of raving democracy. The white horse could hardly move. Through a screaming cortege of carriages, wagons, carts, Jackson pushed and fought, waded forward.

By the time he reached the mansion the throngs were already there. Great barrels of orange punch had been prepared for the reception, but as the white-coated waiters flung open the doors, the first arrivals smashed past them and poured into the house. Waiters and guests collided like two charging armies. The barrels splashed to the floor. Glasses were snatched, dropped, china shattered underfoot. Men in muddy boots climbed onto John Quincy Adams's damask-covered chairs and looked frantically about for their new President.

Meanwhile Chase had skirted the crowds on Pennsylvania Avenue and trotted on a parallel course through the fields near the Potomac. When he approached the President's House from the river side, the people's inauguration had clearly turned into the people's riot. The first thing he saw was men climbing in and out of the President's windows like panicked burglars. A door under the carriage porch was ripped from its hinges. On the lawn every sapling and bush poor Adams had planted was trampled into leaves and splinters, and a vast shoving crowd, two hundred deep, encircled the whole building. Chase struggled toward an open door, was pushed back. At one point, through a window, he saw Jackson backed against a wall, nearly crushed by admirers. Some of the waiters were now carrying their tubs of liquor out into the garden as a kind of decoy or distraction, and people were turning in packs to follow them. Chase passed fainting women, yelping boys. On the back stairs he tripped over an enormous black woman who sat on the floor eating ice cream with a gold spoon. In the *levée* room, where he had shaken hands with John Quincy Adams, a group of senators locked arms and threw a cordon around the exhausted President. Inch by inch they eased him toward a door, which two of them braced open by lowering their shoulders and pushing, as if they were holding back a dam. Jackson waved and vanished; the party roared on.

Later, in a gap where the fence along Pennsylvania Avenue had been flattened, Chase bumped (literally) into the woman he had stood beside at the Capitol.

"A disgrace! A saturnalia!" She held up her skirt to show him its orange stains and muddy tatters. "President Jackson—*King Mob!*"

But then, three hours later, in the dizzying, accelerated pace that Chase had long since come to think of as essentially American, essentially Jacksonian, King Mob gave way in his turn to Queen Decorum. The inaugural ball was by printed invitation only, in the polite K Street assembly rooms of an impresario from New Jersey named Signor Carusi, who specialized in tea dances and banquets of glacial, senatorial pomp, and who had stationed a trio of plume-capped guards at each door to keep out the hordes of the unacceptable.

Chase showed his ticket (acceptable) and stepped into the main *salon,* where an orchestra played discreetly behind a forest of potted plants and where elegant couples, begloved, begowned, and in some cases actually besworded and bewigged, were dancing sedately across a polished floor. Above the floor had been suspended a red, white, and blue banner at least fifty feet long and ten feet high, with Jackson's gigantic oval-framed portrait painted on it (smaller, to one side, Jefferson's hung beside a mirrored bar).

Chase was not interested in banners, large or small. He paced along the walls, drumming his fingers impatiently on his leg. He shouldered his way into the crowd and stopped to look up at the flag-draped dais where the distinguished guests of honor were seated. One of Jackson's young nephews and his wife presided over a long table covered with a white linen cloth, silver candlesticks, and crystal decanters of wine. Men and women in fancy dress lounged around them, chattering over the music. At the far end of the table John Eaton, plumper than ever in his stiff white shirt and black suit, stared in one direction while the red-haired woman beside him stared in the other.

Chase was not interested in red hair, either. He took a glass of punch from a waiter and drank it fast. There was a blond dancer on the other side of the room, beneath a chandelier. Chase rose on his toes. Too tall. Another, dressed in pale blue, emerged from a flower-covered arcade, and he craned his neck the other way. Too short. He paced along the wall again, then on impulse pushed his way up to the mirrored bar. Thomas Jefferson looked benevolently down, unperturbed as Chase ordered a whiskey, drank it, ordered another. Behind him the orchestra started to play "Possum Up De Gum Tree" in honor of the absent President, too sternly in mourning to attend a dance, even his own inaugural ball. If he had published her letters, Chase wondered, abruptly savage in mood, would Rachel have died sooner? Died at all? What particle of difference in the world had he made, except to himself?

His head was pounding with the music. He swung around to leave, bumped shoulders with a waiter, backed one step onto the dance floor—and found himself face-to-face at last with Emma Colden.

She stood directly in front of him, exactly as she had stood in her father's doorway, blocking everything else in his view. "David?"

Chase opened his mouth to speak, but she shook her head. Her face was a mask of ice.

Reflexively he extended his hand as if to invite her to dance. She took a determined step backward. She wore a tight-waisted, wide-skirted blue evening dress, scooped low enough at the bosom to show the tops of her white breasts. A glittering new diamond necklace curled around her throat like a ring of fire.

"You get the *hell* out of here," said Ephraim Sellers, red-faced, drunken, suddenly between them.

Somehow, Chase thought, Emma had gathered all the light in the room to herself. She was an island of pure light. Everybody else had faded away to shadows, the orchestra played soundlessly, the dancers glided by in silence. There were other jewels in her hair, he noticed, more diamonds perhaps, or amethysts, sparkling brilliantly. Rays from the chandelier overhead spilled behind her onto the floor in a wide golden train; her blue skirt floated in a circle of white.

"Out of here! Out of here!" Sellers bellowed and shook his fist before Emma pulled him away.

Trist materialized at Chase's side and handed him a glass of punch. He studied Chase's face, drained his own glass, then snagged another from a passing waiter. "I know that girl," he said. Chase nodded.

After a time they went to the nearest exit and out into the street, where night had long since fallen. Then they walked together along the river and watched the scattered lights of the city receding, smaller and clearer as the hours went by.

EPILOGUE

June 14, 1854—Paris

David Chase pulled the lace curtains of his window to one side and gestured with entirely unjustified pride toward his garden below.

"They're lovely, beautiful," said the young woman beside him, and started charmingly to name the flowers she could see: "verbena, black-eyed Susan, arrow root—why, they're all American flowers, aren't they?"

The young man, her husband—a loutish, undeserving oaf—glanced out the window briefly, nodded curtly, looked significantly at his watch. An insensitive oaf, yes, but what young man was not?

"You don't actually weed and cultivate them yourself?" he asked, indicating with a tactless gesture Chase's bad knee and cane.

"No, no. I have a wealthy man who comes here twice a week to do that for me."

The girl smiled patiently at the joke, but her husband—whose name Chase had utterly forgotten—merely looked puzzled and wandered a few feet away to inspect the paintings.

Kate Sellers Hampton, only child of Emma Colden Sellers of Columbus, Ohio, widow, gave one last admiring look at his flowers and then turned back to him. "My mother said you've written *sixteen* books."

416 / Max Byrd

"Guilty," Chase said. "But a battered and weary world can take heart. I've now retired from literature. The perfectly balanced organism, as one of my Parisian philosophers says, is silent."

"You wrote some of your books in French, some in English," Kate said. "My mother's got them all, except the one about Andrew Jackson."

"Ah." Chase found something quite remarkably interesting in the design of his carpet. He traced it with the tip of his cane.

"But that was a most decisive book, she says."

Chase cleared his throat. "Well, not in the presidential election at any rate. None of us knew back then that the people had decided for Jackson long before."

"When you came back to Paris, she says you started to write novels."

"There is more opportunity for truth in fiction," Chase said, and was rewarded with a laugh. She had a bright, quick mind, he thought, capable of enjoying paradox. She had also, of course, her mother's beautiful blond hair and tall, womanly figure, though her nose was perhaps a little too short and pug and her shoulders a little too square and athletic, American fashion. They lived in southern Illinois, Kate had told him, where her husband was a cotton merchant, and she was going to learn French to beat the band, she said, if they stayed here long.

"Is that the Palais Royal over there?" her husband asked. "That long tiled roof?"

Chase adjusted his spectacles. "Correct. And those trees beyond it, just to the right, belong to the Tuileries, where, now that we've had our tea and sherry, I propose to take you on a Parisian stroll."

"Good," said the young man, reaching for his hat. "But we have to be back at our hotel by six, because we're dining tonight with some quite important French cotton importers and I need to go over my papers."

They entered the Tuileries by a dark, narrow lane running off the rue St. Honoré and emerged into a splendid June afternoon, warm and nearly cloudless. Chase was absurdly pleased that everything appeared so perfectly arranged for his guests. The sunny graveled paths between the trees were dotted with children and nurses. Pretty young mothers strolled nearby under blue-and-red striped French parasols. At the other end of the garden the old Palais du Louvre sat gray and *tolérant* behind a shiny black grille. They stopped by a miniature boat pond to observe a sailboat race.

"I am thirty-two, Kate is twenty-six," the young man said, looking about at the scene. His appalling American bluntness startled Chase. "We've only been married a year, so we have no children yet. I suppose her mother wrote you all that."

"No, no. She wrote very little. Just a note to say that you were coming to Paris and she hoped I would entertain you."

"Well." The young man frowned at the entertainment.

Chase thought he should make a better effort. "I keep up poorly, Mr. Hampton. What is the political situation . . . at home? I read now and then about abolition and disunion."

"Things are very bad," the young man replied. "Terrible. People talk of civil war, the abolition of slavery, states' rights. Everything is coming to a head. The outlook for business is grave."

"Curious." Chase led them down a tree-shaded alley toward the river. He took advantage of an old man's privilege and slipped his arm through Kate's as they walked. "When John Quincy Adams lost the election of 1828 he came back as a congressman and turned into a great crusader for abolition. The Jacksonians always thought that would lead to disunion."

"My mother said you actually knew Andrew Jackson," Kate said, "when you wrote your book. My father knew him too. He was a senator before he died."

Chase nodded. He steered them to a bench that offered a view, to the left, of the Pont Royal and Notre Dame; to the right, a view of the Quai d'Orsay and its tall facade of expensive, elegant houses. Behind them rose the odd black spires of St. Sulpice, which had always appeared to Chase like huge twin inkwells at the service of the Latin Quarter bookstores. He wondered for a moment what Washington City looked like now. When he had returned to Paris in 1829 he had lived for a time on the Left Bank; now he lived on the Right. As usual, he couldn't be quite sure where he belonged.

"Andrew Jackson did only one thing that really counted," the young man said. "Besides quashing the U.S. Bank, of course. And that was quashing nullification."

Chase made room on the bench for Kate, whose fashionable skirt was very wide and full. And blue, of course, her mother's favorite color.

"You mean the famous toast he gave?"

"Yes." Kate's husband chose not to sit but to stand, merchantlike, and survey the long open-topped barges plying coal up and down the Seine. "John C. Calhoun was leading the movement for a state's right to nullify any federal law it didn't care for, even if it meant wrecking the federal Union. And Jackson gave a toast and said the Union would prevail."

Chase thought the young man told a story quite badly. In fact, Chase knew, because Nicholas Trist had written him in elaborate detail, the great toast had taken place in Washington at Jefferson's birthday banquet in 1830, when Jackson's presidency had gotten off to a very uncertain start. All of his numerous enemies were present, smelling blood and snarling and growling like dogs. And the grizzled old general had stood up with his glass in his hand and fire in his eye and glowered ferociously down at them, as if they were the British line at New Orleans. Always the master of the pause, he waited grimly until the whole room had muttered itself into silence. Then—"Our Union!" he had thundered, raising his glass. "It *must* be preserved!"

"People loved him," Kate said. "They still write his name on their ballots, even though he died in 1845."

"People are mad," her husband said.

Chase slowly got to his feet and leaned on his cane. Another privilege of old age was to let your mind wander as it liked. "This garden, the Tuileries, used to be closed to the public," he told them. "You had to buy a special ticket to come in and walk. When Thomas Jefferson lived in Paris, before the Revolution, he liked to rent a chair and sit just about where we are. He took that building over there as the model for Monti-cello." Chase pointed his free hand at the smooth white dome of the Hôtel de Salm across the river. "He carried back a shipload of French flowers for Monticello too."

"I like *your* flowers better," Kate declared with another charming laugh. She helped him down a set of stone steps, toward the path.

"How would you rank Jackson among the Presidents?" her husband asked, finally interested.

"Oh, I would rank him the equal of Jefferson, both of them just below Washington," Chase answered. But he scarcely listened to himself. His legs hurt and his back hurt, and he walked, he knew, with an old man's shuffle. Jackson had died in 1845. Chase didn't remember the date. He did remember that the newspapers had reported Jackson's last words with bewilderment and awe: "Be good children, and I expect to meet you all in heaven, black and white."

They passed one of the ten thousand Parisian *affiches* pasted to a wall, advertising some sort of patent medicine, and Chase thought of the shocking "coffin handbill" he had found one day long ago near Kalorama, and all the others he had seen that summer, and he tried to imagine Jackson lying at last in his own narrow black coffin. He wondered if they had buried or cremated him. In his mind's eye he pictured the old soldier lowered onto his funeral pyre at the Hermitage, like a Roman. Someone applies the torch. His gray hair bursts into yellow spikes. The taut skin of his cheeks turns black as leather. Out of the drifting eddies of smoke, shadows are marching toward him. Here and there a face burns like a star. John Coffee. Sam Houston. And then Jackson's closed eyes are suddenly themselves ablaze with the sight of his dead wife. Golden light pours upward from his open mouth. Love fans it into Rachel's name.

"The consensus now," Kate's husband said, "is that Andrew Jackson was vulgar, violent, bad-tempered, practically illiterate. A *dangerous* man."

"I don't remember him quite that way," Chase said mildly, taking her arm again and smiling with perfect contentment at his and Emma Colden's daughter.

ACKNOWLEDGMENTS

I have invented four characters: Chase, Emma, Hogwood, and Sellers. All the rest are real historical figures doing and saying pretty much what they really did, although of course William Short did not commission Chase's campaign biography and for the sake of economy I have compressed two minor incidents in the Battle of New Orleans. Rachel Jackson did have the affair I describe with Peyton Short; the letters and other documents have mostly disappeared (I suspect the Nashville Whitewash Committee), but there are tantalizing references to them in the historical records. Peyton did gallop away to Virginia, pursued by Robards, and did pay him off. The vile John Randolph's role is simply speculation on my part—plausible, I hope.

I have put together my scenes and conversations from the voluminous diaries, letters, and newspapers of the period. I am particularly indebted to the *Memoirs* of John Quincy Adams, edited by his son, an older and far more sober Charles Francis Adams, and to the edition of Jackson's papers edited by John Spencer Bassett. For the facts of Jackson's life I have generally relied on the excellent three-volume biography by Robert V. Remini, but I have also adapted language and several scenes from earlier biographies by Marquis James and James Parton. I am especially grateful to the director of research at the Hermitage in Nashville, Sharon Macpherson, who has an extraordinary knowledge of nineteenth-century

American history and who has been extremely kind and patient in answering my questions about Jackson. I thank Diana Dulaney Essert for her encouragement and for once again processing my words into prose. Virginia Barber is the Best Literary Agent and Kate Miciak is the Best Editor, no invention there.

ABOUT THE AUTHOR

Max Byrd is the author of six other novels, including *California Thriller*, which won the Shamus Award of the Private Eye Writers of America, and *Target of Opportunity*, a Book-of-the-Month Club Alternate Selection. His best-selling historical novel *Jefferson* was published to wide critical acclaim in 1993. He lives in northern California with his wife and two children and is at work on a new historical novel.